PRAISE FOR SARA WOLF'S

BRING ME THEIR HEARTS

A Goodreads YA Best Book of the Month
An Amazon Best Book of the Month:
Science Fiction & Fantasy

"A zesty treat for YA and new-adult fantasists."
—*Kirkus Reviews*

"Captivating and unique! Sara Wolf has created a world quite
unlike one I've ever read in *Bring Me Their Hearts*. Readers
will fall in love with Zera, the girl with no heart who
somehow has the biggest heart of all."
—Pintip Dunn, *New York Times* bestselling author
of the Forget Tomorrow series

"Thrilling, hilarious, addictive, and awesome!
I absolutely loved it!"
—Sarah Beth Durst, award-winning author
of The Queens of Renthia series

"Everything I need from a story. A standout
among fantasies!"
—Wendy Higgins, *New York Times* bestselling
author of *Sweet Evil*

"Sara Wolf is a fresh voice in YA, and her characters never
fail to make me laugh and think."
—Rachel Harris, *New York Times* bestselling author
of *My Super Sweet Sixteenth Century*

FIND
ME THEIR
BONES

Also by Sara Wolf

Bring Me Their Hearts

the Lovely Vicious series
Love Me Never
Forget Me Always
Remember Me Forever

FIND
ME THEIR
BONES

SARA WOLF

Entangled Publishing, LLC
2614 South Timberline Road
Suite 105, PMB 159
Fort Collins, CO 80525
rights@entangledpublishing.com

Entangled Teen is an imprint of Entangled Publishing, LLC.

Visit our website at www.entangledpublishing.com.

Edited by Stacy Cantor Abrams & Lydia Sharp
Cover artwork by Yin Yuming
Cover design by Heather Howland
Interior design by Toni Kerr

ISBN 978-1-64063-375-9
Ebook ISBN 978-1-64063-660-6

Manufactured in the United States of America

First Edition November 2019

10 9 8 7 6 5 4 3 2 1

entangled teen
an imprint of Entangled Publishing LLC

For the boys with an i and a z.
You've held me together.

"Life rises out of death, death rises out of life; in being opposite they yearn to each other, they give birth to each other and are forever reborn. And with them, all is reborn, the flower of the apple tree, the light of the stars. In life is death. In death is rebirth. What then is life without death? Life unchanging, everlasting, eternal? What is it but death-death without rebirth?"

—Ursula K. Le Guin

1

A REUNION

Princess Varia of Cavanos watches me with the eyes of an amused wildcat. Eyes that should by all accounts be dead. And yet here she is, blinking them and making them crinkle up with her beautiful, slow smile.

A single naked realization rings like a deep bell in my head: *Varia is alive.* She stands right here in front of me—the daughter King Sref of Cavanos mourned so deeply. The sister Prince Lucien of Cavanos missed so dearly. Next to me and yet away from me, Lucien takes a single step forward, reaching for her with a shaking hand.

"Varia. You're…"

"Alive?" she finishes for him softly. "Yes."

"This isn't—" He walks toward her. "This isn't some magic trick by a witch? I'm not dreaming?"

Princess Varia looks around at the pile of bodies at my feet, the blood staining the grass, and the pale yew tree blotched red.

"If anything, it would be a nightmare." Her dark eyes

roam over the corpses to rest on Gavik's body, his glassy eyes blood-smeared and lifeless. "But, since the archduke is dead because of it, I'd call it a pleasant one."

Lucien reaches Varia, the two of them like dark-haired, sable-eyed, golden-skinned mirror images of each other. The same proud hawk nose rests on each of their faces, the same long lashes and razor-sharp cheekbones and brows. My feet won't move; my lips won't form words.

She's dead. She's supposed to be *dead*, killed by Heartless like me five years ago.

Lucien reaches up and touches his sister's shoulder, hesitating at first, as if he's scared to dispel an illusion. But his fingers meet her robes, and he inhales sharply.

"You're alive. *Really alive*. I looked for you, for the Tree you talked about. I looked everywhere for it, hoping beyond hope I would find you—"

Varia smiles at him gently, the same smile King Sref gave me when he and I met while looking at her death portrait—knowing and regretful all at once. She rests her forehead against Lucien's.

"I understand that it's hard to believe," she murmurs. "And you did well. But there will be time to explain everything, especially now that Gavik has been squashed." She pulls away and her eyes roam to me. "You there, Heartless."

Lucien's gaze faintly drifts in my direction, and the joy in his face dims. In a blink he sends up that hard, indifferent shell—his princely shell, the one I worked so hard to penetrate. The one the witches demanded I slip past and steal the heart from even as my own was torn in a million directions.

"Who do you belong to?" Varia asks. It hurts to answer her, to breathe. The locket around my neck feels like it's full of lead.

"Nightsinger," I manage. "The witch Nightsinger." I catch a glimpse of my hands soaked in blood, the taste of it still on my tongue. The things I did—I can't bear to look around me. If I see it with my own eyes, it'll become reality. How many bodies? How many men with families and children and dreams? I ate Gavik, his throat— I can't look. *I can't look.*

And you thought you could escape me, the hunger sneers. ***You can't even resist me. Look at what you've done—***

Vomit burbles in my gut, and I choke out a plea.

"P-Please, Princess Varia. Get Lucien out of here—away from me. Before I turn again."

Lucien's midnight eyes, full of searing affection for me not an hour ago, are so cold now. Unreadable. He doesn't speak, or move, or glance in my direction at all. He is a statue.

In its place in the jar over Nightsinger's witchfire hearth, my heart must surely be bleeding. But I knew. I *knew* it would end like this.

Varia smiles at me, pity clear in her eyes. And yet there's more than just pity there—something inquisitive, something strange.

"What shall we do with her, Lucien?" Varia asks him. "She betrayed your trust, didn't she? I saw that much."

Lucien looks at me then. He *looks—thank the gods he looks*—but I'm not reflected in his eyes. I am glass, a window he's merely peering through.

He's furious. He must be. I burn to beg him to forgive me, but I'm long past forgiveness. I knew that the moment I put on this dark dress to take out his heart. No. I knew that the moment I first laid eyes on him at the Spring Welcoming, and I certainly knew that as I was tearing into the lawguards and Gavik, who threatened his life.

I knew it every moment of our time together.

I had every second to prepare for it. So why do I still arrogantly hope for a happy ending, even with the blood of a dozen men on my hands?

Because you're selfish. The hunger slathers rock salt into my wounds.

Lucien turns, the sight of his back driving me mad in an instant, and the precipice my two halves teetered on for fourteen agonizing days suddenly rips away, tearing me down the middle.

"Don't!" I cry out. "Don't leave! *Please, Lucien...don't leave me.*"

My words ring in the heavy air.

Selfish and mad, the hunger taunts. *What human would stay after what you've done?*

There's a beat, an unbearable moment of crushing nothingness, and then...

"How could I leave something I never had to begin with?" Lucien asks. His disappointed voice is an ice blade snaking through my veins, freezing me solid, every word stabbing me. Disappointed in me, in what I've done, in himself for believing in me. But he wastes no more time on me. He turns to his sister. "She should be questioned."

"By us?" Varia blinks.

He nods. "The truth should be known."

My stomach churns wildly, but Varia just sighs. "You realize Father won't tolerate her in the city. She's a Heartless. He'd sooner burn her over and over."

His obsidian eyes flick to a distant tree. "Unless *you* convince him. He'll listen to you, even if it's to spare a traitor's life."

Traitor.

I sink to my knees. Is that what I am to him? Why isn't

he demanding I be punished, then? Why isn't he demanding I suffer for the lies I've told him, the deceit I've woven around his heart?

Varia sighs, then laughs under her breath. "The Lucien I knew would never care about a traitor's life, let alone ask his sister to beg their father for it."

"People change," Lucien says.

"Or they don't," Varia shoots back. "And they just want to bed a pretty thing."

Twisted shock rises in me. Our kiss in the tent hours ago had dripped with longing. Is *that* why he's being so merciful? Nightsinger chose me to seduce him because he has a type— even now, even after being betrayed, he wants to keep me around to use me before he casts me aside?

The prince doesn't deny it. He doesn't *deny it*, and instead his face softens minutely, fists unclenching. The Lucien I knew—no. He wouldn't.

He could. The hunger slithers through me. *He is nothing more than a human. Selfish, greedy, lustful creatures.*

"This isn't the time for argument, Varia," he says. "You're alive. Let's go back. Father and Mother will be so thrilled to see you."

"Give me a moment," she says. "There's something I must do first."

I watch hollowly as she walks over to the remains of Gavik's body, pulling a velvet bag stitched with black words from inside her cloak. I don't want to read them, I don't want to do anything but sit here and rot in my own misery, but she bends and picks up something soft and leaking and red, and it's then I realize it's Gavik's heart she's dropping into the bag, a bag that reads LEECH.

"It's funny." She laughs softly from her place kneeling

in Gavik's blood. "I've been carrying around this bag for years, hoping I'd get the chance to use it. And now I am. It doesn't feel real." Varia darts her black-glass eyes to me. "You understand, right? Wanting something for so long and then standing on the edge of getting it."

"Yes," I croak. She sighs, and I pinpoint the strangeness in her gaze then. The way she looks at me is almost…hungry, as if I'm a shiny coin and she is the crow who's spotted me on the cobblestones.

"Let me guess: the High Witches dangled your heart in front of you? Your heart for my brother's."

My head snaps up. "How did you—?"

"Because I know them." She laughs, brittle.

Lucien's voice slips between us. "What are you talking about?"

Varia throws him a look over her shoulder. "I knew Gavik would kill me eventually. Every day he stirred up more fear in Vetris, no matter how I tried to stop him. And every day he grew stronger for it. His cleverness and cunning outmatched mine. Father liked to think the royal family was untouchable, invincible back then. But I knew the truth."

I knit my brows, the sudden flash of light from Gavik's mangled corpse nearly blinding me. Varia doesn't blink, her dark orbs soaking the light unflinchingly as she speaks.

"There's a saying in Avellish: *Three enemies means two of them are friends.* Gavik hated me—he knew that when I took the throne, I'd never allow him to have as much power as Father did. But Gavik hated witches, too. So I sought them out." She smiles over her shoulder, her pink lips two halves of a brilliant rose. "Father wouldn't protect me. He relied on Gavik's advice too much to drive him from the court. So I had to protect myself."

She breathes out, long and soft. "I wanted to inherit the power promised to my witch bloodline. But how could I do that, with so much hate for them in our city? The crown princess, asking to meet with the witches? It would've never been allowed. I knew better than to ask Father—I couldn't go through him. I had to go *around* him."

She holds up her graceful hand. All five of her fingers wiggle, even though all five of them are made out of wood. Sleek, polished wood, seamlessly melding with her flesh and moving just like it. She shifts the hem of her long robe in the mud, and where the flesh of her left leg is supposed to be is the same smooth, living wood, bending with her movements.

"I faked my death with a few body parts. Sacrifices had to be made to convince the world—and Gavik—that I was dead."

"But..." Lucien's hawk profile intensifies, all the darkness on his face drawing together. "Your guards—"

"Like I said, brother." Varia's voice is clipped. "Sacrifices had to be made."

The nobles' whispers from weeks ago haunt me—parts of her were found on the road, and all her guards were dead. Torn apart ruthlessly, like a Heartless attack. That means she—*she killed them*, tore them to pieces to make it appear just so.

The prince looks more stunned than I feel, his face slack and his brows knit on Varia's silhouette.

"They won't be forgotten." Varia speaks up again, a new strength in it. "There's a lot I've missed, but if I'm to stop this looming war and save our people, I can't miss anything ever again. Do you understand, Lucien?"

The glow on Gavik's body begins to fade, his flesh I bit and tore apart mending in front of my eyes—shins fusing to knees and skin covering the gaping slit in his belly. Lucien's still riveted to Varia, and then he nods slowly.

"Yes."

Horror starts to dawn brighter than my despair—Gavik is healing. His heart in a bag, Varia as a witch—I clench my fists, looking around for my sword. I can't find it in the blood-soaked grass. I *killed* him. He'll want revenge as I wanted it against the bandits who murdered me. He'll be flush with anger, with the monster's strength.

He staggers to his feet, the glow mending his vertebrae one by one until his neck snaps back into place.

Then Gavik's face swivels to me, long white hair whipping and his every tooth jagged. The monster claws through his skin, nocked straight at me like an arrow, his steps quick and heavy. I shield myself with my arms even though I know it's futile; Gavik's cruel eyes pitch-black from corner to corner and suffused with hate, bloated with bloodlust, his claws bursting through his fingertips and his limbs cracking as they elongate.

He's hideous. He is terrifying.

He's me as I was not seconds ago.

"Enough." Varia's voice rings out, but Gavik keeps stalking toward me. "I said, **that's enough**."

It's just two words, and yet they're pitched so low and so loud that they rumble in my chest. She's a slim, shorter woman, and yet those two words are spoken with all the weight of the world turning. The pain I'm expecting never comes. Gavik is frozen above me, his monstrous, unnaturally tall body not moving a single inch, though his eyes burn and blink down at me. Varia steps up from behind him and smiles at me, a smile too bright for the carnage around us, for the blood-soaked monster just in front of her.

"I apologize about him. You know how Heartless get

when they're first turned."

Over her shoulder I see Lucien, clutching his sword's handle with white knuckles, his glazed eyes now wide and frozen. Fear frostbites his very lips as he stares at Gavik's monstrous frozen spine. Varia just commanded Gavik the way Nightsinger refused to with me. She has total control over him. I swallow and rise to my trembling feet as the princess looks me up and down.

"It's settled, then. We're keeping you. Father won't be happy about it, but I'm sure I can—"

"Zera!" A voice suddenly cuts between us—Malachite. I turn to see his paper-skinned, lanky figure standing on the edge of the clearing, a curly-haired girl with a cane at his side. *Fione?*

"Lady Zera!" Fione calls, both of them running toward us. Fione's expression is fuzzy in my exhausted vision, but I clearly hear her choke on her next word. "V-Varia?"

At my side, Varia's smile grows like the sun rising over a hill.

Exhaustion grips me—iron shackles clamping my lungs. The world becomes a blur of green grass and Malachite's snow skin and Lucien's and Varia's identical midnight heads of hair and Fione's fractured words like a stream—*"A spell, a trick, no, it can't be!"*—and then the sensation of someone catching me before finally, mercifully, darkness.

2

UNBORN AGAIN

You would think I'd be used to waking up in strange places by now.

But the truth of the matter is that no one really gets used to waking up alone. There is bleary panic and utter confusion, until all the brain parts in my skull settle into place and remember for me:

I am Zera Y'shennria, and I have betrayed the Crown Prince of Cavanos.

A prince whose sister is still alive.

A prince who knows I'm a monster.

we are going to be punished. The hunger laughs, somehow quieter and more even than ever, not a trace of the instability I had after I got cut with Lucien's blade anywhere to be heard. ***at last.***

Lucien's cold gaze haunts the backs of my eyelids, the void of my unheart threatening to expand and swallow me whole.

No.

I am Zera Y'shennria, niece of Quinn Y'shennria. I have many weaknesses—a well-made silk dress with just the right number of ruffles, the idea of family, the idea of my heart, a warm cup of chocolate drink and a slice of cake. But I won't allow myself to be weakened by despair.

I shoot up to a sitting position, my spine supported by something soft. My eyes take in everything slowly, methodically: plush carpets, fragile curtains, maroon velvet and white lace adorning every inch of the room. I'm on a sofa propped between a mahogany table and an ironwood sitting chair. Vases of fresh lilies bloom next to gold sandclocks and strangely childish dolls with real curled hair and miniature silk gowns. The room has a haze of dust to it, as if it was tended to but never considered fit to live in. Until now.

I don't recognize the room, but I recognize the walls—how could I not? The pale cream color, the lavish embossing: this is the royal palace in Vetris. How did I get here? I try to shift my legs to the floor, but something metal yanks me back into place. Chains. Someone's cuffed my arms and legs to the feet of the impossibly heavy ironwood sofa.

"Well," I say up at the ceiling, "this is new." I rattle my chains. "*Secure.* I kind of like it."

There's a pause as the ceiling seems to stare down at me questioningly, and I experience several riveting seconds of my new stationary life.

"Okay," I decide. "I hate it."

I twist my entire body, rocking against the cushions. I might not be strong enough to break the chains, but if I can reorient the couch—

My stomach flips as I roll one last time, and the couch heaves, tipping over and sending me crashing to the ground. The cushions smother me, and I cough and blink up at the couch now firmly on top of me. The chains weren't beneath the couch at all but rather hammered into the ironwood legs of it.

I consider the positives as I'm inhaling copious amounts of goose down stuffing. I'm still alive. My body aches with effort, but it's healed of all cuts and bruises. Gavik's sword wound in my chest is gone. I'm left with only the exhausted feeling from fighting Gavik's men.

My iron determination to not succumb falters. Gavik's men. Their body parts, strewn on the grass of the clearing. How many did I kill? Five was my old number—I murdered the five bandits who killed my parents and me. I swore I'd never kill again. And yet…

I swallow regret. *One thing at a time, Zera Y'shennria. You should know by now it's very hard to make amends in shackles.*

I can't send word to Y'shennria trapped like this. Who knows how many hours have passed? It must've been dozens, considering my wounds have been healing slower than normal thanks to the magic-suppressing white mercury wound I sustained from Lucien's sword at the duel weeks ago. To heal such bad wounds with the connection between Nightsinger and me so weak…it must've taken days.

Y'shennria might've told Nightsinger I'm a lost cause already—any moment now, she could shatter my heart. Unlike most, my witch is a soft thing; she doesn't want to shatter me, but for all she knows, I've been caught and am being eternally tortured by the humans.

And that's…not too far from the truth, actually. The fact I didn't wake up in a dungeon is promising. But waking up in the palace could mean anything. Princess Varia and Lucien obviously brought me back to question me, but that could mean torture if I don't cooperate. And when they're done with me, when *Lucien* is done with me, they'll no doubt burn me as an enemy of all humans. Apart from the newly discovered white mercury, burning is the only way a human can slow down a Heartless's magically fueled regeneration.

My head still spins—why did the prince ask his sister to spare me, the traitor? Why did he ask her to appeal to the king for me?

he wants something from you.

The hunger echoes in my skull, as it always has, for the three years since I became Heartless. It's a terrible, dark voice that haunts every Heartless, rushes in and fills the gaps when a witch takes our heart and makes us their immortal thrall. It wants only to kill, to maim, to feast on humans. It thrives on my sadness, my pain, kept at bay and suppressed only by my witch's magic. On every other day that ends in a *y*, it wants to break me. But right now, its words ring true. Lucien is a logical person. And no logical person would ask his sister to spare someone who tried to kill him. He must want something from me. *Something.* What could he want now that I'm a traitor in his eyes?

your body.

The fracture in my willpower yawns wider and wider and then shatters me. Is that all I am to him now? A thing to be trapped and used? I can't get the look on Lucien's face, as he watched me transform into the monster, out of my head, the sheer horrified expressions of those men as I ripped them to nothing but shreds. After everything. After I promised to never kill again.

My eyes brim with hot tears. "Wh-What a way to go," I choke. "Trapped under a couch and crying."

pathetic, the hunger taunts. *it's better this way.*

Once more, the hunger is right. Dying is better—I'll never have to see Lucien again. His lost trust, his disappointment in me—I'll never see it. Malachite and Fione will learn I'm a Heartless from him, I'm sure. I won't have to see their hurt, betrayed faces, either. I failed Nightsinger. I didn't stop the war like I promised Y'shennria. I did nothing but let the people in my life down. I failed them all.

And now I die for it.

I close my eyes, a bitter peace washing over me.

The clicking noise of someone's tongue resounds. "Tut tut. What a mess you've made."

I squint to see through the small gap between the couch and the floor, but suddenly the couch lifts off me, and five pairs of legs in armor reveal themselves as palace guards. They put the couch to one side, the chains yanking me up and contorting my limbs painfully. But at least now I can see who the voice belongs to—Princess Varia in the flesh, her black hair sleek and combed. She no longer wears the dusty traveling robe; a brilliant shimmery purple ensemble hugs her adult curves. She *is* an adult, isn't she? I'm so used to looking at her teenage death portrait, I forgot she would've aged in the time she was presumed dead. By five years, to be exact. Her dark, lustrous eyes look down on me, a faint smile on her lips as she dismisses the guards.

I have nothing to lose. I lost it all in the clearing.

"Is this your room?" I croak. "Terribly sorry. I'd offer to take the dents out of the floor myself, but I don't think I'll be around much longer."

Varia quirks a brow and clips over to me in high riding boots. "Lucien is resting, in case you care. Malachite and Fione have graciously filled me in on everything that's transpired. I knew you had to have bravado to even attempt to infiltrate the Vetrisian court, but I didn't anticipate a sense of humor, too."

"That's all right. After seeing what the court has to offer, I wouldn't anticipate humor, either. Zealotry? For certain. Beauty? In spades. The ability to string two words together and make them funny? Much rarer."

"True," Varia agrees, walking around me at a slow clip. "I could hire you as the court's new laughing boy. But that would be a waste of your...*talents*."

That hungry gleam in her eyes returns as she looks me up and down. I'm reminded painfully of my position—far below her. She's a princess, and I'm a prisoner of war at best. A thing. A body. She could do anything she wanted with me.

I watch her walk over and stroke one of the dolls sitting on the dresser, her delicate finger coming away with dust.

"Shame on you, and shame on the witches for taking advantage of my brother." She sighs lightly. "Though I have to begrudgingly admit—they sent the best one for the job. They hit all his high points—blond, tall, sharp as a tack. He was doomed to lust after you from the start. And you of course went with it, because it seemed like a simple job. A bitter young man, jaded and lonely. Easy prey for someone like you."

She's laid out in plain words what's been haunting me these last two weeks. I flinch but try to sit up higher on the couch cushions.

"How many did I...?" My dry throat breaks. "How many did I kill? In the clearing?"

She brushes her hands off. "Nine lawguards."

I let out a breath. Fourteen men.

I've taken the lives of *fourteen men*.

there will be hundreds more, the hunger taunts.

The princess continues. "I thought it was strange—the trees kept telling me two people had intruded on my clearing. One of them was Lucien; I was used to that. He's been to those woods nearly every year, scouring for me."

I speak, brittle words a welcome distraction. "Why didn't you say hello before, then?"

"He asked me the same thing." Varia shakes her head. "As if the answer isn't obvious."

"Gavik," I breathe, remembering she's made him her Heartless. "Where is he now?"

"Around," the princess says cryptically. "Regardless, I saw Lucien with a girl in my clearing this time, and so I stopped to watch you two. I was thrilled at first—my brother, finally moving on from my loss and embracing love again. And then Gavik made his sordid entrance. And like an Old-God-sent miracle, *you* did what I couldn't. After all those years of hating him while growing up, what I *dreamed* of finally happened. You dragged him out of Vetris, out of the seat of his power, and you so graciously killed him. I didn't need to hide anymore. That's the only reason I even deigned to listen to Lucien's pleadings for me to ask Father to spare you—you freed me, and so I'll keep you from the jaws of Father's torturers. You're welcome."

"I can't take all the credit." I force a thin smile at her. "Fione did most of the 'dragging him out of Vetris' bit."

"So I've heard," Varia muses, pressing on. "Lucien...he's always been easy to read. He was smitten with you, you know. I saw it in his eyes in the clearing, before you turned on him. But that heart wasn't good enough for you, was it? You took what he offered and threw it under a carriage wheel."

Her words might as well be poisoned arrows, riddling me with holes that burn all the way through. I flinch, the chains rattling. Suddenly she kneels next to me, pulling my chin up so my ashamed eyes meet her molten ones. They burn exactly like Lucien's—all dark brimstone.

"I lived with the witches for five years, Heartless. I know their secrets. I know their strengths. I know the way they pull at your strings to make you dance."

Breathing is painful as I speak. "Get your insults in while you can. My witch is going to shatter me any moment now. That was our agreement—if I didn't contact her, she'd assume me captured and mercy-kill me. It's been days. My death is right around the corner."

"Days?" She barks a laugh in my face. "You think it's been *days*?" My muscles go tauter than a crossbow string. Varia drops my chin, her cool fingers leaving my skin as she stands. "Nightsinger, right? That's your witch's name?"

Something in her confident tone makes me uneasy.

"Did you know"—the princess picks up the doll she touched earlier from the shelf—"that a Heartless is never supposed to say their witch's name aloud to another witch?" She twines a finger in the doll's hair lovingly. "Of course you don't. If a Heartless says their witch's name aloud, you're essentially giving other witches permission to steal you away. We can use the sound to create a spell to transfer ownership. But Nightsinger never told you that, did she?"

A cold pit hardens in my stomach. Varia twirls the doll around as if she's dancing with it.

"After all, what use was there? She didn't live in the last witch enclave—Windonhigh—with the rest of the witches. She lived stubbornly alone in a forest. There were no witches who would steal you away. And she knew there'd be no witches left in Vetris to try to steal you, either. She must've wanted so badly to keep you under the illusion that you weren't chained to her. A useless kindness and, in the end, one that sealed your fate."

Varia suddenly stops spinning and drops the doll, the porcelain body shattering into a million pieces, shards of arms and legs flying. A piece slips by my cheek and cuts it, hot blood oozing down my face. But as soon as the cut splits my flesh apart, the familiar feeling of a wound being stitched closed by magic surfaces, knitting me back together again in a blink. Faster than Nightsinger's magic. Faster than any magic I've ever felt. The cold pit in my stomach blossoms into sickly horror as I look up at Varia, the princess smiling down at me.

"Congratulations are in order, Zera. You are now the Second Heartless of the Laughing Daughter."

It takes my brain three frozen seconds to fall into place and begin working again. It hasn't been days. I've healed immediately. If I was still Nightsinger's Heartless, it would've taken much longer.

"No," I blurt.

"Yes," Varia says patiently.

"You can't do that," I snarl. "The Crimson Lady—that tower out there would've detected any magic spell you tried to do—"

"I have someone taking care of that for me," she chimes, kicking through the shards of the doll idly. "It's incredible, really, who your father the king will approve for a position in that red eyesore once you rise from the dead and plead with him."

She has someone in the magic-detecting Crimson Lady—

the polymath-controlled tower that's kept Vetris safe from all magic and witches since it was built. I'm not entirely sure how it works, but it senses magic, and the guards perform arrests depending on the information it gives via the watertell system. The elaborate array of water-fueled pipes ferries messages to and from every corner of the city in a blink—meaning the guards can move on the information even faster. If Varia has someone in the tower covering up the information for her...

"No one knows," I hiss, "that you're a witch?"

Varia's smile is self-satisfied. "No one but you and Lucien. I'm sure Lucien will tell his bodyguard eventually—what's his name? Mallory?"

"Malachite," I snap.

"Oh yes." She shrugs. "And I'll tell Fione when the time comes. But why are we talking about petty interpersonal affairs when we have so much to do? There's a war brewing on the horizon, and you're going to help me stop it. This time, without some risky gamble involving my brother's heart. Something more secure, I think, and without so many High Witches hovering about it."

She sweeps over and unlocks the shackles on my arms and legs. I'm so busy staggering to my weary feet, I barely catch the cotton tunic and breeches she throws at me until they're in my face. "Wear these. We can't have you strutting about in bloodstained things and startling my people, now can we?"

I stand there, paralyzed by fear, my eyes roaming over the stitches of the clean outfit, the holes of the bloodstained dress I'm wearing, and my skin through them. I'm not Nightsinger's Heartless anymore. My reins have been forcefully taken by Varia. It was easier to resign myself to death than to consider living with my mistakes. My betrayal. But now? Now I'll have to keep going. Now I'll have to face the people I've hurt.

And that's far more terrifying than dying.

"What are you waiting for?" Varia's voice cuts through my shellshock. "Put it on. We have places to be. Don't make me command you this early."

Commanding.

A witch can order their Heartless to do anything they want. Nightsinger never used it on me or with her other Heartless—the adorable children Crav and Peligli. Godsdamnit—*Crav and Peligli*. How will I ever see them again? I chew on my lip and desperately try to focus; Varia isn't Nightsinger. I saw how she commanded Gavik. I hurt her brother. In theory, she could command me to jump off a cliff into the maws of a dozen ravenous sharks and I'd have no choice but to do it.

Slowly, my limbs moving like rusted gears, I shed my tattered black dress and pull on the tunic and breeches. The golden heart locket still sits between my collarbones, heavy and somehow comforting. I'm not sure if it works—allowing me to physically go more than a mile and a half from my witch—but just having it around my neck gives me a strange strength, warming my cold, fearful bones ever so slightly. My witch is new, my unlife is uncertain, but the necklace remains.

A guard suddenly walks in when I'm dressed and offers me Father's rusted sword. Just seeing its flaking metal handle has me breathing easier. It's the last thing I own of my parents', and here, at the end of my world and the beginning of a new one, I couldn't ask for anything sturdier to lean on. I take it, pinning it to my belt. I feel doubly protected now, even if I know it's a hollow illusion. Varia points to a pair of black boots near the door, and I lace them up my calves, watching her out of the corner of my eye. When I'm done, she immediately moves for the door and motions for me to follow her.

The palace should look different—as different as my life feels—but it doesn't. Moonlight still streams through the windows and onto both the sleek red carpeting and the marble statues of half-naked women with spears. The guards at every door bow to the princess, and she nods back with perfect regality, as if she wasn't absent for five years. They shoot me wary looks—Lady Zera Y'shennria, with the princess?—but they don't question it. Varia walks ahead of me, and my feet woodenly try to keep up even as my mind spins circles around itself.

"I've told Father you're a Heartless, of course," the princess says softly. "And he's ordered that information to be kept under lock and key, lest panic break out. I've also told him your witch is eager to keep you alive, and I've assured him you can't share any of Vetris's secrets with them. But I'm certain at some point he'll have to question you about Gavik's death. You won't tell him anything, of course."

"You obviously don't know me," I shoot back. "I'm a notorious blabbermouth. I'll tell him you're a witch. Even if you command me—"

"I'm not going to command you to keep quiet," she says lightly. "I won't need to. You won't say a thing to anyone, least of all him."

Her mystifying conviction is iron. How can she be so confident of that? Does she know I can Weep? Reginall—Y'shennria's butler and a veteran of the Sunless War—taught me the framework of a technique the Heartless developed out of desperation during the War. A handful of Heartless managed to resist their witches' commands to fight and kill. They called this Weeping, for the way blood tears stream from our eyes for the duration. Even if it's temporary, the act of Weeping makes the hunger's voice go away. Totally. Not dulling it, like feeding on raw organs does, but *eradicating* it.

It frees a Heartless completely—allowing them to do whatever they want, regardless of what they've been commanded to do, regardless of the hunger's fanatical, blood-lusted voice. It's the closest thing a Heartless can ever come to being human without having their heart again. I Wept that night in the clearing when my monstrous form killed Gavik, his men, and then turned on Lucien. I managed to Weep and control the monster before it could kill the prince.

Did Varia see me do it? Reginall told me the witches in the Sunless War didn't take kindly to their Heartless learning how to defy them. Those who could were shattered—their hearts kept by the witches crushed, which kills the Heartless for good. If I don't want to end up like them, I need to play my cards very carefully.

I almost stop walking. *Can* I still Weep? There are two parts to Weeping: one, the internal calming of thoughts, the clearing of the mind, and two, the external, being cut by a pure white mercury blade. My old connection to Nightsinger had been weakened the moment Lucien accidentally cut me with his white mercury blade during the duel. But this connection between Varia and me hasn't been mangled by magic-suppressing white mercury. It's strong and vibrant.

My stomach writhes as we pass all-too-familiar doors—to the banquet hall, to the throne room, to the gorgeous stained glass Hall of Time and the entrance hall. Lucien's psychic scent lingers in all of them—shadows of memories of when we met for the first (second, really) time. These are places I've been as a different person, as a monster pretending to be a human. He tolerated me then.

He loved me then.

My nerves walk on broken glass—my body had been waiting for two whole weeks in this palace to be reviled and hated, for my secret to come loose. I keep looking around, sick with the thought that I might find Lucien around every corner.

How he must hate me now.

The one boy I felt my unheart beat for, hating me.

The thought tries to drive me madder than the hunger does. It reaches twisting fingers for me, but I focus on every curve of the marble statues, every fiber of the grand carpets, every petal of the vases of impeccable hothouse flowers. The painting in the entrance hall of the New God Kavar looms dark in the night, the scales in his long hands tipping, the hundreds of eyes tattooed onto his divine golden skin glaring down at me as if seeming to say, *There is no escaping justice. You will atone for what you have done.*

Fourteen men. One for each finger on my hand, and then some.

Varia points out the entrance hall, to the gigantic oaken front doors being held open by the guards. Outside, a black-trimmed carriage awaits at the bottom of the grand steps.

"Hurry now. There's something I want you to see." She ushers, sweeping past me and descending the stairs with her skirts held high. Every step of hers is so perfect by Vetrisian court standards that I know even Y'shennria would be impressed.

Y'shennria.

she left you here to rot, the hunger snarls. ***she abandoned you to save her own skin.***

My unheart pangs as I climb into the carriage and seat myself opposite Varia's prim posture. I don't blame

Y'shennria for leaving me here in Vetris all alone, but part of me wants to. Part of me wants to rage and scream at the unfairness of it all—I wanted only my heart. I failed. Why do I have to suffer, to keep living like this, chained to a witch all over again? A part of me is furious. A part of me is scared to the bone. And all of me doesn't want to be alone.

Nightsinger, Crav, Peligli—where are they now? Will I ever see them again?

I look up at Varia's faintly smiling face. Her sheet of black hair gleams in the moonlight. She turns her eyes from the window to look at me, and her smile widens. Calm. Satisfied. In control. She is the total opposite of me.

The city, too, is no different than when I left it. The iron talismans twirl and spin in the midnight wind from every eave and rain gutter—a crescent with three lines moving through it. The Eye of Kavar. Even here, the humans' god is watching me. The spire of the Temple of Kavar broods over the alleyways and streets as we pass through them, drunkards shouting hymns and bedding songs equally as they stagger home from taverns.

Whatever Varia wants to show me, it isn't in the heart of the city. The carriage leads us to what I think is the South Gate, hung with sagging chains of warm oil lamps and choked with the soft hum of murmured conversation as the trading caravans prepare for predawn departures. The princess is silent the entire ride until the carriage comes to a rough stop at the gate.

"We're here." She motions for me to get out. "Try to be on your best behavior."

"Oh, I'll certainly try," I murmur and swing my legs out. "And more certainly fail."

The sleepy crowd envelops us almost instantly, and for

a moment as I push through them to follow Varia, the huge iron-cast doors of the South Gate catch my eye. Ten on the ground, twenty—no, thirty lawguards in shining armor stand rigid on the white wall the gate is nestled in, perched like vultures as they watch the crowd below. The wall surrounding Vetris might keep witches and bandits out, but it's the lawguards who keep people in.

My mind flickers briefly to escape. Even if I scaled the wall by some miracle and got past the thirty guards without being riddled with spearheads, Varia would surely stop me with a command. And I'm not sure of my Weeping anymore. But if I don't run…

I'll have to face Lucien. Fione. Malachite. I'll have to face them as a traitor. As who I really am—a murderer. A liar.

Everything in me wants to run. The scaffolding up the wall is so close. I could *run*. I could sprint like my life depended on it—

Varia's noticed me lagging and turns in the throng. If the crowd recognizes her, none of them shows it. How could they? It's been five years since she was seen last. She's morphed into a young woman, proud and strong.

"Come on," she urges me. "There are things to be done."

I back away from her slowly, and my feet move for the scaffold. I have to try. I can't face Lucien. Not now. Not now that I'm a monster to him. Varia could be bluffing, could be lying about being my new witch, about the entire transferring ownership ordeal, and I could leap that scaffold. The only thing between me and running free at last could be that white wall, the curve of those wooden inclines against it.

"Don't." Varia's voice turns harder. "Zera—I'm warning you."

"What?" I sneer back at her. "Afraid you're not my witch

after all? Afraid I'll escape?"

I spin on my heel, only to be frozen by her words.

"You will follow me."

It's only half her voice. The other half is a dark, deep, visceral tone I know all too well, reverberating up from some jet bell nestled inside my very being. Varia and the hunger say the same words at the same time, and the sound—*the meaning*—courses through me like icy river water, locking me in place. I will follow her. I will follow them—her and the hunger—until I can follow no more.

I spin again on my heels, this time toward her, and like I'm outside my body, hovering above it and observing it like a play on a stage, I watch myself obediently trot after the princess farther and farther into the crowd.

She *is* my witch.

Every single step of my boots on the cobblestones beats it into me like a terrible, inescapable drumbeat.

Princess Varia d'Malvane of Cavanos—the Laughing Daughter—is my new witch.

3

THE WHITE WYRM
AND THE
IRONSPEAKER

"Do you know much about Old Vetris, Zera?" Princess Varia asks as we reach the very back of the South Gate crowd—where the edge of the cobblestone city meets the foot of the white wall that encapsulates Vetris proper. It looms, gargantuan and glowing with unholy light beneath the three moons, but my eyes can barely look at its beauty before my feet steer me uncontrollably after Varia.

Under the effects of the command, I can still move my face and my neck independently. But the rest of my body feels as if it's fallen asleep, like the muscles I move aren't really my own. I can both feel them moving and not feel them. I got drunk once, on cheap mulled mead Nightsinger was brewing behind her cabin, and that feeling of being absolutely haggard drunk is the closest thing I can compare it to. Here but not here. Aware but unable to do anything but gnaw my lip and answer. I'd love to hurl every insult under the sun at her, but fear is starting to win over my anger. What if I'm under her sway forevermore?

My vocal cords are free, at least—a small mercy. I'm not sure what I'd do if I couldn't constantly voice my flawless opinion.

"No," I say.

The princess stops just before a brass door in the wall, flanked on either side by dour-faced lawguards. I've never been this close to the wall before, at least not from the inside—so I'm surprised to see it has doors at all. Now that I think about it, these doors must be how the guards get up the wall to patrol—the single scaffolding at South Gate wouldn't be enough to traffic every guard.

Princess Varia clears her throat and speaks, softly but clearly. "The Laughing Daughter calls."

I've no time to be shocked at the fact she's telling these lawguards her witchname. Maybe they don't know it's hers. Maybe it's just a password to them. The lawguards immediately straighten and then move away from the door to let us pass, Varia pressing through the creaky brass door, and, without any control, my feet follow her into the dimness on the other side.

I crane my head to the guards. "She's a witc—"

Varia's grip on my wrist is instant. "If you want your heart back, you will tell no one that I am a witch."

My heart? Is she…is she tempting me right now? Is she being genuine? If I had my heart, I could escape her grip on me forever—I could escape the hunger. My heart is the entire reason I came to Vetris and betrayed the prince in the first place. Everything up till the moment in the clearing was for my heart.

The princess shuts the door behind us, giving a piercing smile to the guards. There's no command on me to *not* say anything, but the mere chance of getting my heart back has my tongue still. Once again, I'm chained by more than chains. A prisoner in my own body.

I try not to think about it. But like all things one tries not to think about, it's suddenly all I can think about. She could order me to do anything, and I'd be powerless. *Powerless.* Gods, I hate that word. It saps all the hope from me, the hunger laughing and repeating it over and over.

powerless, powerless, it taunts. *just give up.*

No. There has to be something I can do. There has to be some way out. And if it's keeping my mouth shut about her being a witch, then so be it. The idea of another three years or more as a Heartless is *unthinkable.* I barely made it through in the woods, and that was with Crav's and Peligli's calming presences and with a witch who didn't command me. I won't be able to keep sane through something like that again, alone.

Whatever it takes, I have to get free.

The steady rhythmic drip of water grows in my ears, and my eyes adjust quickly; the inside of the wall is cavernous and long and stretches on seemingly forever, like a hollow snake laid over the horizon. Piercing white mercury lamps are riveted to the riblike brass support beams that shape the wall. An aqueduct carves through the floor, flanked on both sides by grated walkways, and by the light of the lamps I can see that over the years, the steady moisture inside this place has worn every inch of brass a brilliant viridian green.

Varia turns, her face unreadable as she walks on the right side of the grating with sure steps, as if she's been here a thousand times. Maybe she has—Vetris was where she grew up, after all. My legs move me after her, even as I crane my neck to look everywhere. Guards patrol inside the wall, too, marching up and down the grating, and among their armor

I spot the odd brown robe of a wandering polymath. A wall this big requires maintaining, no doubt.

"Old Vetris was what the kingdom of Cavanos was called a thousand years ago," the princess recites briskly. "It spanned the entire Mist Continent—from the Twisted Ocean to the Northern Strait, from the Feralstorm to the Avellish Sea. It was the largest kingdom in the world."

"And they say witches aren't nice to their Heartless," I offer, my voice echoing off the high metal ceiling. "Yet here you are, giving me a free, boring history lesson."

She ignores me completely. "But the Old Vetris we know—the one that built this city—was not comprised solely of humans. A wall this size, of this strength, is still impossible for us to build today. Do you know why that is?"

"Magic, right?" I blow an annoying strand of hair out of my face, my hands riveted at my sides. "The humans and the witches built Old Vetris and lived in harmony together."

The princess shoots me a look over her shoulder. "So you're smarter than a schoolchild after all."

She stops abruptly in front of another brass door and opens it, revealing a spiral staircase descending into utter darkness. She steps onto it without an ounce of fear, and my body blindly follows her, strapped tight to the order. Despite the fact that it gets darker as we descend down the spiral stairs, Varia doesn't proffer a light or seem to lose her footing in the slightest. And neither do I.

"Witches hate humans," her voice rings out. "Humans hate witches. My father and the High Witches are mired in a hate far older than any of them could imagine." She pauses, our footsteps echoing nakedly. "Father will go to war very soon. Whether you had taken my brother's heart for the witches or not, he would've gone to war—of that much I'm sure. His father went to war before him, and his grandfather before him. Fighting witches gives Cavanosians purpose. It's built all their traditions, their religions, their culture. Helkyris reveres knowledge. Avel reveres beauty. Cavanos reveres war. It has built itself a life out of killing."

Her laughter rings out, cold and without comfort. "Though the witches are few in number now, they were once mighty. 'Twas not always so that humans chased witches like this—a hundred years ago, humans were very much on the losing side. The witches have built lives out of war, too, just in different ways. They've planted spies. They've thought up new, horrible magics made to kill and wound and poison. They've found ways to build their cities so high and hidden that humans will never find them. They're like two snakes eating each other's tails. I know that now, after having lived with both of them."

My knees start to ache with how many stairs we've taken, but still my legs pump on, the command caring not for how much pain I'm in. Finally, after what feels like a thousand more steps, we even out onto a stone floor. I can barely see the princess anymore—even with my adjusted eyes. I can hear her boots pause, though.

"Before Old Vetris was formed," she says, "Cavanos's annals were riddled with stories of wars between humans and witches. So one has to wonder: What could've possibly forced these mortal enemies to come together and make the walled cities? What could have forced them to work together to build an empire, instead of tearing each other apart?"

I know the answer. Everyone who's picked up a book in the last thousand years would know the answer.

The darkness around us is so deep now that I can close my eyes and open them and not be able to tell the difference.

All I have to go by are the sounds of dripping water and a new sound: a deep, sonorous rhythm echoing off the walls that's gotten louder the lower we've gone. Is it the hum of a polymath contraption, maybe? But that wouldn't explain why there are no lights down here.

We walk for a few more seconds, silently, and gradually the sounds of shuffling and the clank of armor and faint, rough voices start to filter in. Celeon voices—unmistakable in their half-purring, half-hissing tone. Five, ten—there has to be at least a dozen of them all around us. Royal guards, maybe?

There are some celeon lawguards, but most of them directly serve the crown. It makes sense—they have no problem seeing in this dark. Bound with muscle and able to see and hear keenly even with a complete absence of light, celeon are a race of catlike, lizard-like people who were once creatures without sentience. But after a stray magic spell went awry, they were given thought. Since then they've developed a profound hatred for witches, allying themselves instead with the humans. The ones down here might not know Varia's a witch. They likely see her only as a member of the royal d'Malvane family to be obeyed.

Varia must've stopped, because my feet come to a grinding halt.

"Your Highness," a celeon voice says. "We were unaware you were coming so soon. Yorl is on the observation level, taking measurements of the beast. I can call him if—"

"There will be no need just yet," Varia interrupts her smoothly. "At ease. I will inform you when I need you."

Another clanking shuffle echoes from all directions, like all the celeon are doing something at once. Bowing?

"As you wish, Your Highness."

There's more clanking as footsteps pad past me, away from me. I feel a sudden grasp on my wrist as Varia's voice hovers just above my shoulder, a singsong tone to it.

"You haven't answered my question, Zera. What could possibly have driven the humans and witches to work together to form Old Vetris all those years ago?"

My brain thunders in my skull, mirrored by that heavy, sonorous rhythm lathing the darkness. This is no contraption. It's too big. It sounds too...*alive*. The celeon mentioned a "beast." Varia's question, a beast in the dark. But there's no possible way—

Varia's voice seems faint, far away, as she barks to someone, "Open the gates."

"Begging your pardon, Your Highness—but are you sure?" another celeon voice asks nervously. "It just woke up, and it's very hungry."

"Do as I say," Varia bites. "Open the gate."

The screech of metal as something heavy starts to lift makes me jump out of my own skin. Every hair on my arm stands straight up, my entire body covered in gooseflesh. Something huge shakes the ground suddenly, vibrating my very bones, and if I wasn't immortal, this would be the point where I would've most definitely pissed myself. The smell hits me all at once—a wave of putrid death, like rotting blood, carried on a moist sheaf of air. The sound of scales raking across stone.

I understand suddenly, too late and in one horrible swoop—the rhythmic sound is *breathing*, and it's so loud it's like a waterfall's roar in my ears. *No*, it's not possible by any reach of the imagination. But a tiny, terrified voice rings in my mind: *if Gavik kept one in the pipe below the East River Tower for years...*

My feet take me forward, following Varia automatically again, even as the fear crawls up my throat and tries to pull me back. Suddenly my eyes catch a haze of light, growing from one of Varia's fingers—one of the wood fingers she used to replace her lost ones. A flame. It gives off a little halo of orange luminescence, beating hard against the dark. With it, the corners of my eyes catch a sliver of a massive steel gate, of a dirt floor extending for what seems like forever into darkness. And then the flamelight reveals something in the dirt as Varia walks forward: scratch marks, impossibly deep and impossibly *long*.

My breathing is so shallow, it hurts. It can't be—

Something slithers in the darkness beyond the firelight, the hissing sound of scales growing louder. It's huge. I can *hear* how huge it is—how the air moves to make space for it. The rhythmic breathing stops all at once, and so does mine. A heavy spear of air moving fast pierces in front of me, so fast I can see the dust clouds curl before it, and then a mouth lunges into the firelight.

Teeth. Hundreds of them. Thousands.

a fellow monster. The hunger leers.

Teeth, serrated and made for ripping, each one bigger than my entire arm and dripping thick strands of saliva. A forked tongue lashing against the teeth, tasting the firelight. It's not the whole mouth—it's simply a small part of it, the lower corner of a giant, wolflike white jaw—and yet it could swallow Varia and me comfortably whole right this instant. I can't think—all I can do is watch, petrified, as Varia calmly looks at the jaw not three feet in front of her with her dark eyes. The hot, heavy smell of rotting meat and decaying innards intensifies as the creature's breath washes over us, in and out like the tide.

"The answer to my question, Zera," Varia demands evenly, watching as the fangs drop a puddle of drool larger than her on the ground. The firelight flickers over her placid face. "What is it? What was the thing that made humans and witches unite under one banner, again? I'm so absentminded."

Through my gritted teeth, I manage a single hoarse word. "V-Valkerax."

The princess is braver than anyone in the world.

For example, she's standing three feet away from a full-grown valkerax without an inch of terror on her face.

She looks resolute, proud, as if trapping this giant wyrm down here is her greatest accomplishment. It's like she's showing it off to me as a child does a particularly beautiful beetle they've caught or a river stone they've found.

"Don't be afraid, Zera." She laughs softly. "I assure you— it's sedated with the strongest concoctions a polymath can make and held back by the freshest beneather runes. If Gavik is useful for anything, it's for telling me exactly how to keep a valkerax alive and trapped without letting it bite my head off."

I can't see the beneather runes carved anywhere thanks to the darkness, but knowing they're present eases my fear by a fraction. The beneathers—Malachite's people who live beneath the ground in the Dark Below—are the only ones who know how to fight valkerax, how to keep them away. They've been doing both for a thousand years, after all. According to what Malachite told me nearly a week ago, beneather runes can keep a valkerax out of a place, or inside of a place, by binding them with their true name.

"How," I breathe, watching with horror as the jaw

disappears from the firelight and the massive shuffle of scales and breathing resumes as the valkerax moves somewhere else. "How did you—?"

There's an earth-shaking thump that rattles the very pebbles on the ground, and Varia and I start at the same time. I'm relieved to see the princess stride backward—so even she's scared of the thing, deep down—over the lip of the open gate, and I follow her, my body shaking and eager to get away. The metal screech of the gate closes behind us.

"The hows aren't important." Varia sniffs, her face paler in the firelight from her finger but no less serious and composed. "It's the whats I want us to focus on."

I swallow, gulping down stale air. "As in '*what in Kavar's bloody eye socket are you planning to do with that thing*?'"

"Indeed. Yorl." She turns to someone in the darkness. "What *am* I going to do with that thing?"

My heart catches again as another figure steps into the dim firelight—a celeon, blinking his liquid emerald eyes quickly as they adjust to the light. He isn't an adult celeon—his mane too short and bristly along his neck to be fully realized, his features too sharp and lanky, like a tree that's been growing too fast for its own bark with none of the muscle or substance to back it up. The brown robe he wears (a polymath robe without a tool belt—strange) hangs loose on him. It's hard to tell in such a dim environment, but I think his fur is an ochre yellow, spotted with vermillion scales on his ribs and legs. His broad triangular ears are studded with two rows of silver earrings. He carries a bundle of scrolls under one arm and a quill in the other paw. A pair of glasses rests on his face, the bridge wide to accommodate his wider nose.

"Who is this?" The celeon frowns at me, then at the princess. "I won't welcome another distraction in my lab,

Varia. You've given me only one month—"

"She's the Heartless you asked for," Varia chimes, seemingly unmoved by the fact he's addressing her so casually. The celeon narrows his eyes at me, the firelight catching his glasses and making them opaque.

"Hi," I try, wetting my fear-parched lips. "Nice dungeon you've got here. I think. I haven't seen much of it because you appear to have an aversion to interior lighting."

There's a beat as Yorl looks me over and then turns back to Varia. "I'd prefer Gavik over the talkative one."

I bristle internally. I might not have a godsdamn clue what's going on, but anyone who prefers Gavik to me is obviously either a terrible person or an uncaring one—they tend to occur in tandem.

"Yes, well." The princess sighs. "Gavik can't Weep. This one can."

My eyes rivet to her instantly. So she *does* know about Weeping. Then her confidence that I wouldn't tell the king she's a witch is even more mystifying—unless she thinks the shaky promise of my heart is enough to silence me. And it is. But I'd rather rot in the afterlife than tell her that.

"Really?" Yorl scoffs. "This thing? She looks like she crawled out of a gutter."

"And you look like you crawled out of a basement with a lot of valkerax drool in it, but you don't see me insulting you about it," I offer. It's almost nice to be angry instead of devastated, and I let it fuel my tongue. Yorl doesn't so much as blink at the insult, inspecting me from behind his glasses with a cool, unmoving gaze.

"There will be no arguing between you two." Varia clears her throat, her voice every inch a princess's. "We don't have much time to do what is needed. Pray tell her, Yorl, precisely why that valkerax is here and why you need her here, too."

Yorl narrows his emerald eyes on me. "You're going to teach that valkerax how to Weep."

Every word is Common Vetrisian. Every word is one I know, but strung together, they make no sense. I decide to make an inhale instead of a laugh. "I must've misheard you. What you said would imply valkerax are Heartless. And I'm one hundred percent certain there's not a jar in the world that can fit a heart that big."

Yorl scoffs, turning to Varia. "I'm not going to explain everything from the ground up to her."

Varia just smiles at him sweetly. "I beg you to remember— I'm the only one outside of the Black Archives who can give you the polymath title you so desire."

Yorl winces behind his glasses. I've never seen a celeon polymath. Lawguards, sure. But not polymaths. They're either rare or, knowing Vetris, discriminated against. If that's the case, it would definitely be true that Varia is one of the few who can manage to make him one.

He turns his yellow head wearily back to me, his voice a drone. "A thousand years ago, the humans and witches united against the valkerax threat that was razing the kingdom."

"Right, Old Vetris," I agree. "You can skip ahead—I'm not quite as slow as I look."

Yorl just stares at me like I'm a particularly boring piece of art. "With the combined powers of the polymaths' knowledge and the witches' magic, they were able to devise a method to control the valkerax."

"You mean like the beneather runes?" I ask. Yorl's stare turns to a flat glare, and I put on a smile. "Sorry, sorry. You have the floor. Until I decide to lay down on it out of utter boredom."

"Beneather runes simply forbid a valkerax to leave or enter a set area." Yorl's annoyed expression lifts the longer he gets to speak. "Such runes were devised by Old Vetris and given to the beneathers, yes. We have them carved into the walls of the arena we keep this valkerax in. But you are much more familiar with the other method the Old Vetrisians invented."

Yorl holds up his paw, showing me each of his clawed fingers and putting one down for every new point he makes. "Valkerax heal at a surprising rate. It's why they are so difficult to kill. Nothing compared to a Heartless, of course, but faster than any other creature in the world. The Old Vetrisians discovered that by taking a part of the valkerax and anchoring it to a magic-infused object, any witch who touched that object could command the valkerax, and any of their future offspring, to do their bidding."

My unheart goes cold as the hunger slithers through my ears: *just like us. chained like us.*

"You mean…Heartlessness?" I mutter.

Yorl shakes out his half-grown mane. "If anything, it was a prototype of the Heartless curse. But yes. Heartlessness was developed later, purely by the witches and their magic alone, using methods based on Old Vetrisian valkerax control."

My mind races back to the books I've read, the histories I pored over in Nightsinger's cabin with naught else to do. The books were never specific about how the Old Vetrisians managed to save the world from the valkerax rampage, but now…

"*That's* how Old Vetris sent the valkerax into the Dark Below," I marvel. "They *commanded* them?"

Varia nods. "Precisely. Old Vetris forced them under,

and the beneathers sealed them there with the runes. Those of us above can live in peace, while the beneathers act as their jailors."

Beneather jailors for valkerax, witch jailors for Heartless. Pity reaches corrosive fingers into my heart, but I remember the massive fanged jaw I saw not seconds ago, and the fingers curl in on themselves. The books that spoke of burned villages and mountains of dead bodies only glanced over the valkerax's reign of destruction. They weren't always hostile, but one day during the time of Old Vetris they became so and have been ever since. The beneathers are all that stand between them and us.

"Even now," Yorl continues, "the valkerax you saw inside the arena is withering away. The Old Vetrisian command to remain in the Dark Below is eating at its very being, driving it mad with pain. It will eventually die if we do not return it to the Dark Below soon."

"But if I can teach it to Weep..." I trail off.

"If you can teach it to Weep, it could—in theory—resist the all-consuming command," Varia agrees.

I glower at her. "And what do you get from it being able to resist?"

Varia blinks, surprised, the firelight catching the falter in her eyes just before she laughs. "So suspicious." She inspects her flawless nails to regain herself. "Lucien told me you and he found that valkerax skeleton of Gavik's in the tunnels beneath the East River Tower."

We had. Fione needed information to reveal the misdeeds of Gavik—her uncle. She led us to his secret repository, where Gavik had kept a valkerax in the tunnels to guard it. I nod, recalling the beneather runes Malachite read on the wall where its massive skeleton had been. "The runes said it was killed by the Laughing Daughter. Out of mercy."

Laughing Daughter. That was the code word to get down here. And it's Varia's witchname.

"And Lucien's sword fit perfectly in the head wound the skull had," she agrees. "Yes—I killed that valkerax. Gavik was keeping it for study, and the pain of being out of the Dark Below was hurting it horribly. It begged me to kill it."

I pause. "Valkerax...can talk?"

Yorl and Varia share a look. A look I don't like. It reeks of secrets.

"In a manner." Yorl shrugs. "What matters is their minds have been warped by the magic of the command. They speak in fragmented riddles. To stay in the Dark Below is all they care for. If one brings a valkerax above the surface, they are in tremendous amounts of pain. And the fragmented riddles become only more difficult to understand. Unreliable gibberish at best."

My mind skitters around itself as I think. Heartlessness and what the valkerax have gone through might not be the same thing, but they are similar. Not being able to speak, being in pain—it sounds like when I tried to run from Nightsinger at the beginning of my Heartless life. I moved more than a mile and a half away from her and my mind went blank with pure agony. I couldn't think or move or feel anything but the thunderous pain throbbing through my body. It felt like hours passed before Nightsinger found me and brought me back into her radius.

But Nightsinger isn't my witch anymore.

Varia sweeps her black eyes to the gate, the firelight on her finger kissing the steel just enough to see the massive outline, and then she turns back to me.

"I saw you Weep in the clearing, Zera. It took me a great

amount of sleuthing and wheedling, but when I lived with the witches, I managed to get one of the older ones to explain it to me—it lets Heartless have control over themselves again and brings them clarity, even if they are in their monster forms. You will teach the valkerax to Weep, and when it can control itself and speak, it will tell me where their bones are."

I frown. "Their bones?"

"The Old Vetrisians realized controlling the valkerax one by one with thousands of witches wasn't economical," Yorl says softly. "Or statistically possible, for that matter. The valkerax outnumbered the witches greatly. So they gathered as many valkerax parts onto one intensely magical object as they could, to make an attempt at mass control."

"A tree," Varia clarifies. "It's a tree, greatly magical, made entirely of valkerax bones. And entirely lost to time. But the valkerax know where it is. They can feel its presence always, commanding them to remain in the Dark Below. It's what keeps them there."

A tree of bones that can be used to control every valkerax in the world. Varia, who insisted in the clearing she has to stop the war. Suddenly it all falls into place.

"You…" I look to Varia, my eyes working up her legs, her cloaked torso, to her firelit face at last. "*You* want to control them."

Varia's smile widens. "But whatever would I do with them, my cleverest Zera?"

The insult barely pierces through my disbelief. "You're going to use them to force a standstill. An army of valkerax, poised between the humans and witches. No one would dare to fight."

"No one would dare to fight," she repeats softly after me. *"Indeed."*

"You're mad," I blurt.

The princess's eyes go cold, but her smile warms. "No, Zera. I'm simply realistic."

"The valkerax nearly *destroyed the world*!" I throw my hands out. "They could break free someday and they'd raze it all over again! Even if you could keep control over this tree, over them, you'd be feared and reviled even more than witches, more than anyone—"

"Yorl." Varia suddenly looks to him, breezing through my points like they don't exist. "How soon can we send her in?"

"When the concoction is finished brewing." Yorl squints into the darkness. "Which should be tomorrow morning."

"I'm not doing this," I snap. "I'm not helping you play with a power like this!"

"You will," she says. That confidence again. I could rip it apart with my sheer anger, but I chew my lip and hold myself steady.

she holds us hostage like the last witch, the hunger whispers. I lift my chin.

"In no conceivable universe will I help you, Princess."

I expect her to command me to help. But no words come out of her mouth, laced with the hunger or otherwise. With her non-firelit hand, she reaches into her cloak and pulls out something soft and pliable. It sags to one side in her wooden fingers. A bag—a small velvet sack, stitched with black letters; TRAITOR.

Traitor. Just like Lucien called me.

It's identical to the bag I saw Varia put Archduke Gavik's heart in, though his read "leech." She dangles it before me, her smile blazing hot and somehow ferocious on the edges.

"You will help me, Zera, because in return, I'm going to give you back the heart you've always wanted. The one you tried to kill and enthrall my brother for."

My anger snuffs out as quickly as the bag in her hand moves, gently bumping into her palm in a steady rhythm. A *heartbeat*.

She slides the bag off, and there, in her fingers, rests a pink organ the size of a fist. That's... Is that my *heart*? Just there, in her hands? The gap in my chest keens with an aching longing—the same one I felt each time I stared at my heart over Nightsinger's fire.

She has it. Just as Varia took control of my reins, she's standing right in front of me with my heart. No bars around it, no glass between it and me.

I can *hear* it beating. I can see every blue vein in it pulsing with my memories, my human life. The thing I came to Vetris for. The thing I suffered these three years and two long weeks for.

our heart, the hunger whimpers.

"My heart," I whisper.

4

A HEART LIKE A HUNGER

Before I can think, my hand darts out for it, but Varia's command is instantaneous.

"Stand back."

I go rigid, my body automatically making space between us. Yorl watches us with voraciously curious emerald eyes. My mouth still works, at least, even as my fingers are consumed with the maddening itch to snatch the heart from Varia's palm.

"You're lying," I say, hard. I nearly killed her brother. There's no way she would offer me my heart.

"I do many things, Zera," Varia says to me, dully staring down at the bag. "I omit. I plan. But I don't lie. If you teach the valkerax beyond that gate to Weep, I will return your heart and release you from my service."

"You could just command me to teach it to Weep." My words are lightning striking earth and making wildfire in its wake. "Why bother bribing me?"

"Because I *can't* command you to teach it," she lilts,

tilting my heart and bringing her fire-touched finger closer to it, the arteries glowing brighter and hollower. A horrible heat blazes through my empty chest—like the fire is inside me—and I pull back, her command urging me on as the pain does. She nods lightly to Yorl, a command on her lips. **"Tell him what dying feels like."**

My mouth suddenly bursts into movement. "Like nothing. Like a great, empty coldness. There's a white behind your eyes, and then it's like falling asleep, but all at once."

Yorl's gaze narrows slightly at me behind his glasses, his silver-armored tail swishing, but his expression never changes. Varia strokes my heart in her palm like a beloved creature, a pet, her featherlight touch emanating deep inside my chest.

"Now," she commands. **"Tell him what Weeping feels like."**

The hunger mirrors her voice, dark and imperative, and I can feel the magic moving through my unheart like an ocean current—racing for my throat. But unlike the earlier command where everything came out instantly, my body doesn't obey. I expect my tongue to burst into movement and sound and explanation, but there's...*nothing*. I move my jaw experimentally, waiting for words to pour forth. Absolute silence.

I could tell him if I wanted to. I could keep it to myself if I wanted to.

"See?" Varia stops petting my heart and looks up at me, the organ beating earnestly in the dimness. "Anything regarding Weeping is impossible to command. Or, trust me, I would've done exactly that the moment I led you down here. I don't *want* to give you your heart—you don't deserve it after what you did to my brother. I want to teach you exactly the consequences of hurting him. But I'm being magnanimous. I'm putting aside my own wants in order to stop this war." She sighs. "But you...you don't have to sacrifice anything for what you want. I'll give you your heart. You'll have your freedom. All you have to do is teach the valkerax first."

"You could still be lying," I insist, my eyes flickering over to my heart again. "Say I do teach the valkerax how to Weep. What's stopping you from keeping me as your Heartless?"

"My honor as a d'Malvane?" she offers.

"Not good enough." I deaden my gaze.

And then, in one swift motion, she's beside me. She holds my shoulder and shoves her entire fist into my chest with no ceremony, no warning. Like an explosion from an epicenter, the pain radiates out from her fist and I tilt my head down—no blood, no flesh, no wound, only her whole fist, the skin there as black as midnight and embedded deep inside my ribs. Her dark eyes have grown darker from corner to corner, her lips reciting a wordless chant none of us can hear. She's so close to me, I can see the beads of sweat dripping down her temple, her mouth moving faster as the pain inside me blooms.

The firelight on her other hand's finger flickers with an abrupt wind, blowing out and engulfing us in darkness. Every muscle in my body goes limp, but her arm keeps me suspended in air, my entire frame hanging off her fist. My eyelids flutter rapidly, and suddenly I can see it—my life.

Mother's soft, sweet face, her blond eyebrows knitting as she's braiding my hair and laughing. Father's large nose and larger smile, showing me how to tie a caravan knot. We traveled to Helkyris and spent a day rolling snowballs down a hill, the little orbs growing bigger and bigger and crashing into the trees below as we whooped with delight.

My birthday, the sparrows outside the caravan window as Mother brought a dish of sweetrounds covered in maple glaze to the table, the rich and sugary taste on my tongue.

Father and me in the driver's seat, the horses moving at a lazy pace under the afternoon sun, the drakeflies buzzing over the nearby murky lake, and he put his wide-brimmed hat on my head and it was so big it fell over my eyes and all I could see was darkness—

Darkness as the pain recedes, as Varia lights her finger with fire again, her hand retreating from my chest and the memories slipping from my mind like desert sand. It's no use; no matter how hard I try to hold on, they keep getting fainter. But for that moment—that one glorious moment—they were *real*. It was like I was there again, reliving it all at once. And that was only a second of my heart being inside me again.

If I could have the whole thing *forever…*

The urge to get my heart back gnawed at me in Nightsinger's forest. But it was nothing like this. Back then, I didn't remember anything of what my heart held. As the years passed, I got more and more numb to the idea of it—yes, I wanted my heart, but almost entirely for the freedom. I couldn't remember what memories were inside or how dear they were to me.

But now they *sing.*

"No—no!" I grab Varia's wrist, shrieking. "Put it back! *Put it back!*"

The princess wrenches out of my grip with a breathless laugh, sweat dripping down her temples and a cold gleam in her eyes as she relights her finger, the firelight dancing. "You're right, Zera. There's no reason for you to trust my word. But you *will* do this for me. You will teach this valkerax how to Weep, or you will never see your heart again."

I pant, wildly searching for my heart in her palm. There—between her fingers! I can see the pinkness of it.

"You came to Vetris for your heart." Varia breathes raggedly. "All Heartless want their hearts. But you're not all Heartless, are you, Zera? In the clearing, I saw the way my brother looked at you. And I saw how you looked at him, too."

She gently tosses my heart from one hand to the other, like a juggling ball. Like it means nothing to her. I lunge for it, but my body stops me before I can reach her—the command to stay away absolute.

"He will go to war to protect his people. He will be the target of every witch assassin in the kingdom." Concern, genuine and fearful, creeps into her eyes. "But if I stop the war, if I find the Bone Tree and control all the valkerax, I could bring war in Cavanos to a standstill forever. He will be safe."

Safe. Lucien could be safe—Fione and Malachite, too. Everyone in Cavanos will be safe; Crav and Peligli and Nightsinger and Y'shennria—all of them, safe from another devastating human-witch war like the Sunless War. A whine escapes my lips, bestial and pathetic and not of my own control. I can't trust her. But what choice do I have? My heart is so close—it's *right there*. The only thing between my humanity and me is the valkerax behind that gate. Not a lonely prince who must be seduced and deceived but a valkerax who must be taught.

I don't have to hurt anyone. I just have to teach. It's easier than anything Nightsinger ever asked of me. I'm not betraying or lying. I would be whole again; I could stop the war I promised to, without breaking anyone in the process.

Mother's voice—it's fading so quickly. Father's smile—

"All right," I spit. "I'll do it."

Varia's whole demeanor changes in an instant. She straightens, all her haggardness and coldness disappearing. She puts my heart back in its bag, and I watch it go with a longing burn. She wipes her sweat on her sleeves, smooths her hair, and turns to Yorl.

"I'll bring her to you tomorrow morning, then. Anything you need, I'll provide you with. But as of now, we have a banquet to prepare for." She brushes past him and looks at me over her shoulder. "Come."

Without waiting for my response, she sweeps away, the firelight dimming upward as her boots ascend the spiral stairs to the surface. The command doesn't force me to follow, but I do anyway, shuffling after the light.

"Make sure not to get eaten before then," I call to Yorl.

"Make sure not to eat anyone before then," he deadpans back. I scoff as Yorl and the gate disappear into total darkness, the valkerax's breathing still echoing in my ears.

The irony doesn't escape me. It rarely does—I chase irony down like an overzealous kitten hunting butterflies. Varia's dangling in front of me a way to get my heart back, just like Nightsinger did. Is it the nature of witches to wield freedom like a bargaining chip?

Nightsinger struck the deal with me in the first place because I'd been asking to be released for so long. And because she wanted me to have some burning incentive to take Lucien's heart, no doubt. She could've easily commanded me to obey Y'shennria, go with her, infiltrate the court, and take it. But she didn't. She cares—*cared*—too much about me to do that.

In the carriage back to the palace, I ask, "Why choose me specifically for this? Are you that desperate?"

Varia moves her velvety dark eyes from the window

and onto me. "I tried to find other Heartless. Helkyrisian Heartless. Avellish Heartless. Cavanos is the only place Weeping has ever made itself known—the constant wars and the Heartless exposed to battle evolved it naturally. As far as I'm aware, you're the only one still alive who knows how to Weep. The others either died with their witches in the Sunless War or were shattered for their knowledge."

So that's why she looked at me so hungrily in the clearing. Her words gut me like a fish. I'm the only Heartless left who knows? Reginall—Y'shennria's butler—definitely knows a bit about Weeping, but he's a human now. Even if he understood it fully, it'd be difficult to teach without having first done it. So I'm…I'm really the only one.

alone. always alone.

"And then you found me in the clearing," I mutter. "How were you going to locate the Bone Tree if you *didn't* find a Weeping Heartless?"

Varia shifts, her silk skirts whispering as she folds one leg over the other. "Search high and low for it myself. What do you think I've been doing all these years in hiding—knitting baby clothes?"

"Then why haven't you found it yet?"

The princess frowns, her full lips dour. Identical to Lucien's frown, it hits my heart like unwelcome lightning. "The Bone Tree is…*elusive*," Varia says. "The Old Vetrisians pumped it so full of magic, it's developed some quirks of its own. It never stays long in one place."

"It can move?" I marvel.

She nods. "It may look like a tree, but it's more of a magical relic, really. That's why I need a completely sane valkerax in control of itself. They're the only ones who can tell me exactly where it is, *when* it is, with total accuracy."

The carriage rumbles over the cobblestones of the familiar bridge that stretches across the common quarter to the noble quarter. I watch the river move like a lazy black-glass snake beneath the stone arch.

"It won't just be Cavanos that fears you and your valkerax army," I start. "It'll be the whole world. Lucien. Fione. Your father. *Everyone.* You could use it to kill everyone."

Varia speaks, staring placidly out the window. "You've read the Midnight Gifter, right?"

I'm quiet. Of course I have. A hugely popular book series, about a noble in the times of Old Vetris who steals from the rich and gives to the poor and dresses entirely in black. It's the whole reason I thought Lucien, when I met him first as the leather-clad thief Whisper, was so amusing. The resemblance was clear.

"Book three," Varia says. "Page one forty-five, line two. *'That I could give the whole world of Arathess peace, I would. That there was some polymath contraption, some lever I could hit or button I could press that would give peace to all, know that I would die with my hand on it—'*"

"*'And still in death my skeleton would go on, the bones moving of their own accord, and my flesh feeding its furnace,'*" I finish. It's not a common quote, but I remember it well because it struck me so deeply when I was younger. Varia turns to me and smiles faintly. It's a smile different from the ones I've seen from her so far—something much gentler. Something that looks more human and less princess.

"I want my people to live in peace, Zera."

It could be true. Her words, her tone, sound true. Still, I won't let it go.

"The valkerax have had a thousand years to reproduce in the Dark Below," I say. "We're talking thousands of wyrms.

Maybe hundreds of thousands. Can one witch really keep control over all the valkerax in Cavanos? By herself?"

"My flesh will feed its furnace," Varia murmurs again, a fragment of the quote rearranged just so. The carriage jostles us in the uneasy silence.

"The banquet tonight is to celebrate my return." Varia's voice returns loud again. "Fione will be there. And Lucien. His bodyguard, too, I presume."

My fear of the valkerax is buried by a sudden wave of anxiety. They all know now just how terrible I am. I can't possibly face them.

i told you they would turn on us, the hunger taunts.

"I had your measurements taken while you were unconscious on the couch," Varia says lightly. "And my personal tailor refitted several of my old garments for you. I think you'll like them."

A dress means only one thing in Vetris.

"As much as I enjoy a beautiful gown, I'm not going—"

"You don't have to," she interrupts me. "I'm not like the other witches, Zera. I'm not tyrannical. You've agreed to help me find the Bone Tree, so you can do precisely as you please. The guards have been informed, the court has been lied to—you're simply a witness to the terrible murder of Gavik and his men. No one knows you're Heartless except Father and me, and Lucien and his bodyguard. I'll tell Fione tonight, though I'm sure she's guessed as much by now, if Lucien hasn't told her himself."

It's a small, cold relief. I couldn't care less if the noble court knows what I am. They could throw stones and spears all they wanted, if only I could trade their ignorance for my friends' knowledge.

were you ever *really friends?* The hunger cackles.

My unheart splits in half with pain. Were we ever really friends, if I lied to them about who I was the entire time? How can you be friends with someone who isn't who they say they are?

I look out at the buildings of the city, scrying frantically for something to distract myself with. Gavik. If Varia's made sure everyone thinks Gavik was murdered, he can't be in the palace. But neither can he be far. He must be hiding in the city somewhere, doing Varia's bidding in the shadows.

The princess tilts her head, her sheet of black hair glimmering in the oil light of the passing lampposts. "All I'm saying is you might want to be present tonight. There's going to be a rather special announcement at the banquet that I think you'll want to hear."

Announcements can take a flying leap off a volcanic crevice for all I care. But it'd be cowardly, wouldn't it—to run away from the people I've hurt? To hide in Varia's apartments like some sort of pathetic worm cowering in its burrow? I used them. I traded their trust for a chance at my heart, and now that my gamble has failed, the least I can do is face them with the truth laid naked between us. They deserve that much.

"I hope I don't have to remind you," Varia says, "that speaking to anyone of what I am, or what you are doing for me, is the fastest way to lose your one chance at your heart."

I frown. "But you need me. I'm the only one who can teach it how to Weep."

She curls a tendril of shiny dark hair around her delicate finger. "You are merely a means to speed up a lengthy process that will happen, one way or another. Make no mistake—you are valuable. But you are also unnecessary. You are a luxury I would like to keep but would have no compunction sacrificing if you prove troublesome."

My stomach churns uneasily. I should've known better than to get complacent around the princess. I hide my nerves in a scoff. "I suppose being called a 'luxury' is a step up from being called a monster."

She's quiet, and then, "That reminds me. **You will not allow yourself to be cut with a white mercury blade.**"

The command curdles my hunger, makes it rise up dark and swelling inside me, but it has nowhere to go. It simply lingers under my skin, and I hate every inch of it. She knows the only way for me to Weep and get free of her thrall is her white mercury blade. And now, even if I get ahold of it, I won't be able to cut myself, to weaken our magical bond with it and Weep enough to escape.

Varia smiles. "Can't have you running off, now can we?"

The moment the carriage pulls to a stop, I dart out of the uncomfortable atmosphere and take the palace steps two at a time. Mercifully, there are very few nobles out and about in the palace halls—the little Y'shennria now in permanent residence in my head tells me they're too scared for their own well-being after the rumored murder of Gavik. There is one noble, though, looking down on me from a banister as I step into the verdant, flower-strewn entrance hall of the palace. He looms so far above me, pointed dark eyes lingering on places they shouldn't. On monsters they shouldn't.

His hair is short and black and ruffled, his posture immaculate even as mine slinks. There's a moment that feels like years as my eyes drink him in—impossible and out of reach, tall and dark against so much white marble. He shows almost nothing on his noble's mask of icy impassivity. There are no feelings behind his obsidian eyes. It's a familiar look.

The first time he saw me at the Spring Welcoming, his eyes were the exact same. Cold. Impervious.

He's looking at me like he looks at every other noble—with barely hidden disdain. No hint of warmth. Every emotion I'd seen in his eyes once before is now crushed to nothingness.

The prince is silent, his hand gripping the railing. He couldn't speak to me, even if he still wanted to—I wouldn't hear him this far down. It would echo too much. It would be lost. A thousand things flood my mouth and jockey for first place: *I'm sorry. I wanted to tell you. I didn't mean to hurt you—*

but we did. and if it meant our heart, we would hurt you again. does that alone make us a monster?

The high collar of his coat hides his mouth as he turns away, and I'm left with nothing. Nothing but the taste of ash in my mouth.

Here is how my unlife falls apart—one high-heeled step at a time.

Clad in a strangely simple blue dress, modest as can be, I've never felt more naked. My lip tint makes my lips feel gummy, useless, and I half wish it would seal my mouth shut so I couldn't make an ass of myself tonight. As I wander toward the banquet hall and the sounds of socializing nobles and faintly cheery instruments become louder, my breathing starts to fragment. I scoff at myself—even after my training, even after attending these things more than once, I still get nervous.

No one is ever really ready.

With the ghost of Y'shennria at my side, I lift my head high and walk in.

The heat always hits you first—the heat of a hundred bodies packed in close. The smell hits you second—every conceivable floral scent floating through the air and mixing with the smell of sweat and alcohol. This much hasn't changed. And the noise—the noise is a sea of soft and loud voices, of waves and dips and murmurs and roils. The clink of wineglasses on trays, the flash of the candlelight off grand jewelry. Every noble is draped in the most decadent silks and gems, and I'm wearing nothing but a borrowed dress and my own bravado.

Even with a murdered archduke, even with the country on the precipice of war, there is an order to the banquet. Tradition holds Vetris together when no other glue would. The older nobles watch the younger ones walk in, exalting over which of them is most suitable for marriage. The younger nobles do their best to look less nervous than they feel. The Steelrun and d'Goliev girls—Charm and Grace—who debuted with me at the Spring Welcoming, seem older now as I watch them walk in. I spot the Priseless twin boys, ever blond and ever snub-nosed. We lock eyes and, as if they share a skin, both of their faces go a startling shade of green at the same time. Their defeat at my hands in the duel still plagues them, I'm sure. I indulge them with a smile, and they scurry off without so much as another glance.

"And don't come back." I laugh, snatching a flute of wine from a passing tray, but the moment of joy lives short. I down the wine and it gives me courage enough to parse my eyes over the crowd, looking for a shock of familiar white hair, mouse-hair, midnight hair. Nothing. Fione isn't here yet, and I'd know if the prince and Malachite were here.

The wine in turn gives the crowd the courage to whisper.

"*Y'shennria's niece, is she not? And His Highness's favored.*"

"*—mysterious circumstances. She saw Gavik's murder firsthand. Poor thing—*"

"*Lady Y'shennria isn't here with her? How curious.*"

"*I've heard the Y'shennria manor does not stir of late—*"

I hold my head high. Y'shennria's gone—she told me she'd be heading for sanctuary outside of Vetris with the witches the moment I left for the Hunt. Coming back would be pointless; for all she knows, I'm either shattered and dead or reunited with Nightsinger. But if Y'shennria doesn't show up to a noble function soon—and she won't, because it'd be dangerous and illogical—she'll garner more and more suspicion. Especially with news of Gavik's "murder" going around. And that suspicion will shunt right to me, if it hasn't already.

I'm on borrowed time. But I always have been in this city, have I not?

"Lady Fione Himintell," the announcer standing by the door crows. My whole body freezes, and every noble watches the stairs to see her descend. Varia's strong magic no doubt brought me back to consciousness quickly, so it's been only a day, two at most, but it feels like I haven't seen her in years as she walks down the steps in a pearlescent silver gown, her mousey ringlets done up in a cascade. She looks amazing, and yet her face is tense. She clutches her white valkerax-headed cane with equally white knuckles as she moves through the crowd, the whispers coiling around her like snakes.

"Archduke Gavik killed by witches—"

"—she's now the youngest and wealthiest of us by far, and she'll soon be named an archduchess by the Minister of the Blood—"

"Not even married—"

"Only the most suitable man for Her Grace is required, then—"

Man? I'd forgotten how obsessed this court was with pairing children off to sire more. I gnaw my lip. I hadn't even thought about a marriage for Fione, but I'm sure that's all that must be on her mind now. That and the fact I'm a Heartless who lied to her.

Vetrisian society doesn't condemn homosexual relationships, but the court is another matter. All they care about is carrying on their bloodlines. Two women are sometimes more than capable of creating children—but Fione is expected to marry someone who could provide her with heirs, no matter what. Not for love but for cold, unfeeling procreation.

My unheart aches for her, but she turns, and for a moment our eyes meet through the crowd. We're just close enough that she could strike a conversation with me, if she so chose. And *she* has to choose, because I'm a much lower rank than her. I always have been, but now with the mantle of archduchess hanging over her, it's more obvious. Her eyes are so blue—cornflowers at high noon, impassive, and mine, I'm sure, are tired discs of gray. I force a smile.

If she hates me for what I've done, what I am, I'd understand. But I don't want her to. *Gods,* I don't want her to.

Gods, I want to talk to her. To talk *with* her about the stifling court, about their eye roll–worthy expectations and prejudices, would lessen the pressure on my own shoulders. I want to walk around the room with her, arm in arm, like true friends might, like we did in the gardens days ago.

I could. I could bypass decorum and speak to her first, but that's acceptable only if she accepts it, if she still sees me as a friend. She turns in the crowd, so close to me, and I seize the moment.

"Come here often?" I try, addressing her first as a friend might. The people dotted between us fall terse and silent, looking to Fione expectantly. I hate putting her on the spot. I hate this taut string between us at all, but it's here, and I'm tugging on it like a curious seamstress trying to find a mistake. Like a friend, who's trying to tell if she still has the chance to be friends at all.

Fione's face doesn't change, the wax-drawn lines down her cheeks curving into crescent moons around her rosebud mouth. Is she furious? I can't tell. She's always been so immaculate with the noble mask that hides one's true feelings. She was the first friend I ever had. Not only in Vetris but—I think—in life as well.

I take a step forward, and the effect is instant—she promptly takes a step back, her mask breaking and her blush paling.

"I-I'm sorry." Her eyes dart around, anywhere but in my direction. "I have to go."

With a sinking stomach, I watch her push through the crowd, her short frame swallowed up by them in a blink. Hate or fear? Which is it? Both? My presence didn't make her feel comfortable, that much is certain. In the aftermath of what I'd done in the clearing, when I passed out, she must've seen all the blood and the bodies—

how courageous can a mouse be, when it faces a wolf

tearing mice apart? The hunger sneers. *and yet there you stand, foolishly, still thinking a mouse and a wolf could ever be friends...*

I snatch another flute of wine from a passing tray and down it, hoping the bitter liquid will blur the hunger's voice. Or drown it, with any luck.

Watching Fione go, hammers the first and hardest nail into my chest; I can't change what I've done. Is this what life is? Pushing through the days hurting others, making mistakes, and yet left with no choice but to do it again and again? Now more than ever, I want Y'shennria here with me—my eyes search for her face in the crowd, her puffy dark hair set with gems and her easy, graceful poise. She'd know exactly how to deal with such things: what expression to put on and, when we were alone in the carriage home, advice. She'd chide me, too, for believing I had real friends here in Vetris, but I know between the chiding would be kernels of kindness.

alone, always.

I straighten my shoulders. I can't rely on her. Comfort is a luxury I don't deserve. This crushing pain is mine alone to deal with.

There's a hush that runs through the room when the royal family enters. The nobles wait with bated breath to see exactly how splendid the garb is and, more importantly, how to emulate it. Excitement courses through the room as dread courses through me. My body's on point like a foxhound in the reeds, waiting for the slightest movement to send me into a frenzy.

There—King Sref and Queen Kolissa come out first, dressed in matching maroon velvet with deep gold threading. Queen Kolissa looks as beautiful as ever, dark eyes as sharp as her children's and yet soft with obvious happiness. King Sref's long salt-and-pepper mane is braided with red velvet ribbon, but it's the only thing that tells me he's the same man I'd seen before the Hunt. Everything about his face has transformed with Varia's return; his wrinkles are eased, his amber skin glowing from within. His gray eyes, once so exhausted and apathetic, now brim with life. He nods and smiles at nearly every noble he passes, sweeping his grin over them all. He looks like a much, *much* younger man.

And then, the inevitable.

I can feel Lucien's very presence cut the air like a heated knife as he walks in. Dressed entirely in deep indigo silk laced with platinum beads, he looks like the night sky itself. But there's a strangeness about his outline—something missing I'm used to. His hip is absent of his usual white mercury sword. It *was* originally Varia's. I wonder—did he give it back to her? We spoke of it, didn't we? Keeping our family's swords so that when they might return, we could give it back to them.

But that's a distant memory.

His midnight hair is combed back, short and slick, and a wave of horror moves through the crowd when they see it.

"Who would dare cut the prince's hair—?"

"I heard he did it himself, at his Hunt—"

"Does he want *to be a commoner?"*

"It's repulsive and shameful—Cavanos's prince, with the hair of a servant!"

I watch Lucien's obsidian eyes, but they're staring straight ahead without so much as a flicker. He won't give them the satisfaction, and part of me swells with twisted pride. He cut his hair that night at the Hunt in front of all his noble peers as a message—fragments of his speech still ring in my mind.

He wanted to eschew Vetris's reliance on tradition, and on the tradition of hate. Cutting the long hair that marked him a royal had been a gesture. But the nobles don't see any of that. They simply scorn someone daring to do something different.

"Should I ask him to fetch my tea?" a nobleman whispers to another man just beside me, and they share a snicker.

I whirl on them. "You really shouldn't, considering he's still—by blood and birth—your prince. And I'm not sure about you, but I enjoy keeping my head attached to my shoulders."

The noblemen cough, their eyes skittering away from me abruptly. Queen Kolissa suddenly turns to Lucien, his father the king follows suit, and for a moment all three of them smile at one another. Lucien's grin to his father is wide, warm, genuine. It's a different smile from the one I'm used to—more wholesome, more *free*. In the same way Varia's return has lit the king from the inside, so, too, has Varia's return eased the loneliness in Lucien's smile.

He looks so happy, and my unheart warms with it.

Lucien turns his gaze this way and that, searching the crowd. My stomach leaps and curdles at the same time as he lands on me.

His smile fades instantly.

But of course it does. It's imaginary, and impossible, but something circuits between us—like a rope of flame burning back and forth and back again. For a moment, when his eyes meet mine, there's something like relief in their inky depths, but almost instantly they cloud over into unreadable discs of black iron. His word from the clearing rings in my unheart.

Traitor.

I can see the break between us, the gulf in his eyes, the both of us standing on opposite sides. There is nothing I can do to close the gap. He won't let me—or anyone else—see the hurt, but I know it's there, the same way one knows beneath the lid of a cauldron boils a red-hot liquid. He keeps his noble mask taut and lacquered with pure, bristling pride. To the nobles, we're still close. The last time we were both at court, the rumors swirled that the crown prince would choose me as his Spring Bride at the Hunt. In their eyes, right now he should offer me his hand.

And yet all he does is watch me for a moment before turning on his heel.

It's a small movement. It shouldn't hurt as much as it does, like a rusted spear to the chest. The nobles around us dissolve into frantic whispers.

"A disagreement?"

"Surely His Highness picked Lady Zera at the Hunt?"

"The murder might have shaken him—"

A murder has *shaken him,* I want to say. *The murder of nine men whom I killed in front of him.*

tore them apart easily, like rusted old puppets—

Lucien walks away, his smile returning as he and his parents converse easily. In his shadow walks the willowy Malachite in his dress armor—jet black and inlaid with garnets. His snow-white hair and skin stand out even more in the dark armor, the red of the garnets matching his bloodred eyes. His long, bladelike ears can hear every rumor in this room, I'm sure.

The broadsword on his back glints ominously as he looks my way. He's not Lucien—not a noble trained from birth to hide his true feelings. His fury is obvious—no, disgust? Something between the two, etched in his long white eyebrows and slender chin. I'm used to his easy, lazy, joking smile—always, no matter how serious the situation.

But now those lips are set, serious.

I've lost even him, too.

The firehorns suddenly blare a new melody—not the usual introductory one but something grander. More important.

The announcer calls out in a thundering voice aided by the little brass polymath tool held to his lips: "Noble ladies and noble gentlemen of the high Vetrisian court, I present to you Her Highness the crown princess, Varia Helsereth d'Malvane, Archduchess of Tollmount-Kilstead, Lady of the Great People and Forestborn."

I watch as Varia walks in, her sleek black hair oiled to perfection and left long, several small braids tipped with emeralds hanging around her face. Her bright green dress practically glows under the light of the oil-lit orbs hanging from the rafters, cut low to show her smooth shoulders and precise posture. Her makeup is expertly applied, a blush, a lip-tint with hints of strawberry, and the charcoal wax on her cheekbones drawn into two lines of perfect interlocking stars. She keeps her long lashes down, looking at no one as she sweeps across the floor of the banquet hall to her parents waiting on the other side. The white mercury sword is on her hip—her sword—and my chest swells for a brief moment.

He's gotten to return his.

Jealousy wars with happiness; I'll never be able to return Father's sword. But Lucien... I'm glad for him.

I'm so glad he's happy now.

Varia hasn't been seen alive for five years. There's a beat of silence, and then the nobles gathered in the banquet hall implode. The whispers catch flame and burst into shouts, shocked gasps, frantic mutterings, the chatter resounding in the high ceiling.

"Alive?"

"New God Almighty—that can't be her!"

"Her portrait...it looks just like her—"

"Magic? Surely she died, and this is a trick—"

"An imposter? She's the right age—"

"You can't teach an imposter how to carry oneself like a d'Malvane—"

Someone in the crowd faints, and people cluster around to help them. Even the banquet guards and servants seem shocked, their eyes riveted on each step of Varia's velvet-booted feet. Varia is supposed to be dead—killed by witches and Heartless while she was touring the countryside when she was sixteen. All they found were pieces of her. Five years have passed.

And now she stands before them as their new crown princess.

When she draws even with her family, Varia embraces Lucien first. His gaze grows feather soft, his arms around her back careful and his smile into her hair tender. Queen Kolissa embraces the both of them, laying her milky arms over them, the telltale twinkle of tears in her eyes as she draws her children close. Even for royals, trained to never show their true feelings and instead keep them behind masks, restraining the emotions of such a longtime reunion stretches the limits of possibility.

"They are d'Malvanes," I hear someone whisper. "But they are human, too."

I shouldn't, but I watch Lucien's smile for as long as it lasts, letting myself get lost in the fantasy one last time that such a smile could ever be aimed at me.

The royal family parts quickly, as if sensing the court's eyes on them. If Varia's Crown Princess now, that means Lucien isn't. Which means he isn't next in line for the throne.

Which means getting married, all that pressure of leading a country—it's been lifted from him. So why doesn't he look any less burdened?

Our eyes meet again, one last time before he walks into the banquet hall with his family. His lips are a terse line, his eyes fogged mirrors.

It's me. It's *me*, isn't it? I'm the source of his sorrow.

This isn't right. I'm living in a different timeline, the wrong one, where I've failed. I should be gone. I should not be standing here, in a dress, pining after him. I should be gone and he should be smiling. He can rebuild now, his family reunited at his side. He can start to heal. He is *trying* to heal.

But I am the needle, ripping open the stitching on his wounds.

5

THE MASK
MADE TWICE

The rest of the nobles and I file nearer to the banquet hall, seating ourselves in the same way Y'shennria taught me—eldest to youngest, highest blood rank to lowest. Fione sits before me, of course, and the royal family sits before anyone else.

It's strange to consider this normal, to watch the banquet happen without worrying about what spoons to use. I know by now, my hands moving automatically for each delicate wipe of my face and tilt of my bowl. I eat only a little, wary of the blood tears that accompany a Heartless trying to eat human food. I used to be so worried about manners at the table, but now my mind is elsewhere, racing back and forth on a track by itself as my body moves on the track Y'shennria built for me.

The talk of the tables echoes in the high, gilded ceiling; at the forefront of every conversation is Varia. In hushed tones around pumpkin dumplings and game-hen soup, they'll discuss witches, the war, and then look to her, positing among themselves where she's been these past five years and why.

Varia, on the other hand, puts herself above the talk—maneuvering effortlessly through the social rigmarole with assertive humor and grace, talking easily with the ministers and the servants alike. She dotes on Fione, who's seated right next to her, offering her small tidbits of food and touching her shoulder at every opportunity. Their glances to each other are warm, Fione's smile apple-cheeked and rosy, and I'm reminded once more how much Fione loved—*loves*—Varia. And Varia, in return, seems keen on returning the affections. Perhaps now Fione will get the chance to tell Varia how she really feels, and that thought is a spot of brightness in the midst of all my shadowed pain.

Varia doesn't once command me to come to her or do anything at all. She doesn't so much as look at me. Neither does Fione—the few times I find her eyes on me, she skitters them away instantly and focuses on Varia's smiling face. They're utterly absorbed in each other. Malachite, looming on the wall behind Lucien, catches his ruby eyes on mine and flashes them away quickly. Neither he nor Fione can bear to look at me for long.

But at the head of the table, Lucien—

My chest compresses into a hard knot as I find his midnight eyes focused squarely on me. Has he been looking at me this whole time? I can't bring myself to return his stare. My lie ruined everything. My own selfish desires cut down our chances before they could even grow. There is a me somewhere who's not Heartless, who hasn't lied to him, who sits beside him at this banquet and smiles at him, and he smiles back, and they are in love.

But I am not her.

I have, maybe, never been her. And now I never will be.

My eyes skitter to his parents instead—the king and queen. They lavish their attention on Varia, roaring with laughter at her jokes and hanging on her every word. The whole banquet is drawn to her, so when Lucien stands and excuses himself, his parents let it happen. Malachite follows him. The table whispers about it for a moment, but then someone mentions how beautiful Varia looks, and that's the end of their concern.

Varia is probably the reason why, when I get up and excuse myself, too, no one pays much attention, not even Varia herself. She might be my witch, and she might have my body under her control, but I'll be damned if I linger beside her every minute of every day yearning for my heart.

I throw on the cloak that came with the dress—a simple blue thing—and follow Lucien from a forty-pace distance. Somewhere between the deepfish stew and the roast pork, I made up my mind to say something to the prince tonight. An apology? Would that be too hollow? I don't know, but I have to try. I ignore the telltale clenching in my stomach as the food tries to come out as blood tears—in this palace there are no less than a hundred shadowy places to duck into and rearrange oneself if one must.

Malachite pads at his side, and I follow them as far as I can, to the border of the Serpent's Wing, where only the noble family is allowed. The two boys disappear around a corner, leaving me to hover at a window, pacing back and forth. If he's retiring for the night, if he doesn't come out again—

"If you were any more obvious, you'd be wearing a sign with his name on it."

My head snaps up at the voice—Malachite saunters down the hall toward me. The moonlight from the Blue Giant outside catches the rubies in his armor, the combined light flashing violet. His eyes are hooded, and his mouth is set in a flat line. When he reaches me, I'm not sure what to say. Or how to say it.

"I'm sorry," I finally manage. Malachite scoffs, his ruby eyes rolling.

"I'm not the one you need to be apologizing to."

I swallow. "You're...not mad?"

His lips thin in a mockery of a smile. "Oh, I'm madder than a one-legged valkerax. I just don't like to go around showing it."

My unheart stings. "I should've told you I'm a—"

"I could give a horseshit if you're a Heartless, or a witch, or the Old God himself," he interrupts me. "I'm a beneather who lives in the upworld—I know what it's like to be different. It's not the fact you're a Heartless I'm mad about. It's the fact you messed with Lucien's head. You gave him false hope. And that's something I can't forgive."

I chew my lip and nod, all the words I wanted to say stolen from me. He's right. I did give Lucien false hope, didn't I? I forced my way into his life, promised love when I couldn't give it. Malachite's anger is righteous, deserved, and it'd be selfish and pathetic to try to beg for his trust again. Words can only speak so much louder than actions. My stomach curdles, harder this time, the pain no longer able to be ignored. I turn on my heel and start to walk away when his slightly raised voice stops me.

"He's left out the back way in his all-leather getup. If you're quick, you can catch him in the common quarter. Fleshhouse Avenue."

I whirl on my heel, my unheart spasming wildly. "Thank you!"

He's out of the palace. I can approach him.

I dash down the hall and back to the palace entrance. My eyes search for the black carriage of Y'shennria, for Fisher who should be driving it, waiting for me with his large ears and scarecrow body. But he's gone. All the carriages parked here are waiting for their respective nobles at the banquet.

It's strange, that such small things can make one feel so alone. Walking down the palace steps without a carriage waiting for me, I feel unmoored. Out of place. There's no one for me in Vetris anymore. No safe house to go back to. No allies. Two weeks ago I still had Y'shennria and her household. And now I have no one.

abandoned, the hunger insists. **abandoned by everyone.**

I lift my head, wait for an opening in the guard patrols, and dart off into the hot night. The cicadas are the only ones who cry when I am gone.

Vetris's Fleshhouse Avenue is always alive, even during funerals, holy days, and especially during brewing wars. It never closes, never observes silence, because unlike jewelry or shoes or swords, human comfort is always needed. The fleshhouses exist in defiance of all Vetris's suffocating religion and decorum, and maybe that's why I feel a little freer here, even if the hawkers sitting outside shout me down as I pass or the customers give me a leery eye every few steps. The objectification is a double-edged sword; uncomfortable and yet comforting in the sense I'm one of the masses here—not the exception. Not a noble or a Heartless but just a girl. Reduced to my barest parts, reduced to what I've always wanted to be. *Just a human girl.*

I crane my head and search each house's facade desperately for any scrap of dark leather or a tall, proud frame. Prince Lucien's got to be here, dressed in his "all-leather getup," which means he's roaming the streets as Whisper, the enigmatic thief who steals from the rich and gives to the poor. I scoff as I scan the crowd for him, remembering how trite I used to think he was for it. How privileged I was back then, that I could ever consider helping people "trite."

There—on the doorstep of a three-story house. A young man in skin-fitting leather armor, a black cloak over him, emerges from the doorway arm-in-arm with a beautiful, smiling girl in a lace dress. My courage ship springs a sudden hole, leaking everywhere. What am I doing, stalking him like this? He's hired a fleshworker, obviously. He's moving on. This is his business. And I have no right being a part of it anymore.

Come now, Zera. You're better than this. Not much better, but still. At least say sorry to him tonight. And then you can nurse your silly, immature jealousy alone.

I squeeze my fists and march toward the two of them, my unheart in my throat and my mouth bone-dry. I push closer and closer. The girl is so beautiful it's almost hard to look at her—sweet and unassuming, with bright red curls and a round face. She's human, all human. They're talking so openly, Lucien nodding from time to time, his elbow firmly laced with hers. He's free to do anything with whom he wishes. I know that.

tear them apart, the hunger hisses. **eat them together.**

I somehow finally get close enough to hear the beautiful girl speak.

"...don't need that much. But the matron can't afford it—not on top of the polymath bills, too."

"Chillsbane, sleeping draughts, and pain relievers," I hear Lucien's voice rumble behind his cowl. "All right. I can manage that."

The girl's green eyes light up. "Really?"

He nods. "Really."

Chillsbane is a medicine. They're talking about *medicine*? There's a blur of lace as the girl hugs him tightly. He says something to her, too soft for me to hear, and then she minces back through the crowd and disappears inside the fleshhouse again. My first mistake was watching her go—when I turn back to Lucien, he's gone, a gap in the crowd where darkness used to be. Everyone's packed so tightly in this small avenue, and the heat of the day hasn't gone anywhere with the setting sun. I sweat and swivel my head madly.

"New Gods' tit," I wipe my eyes and mutter, the crowd all looking the same. "It shouldn't be this easy to lose someone that tall."

"And yet you continually surprise us all by managing it somehow."

I jump, the deep voice directly behind me as I whirl and come face-to-face with Lucien, his midnight eyes glaring out of his cowl with such brimstone, I almost stagger back. *Say it, Zera. Say it now, before he can walk away or shut you out—*

I gulp down muggy summer air. "Lucien, I'm sor—"

His eyes harden to stone (he learned that from Varia; I can see the similarities now) as his hand darts out and captures my wrist. "You'll be useful. Come with me."

I'm dreaming. I have to be. Except the warmth around my wrist is no phantasmal faceless man's, it's Lucien's—attached to his arm, his broad shoulder, his strong neck as he leads me out through the crowd of Fleshhouse Avenue and into Butcher's Alley. He's touching me, *willingly*, when I never thought he would again. It's simple and small and nothing and yet my body is singing with it. Our cloaks swirl behind us, streamers of blue and black as we bruise across the night.

"Where—" I sidestep a spouting watertell and the courier who rushes over to it. "Where are we going?"

The prince doesn't say anything, his strides lengthening, and I have to jog to keep up. I should tear his hand off my wrist, but it feels so good to be touched. By anyone.

By him especially.

fool. there is no point. The hunger sneers. *he will never trust you again. we are the predator and he is the prey—*

"Lucien," I start. "I want—I want to apologi—"

His other hand abruptly covers my mouth, and he pulls me down behind a line of crates. The feel of his smooth palm against my lips—I swallow hard. A wrongness consumes me, hot and uneasy. I'm the monster, and he's the prince, and he knows that, he *saw* that, so why…?

I give a massive squirm, but he holds me fast, his arms tight around my body. My unheart clenches into itself, my skin buzzing like a wasp's nest.

"Quiet," he growls in my ear. "I didn't bring you here to talk. I brought you here to help me steal. Listen to what I say, and mayhap I'll find it in my heart that you wanted so much to return the favor."

Is that all I have to do? I nod frantically, and he releases every part of me, disappointment lingering where his skin used to be. I let it roll off and catch my breath, watching him peer between the cracks in the crates at what must be his target. When my nerves settle, I look between a crack to see a barrel-laden carriage being unloaded by scores of heavily muscled men. They hoist the barrels into a nearby house, a few lawguards watching their progress.

"A stockpile," Lucien answers my unsaid question. "The royal stockpile, to be more accurate. A royal polymath comes here to check inventory, quality, and to make sure none of it is poisoned, and then they send everything off to the palace."

"All of that," I marvel. "Just for you four?"

"Keeping an aging king on the throne requires a lot of supplements—most of them completely unneeded and overly expensive," Lucien scoffs. "Thankfully, there's some actual medicine included in there, too."

I had an inkling earlier, but now it makes perfect sense. He was seeing what medicines that fleshworker needed as Whisper, not soliciting her as Lucien. Gods, jealousy is a terrible beast that makes clever people so dull. Is this why the bards warn of it so often? I make a solemn pact between myself and I to throw over a cliff the fact I was ever naive enough not to see the truth. Preferably a cliff with a pack of hungry wildcats at the bottom to be rid of the evidence.

I shake myself out and clear my throat. "The last time I checked, Your Highness, the Midnight Gifter didn't gift medicines to fleshhouses."

"Neither did he wear underclothes," Lucien says. "Characters from books don't tend to make a lot of sense in a real world context. Now, talk less and distract more."

He motions to the burly line of men, and I stifle a groan.

"Why can't *I* be the one who does the neat, stealthy things?"

"Because you're the only one currently wearing a dress," the prince says.

"I bet you'd look lovely in a dress." My mouth fires out the jab faster than I can take it back. Something like a smirk quirks at his lips, but I must be imagining it, because it's gone in the next blink. He's giving me this one chance and I joke with it? What is *wrong* with me?

He wants a grand distraction? Fine. I'll give him a grand distraction—so grand he'll have to listen to my hours-long apology. I ignore the stabbing pain in my stomach from the few bites of banquet food and bunch up my hem to tear it—an easy enough feat, considering how fine and old the fabric is. Lucien watches me with deadpan boredom as I smear cobblestone dirt on my face, but when I start pinching and twisting my cheeks, he quirks one eyebrow.

"Not the dirty beggar act, then?" he asks.

"Nay." I rummage in a nearby garbage pile for the glinting empty bottle I'd spotted there. I shake it at him slightly and smirk. "Something far better."

Before he can ask, I stand up from our hiding place and start staggering wildly toward the men, a bawdy song I'd heard a drunkard singing last night from the carriage brewing in my throat.

"Seven men they caught the baker's eye, and seven men they made her sigh, then seven men they came to play, and seven men ate pie that day—"

The barrel line goes quiet, pauses in its motion, and all the men look me up and down suspiciously. The lawguards descend, knitting around me in a tight circle.

"Whoa there, this area is off-limits!" one of them insists.

I squint up at him. "Whaddaya sayin'? This…" I gesture wildly at the house they're going into. "This iz my house! You…you tin men are telling me I can't go in muh own house?"

The lawguards give one another a look, the "better deal with this quick before our superiors hear about it" look. The men unloading the barrels are still, wary, as if they're unsure they should keep working.

"Turn around now, miss, and leave," another lawguard insists, his bushy mustache twitching as I lurch toward him.

"Miss? *Miss?* Do I *look* like a miss to ya?" I stagger into the lawguard on my left. He reflexively pushes me away, and I throw a sloppy punch with no power to it, nearly falling over with the momentum. The lawguards push me back, away from the house. "I'm a ma'am! I'm married...I'm *married, you shiny bastards*! To a pig of a man! An' he's in that house, waitin' for his stew! He's as big as a badger and as mean as a mountain, and if he doesn't get his stew I'm gone for. A doner." I sniff dramatically, blearing my eyes. "If he hits me, you're his fault!"

Lucien's dark outline appears from between the carriage railings, his eyes searching the barrel labels. The working men are beginning to get antsy.

"Ma'am." The lawguard to my right looks thoroughly chastened. "You're drunk, and you've got the wrong house—"

"What are ya talkin' about?" I flail, two of the lawguards having to hold me back at this point. "That's him!" I point at a random man in the line, a barrel clutched to his chest. "What in Kavar's name are you doin' out here workin'? What about the kids? You're just gonna leave them to rot in there?"

The man's face goes slack and white, his mouth gaping like a fish. "Wha— What are you—?"

I cling to the lawguard, the pain of the food twisting my insides. Kavar's tit. I don't have much time.

"Is this your wife?" one of the lawguards asks. The man starts to shake his head, and I lunge for his shirt.

"How could ya, ya oily sack of horse dung!" I scream. "How could ya leave them alone in there—?"

"I have no idea what she's talking about!" the man protests. "I've never seen her in my—"

The pain is piercing now, drilling through my skull. I make a lurch and a gurgling noise not entirely within my control, and the man instantly tries to pull away. I keep my grip hard, and he flounders, the two of us sprawling backward into the line of working men. Barrels go flying, swears and limbs whizzing past my ear. The scrambling commotion bleeds chaos—enough chaos that I hope Lucien can steal what he needs to. There's a moment where the lawguards try to drag me off toward the back of the carriage, but it's that same moment my eyes tear up, hot with blood. I can't let them see that, but I have to keep the distraction up.

I do the only thing I excel at—make believe. I make a lurching gulp and then the wettest, most convincing retching noises anyone's ever heard. I'll be the first to admit—not my most elegant moment, but perhaps my most successful, because the lawguards recoil in disgust even though nothing's there, bouncing off one another as they try to avoid what they think is potential vomit. The man I accused of being my husband—Kavar bless his heart—is a sensitive thing, and starts vomiting for real, right onto the nearest lawguard. His friends try to console him, the lawguards try to get to their own feet again without touching him unduly, and I take the moment and slip back out of the alley as fast as my bleeding eyes allow.

Five streets, four squares—I run until I'm out of breath, until they'd have to sprint to find me, and duck behind a hefty cluster of dye vats. The smell is horrible, like aged mulch and rot. No one will come looking for me here.

"I asked for a distraction, not a mistake."

I look up at the terse voice, only to see Lucien standing

there. Did he follow me? His gaze parses over my face, my blood tears. Old God's gaping mouth—now's not the time to remind him I'm a Heartless. It will never be the time.

I wipe at my cheeks frantically with my sleeves. "Mistake?" I start. "So you didn't get the medicine, then?"

"Do you have any idea how many people could've seen those blood tears?" In one fell swoop he's kneeling beside me, voice burning. "My people are fearful, but they aren't dense. Everyone inside this godsdamn wall knows what it means to cry blood! The temple warns about it, the children sing about it, and you just did it! In front of who knows how many!"

concern for a relic of the past is unbecoming of you, sir prince, the hunger taunts. The hunger is right. I'm his past. Not his future.

I throw my hair back over my shoulder, gold on blue. "Did you get the medicine or not?"

His brows carve deep against the cowl. "They could know what you are! They could be marching lawguards all over the city looking for you right now!"

I breathe deep. I have to take his focus off me. He's moving backward, when he needs to face the truth and move forward. I am a traitor. Closure will help him, and apologies are a good place to start. I need to apologize while I still have the chance. In a blink he could be gone, entrenched in the court again. Beyond my reach.

"I'm sorry, Lucien." I meet his gaze squarely. "I'm sorry for not telling you what I—"

"Save your apologies," he snarls, his hand darting out and enveloping my own. His fingers are so incredibly warm. "We have to go. If they know what you are..."

He stands, pulling me up with him, but before he can

start off, I rip out of his grip. That one movement takes everything in me—to move away from his concern instead of toward it, like every inch of my skin desires.

"*If*—" I steady my voice. "*If* the people of Vetris discover a Heartless in their midst, *if* they tie her up, *if* they burn her alive—it would not do for the prince of Cavanos to care about it."

I pray to both gods he understands. There's a beat. And then...

"It would not do," he agrees, his fury muting to something low and soft.

My breath punctures out of me like a pierced bubble. Of course he understands. It's obvious to anyone with two whits of court knowledge the prince should not care for a traitor.

"But I wouldn't be able to help it," he adds.

My head snaps up. "What?"

The sound of approaching lawguards rings loud in my ears, clanking metal and shouted orders, and in a blink Lucien pulls me in to him, into the shadows behind the dye vats and away from the light. The world fades; I forget the smell of the vats, the blood trails that must be on my cheeks. His every ridge is pressed against mine—our hips digging into each other's, our chests flush and breathing hard. I look up, our faces so close I could count the dark eyelashes around his strangely amused gaze.

"I can't help but pity you, Lady Zera."

It feels like the cobblestones fall away from my feet. A sick coldness rises up in their place.

"I pitied you when we met at the Welcoming," he says lightly, a sigh on the end. "An Y'shennria, without status or parents, being offered as a plaything. Someone as sharp as you didn't deserve to be made a pawn of the marriage game."

If he pities me, why is he holding me so close? Why was he so worried about people seeing my blood tears not moments before?

"Pity?" My voice shakes. Memories of our dance in the street parade, our faces so close in the tavern beneath his cloak, his hand in mine and his head on my shoulder as he shed tears for his lost sister. "Not all of it was pity."

"Of course not." The prince chuckles, the sound so at odds with my coldly burning body. "Only most of it."

The coldness hardens in my stomach like a pit of ice.

"After a few days of deep introspection, I've come to realize: I was infatuated with you because I pitied you. You tried so hard to make me love you, and I pitied you for your efforts. I pitied how alone you were in court, how ignorant you were, how terribly everyone thought of you because you were an Y'shennria. Somewhere along the way, it became affection. But an affection based in a sickly soil can never bloom into a true flower; it can never bloom into true love."

I swallow what feels like metal shavings, scraping my throat on the way down.

"Oh." He laughs softly, hollowly, keeping his mouth by my ear. "Don't look so troubled, Lady Zera. You and I both know it's true. It was only two weeks. What sort of love is ever true after only two weeks? We were infatuated, and nothing more."

His thoughts mirror mine, the truth like needles piercing any joy I held secretly.

"And yet," he says, "emotions aren't convenient pieces of jewelry you can put on and take off whenever you want to."

What does that even mean? That the things we shared can't be removed from memory?

'twould be easy enough to reach around and take his

eyes out, the hunger offers, salivating. *that will make him despise you, for certain.*

Varia had a fresh raw pig liver waiting for me, sequestered beneath the banquet dress in her room, but still the hunger keens. I try to remind it his death doesn't mean our heart anymore, but the darkness unfurls whenever our skin brushes together, like it's been trained to react with violent thoughts to his scent, his feel. The sound of the lawguards approaching crescendos beyond our hiding place, and I feel Lucien's arms tighten around me, his mouth just near my ear. The feel of his breath on my skin chokes me more than the muggy summer air, making my whole body tremble.

"You're shaking." His tone is low, despondent. "How could you be so good at fooling the court yet so terrible at hiding your own feelings?"

He's acting so incredibly different—so light, and amused, and unaffected. I'd seen him do this once before, to the other Spring Brides, the ones he treated kindly just for show, just to keep the court off his back. The farce is lifted, gone. He's supposed to return to his life before me, before my facade. He's never truly happy when he looks at me, and he deserves to be happy.

The red moonlight blazes off the lawguards' armor as they pass us—clanking so incredibly loudly—and then disappear, fading behind a street corner. I arch my back against Lucien's chest in a bid to make space between us.

"What feelings?" I ask.

"That is the question, isn't it?" He releases me just enough that I can turn in his arms, and I spin to face him. "You never answered me in the clearing."

"I told you—you're naive," I bark. "I deceived you—"

"Everyone I've ever met has deceived me," he interrupts

me. "That is what it means to be a d'Malvane. You deceived me. And I pitied you. In the end, I'd call that a draw, wouldn't you?"

"We kissed," I blurt, my mouth running by itself. "You and I—that kiss in the tent. Did that mean nothing to you?"

He leans in suddenly, smiling, a shadow filled with heat and draped in leather, his hands slipping onto either side of my face. It's a farce. He treats people well only when he despises them; the Spring Brides proved that. I swear there's a blink of genuine feeling in his eyes, but then it disappears.

"How can something that was a lie mean anything at all?"

Not like this. I want the real Lucien. Not this one.

"Don't you dare treat me like everyone else," I demand. Lucien's obsidian eyes flicker, the pleasant facade of his nearly crumbling. He drops his hands slowly, reaching into his pocket and procuring a kerchief in his palm, dark blue with red rose embroidery. To clean my face of blood? His black eyes are hard and set with determination as they were the first time we met—him as Whisper, the two of us in an alley not much different from this one.

"Why not?" He tilts his head, a smile carving an impression beneath his cowl. "After all, you treated me like a job."

His words stab right through my tender parts, and my lungs instinctually suck in a bracing breath of air. He ignores it, still that placid, unreal smile on his face as he offers his handkerchief.

"You were the only one who managed to get beneath my armor. I'd ask you to be gentle with me, until I can construct a new set," he says, dropping the kerchief around my hand. "But I know you despise obeying your crown prince."

I barely catch the kerchief before it hits the ground, and

when I manage to look up again, he's gone.

My body aches with the aftermath of the blood tears and the blunt force of Lucien's emotional stabbing. I wipe my face carefully with the kerchief. He was right to be so brutal. Emotions aren't jewelry, he'd said. But they are. I'd put some very convincing jewels on to deceive him—rubies of love, emeralds of affection. What remained when I took them off, that night in the clearing?

Me. Just me.

The monster, the girl, the killer, and the liar in her bare flesh.

undeserving of life, let alone love.

He held me so close. He touched me so tenderly. But he did it because I'm like everyone else in his eyes. I deceived him, like everyone else in the court does.

I am nothing special to him any longer.

Faintly, I hear another commotion start in the street—the lawguards shouting about a "fugitive thief" in "dark leather." They barrel past my hiding place and to the next square over. Lucien's lingered in the streets of Vetris for years—he knows better than to get caught. So why would he purposely flaunt himself in front of lawguards now?

My thief brain hands me the answer neatly; with the guards gone, it's a clear shot from where I am to the noble-quarter bridge. My Heartless brain answers me painfully:

He pities me.

6

THE
WYRM'S SONG

I'm sure of only two things in my unlife: that I have royally fucked up (pun intended, thank you very much) and that Lucien deserves someone far better than me.

I inform Malachite of this the following morning. When I got back to the palace last night, Varia's servant told me I could sleep in her quarters, as she wasn't coming back that evening. The guards let me through. I glared at the princess's perfumed bed and pulled a blanket from the linen closet and slept on the floor instead. It did wonders for my pride and nothing for my back.

"Lucien deserves far better than me," I say to Malachite, cracking my back by holding a banister and twisting my entire spine in the other direction while I wait for my carriage to the valkerax—Varia's servant also informed me of that this morning. The noise of my cracking vertebrae makes a passing noble couple shudder uncontrollably. I hold up a hand and smile at them in a "you're welcome" way.

Malachite, now out of his fancy armor and dressed in

his usual modest chainmail shirt and breeches, rolls his red eyes. "Are nobles always late to the obvious, or just the ones pretending to be nobles?"

"Both?" I offer. "All? Humans are, historically, fools."

"And liars," he fires back, holding his pale, spidery hand out to me like I'm a perfect example.

"And that," I murmur an agreement. "Sometimes. Out of necessity."

"Sorry." Malachite blinks. "What part of attempting to kill a prince and revive him as a witch's servant is necessity again?"

"The point is," I say very loudly, "I tricked Lucien into his feelings. I ruined his view on love. So it's only fair I try to make amends for that."

Pain fractures through my body like ice the moment the words form in the air. My face moves in a numb mask, making a show of winking at Malachite.

"Which means, of course, I'm going to have to find him someone else."

Malachite's quiet, opting instead to stare out of the grand oak doors of the palace entrance. At last, he asks, "Someone else?"

"You know." I shrug, my simple green linen tunic shrugging with me. "He told me he pities me, when the reality is, actually, that *I* pity *him*. He's all but rejected every noble girl for marriage. He treats none of them with any gravitas. He'll never find a wife at this rate! As his best friend"—I point to Malachite—"and his best enemy," I say, pointing to myself, "it's up to us to find him a sweeter girl. Harmless, not Heartless. A girl without razor-sharp teeth or a dark hunger whispering constantly to tear his lungs out."

If Malachite could go any whiter, I'm sure he would, but

instead his thin lips just purse. "The hunger says that?"

"Oh yes. Which is why we need to keep Lucien away. I'm just no good. But you knew that already, of course."

Malachite lets out a sigh. "Zera—"

"So!" I clap my hands. "I'm going to need your help. We need to find someone decidedly less criminal and frequently less homicidal, and steer him toward her."

The beneather looks me up and down, squinting like he's not sure who I am. Finally, he nods. "All right."

"Fantastic. Make sure he and I don't meet in the halls. Make sure he stops staring at me during banquets. If he starts talking about me, change the subject to another girl. Better yet, take him out to *meet* other girls." I beam at him. "If you do it well enough, I might even compensate you."

He raises one brow. "With what? Y'shennria is gone. You have nothing. Not even the dress on your back is yours."

you have nothing.

I laugh. "You used to love flattery, Mal. I'm sure I can scrounge up a blushingly good compliment or three *somewhere*."

The clacking of horseshoes pulls my gaze to the palace steps, where Varia's black carriage awaits. I move to the door when a cool hand grabs my wrist and I'm rooted in place. I look back to see Malachite's pale fingers, his eyes fixed on me like two rain-dimmed garnets.

"Did you ever truly care for him?"

Yes. Of course, yes.

I shrug. "Not for him, particularly. Just for the heart in his chest."

Malachite is quiet, and then, "Was all of you...was all of it fake? Everything?"

No, I want to say. I'm a sixteen-year-old girl, nineteen,

really, but still just a girl. I trained with Y'shennria, not in a theater troupe. I'm not a noble, with a perfect mask learned from the moment I was born. The two weeks I spent with you, Malachite—and Lucien and Fione—the laughter, the anger, the joy; all of it was real.

I was me, even as I was trying my hardest not to be.

But no one needs to know that. Not Malachite, not Fione, and especially not Lucien—it would only make moving on that much harder.

I throw my coyest smile back at Malachite and nod. "Everything."

His grip loosens, and I can feel his eyes watching me down the steps, into the carriage, as far as the last bit of road out of the palace grounds.

I turn Lucien's dark-blue kerchief over in my hands as the carriage moves through the city—stroking the embroidered roses on the edges.

Feelings aren't jewelry.

A heart like Lucien's can't be easily swayed or unswayed. I put the kerchief to my chest, pain winding tight silken strands between my ribs. Apparently unhearts aren't easily unswayed, either. But I can't, under any circumstance, make the same mistake twice. I couldn't afford to make it even once, and yet here we are. He will not stop me again from getting my heart. No matter how badly that heart wants him.

What did Mother look like again? It's on the tip of my consciousness, begging to come out.

I clench my fists. I can lock away my feelings. I can do better this time. I know I can. I can fake it until it becomes reality like Y'shennria taught me. I have to. I *have* to fight back against the whirlpool pull of Lucien's face, his voice, and his scent, or I'll ruin everything and let my heart slip through my grasp yet again.

I have to move on. I can't cling. I can't be deluded by some warm, comforting, hazy idea of love anymore. I have to force myself, with every aching breath, to forget my feelings for him. If that means ignoring them, if that means finding another girl to anchor him upon…

If that means forcing us apart at the seams so that we can never be together by any stretch of the imagination, then so be it.

It will be the hardest thing I've ever done. Harder than deceiving him. Harder than leaving Crav and Peligli. Harder than dying for the first time all over again. Even now, I can feel my own seams screaming to be put back in place.

But I will get my heart back. I will get Mother and Father and my humanity back.

Even if it means I have to tear myself apart.

My hand trembles as I extend it out the window, the kerchief clutched in it. Just a raise of my fingers, and it would slip away on the wind, lost to the cobblestones, the piles of horseshit, the dark corners of dark alleys or the dark pockets of some passerby. If I just drop it, I'll be free.

But my fingers won't move. I envision them opening, but the bones stay locked, cold and numb as I stare at them. I can't. But I have to. *I can't. But I have to.*

"Miss?"

I startle at the voice, looking up to see the carriage driver standing just in front of my extended arm, his eyes concerned. "We've arrived."

Indeed, the bustle of South Gate echoes all around us,

people staring at the girl with her arm straight out of her carriage. I curl my hand in, tucking the kerchief securely into my tunic. "W-Would you look at that. In record time. Thank you, good sir."

I step out, avoiding the strangers' glances, and make for the brass door in the wall. Yorl, Varia's ochre-furred celeon associate, is surprisingly waiting for me outside it, wearing a polymath robe (still no tool belt, the poor thing) and a distinct expression of irritation. I watch his tail swish as I approach, the silver armor on the tip glinting in the sun. Varia essentially threatened him yesterday with his leverage— he wants to be a polymath. Yet he's already wearing the robes of one. It takes the barest bit of psychoanalyzing to realize he believes himself far beyond worthy of being one; he just wants Varia to officiate it. He wants to be official in the eyes of the system, enough to do all this. But why?

Yorl's green orbs narrow as I approach.

"Sleep well?" I tease.

"No," he says, immediately turning in to the door and waving aside the guards with the muttered password, "The Laughing Daughter calls." He says it like it means nothing, just business. "Out of the four gates, South Gate has the least traffic—the only thing south of Vetris is the Tollmount-Kilstead Mountains, and Helkyris beyond that. It's a treacherous journey, so only the well-equipped trading caravans brave it. Which means the clank of heavily armored guards is hideous in the mornings."

"Do you always give detailed explanations for free?" I chirp.

"Only to the people with persistent buffoonish looks attached to their faces."

I wince as we walk along the brass-burnished innards of

the wall, not out of pain, particularly, but out of surprise. I didn't know someone with such an iron rod up his arse could fire back so well. He opens the door into the dark spiral staircase and starts down it without hesitation, his celeon eyes no doubt adjusting impeccably. I follow.

"And here I was, expecting you to be more brainy and less mouthy." My voice echoes off unseeable stone walls.

"Your mistake." He sniffs.

"Entirely," I agree, and graciously flail my hands out in front of me. I catch his tail, and Yorl gives off a keening squawk ending in a snarl.

"Watch yourself!"

"Sorry!" I let go quickly and simper. "I just became so momentarily afraid of the dark!"

I hear a snort, and his paws start to click down the stairs again. I lag behind. It was so much easier going down these steps when Varia's order commanded me to do so. I didn't have to think or hesitate or readjust; my body simply did it all for me. The only benefit of being ordered, I suppose.

"A light would be nice," I offer. "It'd keep me from tripping and potentially smashing my face in."

"If you do, you'll heal." Yorl's voice is emotionless. "There's no need."

I give a watery sniff. "You're even more heartless than I am."

He doesn't answer that. We descend the stairs at as brisk a pace as my darkblind eyes can manage, the sonorous beat of the valkerax's breathing against the stone the only sound.

The moment we hit level ground, Yorl calls out into the darkness. "Get the impalers wound and the archers primed on the wall walk. Teori, Jonall—prepare to open the gates. We're sending the Heartless in at last."

The clank of armor is unmistakable but lacking the cadence of metal boots. The soft padding of celeon paws echoes as what sounds like a dozen scatter to obey his orders. It's strange—judging by his immature mane, he's not very old, but everyone down here is treating him with vast seniority. The perks of knowing the crown princess on a first-name basis, I suppose.

"Heartless," I hear him say and turn to me. "You—"

"I'm Elizera Y'shennria. Zera for short," I interrupt. "But celeon usually call me *a pain in the tail tuft*."

"We have no time for jokes," he retorts. "And even less time for introductions. I am Yorl Farspear-Ashwalker. That is all you need to know. The valkerax is being heavily sedated and can remain awake for only less than a half per day. We must work quickly. Valkerax do very poorly aboveground. It's already been three days—another twenty, and it will die."

"I thought Varia said it would take a month." I tilt my head.

"The longest I've managed to keep a valkerax alive above the Dark Below has been one month. But most don't reach eighteen days."

I start. "How many...how many times have you *done* this?"

"Several. None of them here in Vetris." His answers are succinct and remind me exactly why *I'm* here. My heart. The bittersweet memory of it in my chest the other night rushes through me, heady and sudden. "When we're in the valkerax's chambers, I will give you a vial. You will drink the contents. It will allow you to speak to the valkerax for exactly a half at a time."

"I thought they were mad, that nobody could understand their speech."

"They are," Yorl says coolly.

"So how—"

"It's an Old Vetrisian recipe, an attempt at negotiating with the valkerax to stop their rampage. An attempt that failed. My grandfather had been working on making the recipe functional up until his death. I carried it to completion."

"Your grandfather was a polymath, too?"

"You will drink the vial." Yorl ignores me, very clearly and purposefully. "And speak to the valkerax."

"A liquid that lets you talk to a creature not even the beneathers can understand," I marvel. "That's awfully handy. Why haven't you passed it around to them yet?"

Yorl is suspiciously quiet, but I've no time to ponder it when we suddenly reach the bottom of the stairs. I hear shuffling and the clank of armor and faint, rough voices, and then Yorl's clear call: "Open the gates."

"Are you sure, sir? We could postpone; it hasn't eaten fully yet." Another voice echoes.

"Now," Yorl demands. The clank of armor resounds again.

"Is it all celeon down here?" I ask.

"Do you know of any other races who can see in the dark and lift five times their own weight?" Yorl drawls.

"Uh," I start. "The beneathers?"

He scoffs. "They aren't as strong as celeon. If the valkerax escapes, we are the first line of defense."

"R-Right." I gnaw my lips. "On that note—it's chained up, right? Like, at least one chain? Maybe Varia splurged and bought a thousand or so?"

I can't see, but I swear I can hear Yorl rolling his eyes. The screech of metal as the gate lifts makes me jump, and Yorl pushes me forward into abyssal emptiness, the gate slamming shut behind me. The sonorous rhythm is blaring in my ears now. The valkerax is in here, breathing and alive, and I can't see it at all.

A cold glass tube touches my palm, making me jump.

"Don't drop it," Yorl says, his voice still assertive but now shaking on the edges. It's a small relief to hear even him worried.

"You came in here *with* me?" I snap. "Are you mad? You could die! You know, *death*? Big scary dark unknown lacking the joys of creature comforts?"

"Drink quickly," he presses. "It's already sensed our footfall and is coming this way."

I've never drank anything faster in my life—my throat swallowing with all the frenzied urgency of a dying fish. I can't see—there's just darkness. If I die, it'll be out of the blue. Or out of the black, in this case.

"Say something, damn it," Yorl hisses. "It's in front of you."

Say something.

Say something to a valkerax who needs to learn to Weep, to a valkerax in unthinkable pain. It might be a giant wyrm and I might be a human, but if we're both under magic's sway, we're the same thing wearing different shells.

if you are both Heartless, the hunger pinpricks my brain, *you are both hungry.*

I breathe deep.

"Hi there," I chirp into the dark. "First order of business: please don't eat me. Second order—"

There's a *thwump* of the air, and then something impossibly heavy smashes against my side, and my nerves cry out as I spiral head over heels in the air. Something serrated catches me by the leg and shakes me back and forth, my right hip joint coming loose and leaving the rest of my body to fall. I hit the ground with a piercing jolt of pain and a sickening thud, and with my remaining limbs I manage to sit up through the pulsing agony of the majority of my bones being broken. It's a miracle my spine can still hold me at all.

"O-Okay!" I hold my hand up. "Okay, you can have that leg! That's fine. Hated it anyway. Goes great with a side of dungeon dirt, I bet."

A low, clicking growl moves through the earth, so deep and strong it buzzes the pebbles on the ground around my rapidly healing body.

"Listen! I understand that you're angry!" I wince as my leg starts to grow back, the bones pushing out and the flesh realigning. "But what if I told you I could make the voice go away?"

The growl goes silent all of a sudden, the pebbles going still. Can it really understand me?

"The voice—the one in your head that forces you to do things," I insist. "I can teach you to make it go away."

There's a dense moment of breathing—the valkerax's heaviness and my own shallow panic. Nothing moves. Or if it does, I can't see it.

I don't know where in the afterlife Yorl the madman is, but it better be somewhere outside this godsdamn chamber. There's a keening cry, the sound of an animal being tortured, and the ground shakes beneath me as the valkerax thrashes. I brace myself for it to attack me again, rip me apart, but the thrashing quiets eventually.

"The voice—" A voice like a furious ocean rumbles through the darkness, so loud and achingly old—like an ancient wood door creaking open and closed—that it drowns out my every thought, my every other sense. *"The angry voice, the night voice, the eternal voice. The voice like a song never*

goes. *Never flies away. Want to fly away, but it's always laughing, deep inside. Spiders in an egg waiting to hatch.*"

The words are near nonsense, but my breath catches. "You—you can understand me?"

The growl crescendos, and I hold up my arms like they'll do any good against its thousands of fangs. Its serrated maw still haunts me most. I'm willing to bet dying in there would achieve at least number five on my most painful deaths list.

"I swear, I can teach you how to make that voice be quiet!" I shout.

There's that oppressive breathing silence, and then, "*For...*" The valkerax sucks in heavy, sharp air, like it's been stabbed. "*Forever? Forever like the earth-home? Forever like the moons in our dreams?*"

"Not forever." I gulp. "It's only for a while. But it's quiet. I know a way to make the voice get so quiet, it's like it's not even there."

Another long pause. Then that creaking growl echoes again, this time up against my ear, a hot gust of putrid air blasting into my face. It has its mouth open right in front of me. The valkerax rumbles, heavy *whump*s resounding like a giant dog thrashing its tail.

"*Above-prison-prison. Above stone, still stone. Warm blood inside metal keeps us here to listen.*" The valkerax's teeth and massive jaw snap together abruptly, throwing brutal echoes into my eardrums. It gives a shuddering quiver-hiss as it breathes in and opens its mouth again, the breath wafting over me. "*The song makes great pain. The song will rip us apart. Sing about it to the others. Darkness is the end, darkness to swim-fly within. The little cliffs scratched into shape and stone by mortal fingers,*" it thunders. "*They keep us here, too. Why?*"

Little cliffs? What does it mean? Oh! The runes? The beneather runes—I guess they would look like cliffs in the stone to something very, very small. The valkerax's logic is baffling, considering it's not small at all, but it makes a twisted sense.

"To, uh, to teach you." I try to stand, my new leg wobbling. "The person who caught you wants me to teach you how to make the voice go away. It's called Weeping. And once you learn Weeping…they're going to ask you questions."

The valkerax makes that keening tortured sound again, wheezing after it. *"Pain is the question and going is the answer."*

Going. As in, leaving? Of course the valkerax wants to leave this place where it's being held against its will.

"Is going possible?" it presses, the hot air overwhelming and constant, its mouth even closer now as it thrashes its tail and makes the whole arena shake.

"I don't know," I admit, steadying myself and gulping down the urge to run. "All I know is that I can teach you how to Weep."

The hot air reverses all of a sudden, the sound of inhaling, my clothes flapping as the violent breeze pulls me in like I'm an ant, a bug, something easily moved. I dig my heels into the ground and fight it, but it stops abruptly, and I crash into the dirt. I swivel my head around, trying to get a bearing of which direction it's in, when six points of light slice the darkness and freeze me in my tracks. Six ovals—each taller and wider than me—two symmetrical columns of three stacked on top of each other and glowing white.

Eyes. Eyes in the black.

"You," the valkerax says. *"Little you, alone in the darkness. We see. The song can see now. The bones are tied to me.*

Chimes in the dark wind. The Laughing Daughter is tied to you. Chimes in the dark wind."

"How—" I start. "How did you know my witch's name?"

"Everything that chimes has a true name. Everything that is true, we will know."

I choke on my unsaid words as the pupilless white eyes get closer, so close I can see the gray veins in them.

"You will teach us," the valkerax rumbles. "But first you will die."

I don't quite get my next thoughts out, because every blood vessel in my body goes cold at once, my skin numbing to blank nothingness. Then, a flat heavy pressure in my chest as my lungs collapse, my eyes roll like deadweight back into my head, and the ground rushes up to meet me.

The valkerax is, unfortunately, right.

I die.

7

A HOWL AT THE MOON

I come back to life gasping.

"What in Kavar's left butt cheek—" I press my hand on my chest, trying to slow my breathing. I look down at my body—placed on a sleeping mat of some sort. An eager, yellow-furred face suddenly consumes my entire cone of vision, so close I can see each fine whisker.

"What did it say?" The face breathes heavily.

"Ahh!" I kick at it, Yorl dodging my feet with all the grace of a cat.

"What did the valkerax say to you?" he insists.

"This is no way to wake a lady!" I shove him off and he staggers back, the pad of parchment and quill in his hand clutched defiantly. "Wait—I can *see* your face!"

I twist my head around, pinpointing the source of light—a faint patch of moss growing on the stone wall next to me giving off a purplish glow. It's barely anything, but it's enough. I inspect my body: whole and healed, my green tunic tattered and bloodstained but still mostly intact.

"For the love of the spirits—what did it *say*?" Yorl presses, completely ignoring my insult. His eager green eyes are made more vivid by the mosslight, all hint of his cold seriousness replaced by the enamored gaze of a child in a sweetshop. "Did it address you by true name? Did it agree to the teaching? Did it tell you *its* true name?"

"No, yes, and no." I massage my throbbing temples. "It didn't say much. Or, it did, but it talks like a drunk poet."

"To be expected," Yorl mutters, scribbling on a parchment madly. "In Old Vetris, valkerax, before being bound to the Bone Tree, were said to speak in grandly sweeping stories and metaphors; it was their way of life—" He stops, poking the hem of my bloodstained breeches and wrinkling his nose. "You must go through clothes like a worried minister goes through wine."

"I assure you." I sit up. "If I had my say in it, I wouldn't bleed at all."

"I've heard that from women before." Yorl sighs.

I gasp. "You know what a woman is? And here I thought all you did was stay down here in the dark and order people around!"

"It's my job," Yorl says, inspecting my arm with a prod of his quill.

"Right. Your job is to risk your life walking into a hungry valkerax's chamber."

"It was mandatory I go in, because—"

"You were worried about me. How sweet."

"—my entire life's work is in there. And not just *my* life's work—my grandfather's, too."

His grandfather. He's mentioned him on more than one occasion. He's really very important to Yorl, isn't he? Is that why he's doing all this? I clap my hands.

"I just remembered; you killed me. It was the serum, wasn't it?"

"Yes. It causes critical organ failure after exactly a half. As you're Heartless, you are simultaneously the only being in the world who can use the serum and the only being it won't permanently affect." Yorl offers me his paw up in a startlingly soft gesture and I take it indignantly, brushing dirt off my pants.

"Here's a tip from me to you," I say. "It's polite to tell someone you're going to kill them beforehand."

"I'll keep that in mind." He holds out another vial. I stare at it in his paw, then at him. He clears his throat. "This is going to kill you."

"See?" I tease. "Was that so hard?"

We walk to the gate again together, the mosslight fading so that I have to rely on the sound of his footsteps once more.

"You're sure it agreed to be taught?" Yorl presses.

I nod. "Fairly sure. Although, it somehow knew I was going to die right before I did."

"As they have little need for their eyes in the Dark Below," Yorl says, "they've developed keen senses for temperatures and the minute vibrations of a living thing's body. No doubt it sensed your physical systems withering before you did."

"Good," I mutter. "Great, even."

We come to a stop before the gate, and as the celeon guards raise it with clanking effort, I hear the scratch of Yorl's clawed feet as he ducks beneath it. I scramble after him, reaching wildly and grabbing his tail again.

"Oh no you don't. What if that thing decides to eat *you*?"

"You said it agreed to be taught!" Yorl snarls, yanking his tail away from me.

"I can't *control* it," I hiss. "If it gets hungry, there's no growing back for you!"

Yorl's voice is suddenly granite determination. "I've waited ten years. I pored over every inch of knowledge in the world for this moment; I've sacrificed everything to Varia for this. It's a risk I'm willing to take."

I hear him walk the rest of the way in. He's utterly, perilously mad, but it's not every day I meet a mortal willing to risk their one life for something this strenuously. I'm impressed. And more than a little concerned.

Unfortunately, the celeon have decided against installing lighting in the few minutes I was dead. It's just as dark inside the chamber as it was before I died. I down the vial Yorl gives me, listening to the deep breathing echoing around the massive room.

"Hi," I try into the shadows. "Me again. Are you still up?"

"You could talk to an ancient wyrm with a little more respect," Yorl hisses from across the chamber.

"And you can kiss my very well-developed arse," I hiss back. The slither of scales suddenly echoes, getting closer, and then an intrusive gust of hot, rancid wind assaults my senses. I backpedal, until my spine is flat against the metal wall, cold fear gripping my throat.

"*You,*" the valkerax croaks with its ancient, deep vibrato. "*You stand here. You have escaped death.*"

I put my hand shakily to my empty chest. "You could say I'm an expert at that."

The valkerax gives a resounding snort, and I can feel dirt swell up beneath my tunic with the force. "*This we know. It is like life, like death, like the little cliffs of the bloodeyes—always true. The chimes took our bones, and they took your heart.*"

Took my heart— It knows what I am? The fear coursing

through me suddenly plummets, and the valkerax and I breathe into the utter blackness together. It feels like it's just us in this moment—two monsters below the world.

The valkerax shudders in agony, and I feel the ground shudder with it. The worst part is, I can imagine exactly what it's feeling. Every second must be delirious pain. It's a miracle I can understand the valkerax at all—serum or no.

"Is going possible?" The valkerax breaks the silence finally.

"If I can teach you, maybe."

"Then teach with pretty voice-words. Sing us the ways to silence the song. Metal the blade to its throat."

I close my eyes and cling to the memories of Reginall. The way he taught me—soft and even, calm.

"There are two parts." I open my eyes out of habit, not usefulness. "There's the mental part of it, and then there's the physical part. But the physical part is…*difficult* to deal with."

"Our knowing is unknowing. Sing in child-words." The valkerax thumps its tail against the ground, a little quake running through the entire chamber.

"Child-words. All right." I breathe in. "The first part is all concentration, all up to you. But it won't be enough to make you Weep. You have to be cut with a white mercury sword first."

"White mercury?" it rumbles. *"Cut?"*

"The humans invented this substance—white mercury. It can weaken magic. If we cut you with it, the voice gets out of control. Louder. But at the same time, if you concentrate, your silence can be louder than it. You control the voice instead of it controlling you. That's Weeping."

"Weeping." The valkerax's voice echoes from all directions, accompanied by the sound of it slithering in a circle around me. *"Weeping is to control the song? Weeping*

is the three moons before the tide?"

"Yes. At least I think it is. I've done it only once."

The valkerax suddenly lets out a harsh, barking sound that scares the skin off my bones. Was that a...*laugh*?

"*Only once. Once, the little wolf has howled at the moon,*" it says. "*Wolves do not lie, but your mouth drips with tar. We will kill you for bringing us hope.*"

My body jerks, attempting defensiveness even if it's useless against such a huge creature. "I-I can teach you. I know how—"

"*Death for the wolf is pointless. We will give death to the warmblood instead.*"

All the breath pushes out of me at once.

"Yorl!" I shriek. *"Run!"*

Godsdamn my useless eyes—I can't see *anything*. All I can hear is the frantic rush of scales and footsteps over dirt.

useless. The hunger laughs.

The hunger. The hunger knows heat and scents better than I do. I delve deep into it. It's held far down inside me by Varia's magic, but I reach in and pull up the barest threatening, taunting threads of it, letting it bash against my brain.

pathetic little girl, can't lie when she needs to, can't be honest when it counts. what good are you? how could you teach someone else to Weep when you don't know yourself?

a liar is what you are—

Varia's holding the hunger back with her magic, strong and ironclad. But I know the hunger now. I know it loud, and I know it soft. I know it chaotic, and I know it orderly. I focused for these three long years on holding it back, holding it in, but I know now. I know how to bring it forward.

My teeth grow sharp edges—not long like a full hunger

but just enough. The darkness of the arena becomes distinct spots of warmth and coldness, the air suddenly sharp with the musk of alive things: sweat, blood, spittle. A huge, warm body lunges for something much smaller and running at its full, desperate speed.

The valkerax, chasing Yorl.

It spreads its maw wide, teeth nipping at Yorl's heels, and with pumping lungs and legs, I slide between them, slamming my foot into the valkerax's bottom jaw and wedging my arm against the top, fangs embedding in my palms. I can't run away or overpower it. It's too strong and enormous.

The only way to stop it is to endure it.

The valkerax is a thousand stampeding horses; it is a tidal wave to end all tidal waves. It's angry and hungry and mad and it tells me with its furious shriek close to my ear—so close the sheer volume bursts my eardrums, blood dripping down my jaw—that it hates me. Rank saliva sluices down my arm, one of its fangs indenting into my shin and cracking it.

"We will kill the mortal," the valkerax snarls. *"For the wolf's lies!"*

"I didn't lie!" I grit. "I can teach you!"

"The wolf has done it once. Once is a fly's life. Once is a single drop of water in the lake. Once is a mistake."

"I'm the last Heartless alive," I shout, blinking saliva out of my eyes, "who can do it! I'm not giving you false hope. I'm giving you your *only* hope!"

The valkerax snaps its maw shut, taking my shin and forearm with it. Once the limbs are off, the pain is less— less nerves and flesh as hot adrenaline rushes up to stopper all feeling. I fling myself onto the valkerax's wet black nose, clinging to one of its undulating whiskers with my last good hand. The valkerax thrashes, a sickening forceful whirl to throw me off, but I hold fast, digging my nails into its scales.

"It's not freedom!" I shout. "It will never be freedom! But for a moment, you can go back to the way things were!"

The valkerax tears off suddenly for a cold wall, and at the very last second I manage to pull my bleeding lower body up onto its muzzle, the wyrm reeling in pain. I know this despair—I was just as hopeful when Reginall first told me about Weeping. But he let me down easier than I let this valkerax down. I didn't explain well enough, and it's paying the emotional price. It's been a prisoner to the Bone Tree for longer than Cavanos has stood, and I've toyed with its hope.

"Warmbloods took us into the sky. The song is too loud! THE SONG IS TOO LOUD!" the valkerax cries out, beating its tail against the wall, the stone buckling under the force and a rain of dust pouring from the ceiling. *"Warmbloods tore our earth-home apart. We will tear your sky-home!"*

"I don't have a home," I bellow. "And neither do you!"

we are better off alone, the hunger echoes me in a whisper. The mass of writhing flesh below me suddenly slows its thrashing, its panting harsh. I swallow dust and blood, my broken ears ringing.

"As long as the voice is with us," I heave with my breath, "nowhere is home."

The valkerax gives the wall another beat with its enormous tail, but this one is halfhearted. No-hearted. The ground barely shakes.

"We can't remember who we were," I start. "We're always hurting. Always hungry. That isn't home. This—" I hold my hand to my chest. "This isn't a home. This is a prison."

The valkerax's panting peters off into something like a deep, pained whine. My arm and leg finish growing back, and I let go of its thick whisker, dropping to the ground.

"I can't give you your freedom," I say, my teeth retreating, all my senses dulling to a human's once more. "But I can help you remember what it was like to hold it."

8

THE MAN WITHOUT MERCY IS MADE TO BOW

never get to hear the valkerax's answer, because in the next few seconds, I die. And when I wake up again, only one word is on my lips.

"Yorl? *Yorl?*" I sit up on the mat, the green mosslight glowing down on me as I scrabble past the other faintly lit celeon guards sitting against the wall. "Yorl!"

"Stop shouting for me, Heartless." His voice echoes as he appears out of the darkness, his yellow ears flat to his head. "It's unsightly."

He looks dusty but otherwise whole, and relief floods me. "You're all right!"

"With mild thanks to you." He huffs, pulling out another parchment to scribble on. "The valkerax is sedated. I wrote down everything you said, and pieced the altercation together while you were indisposed." He looks up. "It thought you lied to it, right? According to Grenval Chidon's analytical texts, valkerax hate being lied to."

"I would've loved to see those texts beforehand," I chime.

"It's a fragment of parchment so brittle and old, one touch would dissolve it to dust."

"I would've only folded the page to keep my spot a *little*," I egg on. "I've Wept just once, and I told it that. The valkerax thought that meant I couldn't teach it. But I can. I think. I have to try, at least."

"Maybe instead of saying *I've done it just once*," Yorl says with a frown, "consider trying, *I've done it before*. It gives off a better air of confidence."

I chuckle, the vibrations hurting my throbbing head. "And you'd know all about that. No wonder you're Varia's smartman."

"I prefer the term 'Crown Princess's polymath.'"

"Are you?" I quirk a brow and stand on testy legs. "A polymath?"

He scoffs, the sound almost like a purr. "Absolutely not. Cavanosians don't trust celeon to be anything other than guards and mercenaries. Their distrust of magic means they think us inherently incapable of trustworthy thought, considering the witches gave us sentience. I have no tool belt. I did not study at the Black Archives. I'm self-taught."

I whistle softly. "Self-taught, and you made this Old Vetrisian serum no one else has managed to in a thousand years? Consider me thoroughly intimidated."

Instead of proudly accepting the compliment, he glowers. "Grandfather did most of the work and got none of the credit— not from his peers, and not from the Black Archives."

"Aha. So here you are, determined to get it for him."

Yorl regards me with his incandescently green eyes, his catlike pupils huge in the dimness, but says nothing. Finally, he turns and walks away toward the spiral staircase leading to the surface, and I follow. He leads me back up the steps, but I'm so exhausted from being masticated repeatedly by the valkerax that I stumble on a stair.

I feel something warm encase my hand immediately, too bulky to be human fingers. Leathery pads, the tips of claws. Yorl's paw.

"Don't fall behind." His voice is gruff.

Secretly pleased, I strut behind him. "You could just say 'thank you for saving my life' like everyone else does."

When we reach the top of the stairs and emerge into the white mercury–lit hall, he tells me to meet him at the same place, same time tomorrow, and then disappears back into the dark stairwell. I can't stand the thought of being trapped in more stuffy dimness, so I decide to walk back to the palace instead of flagging a carriage, gulping down fresh, warm air the whole way.

One step.

I'm one step closer to my heart. The valkerax can kill me all it likes—but I won't give up.

Dying hurts much less than lying.

The sunset is a brilliant orange gem against a sky banded with gold and platinum. I meander through a Vetris preparing for dinnertime—the smell of roasting fish and barley ale on the air as crowds of bedraggled workers shuffle toward home. Meat has been scarce lately, with most game hunters unwilling to make the long, dangerous journey to Vetris, and the caravans slowing due to avoiding the forested roads—any chance of encountering a witch and their Heartless a constant fear. All that means the meat vendors sell scraps of hare and not much else, while the vegetable vendors flourish—selling cheaper heads of crisp sugarleaf and great bouquets of red summer mushrooms.

The fish vendors are even better off, fat perch and oily flatfish from the rivers within the city piled high.

For a second, I worry Varia won't be able to get the raw organs I require, but then I remember she's a princess. Anything she wants is hers, even with wartime looming. And while fish organs don't satiate me much, they would do in a pinch. Still, I can't help but read far ahead and between the lines—if a war does break out, it won't be long before Vetris's native supply of fish is used up. And that's when the real horror begins. War is terrifying. But I know better than anyone that hunger is the true thing to fear.

Despite my dark thoughts, delicate gouts of white summer pollen float heavy on the wind, mixing with the great plumes of white mercury smoke to envelop the city in a murky haze. I had my leg torn off by a valkerax barely a half ago. I'm still alive, despite the fact I deceived the royal court that lords over these people. Nothing feels quite real, as if I'm swimming in a dream.

A familiar face grounds me back down to the earth. There, on a stone wall covered in wanted posters, is a long row of posters lined up beside each other with Y'shennria's face painted on them. Her strict eyes and puffy hair glare out at me, the scar on her neck so well drawn I feel a twist of nostalgia. It's like ten of her are here, each staring me down, each disappointed in me for how badly I botched all her desperate efforts to stop the war. Bounty hunters linger in front of her posters, armed to the teeth with swords and knives and crossbows. She's safe, I hope—from them, and from the war. She has to be.

"If you could see me now," I mutter to her, and catch a glimpse of my stained self in a passing window. "You'd...well, I'd rather you not see me right now, actually."

I smooth my hair flat in a pallid attempt to make myself look Y'shennria-presentable. The bounty hunters leave, eventually, heading to taverns and inns for the night. I look over my shoulder this way and that, and when I'm sure there are no lawguards about, I tear at all of Y'shennria's posters, quick and furious. Parchment fragments rain down like ragged snowflakes. My boots pause before the last poster of her. This one I peel off as carefully as I can. I open Lucien's kerchief, and fold them both together away in my pocket.

Now hyperaware of the people around me, someone in a simple gray robe catches my eye. They'd been watching me tear the posters, I'm sure of it. I glimpse white hair in the hood, a familiar cruel mouth, but when I turn on them they start off, disappearing around a corner.

That isn't... That can't *possibly* be...

Before my mind can make a better decision, my body slinks after the gray robe's trail. They carry a huge basket on their arm filled with what looks like loaves of bread, and I watch as the gray robe stops near every huddled vagrant and urchin child and offers the basket to them. They dive hungrily for the bread, looking up as if unsure it comes without cost, but the gray robe simply offers.

I follow them until the basket is almost empty, through the poorest winding streets of Vetris, and after passing a ramshackle house of thin boards and cheesecloth windows, they freeze in a small thoroughfare, turning to face me. They don't lower their hood, but they raise their head, and I can see their face clearly.

The cruel twisted mouth, the dignified nose, the watery eyes. His hair is silver-white and cropped short now, and his beard is even shorter on his wrinkled chin.

"Gavik?" I hiss through clenched teeth. "What are you—?"

"You have the wrong person. My name is Kreld," Gavik says instantly, almost far *too* quickly, as if he's been deflecting such a question frequently. He breathes in. "You. What do you want?"

He sounds irritated. Not furious, like I'd expect him to sound when facing down his murderer.

"Oh, nothing," I cross my arms behind my back. "I'm just following a particularly charitable citizen of Vetris and watching him work."

"You think I'd pass out food to these insignificant lowlifes of my own free will?" he snarls.

"Not by any stretch of the imagination." I lilt.

Gavik's face contorts, his glare aimed at the basket as if he wants nothing more than to burn the thing. "I could be doing so much more, but that...*girl*"—he spits the word like poison—"has commanded me to do this denigrating work, day and night without rest."

Ah—that's why he's here. He's been commanded. Power has been lorded over him like he lorded it over the entire city of Vetris. Fury is etched into every inch of his face, and I take a sick pride in knowing there's nothing he can do about it. He couldn't stop even if he wanted to. The idea of a witch commanding a Heartless completely and totally still makes me nauseous, but this feels deserving.

"Is that why you aren't trying to rip my throat out right now?" I ask. "Because she's commanded you to play nice?"

Gavik just glowers, but it's confirmation enough. Varia's sentenced him for his crimes in a way no one ever could when he was a human. He was Archduke Gavik—the most powerful man in Cavanos, which is the most powerful country on the Mist Continent. He was above the law. The crown princess might be dangling my heart in front of me cruelly, but she's also punishing someone who would've never been otherwise. Half of me is bitter at her, and yet the other half is utterly delighted.

"In all truth, *Archduke*..." I wield his old title like a razor as I smile at him. "If I were in your shoes, I would be grateful. Handing out bread is hardly taxing work. Publicly drowning innocent people takes much more effort."

His face goes blank. "Drowning? What do you...?"

He trails off. He doesn't remember his human life. He doesn't remember why he's being punished so. He's been commanded into these streets without knowing how much damage he did to the people who live on them. I wish he remembered. I wish he knew what he'd done so he could learn. But people like him—people with hate deep in their veins—never really learn, do they?

"The hunger never leaves, you know," I say. "It gets quieter, but it never, *ever* goes away."

Gavik doesn't speak for a moment, and the stares of a passing couple force him to warily draw his hood closer to his face.

"You don't even remember drowning those people," I continue. "But you did. I saw you do it the first time I came here. You kept this city under your thumb, terrified that one wrong word, one wrong move, would have them all killed. That's the kind of person you were as a human. A tyrant. A mass murderer. And I'm never going to let you forget it."

I walk away from him with grim satisfaction in my chest, but it fades when I pass the Temple of Kavar and see the ruined, blackened houses—still singed from the fake witchfire Gavik himself planted. His crimes are many, and even if he can't remember them, punishing him for them is justice. But it will never bring back the people he killed.

I clench my fists. I've killed fourteen men. And they are never coming back, either.

so fearful they were, when they saw the end of their lives coming, the hunger oozes from between my ears. ***as fearful as these people were under the archduke's rule. how can you hate him, when you have done much the same?***

The dying sun shafts into my eyes, and I welcome the burn. My crimes are many, but there is no witch forcing me to atone.

If no one will punish me, then I must do it myself.

"Zera!"

That voice—never in a million years did I think I'd hear *that* voice call my name. I turn to see Gavik striding up to me, his hood still close but his basket now empty. Freed from his commanded duty, he no doubt was finally able to come after me. I wrinkle my nose in distaste at the mere sight of him.

"What do you want?"

He draws even with me, leaning in as I lean away, his breath smelling of rancid wine. No doubt he's found that wine is one of the few human things we can consume without crying blood. Up close, he looks so haggard—the deep shadows beneath his eyes deeper, his beard tangled and smeared with dust and detritus, his watery blue eyes glaring out of mud-smeared skin. I'm not entirely sure Varia hasn't commanded him to be unable to clean himself.

"I know," he says, low and rapid. "The Bone Tree. I know of it. I know what she plans to do with it."

"Did you learn about it after you lost your heart? Because you're not supposed to remember anything of your old life."

"I don't—" He winces. "I don't know. I don't know why

I remember it and nothing else. I remember the Bone Tree, yet everything else…it's lost. But Varia told me some things. She told me I tried to kill her. And I'm certain it was because of the Bone Tree."

I freeze down to the last twitch of my fingers. I know why he tried to kill Varia—Fione told me it was because he wanted Varia's white mercury sword. And because Varia was always getting in the way of his plans to accrue more influence. But that doesn't change the fact he shouldn't remember anything.

"You knew about the Bone Tree in your human life?" I whisper, and he nods.

"Yes. I don't know how or why. But I am certain I would've written it down. The urge to keep a diary has been coursing through me even now as I'm this bloodthirsty monster, stronger than a tobacco habit. All my memories—I must've written them down somewhere."

"You tried to kill her," I snarl, "because she had a sword you wanted. Because she opposed you."

He barks an unpleasant laugh. "Do you really think I'd spent years trying to kill a little girl because I was *annoyed* with her? Because I wanted some trifling weapon from the Sunless War? I may have lost my memories, Zera, but I know what I would and would not do."

I'm the same. I hate it in my bones to even admit it, but I'm the same as him. I have no memories of my old life, but I know what I'm capable of. Who I am has never changed, just what I remember.

I look around at the passing crowd, careful to mutter, "It's hardly a trifling weapon when it can stop Heartless."

"Many things can already stop Heartless, you pathetic dullard," Gavik insists. "Fire. Killing their witch. Pure white mercury pumped into their veins acts nearly as well as any white mercury sword, or so I've heard the polymaths in the streets say. No—I didn't try to kill her for the sword. I'm certain of that."

Confusion roots me in place. "Then what—"

"The Bone Tree," Gavik interrupts, his eyes snapping to mine. "Do you understand? It must've been for the Bone Tree. It must be important, if I can remember it even now."

"Because you wanted it, too," I snap. "You wanted its power—"

"No." He shakes his head, his gaze now glazed and focused in the distance. "No, it's not that." He struggles, his face twisting with his efforts. "I can't remember. Godsdamn it all, I can't *remember*!"

His growl reverberates, and a passing mother pulls her child closer to her side. Gavik sneers at the child and looks back down at me.

"I can't remember. But there's some terrible feeling deep inside me. As if I'm missing something crucial. Something vital."

I scoff. "Are you sure it's not just indigestion, Your Grace?"

He spits then. Right in my face.

I wipe the wetness off with the collar of my tunic, and the look I throw him burns hotter than the sun and dirtier than a pile of refuse under said sun.

"Laugh all you want," he says. "Laugh for what I've done, mock me as much as your unheart desires. But when Varia betrays you, you will come groveling to me. And I will give you nothing."

Before I can retort, he turns and skulks away into a dark alley, his basket clutched in his white-knuckled hands.

I don't let Gavik's words haunt me any more than is necessary. The man can't be trusted. Malachite's name for him rings in my head—he's a "genocidal old coot." He hates Varia, and me, and every witch in Arathess. Anything he says is out of spite, not truth. Still, it *is* strange that he can remember the Bone Tree from his old life. Not only is it strange, but it's impossible. Heartless don't remember much, if anything at all. It's usually just fuzzy scraps of memory—nothing solid. It's far more likely Varia let something about the Bone Tree slip after he was changed.

There's no banquet tonight at the palace, so the halls are not nearly as bustling. I make it one step into the front hall when Ulla the Headkeeper approaches me, her bun tight and her eyes downcast as she bows, her gold mantle around her shoulders that denotes her position glinting in the sunset.

"Lady Zera. Princess Varia has requested I offer you this outerwear when and if you returned through the main entrance."

She holds open a dark blue robe, the few scattered nobles walking behind her and in the gardens downstairs sending glances my way. My tunic is streaked with mud and blood, and while that doesn't catch much attention in the common quarter, it does here. Rumors could start quickly if I don't cover up as fast as possible.

"Lady Zera, please," Ulla insists, holding the robe higher. "You have a reputation to maintain."

"Do I?" I smile at her.

"You are a Spring Bride, and Prince Lucien's favorite besides."

Her comment acts like a barbed arrow, settling deep in my flesh and refusing to be pulled out. No—I can pull this arrow out. By myself. I have to, or it will fester into love again.

"I was," I agree, patting her on the shoulder and brushing past her. "Wasn't I?"

I stride the halls with my besmirched tunic, ignoring the soft gasps of nobles as they see me. So shocked are they by the sight of blood that several of the women even collapse, one fainting cold on the carpet when I approach closely. Young gaggles of noble children stop and gape at me, pointing wildly. I am filthy among shining crystal. I am bloodstained among immaculate white marble.

"No better than a butcher's daughter!"

"Does she think she's fighting in the war or some such?"

"—a violent girl!"

"So ugly a thing for a Spring Bride—"

"A potential princess of the kingdom covered in blood?"

With every word of disgust, I can feel Lucien slipping away from me. It's a tiny step. It's small, but this moment, their disapproval—it will all circle back to the king. This is just the first incident, but when I am done, the court will riot at the mere thought of making me a part of the d'Malvane family. Whatever clout I have left as a Spring Bride, whatever delusions the nobles still hold with me as Lucien's favorite—it will all dry up.

Y'shennria taught me the importance of small things, of appearances, of rumors, and now I'm using all her knowledge to do the exact opposite of what she taught me for: to remove Lucien from me, bit by inexorable bit. Every rumor will be a cage for him, and every scandalous thing I do will be the impenetrable lock over the door. I'll seal him in the palace again, putting the entire court between him and me.

I will never touch him again. And neither will he touch me.

His days of weakening me are over.

I arrive at the Serpent Wing, and the guards graciously allow me to dramatically throw the doors open to Varia's apartments. But the rooms are empty. She's gone.

A note rests where she left my dress earlier, in perfectly curled handwriting;

When you return, join me at the shooting range. I've planned a lovely picnic.

I snort. How noble of her—a picnic, while I was being eaten by a valkerax in the pitch dark. The Y'shennria in my head insists I change into a proper dress from Varia's younger closet to look presentable, but I push the thought away. The last thing I want is to look presentable. The uglier and wilder, the better.

So I make it a point to smile and bow at every noble on my way down to the shooting range—the garden full of them at this beautiful time of twilit night. The nobles have the good sense to make sure their whispers don't reach me, this time. This time, they have obviously been warned of me—peering over hedges and bushes to get a good look at the indignity I'm perpetrating on their grounds.

Because the gardens are so full, the shooting range is nearly abandoned. The groundskeeper circles around the range's brightly colored targets far out in the field, adding fresh coats of paint with a horsehair brush. One can tell where the princess is by the entourage of guards—even being the crown princess can't free her from the king's worried order to protect his daughter lest she disappear again.

I follow the glint of armor faithfully. There, on the edge of the range where the woods begin, is Varia, seated on a striped blanket with a dizzying array of fruits and wines and pastries laid out before her. And, to my surprise, she has a guest.

I watch as the crown princess raises her hand, tucking a strand of stray mouse-curls behind Fione's ear. I watch, too, as Fione's face alights with a rosy blush, a smile pulling her face like the petals of a blooming flower. I've never—not once—seen her so honestly happy. She's not giving the sardonic little kitten-smiles she used to give but truly, brilliantly *happy* ones.

"Zera," Fione breathes out softly upon seeing me, her cornflower blue eyes widening at the state of my tunic, her rosy cheeks and smile vanishing all at once. I've done nothing but rob people of their smiles lately. It's a shame she has to see me like this, all bloodied, but it's a sacrifice I'm willing to make.

Varia notices me then, too, but her smile doesn't fade. Their hands are joined on Fione's lap, but they part instantly, and I feel more than a little sorry for interrupting their clear affection. Fione scrabbles with the thing they were holding together—the beautiful gold-kissed dagger lined with rings of sapphires and pearls. She shoves it into a scabbard on her hip. That's the dagger Fione would admire when talking about Varia.

Out of all of us, I realize now that Fione got the happiest ending, and my unheart can't help but glow for her.

"There you are! I was beginning to worry," the crown princess simpers at me and pats the blanket next to her. She pauses when she sees my tunic. "I thought I told you not to startle my people with any blood." She sighs. "No matter—sit down with us, will you?"

I dart my eyes to Fione's face, but she refuses to look

at me, her blush long gone. She shifts in her seat, stroking one thumb over the other. It's a tiny movement, something I'd never catch before Y'shennria's training—nerves. Her refusal to look at me hurts, but not as much as the fact that my very presence is clearly making her unbearably uncomfortable in a way that can't be hidden by her usually perfect noble mask.

"I really shouldn't." I gesture down at my tunic.

Varia quirks a brow. "Sit."

Fione suddenly gets to her feet, leaning on her cane to do so quickly. "I should go. Thank you for the food, Your Highness—"

"Oh, please, Fione. We can all share a meal together, can't we?" She blinks between us. I steal a glance at Fione's terse face.

"I'd—" I swallow. "I'd like to, yes."

"See? She doesn't *want* to bite you, Fione." Varia laughs. "Please sit back down."

Fione starts, this time pivoting. "I can't—"

Varia lets out an explosive sigh. "Fione, *Fione*. So brave, so smart, and yet so scared when it comes to Heartless. Did you ever tell her?"

My stomach plummets. Tell me what? Fione won't face us, or more precisely me, but I can faintly see her thin shoulders beneath her muslin dress shaking. Varia looks to me pointedly, taking a long sip of wine.

"Heartless are her greatest fear. Not that I blame her. The storybooks and bards' songs love to make them seem pants-wettingly terrifying, don't they?"

Things click into place in my head like a polymath contraption starting up. That's why she wouldn't look at me at the banquet. That's why she can't look at me now. I thought it was a fear of what I'd done, but no. It's a fear of what I *am*.

And that hurts far deeper down.

"Fione," I start, my mouth moving rustily. "I would never hurt you—"

"I've seen the Sunless War veterans," Fione says softly. "The men with their legs and arms chewed off. Most of them were not as lucky—some have pieces of their torso missing. Vital organs, eaten. I have seen them die early, because they have barely any liver left at all."

I swallow acid, but Fione continues, her voice trembling.

"Lady Y'shennria's scar. Do you know how she got it?"

I brace myself, knotting my hands in the picnic blanket for stability. "No."

"She was trying to save her infant girl. She bared her neck to them, so they would go for her instead."

Everything inside my chest plummets—every bone, every muscle suddenly weak. Y'shennria never told me. She alluded to it, but it was never said in plain words.

I knew she had lost her entire family, but this level of brutality and sacrifice...

Fione pivots then, slowly, her blue eyes carefully fixed to my boots as she speaks. "She knew there was nothing she could do to stop them. They always come back. They always heal, no matter what injuries one inflicts. *She couldn't fight back.*" Fione's hands, clasped tightly around each other, are white down to the veins. "That is the part I am afraid of. Not the hunger. Not the monstrous form. But the fact that one cannot fight back against them. Against...*you*."

the mouse is smart. The hunger laughs. I search for words, any words of comfort at all, but nothing comes. Any attempt would be hollow; I am the monster she fears.

"Fione, I'm asking this as a favor—" Varia works herself

to her feet, waltzing over to the two of us with mincing steps. She sloshes some of her wine from her goblet as she stops beside me, sweeping her eyes to the guards. "Leave us."

"But, Your Highness," one of the guards starts. "His Majesty has ordered—"

"I know damn well what he's ordered," she snaps, then composes herself. "You can still watch us. But you will do so from the firing line."

She points at the distant line of rails where the shooting range begins. The guard looks to the others, and wordlessly they trot off in that direction. When their metallic cacophony fades, Varia turns her smile back to Fione.

"Give me the dagger, Fi."

Fione looks up at her, wide-eyed. "What?"

"Our dagger," Varia corrects. "I want to show you something, and that sword on Zera's hip will not do."

"I know it's a bit rusty, but it still cuts as well as any fancy cheese knife." I make a feeble attempt at a joke, but it falls flat—it doesn't make Fione look less serious in the slightest. She warily unsheathes the dagger and hands it to the crown princess, ever careful to stay out of my arm's reach. Varia inspects it, then hands it to me, focusing her dark gaze on mine.

"If you ever touch Fione, you will immediately find a secluded place and use the nearest sharp object to stab yourself three times in the stomach." The command and the hunger well up as one in my head. Varia's obsidian eyes lose their intensity as she turns to Fione with a smile. "There. The stomach should be a painful enough place."

Fione's shakes have only gotten worse, her rosebud lips paling. "Varia—how could you—?"

"Hush," Varia chides her. "This is for your peace of mind

as much as mine. I won't let her, or anyone else, hurt you. Go on. Try it out. Touch her."

I stand stock-still, petrified. Fione looks nervously between Varia and my shoes, then back to Varia again, her cheeks whiter than bone and her small frame quaking uncontrollably. She's nervous but not surprised, which means Varia's already told her about being a witch.

her fear is sweet. The hunger licks its lips. She's right to fear me, to fear this emptiness inside me.

She's right to fear, but she shouldn't *have* to. She was the closest thing I ever had to a friend. She doesn't deserve to be held captive by fear. She has to see just how much control Varia and the command has over me. She has to see she's *safe*.

With my hands outstretched, I move toward her. She pulls back far too late—my fingers brushing her mouse-brown curls. The command has me in its jaws in the time it takes to blink, wrapping its tendrils about my arms and legs and forcing them to move toward the forest that touches the shooting range. The command must think the relative isolation of the shadows between the trees is secluded enough, because I stride quickly and purposefully through the grass, over the picnic blanket, around trunks and branches until I am alone.

My hands poise the bejeweled dagger on their own, and I suck in a breath and watch the blade's beautiful tip kiss the fabric over my stomach. I steel myself, but Varia was right—the stomach is an awful place to be stabbed. Things tend to rupture and twist, and blood pools inside abdominal cavities. I grit my teeth and watch the dagger fly, once, twice, thrice, and the last stab catches something vital in me and my legs buckle out with the pain. My cheek presses into the pine needles, suddenly warm and wet from my blood, and my eyes start to dim as my ears do.

The sound of a horrified gasp cut short resounds in the forest, and then Varia's calm, fading voice.

"...see—this will deter her from ever touching you. You have nothing to fear, Fi. She's mine. Magic has made her mine. And I'll never let her hurt you."

9

GLASS AND BONE

The Laughing Daughter's magic is so incredibly *strong*, I'm almost offended by it. It gives me no time to sit and languish in pain and throw a pity banquet for myself at all. The three stab wounds in my stomach stitch themselves together, the skin warming on the edges where it entangles over itself. Those little lines of warmth are what yanks me out of the blank white precipice of death and plops me back into unlife. I crawl to my knees, slipping on the pine needles as I look around for Varia.

I find my witch (*gods, so strange to call her that*) idly sitting on a log not a few paces away from me, her heels beating against the wood like an impatient child. I scour the forest around her.

"Just you?" I start. "What a disappointing welcome back party."

Varia shrugs, midnight sheet of hair spilling over her shoulders. "Fione left. She saw your body and ran in the other direction looking sick."

"Poor thing," I murmur. "Probably best that way. No

human *likes* to watch flesh mend itself again."

But at least now she knows—I can't touch her without very painful consequences. That should ease her mind, at least a little, and that in turn makes me feel a tiny bit better about it all.

Varia clears her throat. "I appreciate the gesture, by the way."

"Which one? The dying?" I brush dirt off my mouth and motion to my tunic that's now horrifically bloodied. "Or crashing your gorgeous picnic whilst covered in blood?"

Varia's smile is strangely absent as she speaks, her wide lips serious. "You reached out to touch her first. I wasn't relishing the idea of ordering you to do it."

"Because *that's* where you draw the line." I snort.

Varia's eyes flash like black witchfire. "Fione is my dear heart. Obviously that's where I—"

"She's an eighteen-year-old girl who's never left the court's influence," I retort. "And you're a twenty-one-year-old witch plotting to use the world's most terrifying army against it. She spent five years looking for you. Lucien spent five years. Both of them suffered horribly for *five years* because of you."

Varia suddenly laughs, the sound bitter. "Oh, this is rich. The Heartless who earned their trust and then betrayed them all—lecturing *me* on hurting them? You truly are the only funny noble in Vetris, *Lady Zera*."

My blood boils at the way she says it. I worked my arse off for Y'shennria to be called that. She was proud of me. No matter how huge a facade it was, I held it up with my own two arms. I *earned* that title.

"Have you even told her?" I snap back. "Have you told Lucien what you're going to do with the Bone Tree, either? Or are you keeping that a secret, too, so they can suffer when you transform overnight into the world's most powerful—most *terrifying*—person?"

There's that brimstone flash in her eyes—the same as Lucien's. I inhale hugely.

"I might've betrayed them. But at least I didn't abandon them."

She stands abruptly from the log, skirts swirling. "I'm *protecting* them!"

My mouth falls silent as Varia's chest rises and falls with her furious breathing. She quips, she smiles, she deflects, but she doesn't get truly angry. Until now.

"I am the one who will stop the eternal spiral of war in Cavanos," the crown princess says, softer but with no less hard an edge. "Because it's what must be done. But I will do it alone."

"The world will fear you," I snarl. "And take it from me, Princess—that always leads to hatred."

"Then they will fear only me." She raises her chin haughtily. "And they will hate only me."

I almost blurt a laugh then. Bullheadedness must run thick and undeniable in the d'Malvane blood.

"You could call a truce," I press. "You're the crown princess *and* a witch. You'd be the perfect person to negotiate a peace talk, as an ambassador to both—"

"So that what, Zera?" Varia slices through my words. "So that some ignorant human in a village can 'accidentally' drown a witch one day, and Cavanos can go to war again in ten years' time? No."

"But…raising the valkerax—"

"I have considered everything," she interrupts me coldly. "And this is the best option."

"Best?" This time I do blurt a laugh, though it sounds half

hysterical. "What madman would ever think commanding a ravening valkerax army is the *best* option?"

Varia's quiet, the forest wind playing with her hair, and then, "This is what the crown princess must do for her people."

The rising Blue Giant catches her face, lacquering her gold skin with pale azure. Her proud nose gleams, her brows knit, and fierce determination is etched in her every pore, and yet her eyes are piercingly lucid. Where Lucien is a hawk forever hunting, she is an owl—watching, waiting, a sentinel in the night.

I'm awestruck for a moment. I see her for the first time like a younger Lucien might've. I understand now why he looks up to her so much. Why he took up the mantle of Whisper to try to behold her ideals while she was away. Lucien grew himself in her image over the years she was gone. She is a pillar of conviction, a pillar lit with flame and blazing alone into the night.

The moment passes, and Varia covers her raw self with a lid of a smile.

"How was your first valkerax session?"

I manage an inhale. "G-Good. I died twice, but that's just business as usual."

"Do you think you can teach it?" she asks.

"No idea. But I'm going to kill myself trying."

It's not my strongest joke, but it earns a tiny chuckle from the crown princess, granting a breath of levity to the dense air. The wind whistles through the trees and between us, and finally she turns to walk out of the wood.

"Father is planning to call you in soon for questioning about Gavik's death."

"*Vachiayis.*" I exhale the beneather swear.

Varia presses on. "I'd refrain from telling them the truth of who killed him. Whether or not Gavik was a danger to me, if you tell Father you killed a blooded noble, he is oathbound as king to punish you appropriately. Even I wouldn't be able to get around that. And, of course, it goes without saying—if you tell Father I'm a witch, you will never get your heart."

I swallow hard, and Varia raises one hand in farewell as she walks away toward her ring of guards. I walk out and stare at the abandoned picnic blanket, disheveled but still beautiful, and I do what any sane undead thrall about to go on trial for their unlife would do.

I pick up the half-empty wine bottle and chug it.

That night, I have that dream again.

I'm walking in the Hall of Time, the stained glass embracing me with brilliant colors from every which angle. The stained glass tells the history of Vetris in perfect detail—of how it was built by the Old Vetrisians, of how the Cavanosians once fought the neighboring country of Helkyris, of the Old God and the New God worshippers warring; the humans and celeon versus witches and their Heartless.

I recognize I've had this dream before—faintly, in the back of my mind as I watch history pass me, I recall this dream. Last time, the Hall of Time fragmented, and I dragged myself through the shards to reach two rosaries with trees on them, so convinced if I didn't reach them, something horrible would happen.

But this dream is different.

Beyond the stained glass is a dark shadow. Outstretched branches. A tree. By that convincing, totalitarian logic one has in a dream, I know that tree outside the Hall of Time is alone. I can feel loneliness physically emanating from it like waves, repeated and undeniable. My unheart aches for it, for how desperate and deep its loneliness is.

Suddenly, there's a screeching bestial roar, and the Hall of Time implodes on itself above me, all around me. The stained glass fragments into a million glittering petals of all colors of the rainbow. Razor sharp, they cut me on the way down, scoring my cheeks, my upturned palms.

At last, there's no Hall separating the tree and me. It's a naked tree, dark and small and still young, barely taller than I.

I run toward it, the shards of glass serrating my feet. Blood everywhere. But the bloodstained shards begin to move as I do, racing faster than I ever could toward the tree of their own free will, dragging crimson lines of my blood in the ground behind them. I run, but the glass shards run faster, chittering against one another like short-lived bells, like thousands of birds. They reach the tree first, and I watch as they settle against the trunk, securing themselves to it as if they want to be the bark instead. Like chaotic puzzle pieces, they assemble themselves over the tree like armor. The entire history of Vetris, fragmented and broken, gleams up the branches, curls down to the roots. The tree glitters so brightly, I'm nearly blinded, my bloodstains on the glass the only thing daring to dull it.

Still, the waves of loneliness from the tree do not ease. Still, I reach out for it, and suddenly, all at once, like a thousand spears of an army, the glass shards all raise like spines and point square at my face—

I bolt awake on Varia's couch covered in a cold, clammy sweat. My blurry eyes focus on the room, and I stare at the gorgeous silk curtains, the gold-leaf paintings, the sheer beauty of the princess's room to ground myself, force myself to calm down. My breathing evens out slowly as my eyes drink in the breathtaking sight of the white marble balcony in the moonlight.

I blink when I find someone standing on it, their long raven hair let loose and tangled as if they'd just woken up. Varia. She's in her muslin nightgown, facing away from me and toward the Blue Giant half-moon in the sky. I sit up to see her face and freeze.

Her eyes are glazed, far away. Her whole body is still, gently swaying in a way I've never seen before. She always stands straight, her posture perfect. But it's neither her eyes nor her body that alarms me most.

It's her mouth. Her mouth is moving, quickly and silently. At first I think she's casting a spell, those wordless spells that only the Old God can hear. But then, slowly, I lift myself off the couch and linger at the balcony's door, and I hear her monotone words.

"The tree," she says. "The tree...the tree. The tree."

Terror grips me, irrational and mind-bendingly strong. How does she know what I dreamed? Or is she dreaming, too?

I back away from the balcony, wrap myself in a fox fur throw blanket, and spend the rest of the night in the corridor with the unquestioning guards.

In the morning, Varia is long gone. What would I even say? That I saw her on the balcony being objectively unsettling? That I, too, dream of a tree? In the cold light of morning, my fear seems childish and unreal. So I push it away to focus on the reality in front of me.

I wait for the king to call on me. Waiting is the worst part of life; it feels like walking on a bed of rusted nails, every step painful.

But the king doesn't call for me. First, he calls for his army.

King Sref sends for the bulk of the Vetrisian army to gather at the capital. He also calls the farmers and the tradesmen to consolidate resources in Vetris—in no time the streets crowd with grain wagons moving back and forth to storage towers. It's a grim reminder that I can cocoon myself in my worries all I want, but the war outside will move forward inexorably.

Varia barely returns to her room—either in meetings with ministers or with Fione spending time together in the library—which means I have free rein of the apartments. If I wanted to appear proper to the court, I would go back to Y'shennria's manor to live. And I'm sure Varia would be fine with it. But living in that empty mansion, full of so many memories, would gnaw at me. I know that. So I stay among the silks and the marble, watching the darkwood manse from afar. The nobles approve insomuch as they can—praising Varia for taking pity on me when Lady Y'shennria's all but "abandoned" me.

Fione avoids me at all costs, darting out when we enter the same rooms, making muttered excuses to flee any social situation I exist in. Malachite still won't look at me straight when I'm around. Lucien, on the other hand, acts the opposite. He looks up when I pass and makes a point to shoot me the most grating, placating smile I've ever seen each time we meet in the halls. The sort of smile he gives to people he dislikes. It itches, burns like an acidfire under skin—a fire I can't escape no matter which way I turn or how far I get. He addresses me once, as we meet on the stairs of the palace entrance—me going to the valkerax, and him returning from riding, his hair sweat-beaded and his cheeks flushed.

"Lady Zera." He smiles bitterly, his shed riding jacket under his arm. "I hope I find you well."

It's such a trite thing to say, a furious laugh starts to bubble up in me. It's for girls much more gullible than I am. Girls much younger than I am. Girls much more human than I am. It's not a pleasantry; it's an insult. And we both know it.

His disdainful smile pushes me away, the white dress shirt clinging to the muscles of his arm, drawing me in. His face is handsome as always, but his faked smile isn't enough to hide the faintly purple circles under his eyes. I blink, throwing him a more brilliant smile than ever before, constructed out of sheer anger-cut glass.

"You've found me incredibly fine, Your Highness. Whatever can I do to repay you for your inquiring kindness?"

This doesn't throw him. Of course it doesn't. He's endured these sorts of exchanges all his life. He blinks and runs a hand through his short black hair, mussing it more.

"Your smile, Lady Zera," he says, voice dripping with honey-laced wrongness. "That's all I'd request from you."

For a second, I have no idea what to do or say. For the first time, I feel as if I'm squaring off against him as an equal. We're both standing here, smiling at each other, knowing exactly what we both are. It's no longer me deceiving him, secrets always up my laced sleeve. This is the two of us on equal footing.

At last.

His dark eyes hold me. He's won this time. I can feel it as he walks away—his shoulders broad and proud. He's won something invisible back from me. Something I didn't even know I had taken.

I linger on the steps, staring at the one he'd been standing on. If I had a heartbeat, I know it would be painfully loud in my ears.

Sometimes, I catch glimpses of Lucien around the palace with Varia. Usually the two of them are accompanied by Fione. I watch them walk the gardens, laughing and teasing one another. Varia tucks daisies behind Lucien's ear, and he grins sheepishly. Fione trips over roots or brick walkways, and Lucien reaches out to catch her before she falls. Varia never hesitates to kiss Fione's hand at every opportunity. They ride horses together, Lucien challenging his sister to a race. Fione insists on riding the same horse as Varia, clinging to her back for dear life with a delighted red flush on her cheeks.

They are...happy. Lucien is happier than I've ever seen him before. I feel somehow guilty for watching them like this. But it's the only time I can catch glimpses of his rare, golden smile, the true one, the one that squeezes my chest so hard it feels as if I have a heart again.

I watch, and I wonder, wistfully, what it would be like to join them.

Malachite must've taken my plea about introducing Lucien to other girls to heart, because I start to see Lucien walking with someone who isn't Varia or Fione; a beautiful girl with pale milk-blond hair and warm brown eyes of cinnamon. She's as graceful as Y'shennria and far quieter than I. On the first day, Lucien is as cold as winter toward her—ignoring everything she rarely says, walking fast as if trying to ditch her. But she keeps coming back. Malachite keeps smiling at her when she walks up. He approves of her, that much is clear, and I feel a pang of regret that I can't be the one he's smiling at.

The beneather is smart, and he knows how Lucien works—he keeps talking to her long enough to force Lucien to engage with her as well. She walks quickly to keep up with Lucien, sometimes running—an unsightly thing noble girls are never supposed to do. But unlike the other noble girls, she doesn't seem to care how she looks. Her dresses are simple, her hair even simpler. She trips over carpets as she runs, but she always gets to her feet instantly and determinedly continues after Lucien, apologizing for her own clumsiness.

It doesn't take long for me to overhear exactly who she is—Lady Ania Tarroux, a Goldblood whose father's money is funding a great deal of the war effort. The nobles call her *simple* and *rather hopeless*, but the way she so genuinely tries to keep up with Lucien despite him ignoring her—something about it plays on my unheart strings. She doesn't laugh excessively, or bat her eyelashes, or desperately try to get him to talk. She's just...*there*, steady and gentle. I'm half in awe of how well Malachite knows Lucien—steadiness and persistence are the two things a girl pursuing Lucien needs more than anything, and she has it in spades. He's picked well.

Sometimes, it gets hard to breathe when I think such thoughts. But I like to blame it on the dust in the palace.

I ask around about her—the kitchen maids more than happy to gossip with me. Lady Tarroux lost her mother at a very young age, and by all accounts she's the one raising her four other sisters. She's very devout—spending most of her time in prayer in the Temple of Kavar in the center of the city—and often she's spotted handing out food and clothing with the priestesses. She's due to debut next year at the Spring Welcoming, and the rumors are, of course, already circulating about it, seeing as Lucien hasn't announced his engagement to me. Or to anyone.

Lady Tarroux is the exact opposite of everything I am— quiet, gentle, easygoing, innocent. And best of all, she's humble. She's different from the other nobles, enough that she could catch Lucien's eye, if he just gave her a chance. And Malachite seems dead set on providing that chance.

She's *perfect*.

The perfect wedge to drive between Lucien and me—so perfect I almost pity her. I'm going to use the poor girl like a tool, and she'll never see it coming. But maybe that's for the best—she'll have a princely husband out of it, if all goes well.

But I don't have the time to help Malachite orchestrate anything between Tarroux and Lucien. For four days, my life is consumed entirely by the valkerax. First thing in the morning, I wash and dress and head to the South Gate via Varia's carriage. In the dark arena below the city with Yorl, I try desperately to teach the valkerax how to sit still (an increasingly impossible feat, considering how much pain it's in) while simultaneously trying to understand its lyrical, half-mad poetry. Each day I walk into the arena, its voice gets a little softer, and that worries me. Yorl insists the valkerax is stable, but it's hard not to think otherwise. On the second day, its voice is barely loud enough to hear. Yorl's there with me every step of the way, unflinchingly brave even when the valkerax thrashes around violently in fits of pain. We barely make any progress—and I hardly even manage to get two coherent words out of the valkerax. The sound of it whining in sheer agony makes my stomach sink and pity rise.

"Can't you, I dunno, give it some permanent polymath painkiller? Or have Varia magic the pain away?" I ask Yorl as we ascend the stairs after the session, his paw in mine. I feel Yorl's immature mane brush my shoulders as he shakes his head.

"I've tried. But the Bone Tree was made with the most advanced Old Vetrisian magic available. That sort of forging is lost to us. There are temporary solutions, but nothing works permanently to relieve their pain. It's almost as if it's a fundamental agony the Bone Tree has written into the laws of valkerax existence."

"Couldn't I just…" I stumble over a stair and Yorl tenses his arm, and I pull myself up by it. "Couldn't I just go down to where the valkerax live, then? Into the Dark Below? I could teach one that isn't in pain."

Yorl snorts. "No one goes into the Dark Below and survives—not humans and not witches. Perhaps if you were a beneather culling party, but even then there's a good chance half of you wouldn't make it back."

"And my locket." I clutch the gold heart around my neck. "I'm guessing valkerax live way more than a mile and a half down, huh? Varia wouldn't want to risk her death going very far."

Yorl blinks at me with his huge green eyes. "I must be rubbing off on you. You almost sounded *intelligent* just then."

I can't see my own rude gesture, but he can. We're quiet as we walk the rest of the way up the stairs, and Yorl leaves me at the top.

"Tomorrow," he says. "I'll feed it well and sedate it as much as I can. We can try again tomorrow."

"And if that doesn't work?"

Yorl stares at me steadily. "There are other Old Vetrisian methods I can try. But they are...brutal. I'd prefer not to resort to such things."

"Brutal how?" I swallow nervously.

"It involves taking off parts of the valkerax's body."

as always, the hunger sneers at Yorl. *we are forever expendable to them.*

"Is there any way to not dismember a living thing for what we want?" I ask lightly.

"I will do it if I must," he says, resolute, his tail swishing. "I will become a polymath, no matter what must be done. And you? Will you do it, for your heart?"

The taunting gap where the memories of my heart were inside me widens, yawning open. To never eat raw things, to never have to kill again. To never have to take orders, and to remember everything I once was, at the cost of a creature's pain.

"These methods won't kill it?" I narrow my eyes at Yorl.

He shakes his head. "No. It would temporarily inflict great pain, and the valkerax may never regrow them back."

I have to try everything I possibly can to make the valkerax talk cohesively, to teach it, to make sure it doesn't come to that. But if it does...

if it does, you would, the hunger insists with rock-hard truth. *you desire your weak humanity as a moth desires flame, and it will be your undoing.*

I stare into the darkness of the doorway behind him and think of the majestic creature that sits there at the bottom, alone, in pain, half dead and all mad. If I was a good person, I would say no. If I was a dishonest person, I would say no.

But I am done with lies.

"Yes," I start. "If that's what it comes to."

Yorl and I share a long glance, our twin goals laced in the abject silence of dirty deeds, and then he turns wordlessly and descends back down the dark staircase, the door creaking shut behind him. I take a deep breath to clear the heaviness in my chest, turn on my heel, and leave the wall. I blink as my eyes frantically adjust to the bright, late-afternoon sunlight. Not as many people stare at me this time as I walk through South Gate's crowd, entirely because I'm not covered in blood. The valkerax hasn't had the presence of mind to speak two sensible words to me, let alone the energy to try to bite me again.

There was something the valkerax said today, though, that stuck with me.

The branches cry out in the night to those who will listen in slumber.

It had no context, blurted between bouts of pain, but it echoes in my head. It would be easy to write off such a sentence as gibberish if I hadn't had that dream of the tree the other night. To *listen in slumber*—that could be dreaming. And there had been branches in my dream, covered in bloodstained glass. Glass that pointed itself at me when I tried to come near.

But Vetris is no place to dream for a Heartless.

The war, the valkerax, how to push Lady Tarroux at Lucien—I mull it over every hour of the day, barely falling into the mockery of sleep Heartless experience. Varia's maids send a pitcher of wine to her room every night, and I find myself dipping into it more than is healthy, the wine the only thing capable of slowing my racing mind. But soon—like all places I stare at the walls of for more than two days—the palace starts to feel like a prison. And so I turn to the only place left to me—the city.

The looming war permeates Vetris as thoroughly as the stink of white mercury; the blacksmiths never quiet their anvils as they produce piles of swords and armor. The polymaths gather in groups, in taverns and on the cobblestone streets, gesturing wildly with their baggy sleeves at buildings and walls and arguing over how to better fortify them against magical attacks. The Vetrisian army trickles in from all over the country thanks to the king's summons, gathering outside the white wall in little nodes of tents that rapidly grow to sprawl over the grassland.

The soldiers run drills during the day, the sound of their boots most prominently heard near the gates, and at night they stagger through the alleys and roads of Vetris, drunk and blustering about how many witches and Heartless they'll kill soon. I allow myself a single flinch when I hear such things for the first time, said with such venom and bravado all at once. Said as if they were convinced it was the right thing to do. The children follow on their heels, excited to see so many uniforms, their voices rising up as they joyfully sing the little songs they do while playing games:

"Dark clouds, dark clouds,
Kavar break them all,
Water for a witch and fire for their thralls!"

I swallow down, sick. The humans kill witches with water—drowning them, to stop them from speaking spells and escaping. And fire works better than any other weapon to slow down a Heartless—burning a body gives even magic a difficult time regenerating it. Hearing methods to kill witches and Heartless spill from the mouths of children sends shivers up my spine.

Why do the humans and witches hate each other at all?

I realize almost immediately that it's a pointless question to ask. Old Vetris fell to ruins about a thousand years ago. They united against the valkerax threat, but their differences eventually tore them apart. That's what the books say, anyway, written by polymaths well versed in history; their differences were just irreconcilable. The more I try to ask myself why the humans and witches hate each other, the more juvenile it sounds; magic is power. Power causes fear. Fear curdles to hate. Wondering where the root of all these wars began is pointless; witches are witches. Humans are humans. They fear. They hate.

Even if the initial disagreement was small, the thousand years of bloodshed between witch and human have turned it into something far, far larger—a web that feels like it can never be destroyed or escaped from. Suffocating us all.

It's the third day when the valkerax finally says something that makes a drop of sense. It curls around itself, panting, and wheezes, *"The tree of bone will always call to the chime strong enough to become its roots."*

There's a moment of breathing, mine and its, and I dare to hope that I've gotten through to it, that the next few sentences it says will make sense just like that one.

"You have to fight it!" I call into the dark. "I know it's hard, but you have to clear your thoughts of the pain!"

I wait on needles, praying it will acknowledge me at all. But instead it groans, the sound like wood being bent until it breaks.

"Immortal hate, immortal anger. Life squirming in a world of undeath. Below the sun and above the moons, together at last." The valkerax's voice is a bare whisper. *"The mother calls to the son; two long to become one. A daughter like a weapon. A rose between them. A wolf to end the world. A*

WOLF. TO END. THE WORLD!"

Its voice is suddenly so earsplittingly loud, booming around the arena and dislodging pebbles from the ceiling. Dirt rains down, and I duck beneath its thrashing tail just as the serum overtakes me, cold death waiting with open arms.

Yorl looks tired for the very first time when I wake up again, his whiskers drooping even as he scribbles on his parchment, his mouth a thoughtful line.

"It's not reacting to the painkillers the same way the last one did," he mutters. "Unusually willful."

"I could try to dance for it," I quip. "I've been told that takes all the fight out of people."

I smirk, thinking of Y'shennria and how exasperated she was when she taught me to dance. Yorl doesn't bite. He's quiet the whole time we walk up the stairs, and even when we part at the top, his emerald eyes are deep in racing thought.

"You're not going to do that whole body part thing—" I start.

"I will do what is necessary." He interrupts me coldly without looking up. "Better the valkerax be in pain than die and give us nothing."

"Is it…really that bad?" I swallow, my throat dry.

"You've seen how weak it's getting," Yorl says, pushing his glasses up on his nose. "The Bone Tree's command is eating away at it like the basest acid. It will not survive aboveground much longer."

I watch him go back down the dark stairs with a twisting in my stomach.

"The tree of bone will always call to the chime strong enough to become its roots."

That one sentence, among all the gibberish, haunts the space between my ears. I know the tree of bone. Varia's after it. A chime—the valkerax uses that word for witches. Based on what the valkerax said, can the Bone Tree call to a witch? How? And why would it? It's an Old Vetrisian magical relic, for the gods' sakes, not a person with sentient thought.

Would it—*could it*—try to use a witch for its own purposes?

I shake my hair free of dust. No, it'd be foolish to take anything the valkerax says in those throes of pain seriously. It's under so much stress and agony. If anything of what it says while suffering from the Bone Tree's command were true, then Varia wouldn't need me to teach it to Weep in the first place. Gibberish. That's all it is.

I'm walking past a dark alley tavern when I see a familiar figure in a gray robe backed against a wall by half a dozen angry men. Gavik. The men palm wooden clubs and the hilts of swords, the air thick and tensely wound, like an invisible nest of threads pulled tight enough to cut.

"—not as dense as you think we are!" One of the men gets in Gavik's gaunt face. "I saw you with my own two eyes, that night in the black market!"

The men behind him shift, some of them nodding along, others grunting. Gavik refuses to blink—staring down at the shorter man over his nose. Is the man talking about the night Gavik made the raid on the black market here in Vetris, the one Lucien showed me? The one that traded vital food and supplies beneath the radar to escape the crushing taxes Gavik had enacted?

"Don't waste your energy on the wrong man." Gavik

sneers, his words slurring as if he's…drunk? I squint, and sure enough, I see him tottering from one leg to the other. "Whyever would an archduke be here, in a disgusting alley, with a disgusting pack of sniveling dogs?"

"That's it!" the man in his face barks, pulling out a club. "Get him, boys!"

The men descend like ravens on a corpse, the dull smacking sound of heavy blows meeting flesh resounding. Gavik, as self-contained as he is, as I always saw him be in the palace, isn't immune to the pain. Pain is the great equalizer. It makes us all look foolish and weak. It makes us all cry out the same, and Gavik is no different. He bellows like a wounded buck, and in the glimpses between the men's flying limbs and flashes of swords, I see him gnashing his teeth, blood and spittle running down his chin.

I wait.

Varia's magic is too strong even for me—I can't bring out the monster much further than a few claws and teeth. I'm sure letting the archduke wander free among the people of Vetris means Varia's taken precautions against him turning, but one can never be too sure with the hunger. I'm the only one who could feasibly stop him if worse came to worst.

But…neither do I stop the men. All I can see is the boy I first met when I came to Vetris, his terrified face as he was forced to ascend the stepladder into the water coffin on Gavik's orders and drown. My wrist aches with the phantom memory of the pain when Gavik, that same fateful black market night, ordered one of his men to shoot me with a crossbow.

"I wonder if the West Star is out tonight," I murmur lightly, looking up at the glittering sky between the alley's roofs. The cries of pain ricochet, and I almost laugh.

Lady Tarroux would, surely, help anyone in pain. And here I am, just enjoying myself.

evil, the hunger cackles. ***evil down to your core.***

"No," I argue softly. "I'm not the evil tonight."

When the men finally run out of steam, they spit on his crumpled body and walk off. Blood seeps between the cobblestones as I approach the figure of Gavik slumped against the wall.

"My, my, *my.*" I lean next to him on the wall, my eyes on the warm lights of the tavern opposite us. "I had no idea this place served just desserts."

It's merciful the men didn't stay, because my eyes catch the wounds on Gavik's legs mending already. The bruises fade from deep reddish purple to green, to yellow, and then to nothing. The cuts close up, sewing skin against skin. Gavik just shudders and holds himself.

"I thought you were supposed to be dead," I try. "Don't the common people know that you've been declared murdered?"

Gavik says nothing, his voice rasping in his injured throat with a weak noise.

"You're right," I agree. "Why would the nobles tell the common people anything? And why would the common people care about one murdered noble, when their sons and daughters are poised to go off to war and experience the same a thousand times over?"

My instincts hone in on a shadow in the corner of the woodwork, just outside the tavern. An opportunistic vulture, waiting for the right time to strike.

"Unfortunately, he's not dying tonight," I call out to it. "And his soul is emptier than his pockets. So move along."

The shadow rescinds, and I sigh lightly and look down at Gavik.

"It's cruel of Varia, isn't it? To send you out here and not give you a new face? You've been starving and torturing and killing these people and their loved ones for years. They're bound to know what you look like. You're a smart man. The first thing you'd do is put on a mask. Which means Varia must've commanded you to keep your face clear."

Gavik coughs, the sound wet but healing. His breath reeks of stale wine.

"It's a song," he rasps.

I wrinkle an eyebrow. "You've certainly gotten worse at conversational segues since your time away from court."

He leans his head against the wall, gray hood falling to reveal the bloodstained skin of his old, drained face as his watery eyes move to me.

"I know how I remember the Bone Tree. It's a song."

"It must've been a terribly memorable song," I lilt.

His creaky voice warbles out, low and off tune, the lyrics echoing among the alley's walls. *The tree of bone and tree of glass, will sit together as family at last.*"

My unheart clenches. A tree of glass. Like the one in my dream. I keep my face cool, composed. "What sort of song is that?"

He narrows his eyes. "I don't know. I don't remember any more of it. But I heard it a long, long time ago. And it was important. I pursued it—I must've. I couldn't remember anything of my human life when I first woke up as a Heartless. But over time, the single line of that song broke through my mind. I caught myself humming it, and then the words came. After that, the memory of the Bone Tree flooded in."

I frown. "What sort of memories about the Bone Tree are kicking around in that hateful old skull of yours?"

"None." His watery eyes dim, and he looks down at the

bloodstained cobblestones. "I don't remember anything about it. But I remember it exists and that it's dangerous. A terrible, dangerous weapon."

I blow out air. He's not technically wrong. I realized that, too, the moment Varia and Yorl told me what the Bone Tree is, and does.

"I know that," I bite. "What's your point?"

"Varia can't have it," he insists.

"She's going to get it," I say. "And I'm going to help her."

"You have to stop," the archduke insists. "I don't remember—" He slams his fist on the ground, knuckles skinning themselves and healing all in a second. "I don't remember why, but the Bone Tree is terribly dangerous. More so than you think, more than anyone knows."

Doubt starts to creep in, but my unheart burns. Of course it's dangerous. But it's the one path left to my heart. It's the last road left open, the last one I can walk on my own. Mother's face lingers, an outline that I know can be filled in so easily, so warmly, if my heart returns to my chest.

"You don't say," I drawl. "It's almost like it's a tree that can control all valkerax."

Suddenly, to my utter horror, I feel something tug on my breech cuffs. I look down to see Gavik...*begging.* On his knees, folded in half, his hands clinging on my boots and his face downturned. I stagger back in alarm.

"Please." His voice is thin, all traces of sneering superiority gone. "You must stop helping her find the Bone Tree. I don't know how, or why, but I can feel it—if she finds the Tree, it will mean disaster."

An archduke. Not just any archduke—the most powerful archduke, the most influential noble in Vetris. The most proud, arrogant man in all of Cavanos, the man who hated me with a burning passion as Y'shennria's niece and an outspoken girl, now *begging* me.

He could be lying. But why would he? He's lost his memories. He's lost everything. Is this some bid to make me pity him, to get his heart back eventually? I killed him, for the gods' sakes. He should be consumed with revenge and fury toward me, but this… Is he truly *that* scared? Scared enough to beg?

And if he's this scared, then shouldn't I be, too?

I shake him off my boots like a slug.

"Don't you dare ask me for favors," I growl down at him. "Not after everything you've done."

I leave him in the alley, his song ringing eerily in my head.

The tree of bone and the tree of glass, will sit together as family at last.

Two trees. Not one, but two.

My nightmare was about two trees. Running through the broken shards of the palace's stained glass Hall of Time, the shards ripping at me, my hands reaching for two rosaries with naked trees on them, like the one Y'shennria carried. I remember it as if it were real. I remember it for the terrible certainty it made me feel.

A certainty that, if I didn't reach those twin rosaries, something horrible would happen.

If she finds the Tree, it will mean disaster.

I do my best to keep Gavik's unsettling words out of my work. Wine helps, but working with the valkerax is better. It's easy to lose a scared archduke's nonsense within more nonsense. But my questions still linger, my nightmare still lingers, unsettling me down to the bone. Gavik said he had the urge to keep a diary coursing through him, and he seemed convinced on our first re-meeting that he'd have written about the Bone Tree somewhere.

On one of the rare nights Varia returns to her apartments, I lean in the doorframe of her bathroom. She's languishing in a full silver tub of rose- and violet-perfumed water spiked with goat's milk, the petals swirling in the murky white.

"You...wouldn't happen to have Gavik's things on hand, would you?" I ask. "I want to frame some of them for posterity."

Varia sighs, leaning her head against the tub so her sheet of wet hair hangs over the lip.

"Fione and I agreed it would be cathartic for her to burn it all."

"Everything?" I try to sound as uninterested as possible, but Varia catches on. She sits up, turning to look at me with mild irritation.

"You expect a girl who's been abused by her uncle to keep even one thing of his?"

"No," I blurt. "Obviously not."

Now I look like the horse's arse for asking. Of course I wouldn't deny Fione her catharsis about Gavik's mistreatment of her. But I still can't keep myself from feeling disappointed. *a friend only in name, wishing for her pain over your curiosity.* The hunger laughs.

Seemingly satisfied with my answer, Varia relaxes back into the tub, pulling her slender living wood leg out of the water and rubbing it down with a bar of gold-flaked Avellish soap. It's easy to forget sometimes that she's only two years older than I am—my technical nineteen years and her twenty-one feel so far apart when her body looks so much more mature than mine. It's hard to feel around her age when she's a princess. *And* my witch.

"Your Highness?" A maid's voice filters through the apartments. "A letter has come for Lady Zera."

"What rich fool would waste paper on me?" I trill, plucking the letter from the maid's offered tray. The parchment is thick and creamy—high grade—and the wax seal on the front is embossed with a serpent. Just one.

Lucien.

I should throw it in the fire to keep up appearances. The maid would surely tell everyone she could that she saw Lucien's Spring Bride (the mere sound of those words strung together stings, nowadays) throwing his letter away like trash.

I *should* throw it away. For my heart. To keep him at arm's length, mile's length. To make sure he has no hold over me ever again.

My fingers peel under the envelope before I can stop them.

There is a derelict grain tower by the West Gate with a perfect view of city and stars alike. Your prince requests you join him there tonight, at the fourteenth-half.

I look up at the maid waiting expectantly.

"Shall I fetch you a quill and parchment, milady?" the maid asks, wide-eyed. No one would dare refuse to respond to a missive from the prince. She knows that. The whole court knows that, down to the last stable boy.

I stare longingly at the ink spirals of his large, neat handwriting. We exchanged letters like this not two weeks ago. How my blood had warmed at the sight of his words. I was a fool then. He is a fool now. There's a whole world of women waiting at his feet, none of them murderers and none of them liars. A true love—*a real love*—based in truth and kindness, instead of deceit and darkness, is out there somewhere for him. Her name could be Lady Tarroux. It could be anyone. All I know for certain is that it's not me.

I turn to the maid with an Y'shennria-perfect smile. "No. That won't be necessary."

The maid starts. "But, milady—"

"I think it'll make a lovely piece of kindling," I say airily, walking over to the fireplace. My fingers hesitate, the letter hanging above the flames.

My heart is mine, and mine alone. I will not let him have it this time.

The letter tips from my hand and falls gracefully into the fire, the flames consuming it eagerly and instantly, leaving nothing behind but ash.

10

THE DREAM WITHOUT END

Whoever said it's easier to destroy things than to build them was a scammer, and I want my coin back.

I should be sitting in the castle, worrying about the valkerax. I should be thinking of what to do after I get my heart back. How Crav, Peligli, and Y'shennria are. But here I am, against my own sound judgment, tucked behind a brick wall and watching the broken tower near West Gate like it holds the key to all my problems.

Whichever natural disaster destroyed this tower was a very angry one—scorch marks blaze black across the crumbling parapets. The blackened stone looks familiar somehow, and then it hits me: Ravenshaunt, Y'shennria's ancestral home that was consumed by witchfire. She showed me the ruins of it when she retrieved me from Nightsinger's woods and brought me to Vetris. They're the same marks. That means this tower, too, is a survivor of the Sunless War.

In my shadowed hiding place, I go still. Y'shennria. The truth Fione revealed to me—the idea of Y'shennria baring her throat for the Heartless as a lure away from her child freezes my blood. From here, my view of the West Gate is clear. Soldiers tromp through the streets, the clash of their swords in practice combat reverberating from their camps just outside the wall. Caravans loaded with grain and other dried rations come into Vetris in a constant stream, the lawguards unloading their contents and taking inventory. The molten glow of the blacksmiths' forges never goes dark.

I promised her. I promised Y'shennria I'd stop the war. And yet it grinds its gears just in front of me.

If I teach the valkerax, if Varia gets the Bone Tree and controls it without an issue, if it works the way Yorl and she say it will, if Varia isn't lying about using it only to stop the war—all these *ifs*. I try to imagine an army of white valkerax swarming over the white walls of Vetris, easily, effortlessly, like serpents over a forest floor. A hundred copies of the valkerax below the South Gate, no—*thousands* of them, just as large, just as riddled with teeth and claws.

Such a thing would, in no uncertain terms, stop the war cold.

I can still stop the war *and* get my heart. I can still do everything I told Y'shennria I would. I just have to trust that what Varia says is true.

trust is a comforting delusion, the insipid sister of hope.

Lucien is waiting in that broken tower. I can't see him, but I know he's there, dressed as Whisper, no doubt. He's waiting for me. Whatever he wants to say couldn't be said in the palace, which is why he sent the letter and arranged this. Who does he want to avoid in the palace? He and the whole court know I've been taking shelter in Varia's apartments since Y'shennria's disappearance. Could he not just come speak to me there?

Unless he doesn't want Varia to hear it.

But why? She's his sister. He loves her. The admiration in his eyes when I see them together is undeniable. He trusts her, doesn't he?

The lawguards largely ignore the ruined tower, their attention taken up by the caravans. One or two still patrol near the tower, but they pause to speak with a few soldiers. I take a deep breath and dart over the grass to the tower. I pick through the rubble, finding nothing on the ground floor but stones overgrown with wildflowers. There's a spiral staircase ascending to the roof, but it's missing the bottom six feet of steps. I perch myself on a little hill and jump with all my might, my arms barely hooking onto the stone. Pulling myself up, I wince at my bruised ribs. I'm sure Lucien had no problem with that jump, if his performance scaling an entire building during the fake witchfire scare at the Temple of Kavar a week ago was any indication. He's more in shape than I am. And I'm more immortal than he is. It balances out.

"There's no use comparing us," I mutter as I scale the worn steps. "I'm clearly the more attractive one."

As I get to the top of the tower, the sight of a bare chest gleaming in the moonlight stops me in my tracks. The whole of Lucien lazily lies on the demolished stone lip of what remains of a wall, body splayed along it like it's the most luxurious palace settee. The moonlight embraces the faint lines of his muscles and smooth expanses of his golden skin with overzealous glee. I roll my eyes up at the sky, at the Old God and New God who are clearly laughing at me and any assertion I've ever dared to make of my own attractiveness.

"Good to know you two are on *my* side," I grumble.

Even my begrudging self has to admit it: he's beautiful. His eyes are closed, dark lashes laid long against his cheeks and his black hair scattered around his forehead. My unheart skips a traitorous beat. In this moment, framed against the starry sky and the double crimson discs of the Red Twins, he's like a painting of the New God—untouchable and exquisite.

"I usually charge for extended viewings." His drawled voice fractures my shock. I can move again, and I pad with as much dignity as I can up the last few steps. Is he here alone? Where is Malachite? He doesn't usually come with Lucien on his excursions into the city as Whisper, but there's always the chance.

"I was hoping you'd consider a discount for me." I throw my hair over my shoulder with a smirk. "Considering how long we've been together."

"Two weeks *is* nearly a lifetime," he agrees drily. He sits up, his leather pants crinkling as he swings his long legs around and stands. The moonlight highlights his strong cheekbones, and through my stupor I'm taken aback at the purple circles under his eyes, now much deeper than before. Is he sleeping at all these days? He should be sleeping well. He should have hardly any worries to keep him up, with Varia being the crown princess and all. His family is whole again.

"Do you often call girls out to secluded locations to admire your naked chest under the moonlight?" I quirk a brow. "Or am I a special case?"

"'Special' is rather generous and grandiose of you." He throws me that brittle smile as he pulls on his buckling shirt again, the slice of his skin from neck to navel standing out starkly against the black leather. "I don't typically think of traitors as special. In fact, they're rather common in my line of work."

I hide my flinch expertly—*gods bless you, Y'shennria.*

"I'm sure being a prince is truly backbreaking work," I jab. Why is he wasting my time like this? Why would he call me out here and shed clothes while waiting for me? Is he trying to distract me? This is more tormenting than it should be, than I promised myself it would be.

"It is when girls like you test my patience." He buttons up the leather shirt, one by one, dark eyes meeting mine coolly. With that look in his gaze, I suddenly understand. I don't affect him at all in this moment. But he's proving, undeniably, that he affects me. His shirtless ruse is something to rile me. To prove he can control me, instead of the other way around. To lead me the way I led him around for two weeks. I gulp my anger down with cold purpose and give him a smile.

"I assume you called me out here for business, Your Highness. After all, we both know it's not for pleasure."

I take one step toward him, and the world moves.

From the shadows, metal spears through the air, a sharp *whizz* streaking past my ear and sinking into the deteriorating clay just an inch from the toe of my boot. A crossbow bolt. Metal swings through the air, a weighty arc that stops just before my throat. A broadsword.

Malachite stands to my side, ruby eyes glinting determinedly as he holds his sword before my neck. Not to it, like a total threat, but just before it—at most an unfriendly reminder. From behind a stack of rubble, Fione stands, her cherubic face deathly serious and a crossbow clutched in her white-knuckled hands, made of the same polished wood as her cane. A familiar ivory valkerax head is carved into the beak of it, and it supports another gleaming belt bolt aimed right at me.

"Apologies." Lucien smirks. "They insisted on coming.

Something about refusing to leave me alone with a Heartless."

Father's sword is too far away on my waist. I chide my own brain for even considering drawing it against Malachite and Fione. They aren't my enemies.

but neither are they your friends, the hunger assures me. *you saw to that with your lies.*

I put up my hands slowly. "If I knew it was going to be a party, I would've at least put on some blush."

Fione and Malachite don't move, don't even blink at the quip. Lucien is the only one who dares approach me, his footsteps slow, each one beating like a drum against the stone. He puts a hand over Malachite's blade.

"Easy, Mal."

"I don't care how many times you two have stuck your tongues down each other's throats—if she tries to hurt you, I'm slitting hers." Malachite narrows his eyes at me. The threat should burn, but it's not hate in his eyes—it's just a protectiveness for Lucien. It blazes bright in every corner of his paper-white face. He doesn't hate me, per se. He just cares for Lucien more.

Lucien's voice goes serious. "Be reasonable. Asking her questions would be much harder that way."

"*Reasonable?*" Malachite snaps. "After all she's done to you?"

"She'd heal soon anyway." Fione stands up, crossbow steadied expertly on her forearm. "But she would feel everything."

Malachite's eyes don't flicker, but Lucien's do. No—I must be imagining it. Surely he knows better than to care for the pain a traitor could go through. Feelings aren't temporary jewelry, but neither are they permanent tattoos, and he's doing a miserable job of making either disappear.

"We can stop talking about me like I'm not here," I lilt. "And start talking about why you called me out. Couldn't we have conducted this nasty business inside the castle? Or is there someone there you don't want knowing about this little inquisition of yours?"

Fione's gaze flickers to Lucien's, but the prince keeps his dark eyes steady and on me.

"You take a carriage every morning to South Gate," Lucien starts. "You go in a door, and you come out roughly an hour later. Why?"

"Tourism?" I offer with an innocent smile.

"Answer his question straight," Malachite barks, raising his sword higher at me. Lucien exhales, his hand gently pressing Malachite's blade lower.

"Put it down, Mal."

"She could hurt you, Luc," Malachite argues. "She's fast, and I have to be faster—"

"Put it *down*," Lucien quietly demands, his fingers clutching the sharp edge of the beneather's blade with more insistence. I start at the rivulet of blood that seeps from between his long fingers. Why would he—?

"Your Highness—" I blurt. "You're hurting yourself."

Malachite's irritated ruby eyes war with Lucien's calm obsidian ones for a moment.

"You trust too easily," Malachite finally mutters at him.

Lucien smiles wanly. "I know."

It's a joke between them, among the four of us. Even I know Lucien isn't trusting in the slightest. Finally, the beneather drops his blade away from me but keeps it tight at his side, ready to spring into action. Lucien wipes his wound on his pants and looks to Fione, still aiming her crossbow at me.

"You, too, Archduchess," he says. "Ease up."

"No," I start. "It's smart to keep at least one weapon trained on a Heartless at all times. You never know when the monster will come out."

The fear-etched lines in Fione's face harden. Lucien's composure weakens, his jaw going slack for one moment. He must be remembering the clearing, the sight of me, all fangs and claws and blood.

I smile at him. "So? What questions are burning up those precious mortal bodies of yours?" Lucien opens his mouth, but I hold up one finger to interrupt him. "Keep in mind that anything you ask me, any answer I give—all of it could be commanded out of me by Varia. What you say will be far from secret. And I'd hate for all your efforts to call me out here to go to waste."

Lucien seems to think twice, then motions Fione forward. She doesn't move, her cornflower blue eyes hard and on me over the sights of her crossbow.

"You're Varia's Heartless," she says.

"Oh, c'mon." I laugh. "We all know I am. Give me one of the harder questions. I can handle it."

Fione's frown only gets deeper. "You go to the South Gate and in that door. Varia's told me you do it because you're helping her train our soldiers on how to fight the Heartless. Is that true?"

I look up at Lucien, whose face is suddenly unreadable. Malachite is packed to the brim with equal parts suspicion and hair-threaded readiness.

I give another laugh, this one lighter. "You're Vetrisian. You know a lie when you hear one. I'd say yes, but the three of you are smarter than that. Well, maybe not Malachite. People like him and me have to work to be smart. You two were born into it."

"Don't lump me in with you," Malachite instantly fires out. "I didn't betray anyone."

"We're very different creatures," I agree. "Your honor is pristine, and I never had any to begin with. I suppose it left with all my memories of my old life."

"Memories?" Lucien asks, quiet.

"Oh. You didn't know?" I examine my nails carelessly. "When our hearts are taken out, we forget everything about our human lives before that moment. Mothers, fathers, growing up, sad memories and happy ones, loving ones and hateful ones—all of it. Gone."

None of the three speaks. The muggy summer air chokes us all silent, the droning of the cicadas filling the quiet.

Malachite, ever the brave one, blurts, "If I didn't know better, I'd say you were trying to make us feel sorry for you."

I snort. "I'm long past trying to make any of you feel anything for me. It won't get me my heart anymore. So there's no real point."

"Then what are you doing beneath South Gate?" Lucien asks sharply. "I've tried to get in. I've gone by every route, old and new, but the security is impenetrable."

"And I've tried to bribe every last guard," Fione offers. "Every polymath, every adjacent laborer. But no one budges. Someone always budges. *Always.* But not this time."

They've been working so hard. They can't just leave well enough alone, can they? I smile sympathetically. "And that worries you, doesn't it?"

"Answer their spiritsdamn questions!" Malachite demands.

I shrug.

"She might not be able to," Fione murmurs. "I've seen

Varia command her to do…terrible things. She could have command her to stay silent."

"She hasn't," I correct. "But why would I talk?"

Fione and Malachite share a look, and Lucien's eyes harden. It's never been clearer than in this moment that they think of me as an enemy. I could wipe away all their suspicion, all their wariness, if I just told them what was going on. If I told them about the valkerax, surely their feelings for me would soften. We wouldn't go back to the way things were, but at least it wouldn't be this crushing mistrustfulness anymore.

But the valkerax is dangerous. The Bone Tree is dangerous. Varia's keeping them in the dark for a reason—she doesn't want them to be associated with the fallout of it. She wants to take all the power and all the hate and fear that come with it. And she's right. Anyone involved with the Bone Tree will be public enemy number one when Varia finally gets it.

They'll be safer not knowing.

I breathe in. "Varia's offering my heart to do what I do, quietly and quickly. And you three are offering me, well." I smile wider, looking Lucien up and down. "Nothing but heartbreak and threats."

The prince suddenly moves in, our chests perilously close to touching, our moonlit shadows mingling on the ruins of the tower. He looks down at me with a soft edge to his black eyes—an echo of the softness in his gaze I beheld in the Hunt's tent, just before the kiss that lit my soul on fire. He smells faintly of not ash and clearwater, but of something like white mercury. Perhaps that's just the city's smell.

"Zera." He says my name gently, like fingers on a

windlute's deepest notes. "Please. Tell me—what are you doing for my sister?"

I want to trust him. I want to trust the warmth seeping into me from beneath his skin. I want to trust his lips, so close. I want to trust that he holds enough affection for me, still, to be this close willingly, to believe me when I speak.

"You actually think I would tell you the truth? After everything I've done?" I whisper up at him.

"I'm giving you another chance to," he says.

I want to believe in another chance. But I know. I know this is just an act—the same one he uses to fool the court, the nobles, the girls who dare bat their eyes at him. Beneath this softness is a brittle disappointment, a deep and betrayed hurt. I can see it, sharp and ever-growing, like rose thorns taken root in his eyes.

No amount of petals can cover the wounds I've inflicted on him. On us.

There is no going back.

My sadness and guilt give way to disbelieving fury. He's using me. He's using our attraction against me right now. Is he that desperate for information about what his sister is doing?

With perfect, enraged control, I tilt my face up to his, our lips nearly touching as I murmur, "Don't you trust your sister, Your Highness? You heard her in the clearing. She's going to stop the war. Isn't that what you want? A peaceful country for your people?"

He doesn't step away. On the contrary, he puts his hand on my hip, and my whole body ripples with a shudder from the epicenter. "She can't do that alone."

To melt into him right now would be so easy. Malachite might as well not exist, Fione likewise blank. Right now, it's just him and me and the stars. But our chests pressed together would beat with the sound of only one heart.

he's using us like everyone else does, the hunger sneers. *we are nothing to him but a doll.*

I tear myself away, my skin enmeshed in his crying out at the pain of being pulled apart. I turn to Fione, whose cheeks are tinged with the slightest red, her eyes wide. Lucien is trying to use me. All three of them are. But I can use them, too.

"If we can't be friends," I start, "we can at least be one another's tools. Don't you agree, Your Grace?"

Fione jumps slightly when I address her, her crossbow still clutched in her petite hands. When she knits her lips, I smile.

"Gavik's things. Varia said you and she burned them all."

"And?" Fione mutters. Varia might've been convinced Fione burned it all. But I know Fione better than that—she spent five years collecting important information about important people on the streets of Vetris in order to avenge Varia. Habits like that don't die easily.

"Did you really burn it *all*? So quickly?"

Fione's blue eyes dart around. "I don't see how this concerns you—"

"Gavik told me he kept a diary," I say. "You've seen him, I'm sure—walking around Vetris handing out bread to the poor."

"I have," Lucien cuts in. "But she hasn't. He turns tail and runs whenever he sees her."

Varia's commanded me to stab myself if I ever touch Fione, a command Varia is convinced will protect her, make her feel at ease. She's probably commanded Gavik in the same manner to stay out of Fione's way.

"Bring me his diary," I say. "If it still exists. And maybe I'll tell you what's going on."

"The one that speaks of the Bone Tree?" Fione blurts. A hush falls over us, and I smile with all my teeth—the human ones, not my hungry ones. So she did keep some of his things. And she read them. The Bone Tree—Gavik really *did* write about it. His instinct regarding his human self was right.

"Yeah. That one."

"It's not real," Fione insists quickly. "It's just a delusional excuse he was using to persecute Varia. He was paranoid. All he wanted was the white mercury sword."

"So you've told me," I lilt.

"The Bone Tree doesn't exist. It's just a bedtime story once meant to scare Old Vetrisian children."

"Just as Heartless are a bedtime story," I say. "Meant to scare New Vetrisian children."

"The evidence for its existence is anecdotal at best," she presses harshly, sounding so much like Yorl when he gets onto a subject he knows much about, and some part of me wistfully realizes they'd get along amazingly. "Anti-witch propaganda at worst. No one has ever been able to conclusively prove it exists. It's just a religious symbol the Old God followers worship."

The naked tree rosary clutched in Y'shennria's hand when she and I were forced to go to Kavar's temple. My nightmare of the two tree rosaries—not one. Two.

I shake my head. The urge to tell them everything almost overflows, like an overfilled cup. The urge to trust them again, to confide in them. To rely on anyone other than the hunger—to trust someone fully instead of halfheartedly like I do Varia—it sounds like paradise. It would make the burden I carry so much lighter.

Not again. I won't let human weakness steal my heart from me *again*.

I give a proper bow fit for a prince and archduchess and start down the stairs with an uncaring wave of my hand.

"Bring me that diary, my good nobles. And then I'll consider telling you a story."

The patrols in the palace are more alert than usual, perhaps preparing for the war. Being caught wandering the halls in the dead of night isn't illegal for a noble, but still the guards stop me, asking questions. I give them the excuse that I'd felt sick and went to visit the royal polymaths in the palace's Sun Ward. I smile brightly, and while I'm positive they know I'm lying, they don't dare stop me—the crown princess has told them I'm allowed in her apartments, and to stop me might mean invoking her ire.

When I slip into the sitting room, the oil lamps are all snuffed out, the apartments engulfed in dimness. The blue moonlight filters through the glass windows, and I carefully tiptoe past the bedroom. My eyes catch on the dark figure in it. A dark figure, moving. No—*thrashing*. Varia's black hair is slicked to her head with sweat, her limbs twitching, struggling to be free of the sheets. Her eyes are closed—she's fast asleep, and yet moving like she's fighting something.

I should leave her. She's my witch—holding me hostage by my heart. At the very least, she deserves nightmares. But...the soft whine that escapes her lips suddenly tugs at me. Peligli used to have nightmares like these, mewling like this, and I'd always wake her up.

She means so much to Fione. To Lucien.

I gulp down a breath and walk over to her bedside. This close, I can see just how pale and tinged green her skin's become, as if she's sick, her eyes moving frantically behind her eyelids.

Gingerly, I put my hand on her shoulder. "Your Highness?" I say. She doesn't respond. *"Varia?"*

Suddenly, her thrashing gets violent, her limbs bashing against one another, quaking the mattress. Her shin hits a wooden poster of the bed so hard it vibrates through the floor, blood pooling instantly crimson beneath her skin. I put both hands on her shoulders and shake her.

"Varia!"

Her dark eyes snap open, her thrashing going still at the same moment that she sits straight up in the bed.

"The Tree!" She gasps, sucking in air like she's been underwater for far too long. Was she dreaming of the tree again, like she was that night on the balcony? Her eyes are wide black discs, terrified and fervid all at once, like she's seen into the face of the New God himself. She notices me out of the corner of her eye, and she flicks her sweat-sheened face to me.

"You. What are you doing here?"

"You were having a nightmare," I say, pointing at her leg. "And beating yourself up about it."

Varia's disoriented gaze moves down to the injury, her face twisting with irritation and her chest rising hard and quick as she tries to catch her breath.

"Get out."

"You—" I start, my throat dry. "Were you dreaming of the Bone Tree?"

"I said get out!"

Her eyes are embers—hotter even than the moment I

saw her in the woods. She isn't a wise, waiting owl now. She is carved in anger and something like panic. The command is a chokehold—the hunger gripping my legs and arms and forcing me out of the room in an instant. The bedroom doors in front of my face slam shut with some invisible force—magic, no doubt. The slam echoes and then settles.

The command releases my rigid body and confused mind, and I collapse on the nearest love seat. I've never seen her command so quickly, so ferociously.

Why would she react like that to a simple, innocent question?

11

THE WEIGHT
OF UNLIVING

The next morning, Varia acts like nothing at all happened.

It could be that she doesn't remember it. Or it could be that she's purposely pretending it never happened. Either way, the crown princess is ensconced in her closet, being dressed by her maids, when Fione walks in, her hair left long and curled and tied with daisy-yellow ribbons to match her dress. She looks lovely. She looks uneasy. The full fear I saw in her face the first few times we met again after the clearing is much less—no doubt thanks to Varia's command. If I touch her, I stab myself. And I can see, tangibly, that idea is giving Fione some measure of security; her eyes still avoid meeting mine, but I catch her staring at my profile every so often.

"Where are you two off to this fine morning, Your Grace?" I play the polite noble card, hoping to put her more at ease. Fione's lips purse slightly.

"A breakfast," she says. "At my manor."

"That's right." I whistle. "You have the whole of the Himintell estate to yourself now."

"It's nothing much," she says modestly, and I laugh, picking up my morning chocolate drink and sipping at it, washing away the taste of the liver I'd consumed not minutes before she and the maids walked in.

"When we first met at that banquet," I start, "you were Lady Himintell, being picked on by those frilly walking dung piles and ridiculed by Gavik. And now"—I motion to her dress, her stiff posture—"you got rid of him. Now you're an archduchess. Give yourself a thimbleful of credit, will you? You've done well."

Fione breathes out, her gaze skittering over the floor as she thinks of what to say. Finally she looks up, and this time it's right into my eyes. For the first time since the clearing, her cornflower blue eyes look *at* me.

"Thank you," she says.

It's like the first sprout of spring breaking through a snow bank. My chest warms, and I smile back. It isn't a long moment, and soon her gaze is out the windows again, but at the very least, it happened. My unheart doesn't feel so heavy suddenly. Encouraged by it all, I open my mouth.

"Does she usually have nightmares?" Fione's head snaps up, and I continue. "It's just, she spends most nights at your place, so I don't see it often. But last night—"

"She hurt herself. And talked about the Tree," Fione finishes for me. "Right?"

It's my turn to look surprised. "How did you—?"

Fione lowers her voice, her face suddenly expressionless, as if she's trying hard to keep it together. "It's happened every night since she's been back. She flails, she screams, she cries. And she mutters about the Tree the whole time."

Quietly, we watch the maids flicker in and out of the dressing room with long lengths of purple ribbon. Fione's face is so drawn, so tight with worry. I can't imagine what it must be like—to have your beloved back, only to watch them struggling so in their sleep.

I lean in to Fione, careful not to get close enough to scare her, and murmur, "If the Tree isn't real, as you said in the tower, then why is she having so many nightmares about it?"

I know the Tree is real. Or, at the very least, I know Varia thinks the Tree is real. I know Yorl has given me explanations and evidence as to why the Tree is real. The valkerax has talked about it. But I've never seen it. I know the Tree is real in the same sense one knows the gods are real—belief. Fione has never held such beliefs for the gods; if anything, she's shown disdain for them. She's a lady of facts and evidence, resisting the unquestioning faith most of Vetris has been scared into by Gavik and the sheer intimidating threat of magic itself.

So my question hangs, and she's unable to answer it.

"She'll be all right." I make a smile. "I'll wake her up if it ever gets too bad. You'll wake her up at your place. Together, we'll keep our crown princess unbruised yet."

Fione's expression crumbles, worry tingeing it. "Yes."

The guards come in then and announce that my carriage to South Gate is ready. I resist the urge to hug Fione, to put my arm on her shoulder, even, and make a bow to her instead.

I watch the city flash by, the older parts of the common quarter bustling. Construction noisily tears down old buildings and erects new ones as barracks for soldiers, and more construction still happens between the streets and alleys as emergency barricades are put in place, in case of invasion. The Temple of Kavar is being particularly insulated by such barricades, a priest standing on the steps and blessing the workers as they haul wood and metal, his sermon ringing out as my carriage passes.

"The weight of living belongs to us all!"

"Indeed. But," I murmur to the carriage's ceiling, "what about the weight of unliving? Who does that belong to?"

The crown princess hasn't told Lucien or Fione what she's doing with the valkerax, for their safety, no doubt. She wants to keep the valkerax to herself—not out of selfishness but out of a desire to protect those closest to her. I can't find it in me to blame her. I'd do the same. But the urge to tell Lucien and Fione this one truth still burns, even in the morning light. If I do, if Lucien and Fione even believe me, I'd have a hard time believing the crown princess would be pleased. And she holds my heart in the palm of her hand, literally.

If Fione does bring me Gavik's journal, it's not safe to tell her the truth. But she deserves that much, and my two inclinations war with each other even as I teach the valkerax for the day. Yorl pushes me hard—we try the serum three times, and I die three times. But the valkerax has other plans: namely, lying there on the ground and wheezing. It doesn't even move to snap at me. It doesn't answer me, except to mutter nonsense once more—about sky-homes and earth-homes, about flying below the sun. My unheart feels like a pincushion as I listen to its labored breaths, and right then it finally hits me: it's not going to last long. All of Yorl's warnings were easy to ignore when it wasn't collapsed in a heap on the ground. But now, listening with my own two ears as it struggles to live, I brutally understand.

It might die for this.

It *will* die without my helping it to Weep. It will die because I wasn't fast enough or correct enough in my teaching.

And the most naked truth: I might not get my heart back.

even at the end of all possibility. The hunger sneers at me. *selfish to the last.*

I bask in the low, late afternoon sun aboveground, trying not to think. But it's all I can do; if I don't get my heart, where does that leave me? As a pawn for Varia for how many more years? Will she make me fight in the war?

A shadow catches my eye in the sparse South Gate crowd. Beneath the eaves of a hat shop, a dark figure in all leather leans against the wall. Lucien. What is he doing here? I turn and hide my face. Being alone with him again isn't what I need right now.

but it's what we want, the hunger insists, lolling its pitch-black tongue.

Suddenly, something black and small catches my eye. A flower? No, a rose. A black rose. It's held by a leather-clad arm, and my eyes meet Lucien's cowled face, his eyes full to the brim with detached amusement as he holds the rose out to me. My twisted mind tries to celebrate—he's offering me a gift.

don't be naïve. The hunger laughs. *the little prince is already naive enough for the both of you.*

"A beautiful rose for a beautiful lady," he says. A pair of noble women passing by looks me up and down, giggling madly and clucking their tongues in equal turn. A rose given to a noble lady by a commoner is scandalous in the extreme. Lucien holds the rose out more insistently when a flustered courier boy walks by, and I tempestuously fight the urge to take the flower. There's only one place in Vetris black roses grow—in front of Y'shennria's manor. This is a ploy. He's trying to remind me of my mistakes, of my lie of pretending to be an Y'shennria—a Firstblood noble. Any gift from him isn't because he particularly likes me—we established that in the tower. He must be doing this to get to me. To hurt me.

you lied. you deserve this pain—

I smile as I take the rose, careful not to touch his gloved hand. I look at the soft petals for a moment, enjoying the familiar scent that tugs at my unheart, and then throw the rose over my shoulder, directly into a muddy puddle.

"A terrible gift for a terrible gifter." I smile at him lightly.

There's a moment where I think I can see the true Lucien—hurt running across his face. But it evaporates like a raindrop in the sun. He half sighs, his eyes now amused again.

"We have things to clarify."

"Do we have to clarify them here, in front of *everyone*?" I ask.

"How improper of me," he drawls. "You're right. A true thief never does business in the light. My hiding holes are, of course, your hiding holes." He motions to an alley behind the hat shop. "This way."

Half wary, I trail after him over the cobblestones, thick with grime the farther we get from any main road. Is he guiding me to a setup with Fione and Malachite waiting again? He leads me through a dizzying pattern of turns: betwixt barrels and crates, beneath laundry lines, and around wells and giant water-spewing snake statues, and finally to a derelict building in a forgotten square—still standing, but molded and nearly eaten by termites, the doorframe remaining on what seems like toothpicks as we duck beneath it.

The late sunlight plays dappled beams of gold through the ruined roof and onto the creaking floor as Lucien crosses it, seating himself on the only sturdy thing on the premises—a stone hearth in the center.

He holds his arms out. "Welcome. You're the first visitor

I've had here. I'd tell you to take your shoes off, but at this point, a dirty boot would be the least of this place's problems."

"Does it have an ambush set up in it, too?" I ask.

Lucien shakes his head. "I know I might seem a little dense to you, after you deceived me about being human for two entire weeks," he says. "But even *I* know not to use the same surprise twice."

I tamp down the instant urge to flinch. He really won't let me live it down. And for good reason. But still, he could be lying. Malachite could be behind any corner again. Half of me bleeds with the pain of not being able to trust him as he can't trust me. He doesn't owe me honesty, after all. Soft cooing makes me look up just then—a flutter of dove wings beating the air above the roof. I watch a white feather float down to the floor, and I reach out just in time to catch it. I can feel Lucien's eyes on me, like two spots of uncomfortably hot fire, even as I stroke the soft thing for some comfort.

"That black rose," I say. "Was it from Y'shennria's manor?"

I hear him chuckle. "Obviously." There's another moment of quiet, and then, "On nights it was hard to be in the palace, I would stand outside the manor and watch the lights of your bedroom. The black rose bushes were always in my way. But over time, I began to feel a fondness for them. Seeing a black rose meant I was near you, near the one person who understood me."

The sharp pain in my lungs makes my breathing ragged, but I recover. I have to recover.

"What is it we need to clarify?" I ask stiffly. "As you might've guessed from stalking me every day to South Gate, I'm a busy woman."

Lucien swallows hard. "Very well." He stands but keeps

his distance. "The Tree."

I snort. "That's all anyone talks about anymore—"

"I knew about the Tree before anyone," Lucien interrupts. "Before even Varia knew."

I turn the dove feather over curiously. "What?"

"Fione told me Varia's been having nightmares about the Tree. That you saw it last night. I was the first one to ever see her have a nightmare about it."

I try not to betray the interest in my voice. "When?"

"I was seven," he says. "She was ten. We were in the palace's nursery."

"That's so *young*. She wasn't a witch then, right?"

He shakes his head, the sun catching on his black cowl and illuminating the rich darkness. "No. But I remember the night it happened for the first time. And it kept happening. Mother brought every polymath to her, desperate to diagnose her, to 'fix' her. It was the best kept secret in the palace—that Varia was 'sick.'"

"Why?"

"Father was worried," Lucien says, and cracks his neck leisurely. "You've heard of the assassins Malachite deals with, trying to kill me. The royal family isn't liked. And the whole court knows the rumor that we are a witch family. Any display of oddness was Father's greatest fear."

"So he didn't want rumors of Varia's nightmares to get out," I muse. "Because it would make the nobles uneasy."

"Uneasy at best," he agrees. "And at worst, it would give them cause to dispose of the d'Malvanes. Witches are never trusted in Vetris—no matter who they are."

"So your mother brought polymaths to her?" I lead. He nods, shaggy bangs nodding with him.

"They all said she was mad. Father refused to believe it,

but it kept happening. He used to order the servants to drug her with moonroot every night so she could sleep without hurting herself."

I'm silent. Lucien isn't.

"On bad nights, she used to sleepwalk." His eyes get a glassy, far-off look in them. "I remember waking up and finding her on the balcony staring off into space more than once."

I go still, my fist clenching around the feather. So that night...she *was* dreaming.

Lucien presses on. "I'd try to wake her, but all she would do is mutter about the Tree. They got worse, the older she got. She broke both of her wrists when she was thirteen."

"Are they just nightmares?" I ask. "Or could they be magical?"

He shrugs. "I have no clue. The polymaths had no clue, either—they study magical symptoms in order to combat them, certainly, but they'd never seen anything like this. So we were led to believe they weren't magical. They were just part of the way her mind worked in sleep."

The dust swirls in the light, like thousands of miniature fireflies. I understand something then. "And you— So when she died, you went looking for it. You used the annual prince's Hunts to search the woods, thinking you could find this Tree. You thought—"

"I thought it had something to do with her death," he agrees, eyes focusing on me again. "That it lured her somewhere. That sounds equally mad, I know. Part of me was using it as an excuse. But another part of me was—is— still suspicious. The polymaths said her symptoms weren't magical. But I've seen it happen too much to think it's just a human symptom, either."

He breathes out, heavy and long, looking up at the blue summer sky through the shards of roof. "She was gone for five years. And she came back. And still, *still* she dreams of that godsdamned Tree. I'd hoped she'd gotten better. Fione and I—after we got over the joy of having her back—we both dared to hope, but..."

For a moment, I admire the way the shafts of sunlight illuminate his proud nose, his thick brows. Prince Lucien flits his eyes to me.

"There was one polymath," he says. "One, out of the thousands, who didn't think Varia was mad."

"Just one?" I quirk a brow.

"He wasn't an official polymath," the prince says. "But Mother and Father were so desperate to find someone who knew something, they called for anyone who could pass a basic test. He was an old celeon. I've always remembered his name—he was the first person who dressed in polymath robes and smiled at me kindly at the same time. Farspear-Ashwalker. Muro Farspear-Ashwalker."

My blood goes cold. That name is chillingly familiar—it's Yorl's last name. Yorl's father? No—his *grandfather*? The one who did all that polymath research and got no credit for it? The one who all but made the serum that lets me talk to valkerax? The one Yorl is working so hard to vindicate with the valkerax—with Varia?

"What did he say about Varia's nightmares?" I blurt.

Lucien sighs. "I don't know. I was young. I was playing with some toy at Mother's side while they talked. I assure you, over the past decade, I've tried to remember. It all blends together. But one thing did stand out."

My feet take me to him, burning with curiosity. "What is it?"

Lucien looks up at me slowly. "A song. I don't remember what they were talking about, but I remember at one point this old celeon just started singing."

A song. It can't be—this *can't* be a coincidence.

"What were the words?" I demand.

"I don't—" Lucien runs a frustrated hand through his hair. "I don't remember. If I could, I'm sure it would make more sense. I just remember he started singing—"

"*The tree of bone and the tree of glass will sit together as family at last.*" I let the words tumble from my mouth, my voice shaky and the notes a bare skeleton of what I can remember Gavik singing.

Lucien's face lights up instantly. "You know it?" He grabs my shoulders. "Kavar's eye—how in the afterlife do *you* know it?"

I look up, my eyes sparking into his, both of us flushed with discovery. The facade of his lofty effortlessness is gone now. He's treating me like someone he genuinely likes again. It's then I realize just how close we are. Just how high my words could stoke him. He can't know what I know. The valkerax is dangerous.

"Zera," he insists, fingers trembling on my shoulders. "You're hoarding all this information—why? Varia can't do everything herself. I know she's trying to. I know she'll kill herself doing it. *Please*—you have to help me help my sister, before she hurts herself."

Varia's words, her recitation of the Midnight Gifter, ring in my head. *My flesh will feed its furnace.* He's right to be worried. She'll do anything for her people, just like him. The care in his voice is a velvet knife plunged into my chest. His love for her is so obvious and untethered by guilt or complicated emotions. It's so strong it even glows through his disdain for me, forces him to ask for help from someone he holds his pride like a shield against.

"If you tell me what's going on," he presses, "Fione and I can help you—"

"Why would you?" I laugh. "We're not friends anymore. I'm a monster, not your Spring Bride. You have no obligation to me. In fact, you hate me."

Lucien inhales, this time sharp as a spear. "Zera—"

I start moving to leave the ruined building, the sun shafting through my eyes.

"If I could convince my sister to free you—" the prince's voice suddenly calls.

"No. I won't be freed by your hand." My voice is sleek steel.

"Why not?" he presses. "I could free you—"

"I'll free myself."

The silence lingers, my body on the edge of collapsing if I don't get out from under his gaze. My boots take one step over the dusty floor, and Lucien's words this time aren't soft at all—they're strong and clear to my back.

"I don't hate you. I *can't* hate you."

My chest caves. To turn and face him right now, to talk through our problems and mistrust, to try to heal the wounds I've made—I want that.

he's manipulating you. The hunger sneers. *reeling you in with bait to help the sister he cares so much more for.*

I speak without turning to look at him. "It's better if you do."

Every cobblestone I walk over and put between him and me, the easier it is to breathe. The pressure on my chest is crushing, but the emptiness in my unheart is cold and hollow. He will not stand between my heart and me. Not again. Not this time. I will not be weak anymore.

My feet take me back, determined, to South Gate, but when I emerge into the sunlight of the main road, my ears catch the sound of lawguard footsteps approaching. They pause just behind me, and a lawguard calls out, "Lady Zera?"

Did Lucien order them down on me? No. He's fast but not that fast, and he wouldn't risk revealing his identity as Whisper. I turn to face the lawguards—an astonishing number of them, at least a dozen, and six of them in the back are royal celeon lawguards.

"Yes?" I ask innocently.

"His Majesty the king has requested your presence in the throne room."

Gooseflesh crawls across my arms. It's time, then, for the inquiry into Gavik's murder.

The sick feeling in my stomach intensifies, but I keep my posture tall as I sigh. "Very well. Lead the way, gentlemen."

To my surprise, the lawguards flank me, separate, and then close in, the two halves compressing around me in a protective—and inescapable—formation. As they march collectively forward and I walk in the center of the iron flower, we pass Lucien's shadowed lurking place near the hat shop.

I can feel eyes following me, two obsidian needles prickling into my skin, the air ringing with the words I can't say to him.

I've learned, Your Highness, that it is easier to hate than it is to love.

12

A FIRE MADE REAL

The throne room isn't nearly as intimidating as it used to be. This, I presume, is what it means to grow up, to stop being afraid of things that used to terrify you.

As the lawguards lead me through the stained glass beauty of the Hall of Time, my body starts to tingle with the familiar court-related anxiety, but I breathe deep and let it pass me by. I have nothing to lose anymore. I've pushed Lucien away. Fione and Malachite's friendship is long buried. All I have is my heart to hold on to, and that makes everything so much simpler.

lonelier than ever.

The rainbow glisten of the Hall of Time, being beneath it—I used to be in awe of it, but now, all I can think about is my nightmare. Varia has nightmares about a Tree. And I had a nightmare in which this hall collapsed, and I had to wade through the glass shards as they cut me to reach two Old God rosaries with naked trees on them. I watched the glass shards of this hall arrange themselves on the bark of a tree, becoming it. Unease crawls through me as the summer sunlight glitters into my eyes, throwing crimson and azure shadows over my skin.

In comparison, the small stone hallway that opens into the throne room, and the throne room itself, feels like a lifting of a thousand pounds off my chest. The grand stone cavern that houses the throne makes me feel at peace. Perhaps because of the Hall of Time nightmare, but also because the place is nearly empty of people.

The vaulted ceilings of the cavern are held up by polished stone pillars, everything illuminated by the glass circles etched high above that let in several concentrated beams of searing white sunlight from outside. The light catches on the gold braziers but sprawls itself over the crystal throne at the back and center of the room. The lawguards march me up the long carpet walk and stop me in the very middle of a large beam of sunlight.

My eyes adjust, sunlit dust swirling around me as I capture each face—King Sref, relaxed and handsome on the shining throne, his hulking celeon royal guards at his side, and then scattered around the throne in smaller chairs are the three Ministers of Cavanos. I recognize them all from the banquets and Y'shennria's training—the Ministers of the Blood, Brick, and Coin. The Minister of the Sword's chair is empty—the space where Gavik should be sitting somehow seems to grow larger with each passing second.

I thought I wouldn't be nervous. But King Sref is still a king. He carries himself like a true ruler, a true d'Malvane, and his sharp gray gaze on me has my palms sweating. I slowly make a kingworthy bow to the floor and lift my head only when his voice rumbles out, "Rise."

"Lady Zera Y'shennria—" The Minister of the Blood,

a short mustached man stands from his chair, his voice far louder than his stature betrays. "Niece of Quinn Y'shennria, you come before us as the secondary witness to the murder of Archduke Gavik Himintell. The evidence you provide here will be used in the investigation of unearthing his killer. Under the New God's many watchful eyes, you are beholden to speak only truth. If this you do not do, the court of Vetris will be compelled to move rightly. Do you understand?"

Secondary witness. That means Lucien's already spoken to them. Did he tell them the truth? No—if he did, I would already be in chains. So he must've lied. But if I don't tell them the same story, then I'll suddenly become a magnet for suspicion. And if the ministers dig into my story, they'll surely find who—what—I really am. And I can't afford to be thrown in the dungeon and tortured. Not while the valkerax is on such a short lease of life.

I focus my eyes on the throne, on King's Sref's still, expressionless face. Lucien learned that particular move from his father, not Varia. The other ministers watch me with judgmental eyes. The Minister of the Blood was the one who sneaked me into the Vetrisian court with some bribes on Y'shennria's part, undoubtedly not knowing I was truly a Heartless, but he's definitely not on my side anymore. At this moment, I have no allies at all.

you have me and only me.

Even though Varia has returned, even though the king is happier now, he still retains that persistent air of perfect calm. His mask is, and always has been, impeccable. He knows I'm a Heartless, a creature he's spent his whole life fighting and killing, and yet nothing betrays on his face. Varia told him I was benign, and it shows. He trusts Varia wholly. How can any father not want to trust his child?

"I understand," I say quietly. The Minister of the Blood sits back down in his chair and motions to the king.

"Your Majesty, we may begin with the inquiry."

The king's gray eyes move over my face as he straightens in his throne. His voice is quiet, somehow downtrodden despite the fact that he's been so happy lately. Is this because of Gavik, perhaps? In the king's eyes, Gavik was someone for him to rely on. My mind flashes to Varia. How much self-control must she have had, after being forced to hide for five years, to not tell her father who forced her to hide in the first place?

My lips open, and for a moment I think the barest thought of telling the king Varia is a witch. It rests ready and willing in the fibers of my tongue: *Varia is a witch.* It sears through my blood and surfaces into my throat, but as quickly as it rises, the heavy, total iron block of the thought of getting my heart back snuffs it out.

"Lady Zera," the king says slowly. "I will ask only once. In that clearing, did you see who murdered the archduke?"

I have to lie to the king. Anything less and he'll have me arrested, tortured, used as a wartime test subject for the polymaths within Vetris.

I inhale, pause, and then, "No, Your Majesty. Everything was a blur."

My answer rings in the high cavern and between the carved stone pillars ominously. The Minister of the Coin is the only one who dares to make noise—his snort soft.

"By all accounts, Your Majesty, she has been revealed of late to be less than a reliable source," the Minister of the Coin says. "She consorts with commoners in her leisure time."

"Walking around the common quarter does not inhibit one's ability to tell the truth, Sarcomel," the king responds dully. The Ministers of the Brick and Blood shift in their seats, and Sarcomel shrinks in his. I let out the tiniest of breaths. King Sref turns back to me, his long salt-and-pepper hair waterfalling over his shoulder.

"You will tell us what you did see, then," he says. "As best you can."

I nod, even though my insides are scrambling. He knows I'm Heartless, but I can't make up any witch or magic things in front of the other three Ministers.

arrogant! the hunger squeals.

"I...I invited Lucien to walk with me in the forest." I try to make my voice as steady as I can. "When the hunting party was bathing, I saw a beautiful yew tree and thought it would be nice to look at in the moonlight."

Sarcomel scoffs, this time with a toxicity to his words. "Your Majesty, I have no idea why we're entertaining an Y'shennria's word. They are Old God traitors, and the temple says—"

"I will not be bothered by what the temple says in an independent investigation pursuing the truth of the murder of one of my ministers." King Sref raises his voice a hair, and the ministers fall silent again.

The Minister of the Brick speaks up. "With all due respect, Your Majesty, Minister Sarcomel has a point. Lady Quinn Y'shennria has been missing from the capital for six days now. The timing of her absence is undeniably questionable. We should be focusing less on interrogating the hazy witnesses—both of whom are children incapable of much—and more on bringing her back to Vetris."

I nearly take a step back. The gall of this moldy old skunk! The self-assured certainty with which he views Lucien and me as "incapable" has me *reeling*. It staggers me again and again with how little Vetrisian nobles care for their children.

"Are you insinuating my son the prince is not capable, Minister Polsk?" the king asks coolly, and I celebrate vicariously through his words for a moment.

"N-Not in the slightest, Your Majesty," Minister Polsk's ancient, liver-spotted face sours with a faint greenish hue. I can only watch as the power balances tip back and forth. As Minister Polsk stumbles over his next words, Minister Sarcomel stands from his chair and points at me furiously.

"Did you or did you not see Archduke Gavik murdered, Lady Zera?" he shouts. "If someone managed to get to Gavik and kill him, we could be next! Don't you see? No one is safe! This is a deep-set plot by the witches to destabilize the power within Vetris and crumble us from the inside! And you're all sitting here entertaining the actuality of talking to one of their sympathizers as if it's logical, as if she poses no threat at all!"

The king's gray eyes meet mine for a brief second, and the truth circuits between us. Sarcomel is a fearful little horseshit, but he's partially right. I do pose a threat, far more of one than he could ever dream of. A Heartless being tolerated in the Vetrisian court? Outlandish. Impossible. But I've always been a bit of an impossibility; impossibly good-looking, impossibly well dressed. Impossible girl stands here in front of a Cavanosian king, existing exactly where she shouldn't, *when* she shouldn't.

The ministers quickly devolve to arguing, Sarcomel the loudest of them all. I knit my fists in my skirt, nerves buzzing through me. Whatever they decide, I am at their mercy. Varia said it herself—she can do only so much for me. Their voices ricochet among the stone walls, the lawguards surrounding them unmoving. With the display the ministers are putting on, I'm almost certain Gavik was the faux leader of them, and now without their head, they're rudderless, flailing.

Sarcomel breaks out of the argument and points at me wildly. "Your Majesty, she is a threat until Lady Y'shennria can be found and cleared. I demand under the Sunless Concordat that you arrest her as an enemy of the kingdom!"

No—not the dungeon. They'd find out I'm a Heartless eventually, if I was caught in a cell, healing quickly and growing hungrier and more mad as they insist I eat their human food instead of organs. The king leans forward, and just as I open my mouth to defend myself, the door to the throne room bursts open. The clap echoes in the cavern and sends Sarcomel yelping.

Four lawguards come rushing into the throne room, led by a winded-looking Malachite, his white brows drawn tightly. He strides by me without so much as an angry glance in my direction—and that's how I know something's very, *very* wrong.

"Your Majesty," Malachite says, and it's the first time I've heard him willingly use an honorific, but he doesn't bend the knee. "There's a witchfire in the common quarter, near South Gate."

Witchfire? *Real* witchfire? The air grows so thick, it feels choking. Sarcomel starts to exclaim something, but King Sref stands from the throne, descending the stairs and drawing level to Malachite quickly.

"Lucien?" the king demands of Malachite, searching the beneather's face as my struggling lungs collapse on themselves. Lucien was by South Gate. I just saw him there—

dying. The hunger laughs. *he's burning alive without ever knowing how you feel about him—*

"Not in the palace," Malachite responds. "I'm going."

The king nods, the whole exchange clipped and with much unsaid. Malachite immediately turns on his heel, sprinting with his long gait out of the cavern.

"W-Witchfire?" Sarcomel stammers.

The Minister of the Blood and the Minister of the Brick share a tense look. Gavik's witchfire around the temple of Kavar two weeks ago was fake. But this? Gavik isn't able to orchestrate such a thing anymore, and the Ministers look too shocked to have done it. Varia would never let Gavik do it again, and she would never do it herself and draw all that attention.

Which means the likelihood it's real witchfire is…

I turn to King Sref. "Your Majesty, I'm going, too. I'll come back for the inquiry, but Lucien—"

"As long as I draw breath, Lady Zera, I will never allow one such as you to be his bride," King Sref murmurs, so close I can see the crow's feet wrinkling his serious eyes. "Even so, you would protect him?"

"Yes," I blurt. The king burrows his gaze into me, like a burr stuck beneath skin. I can feel every movement of his eyes like a polymath's scalpel slicing inside my body. And then, when he's torn me to pieces, he nods.

"Then go. Do not let my son come to harm, or it will be the last mistake you make."

I spin and leave his cold threat lingering behind in the colder throne room.

I hear the chaos before I see it.

The footsteps of servants rush about frantically, all of

them gathering to press themselves against the north-facing windows of the palace. Their chittering is hushed and wobbly, the words *witches* and *the war* dancing frantically in the air. The crowds are so dense and tightly packed along the hall windows that I couldn't worm my way into any of them even if I wanted to.

I can't afford to stop and gawk, regardless. Lucien is down there.

Was it Varia? Or have the witches launched the first attack of the war? The lawguards of the palace seem to believe the latter, and we brusquely sidestep one another as they rush to arm themselves and establish a perimeter. It's been thirty years since any Cavanosian has fought Heartless, and only the elder ones seem to be able to keep their heads, walking calmly.

I hear several younger guards in passing as I race down the hall.

"—barricade the doors and windows?"

"Barricades don't stop witches, fool, they teleport right in—"

"—the full army hasn't arrived yet. If they brought enough Heartless, they could overrun us—"

"Get yourselves to your posts!" a commanding officer suddenly shouts, and the chittering lawguards all scatter like well-armored flies.

I finally make it to the palace entrance and freeze.

From the steps of the palace, the height of it, it's easy to see where exactly the witchfire is—smoke billowing up in huge plumes from the area near South Gate. The plumes are so high they dwarf the magic-detecting Crimson Lady in the middle of the common quarter. If I squint, there, against the ominous crimson sunset, I can see the barest lick of a dark, shadowy flame flickering among the wooden rooftops. I quash panic and try to think. Do I even have time to find Fione or Varia? Would either of them even be able to make a difference? Varia could teleport us to South Gate, but anyone seen doing anything slightly magical at this particular moment would probably be beaten to death. I have to go alone.

If Lucien dies...

I swallow cold fear and move my feet faster down the palace steps. He won't die. I won't let him get in the way of my heart. But neither will I let him die.

Taking a carriage isn't the right move; too much panic will clog the streets. The lawguards at the bridge crossing between the noble quarter and the common quarter likely won't let anyone through either way. Which means the only viable option to get to Lucien is the one Y'shennria showed me—across the aqueduct pipes of the river that separate the quarters. I race down the steps and over the palace grounds, heaving by the time I reach the riverside.

Even the noble quarter roads are frantic—carriages and lawguards on horses racing to and fro. But it works in my favor; no one stops me on my way. I slick my sweaty hair back to see properly and clamber down the side of the algae-covered wall, letting myself hang before falling onto a brass pipe. I follow the pipes as they intertwine, hulking and massive and rusted green, like petrified snakes.

I've almost made it across when I hear a lawguard from the noble shore shouting, "You there! No one's allowed on that! Come back at once!"

"Gods, I wish I knew more than one beneather swear," I mutter under my haggard breath, pulling myself up and onto another pipe. My eyes catch a far-set pipe on the common side of the shore—if I jump far enough, I could make it and throw the lawguard off. But it's a *massive* jump, the river rushing furiously below. If I don't make it, I'll be swept away and lose precious time.

"Stop!" The guard's shouting grows louder as he determinedly crosses his first pipe.

"You obviously don't know me, sir," I shout, pushing my sweaty hair off my eyes again. "I need at least three 'pleases' and one grovel before I do anything at all!"

Pivoting to face the pipe, I breathe. In and out.

Of the silence, in the silence.

Standing on a rusty pipe, fleeing a guard while running toward a boy I cannot possibly have is an awfully strange place to get a revelation, but I've never been one for normality. This is what it means to be silent, what Reginall, who taught me to Weep, meant—in the middle of cacophony, in the midst of the chaos of living, to find that moment where the only thing that matters is what one does next. The past doesn't matter. The future doesn't matter. All that has meaning is the moment.

This is what silence means—to live only for the next moment.

I brace my legs and shoot forward. My thighs pump with all my condensed might and the world falls away as I leap off the edge of the pipe.

The river churns and peaks white below me in what feels like slowed time, my arms and legs flailing as if they were submerged in sugar syrup, and then all at once my palm bashes into hard metal, my fingers giving off faint cracks as they break. My momentum swings me forward, into the curve of another metal pipe level with my chest, all the wind knocking out of me as my ribs shatter. The Laughing

Daughter's magic gets to work instantly, but pulling myself up with broken fingers and a fractured palm...the pain is blinding tridents of lightning pulsing up my arm, into my spine and back again. I inhale wetly and pull up blood from my punctured lung, but that breath is just enough energy for me to throw my other hand forward and pull myself up the rest of the way.

By the time I struggle to my feet, I'm healed. The smell of smoke burns my nose, the shouts and screams of Vetrisians ringing between every building in the common quarter. I get my bearings quickly—the Crimson Lady to the east of me means South Gate is down the next road.

My earlier hunch was right—the roads moving away from South Gate are entirely congested, men shouting as they elbow people out of the way, wide-eyed celeon with their ears flat on their heads and their hackles raised, babies bleating cries as terrified parents shuffle them farther from harm's way, and lawguards trying to keep all the chaos from erupting into full-blown panic. I'm the only one moving *toward* the gate, and thankfully the lawguards are too preoccupied with preventing the imminent stampede to stop me.

My eyes frantically search the crowd for Lucien, but there's no hint of a dark leather cowl anywhere to be seen. He can't still be at the hat shop? I head toward it, the smoke growing thick as winter fog as I fight against the current of people.

Unlike the roads leading into South Gate, the very heart of it is empty. The crackle of flames roars loud in my ears, waves of heat battering my exposed skin, and as I turn a watertell corner, I finally see it for the third time in my life.

Witchfire.

13

PRAYER

Nightsinger kept a hearth of witchfire broiling at all times, the black flames keeping the three hearts of Crav, Peligli, and me warm in their jars. The hearts of Heartless must be kept warm at all times, by spell or by flame, or in Nightsinger's case, both. Witchfire is a spell-flame. I watch the great gouts of shadowy black fire devour the modest wood of the Vetrisian buildings, cracking beams and scattering embers, knowing that no amount of water can douse them. Witchfire only ever stops burning when the witch who sparked it desires it, or if they die.

If Lucien is burning, he will never stop burning.

if he dies, he will leave you behind just as you so wish.

The hunger's words only spur me faster down the road. I refuse to even entertain the validity of what it says this time. He won't die. He won't.

He might not be mine ever again, but I refuse to live in a world without him in it.

Stray embers catch on my hair and on my dress, burning

through cloth and skin—forever burning—but I ignore them and press onward into the sunset-lit alleys.

I don't want him to die. I don't want him to forget me. That thought burns hotter in me than the witchfire burns on me. For all my insistence he move on, he hate me, I don't want him to. I want him to be with me, for us to be together. I don't want to lose him, even though I know I must, and it's tearing me apart.

The thick smoke obscures my otherwise keen sense of direction, and the vague outline of the white wall surrounding Vetris looms into view above my head. I hurriedly look for any distinctive markers and find the very edge of the South Gate, the scaffolding sticking out of the smoke. I briefly glimpse the door leading to the valkerax, and pause. Yorl and the other celeon are too far down and surrounded by stone and metal—they'll be safe.

The smoke is so thick now, it blears my eyes, my lungs struggling to breathe. I know I have only a sliver of time before I die from inhaling this much smoke, but so does Lucien. And *he* does not grow back. The heat slicks my skin with sweat, and I stagger as I draw close to the hat shop. The fire condenses here in a suffocating pit, the eye of the inferno. A building collapses as I pass, wood and tile crashing to the ground, and sharp screaming cuts through the fire's roaring as people pour out from the building's basement, led by a familiar figure in black leather.

He's still alive! Thank the gods! My unheart soars, the hunger mocking it.

traitor.

"Go!" Lucien bellows, motioning to the open road away from South Gate, and not needing to be told twice, the people flee, aprons and coats clutched to their mouths and noses.

Lucien's cowl protects him somewhat but not enough, and I watch in horror as he immediately turns to enter another burning building. I dash up to him and pull his arm.

"Hey! Your Foolishness!"

Lucien staggers, his eyes widening. "You—what are you doing here?"

"Vacationing! What do you think?" I shout. "We need to get out of here!"

The black witchfire flickers off his darker hair. He says nothing, his eyes flat. He's not wearing the princely mask or purposefully ignoring me, he's...not *seeing* me. His eyes are unfocused, glassy. Before I can ask what's wrong, he turns, going for another building on fire.

"Oh no you don't!" I lunge for him, pulling him back by the arm. To my surprise, his body gives easily, with so little resistance he nearly staggers backward into me. He's panting, sweating, and clutching my arm like it's the last rung of a ladder dangling over a pit. How long has he stayed here, helping people out of the fire? He's on the edge of exhaustion—his heart for his people bigger than his body can sustain.

"Hold on!" I shout, lacing his arm over mine and shouldering his weight as I lead him backward. We need fresh air, and fast.

"You," Lucien murmurs, his face so close to mine I can see the sweat carving over his cheekbones. "Do you hate me?"

"Right, yes—because now is a great time to discuss our relationship! When everything is on *literal fire*!" I snap, dragging him over the cobblestones. "Where in the afterlife is a super-strong beneather when you need him?"

Through the loud cracking noises of fire-eaten buildings and the blood thrumming in my own ears, I startle at the feel of something smooth and callused on my cheek. A hand. Lucien's hand, missing a glove and resting there lightly as his unfocused eyes focus on me all at once.

"Please—stay in my dreams, at least."

My chest constricts with an irrational pain. He's talking gibberish, and uneasily I fear he might be beyond help. His hand falls limply to his side, and my insides fall with it. No, *no, **no**—*

"Stay alive," I shout at him, hysterics thinning my voice. "You hear me? I haven't given you permission to die, Lucien!"

"Luc!" a sudden voice bellows. Malachite comes sprinting out from a wall of fire, the flames rolling off his skin and chainmail like water off oil. He grabs the whole of Lucien's body from me and throws him over one shoulder, the prince's deadweight nothing to the beneather. "This way!"

Too tired to question, I follow his long-eared, hazy outline through the smoke. The world spins, but I clutch at Malachite's hot chainmail, looping my fingers through it as a lead even as it scorches my skin. There's a break in the fire thanks to a stretch of old stone buildings, and by the time we get through it and into a street dotted with confused, wailing citizens watching the flames, my dizziness is gone.

Malachite puts Lucien into a waiting carriage and motions frantically for me. "We have to get him to a polymath! Hurry!"

I grant myself one moment of staring at Lucien's resting eyes, his eyelashes against his cheeks, the outline of his slack body on the carriage seat. He wanted to save his people. He drove himself to this edge to get them out of the fire. He's maybe died for them.

But me? I can't die at all, and the fire still rages.

"Go on without me." I wave. "Go!"

Malachite doesn't need to be told twice. He slams the

carriage door shut and the driver maneuvers around the crowd at an alarming speed. I watch them go, and then turn back, walking into the fire and the flaming buildings the prince was so worried about.

killing yourself for him, to the very end.

I manage to get four more people out of the top level of their buildings, drawing on what little I can of the hunger to push beams aside and pull grown men over the cobblestones. Finally, as the fourth person staggers away, I collapse in the entryway of a building, the smoke making the world go black. Faintly, through my dying eyes, I feel burning and see the black fire spreading up my legs, over my body. It burns. I can feel my hair burning up, blood and pus and fat baking beneath my skin.

"Fire..." I whisper. "For their thralls."

The smoke doesn't kill me fast enough, the fire consuming my sluggish body in a wave of agonizing heat I can't even muster the energy to escape. My skin goes black, cracking like dried earth, my body twitching as the fire eats through my muscles and bone. Varia's magic tries desperately to heal me, but the fire is never satisfied, roaring through my body as if it's nothing more than kindling, energy for it to feed on.

Finally, a hunger greater than my own.

Sometimes, when death hurts especially hard, my mouth whimpers unbidden things, begging the gods for my mother. My father. Someone. Anyone.

The fire rages, consuming me, consuming my small, scared voice.

The last thing I see is the white wall surrounding South

Gate, the brass door I walk through every morning taunting me. The valkerax is down there. I'm so close to my heart, and yet still so far.

Finally, *mercifully*, I die.

I t takes magic longer to heal a burned Heartless, but eventually, it does. I wake up to ashes surrounding me, the house I collapsed beneath now nothing more than a pile of black. The fire continues to rage, but it's moved on, beyond South Gate's immediate vicinity, eating up the roofs of distant buildings. My clothes are gone but Father's sword is at my side, the metal hot and singeing my hands as I pick it up. The brass door that leads to the the valkerax still stands strong, taunting.

I stare at it as best my re-forming eyes can. I've died a dozen ways. And fire is, still, the worst of all. My head is reeling, my body tingling like it's being stabbed countless times even as it heals. Someday, *someday soon*, I won't have to keep dying like this. Someday, the agony of being brought back after terrifying pain won't ever be a part of my life again.

"I'm coming, Father," I murmur through my chapped lips, staring at his rusted sword in my hand. "For you and Mother."

My body is nearly whole, and I stagger to my slowly healing charred feet and make for the road again before the smoke can kill me once more.

By the time I make it to the bustling street, every last bit of my charred skin is healed. A kind celeon sees me walking out of the flames and throws a blanket around my naked body. I stagger back to the palace among flying rumors, displaced families, and fearful, heavily armed guards harassing the populace. They beat down doors, loudly interrogating anyone who catches their eye. The Vetrisian soldiers from the army outside the walls trickle in to give support in the form of more intimidation and patrols wandering the streets, and between the waves of my exhaustion, my heart sinks—the knife's edge the war has teetered on will come ever closer in the wake of this witchfire. Nightsinger, Crav, Peligli, Y'shennria—the danger of war and death is looming ever closer to them.

I manage to trudge back to the noble quarter and cross the tightly guarded bridge by displaying Father's rusted sword to the lawguards—an item the entire Vetrisian court knows Lady Zera Y'shennria owns, and the only thing of mine that survived the flames. The nobles are gathered on the palace's front lawn in close-knit groups, all of them watching the fire with drawn and worried faces. No invading Heartless have been spotted from over the wall, and so the initial panic has died down, but still it simmers just below the surface.

I'm halfway up the gravel road to the palace when I hear the gasp of a nearby noble group gathered around a large brass tube, not unlike the small one Y'shennria gave me to see into the distance with the first time we met.

"The fire!"

"It's gone out!"

I turn my head over my shoulder, and for once the nobles have decided to speak truth. The sun, beginning to set in bright shades of violet and ice, illuminates a smoky South Gate free of any black flames, ash and char the only evidence left. Whoever the witch was, wherever they are, they've either willed the fire to stop or they've been killed. Knowing what state the city is in, I'd hazard a rough guess at the latter. Varia would know. She has to—she has people up in the Crimson Lady, scrubbing her magical doings from detection. Surely they picked something up about this rogue witch.

I walk through the Serpent's Wing back to Varia's room, and briefly my eyes catch on the hall leading to Lucien's apartments. A gaggle of royal polymaths linger outside, whispering with concerned looks on their faces. I want nothing more than to walk into his room and see him, see with my own two eyes if his chest still rises and falls.

"Lady Tarroux!"

I look up to see the polymaths fussing over a breathless Lady Tarroux. Her face is white, her hands clutched in front of her chest and her soft voice just loud enough for me to hear.

"Please, I beg you," she pleads. "Tell me—will he live?"

My unheart sinks as one of the polymaths shakes his head. "I'm sorry, milady. It is still too early to tell."

Lady Tarroux's round face crumples, but she tries so hard to remain strong, her posture straight and true. "Please, there must be something I can do to help. Allow me to assist you in any way I can."

"I'm sorry," the polymath insists. "There is nothing. His condition is very delicate. The king and queen have already visited him—he must remain alone now. The only ones permitted inside are his polymaths and his bodyguard."

My stomach sinks and then rises. Malachite must be inside. That's good—I'm certain he won't let Lucien die that easily. The king and queen have visited, but not Varia? Where is she? Maybe running damage control—trying to find out which witch did this?

Lady Tarroux swallows, her long, elegant neck bobbing. "Then I will remain here, as close as I can be, and pray to the New God for his life."

The polymaths and I watch her settle on the carpet, the polymaths scrambling and insisting a noble lady such as she shouldn't go on her knees in such a public place, but Tarroux ignores them. She sits with her back against Lucien's wall and clasps her hands, her lips moving silently in fervent prayer. Something like affection for her springs up in me unbidden—pride means everything to a noble, and here she is, prostrating herself in the hopes it will bring Lucien back to life with no regard for how she looks.

I go to Varia's room and throw on the nearest dress I can find before venturing into the hall again. As I approach Lucien's door, the polymaths warily watch me, but when I make for Lady Tarroux, they seem to relax. Lady Tarroux doesn't look up until she hears my boots in front of her. She blinks her large brown eyes up at me and gives me a wan smile.

"Oh, Lady Zera. Have you come to visit the prince, too? He's very fond of you—your presence will no doubt strengthen his spirit."

I clear my throat. "I'm not so sure about that."

"I am." She sets her mouth in a determined line, her brows drawn. "He speaks very seldom to me, but when he does, it is about you. He cares for you deeply. From what I have gathered, you are a very wonderful person."

It's such a strange thing for a noble to say—so different from the backstabbing compliments I'm used to from girls my age in the court. Coming from her, and from a face that serious, her words don't feel manufactured at all. She's so genuine, no noble mask to be seen. Is this how all Goldbloods are, or did she just never develop a mask to begin with? I almost laugh but manage to keep it to myself as I settle beside her.

"I've never prayed before," I admit. "You'll have to teach me."

Tarroux's eyes sparkle with joy. "Yes, of course. I would be honored."

I sit by her side and repeat her prayers, my hands clasped. She prays for Lucien's well-being, his strength, his longevity. She prays that he will live a long and happy life, going slightly out of breath with the effort of saying so many things so quickly. Her earnestness is obvious, and more than once I have to smother a laugh at how adorable it is.

We sit there for a half before I get tired and thank her and excuse myself to Varia's apartments, where it's easier to sulk and worry about Lucien without battling the urge to barge inside his room. The image of him unconscious and unmoving in the carriage is burned into my eyes, perhaps literally. Even when I come out, hours later, Lady Tarroux is still there, not having moved an inch and praying fervently. Her hair's plastered to her forehead with sweat, her shoulders sagging from holding that one position for so long.

She's staying by Lucien's side. She's unwavering, while a traitor like me contemplates, every hour of the day, retrieving my heart and leaving Vetris for good.

"Has our little lady eaten?" I ask the guards. They shake their heads. New God's eyelash, she might be more stubborn than Lucien himself—they'll give each other a run for their coin. But she has to eat, or she'll do no running at all. I turn and make a trip down to the kitchens. A few words and a lot of careful steps later, I return with a plate laden with cold meat and warm bread, sweet fruits and dark, dense nuts. Kneeling, I place it in front of her and smile.

"Hey, milady priestess," I tease. "Take a break and eat.

I'm fairly certain the New God doesn't listen to the prayers of shriveled-up corpses."

Lady Tarroux's eyes blink open, falling on the plate, and then my face. "You—Lady Zera. You brought this for *me*?"

"Do you see anyone else around here silly enough not to eat for seven hours?" I smirk.

Lady Tarroux's milk-blond hair catches the moonlight as her lips pull into a gentle smile. "I see now. His Highness was right—you truly are kind."

"All I did was pile some things on a plate." I sigh. "It's not as if I grew the fruits out of my own arsehole."

I expect her to recoil at the word, but Lady Tarroux just laughs, like a thousand little happy birds in a tree. "And it is also true that you are very funny!"

I flush red—hearing it from someone so straightforward is different than hearing it from the usual noble flatterers. "Just hurry up and eat before you faint."

"Yes, thank you," Tarroux agrees, tearing apart a piece of bread and offering me the other half. I shake my head with a wry smile.

"I'm a...*picky* eater. It's all yours."

She speaks around mouthfuls, an unexpectedly delightful breach of etiquette that reminds me so much of Crav, who could never stop talking with his mouth full.

"You said you've never prayed before today," she says. "Are you not religious?"

"Not particularly," I say warily, waiting for her admonishment. But it never comes. She just nods sagely.

"My father is like you. We're originally from Helkyris. Religion is less of a priority there than polymathematics. But when I came of age here, I found Kavar's light. His temple just called out to me. My father is a little disappointed in me, but he has my other sister, at least. She's the smart one."

"Don't be modest. I've seen those hymn books in the temple," I say. "You've gotta have at least a cupful of intelligence to memorize so many words. And it's all Old Vetrisian, too."

"Oh..." She goes a little red on her cheeks. "But I enjoy it so. It barely feels like effort."

There's quiet as she chases the bread with a gulp of water, picking up a grape and looking at it thoughtfully. She sings something soft and under her breath, the language like nothing I've heard before.

"Is that a hymn?" I ask.

Tarroux nods. "My favorite one. It's very flowery, compared to the other hymns. It uses many metaphors, most of them about the natural world." She repeats the lyrics in Old Vetrisian, speaking them more than singing now.

"What does that line mean?" I quirk a brow.

She smiles brilliantly. "It's the main chorus. The priest told me it means *glory to the first tree and no others.*"

I stop fiddling with my dress hem. "The first tree?"

She nods. "The priest said it's an old metaphor for Kavar." She leans in and whispers conspiratorially. "One time I was looking for the song in the hymn library of the temple, and I found an old version from before the Sunless War. It talked about all manner of strange and wonderful things. But the priests don't use that version anymore."

I lean in. "Why not?"

"It mentions the— Well." She frowns and whispers even softer. "The *Old God.*"

"How heretical," I whisper back, feigning awe. "But fascinating."

"Isn't it?" She smiles. "I know we aren't supposed to

speak of him because Kavar's eyes are always watching, and I try not to. But it's my favorite hymn. It was being sung when I first walked into the temple here in Vetris, and so I've always had a soft spot for it."

The first tree. It could, like Tarroux says, just be a metaphor. But something about it doesn't sit right with me. The first tree in the hymn, the song Gavik and Yorl's grandfather know...

"Do you remember how the old hymn you found went at all?" I press. "In Common Vetrisian, of course."

The sudden opening of the door next to us has us both jumping up to stand as a polymath scurries out of it.

"He's awake! His Highness is awake! Inform the king, quickly!"

The tight undercurrents of anxiety loosen within me instantly. Sheer relief floods me down to my toes, weakening the bones keeping me upright. Lucien's awake. He'll *live*. One of the guards trots off to tell the king, and next to me, Lady Tarroux steadies herself on a nearby wall with one of her hands, making the sign of Kavar by touching her other hand to both her eyelids.

"Oh, thank the New God." She turns to me. "Lady Zera, should we greet him together? I'm certain he'd be pleased to see you."

I stare at the dark crack in the open door. To go in, to see him awake and alive with my own two eyes— No.

I've heard he's alive. That's enough for me.

I smile at Tarroux. "You go on. I have business to attend to."

Her face is hurt, but only for a second before she makes a bow. "Of course. Thank you for your companionship, Lady Zera."

"You can thank me, Lady Tarroux"—I make a deeper bow—"by staying by his side."

The words sting coming out, as if I have cuts on my lips and each syllable is salt and vinegar. Her pale brows knit, and I can hear the courtly cogs working in her mind; Prince Lucien's Spring Bride, the one he was rumored to ask to marry him at the Hunt, asking another girl in turn to stay with him. It's a strange pivot, a bizarre path for a Spring Bride to take—rejecting the prince, pushing him away from her when her very existence at court is meant to pull him in.

I'm gone before she can speak.

The king doesn't send for me to continue the inquiry, other things clearly taking up his plate right now—Lucien, the witchfire, the war. I pace back and forth over the carpet in Varia's room, the urge to find Malachite and demand to know if the prince is recovering well gnawing greater than the hunger. The briefest flicker of possibility from the other timeline of my life flashes through my mind—visiting Lucien's bedside, holding his hand. Bursting into tears with relief, and his soft smile as he embraces me and tells me not to worry.

fourteen days of lies and fourteen men, and still you expect a happy end—

I snatch up the nearest wine decanter and down the glass I pour in one swallow.

The hunger blurs into a smooth river, but guilt is the sharp rocks waiting at the foot of the waterfall.

14

THE NAME
OF THE WOLF

Princess Varia doesn't return to her apartments until the early hours of the dim melon-pink morning, when the sunbirds first start to screech. I jolt awake from my wine-induced slumber to see her standing at the shelf of porcelain dolls, stroking the ribbon hat of one absently. Somehow, using that witchy awareness Nightsinger had, too, she knows I'm awake and speaks without turning around.

"No one died in the fire, but several dozen were injured. A great amount of property was lost." She pauses, her languid sheet of dark hair quivering, and then, "My father has drawn up a formal declaration of war. It was announced at midnight."

My insides sink down to my knees. *War.* The war the witches and Y'shennria and I dreaded for so long. Part of me knew it was inevitable after the fire, but I never thought Vetrisian bureaucracy could move so fast.

People will die now. Maybe not because of me, but neither did I do anything to fulfill the witches' plans to stop the war. I try to put the guilt behind me, slowly, like a freshly whetted knife—always aware of its ability to harm, always aware of its usefulness as a tool.

"Was it real witchfire?" I finally ask.

"Yes," she says.

"You didn't do it. You *wouldn't*. That would sabotage all your plans to lay low. So who did?"

Varia picks up the doll, and my memory of her breaking the other one has me instinctually leaning away.

"Whoever the poor fool was," she mutters. "They let their magic spiral completely out of control."

"What?" I blink.

"The bulk of the soldiers currently gathered will be deployed to raze the forests east and west of Vetris." She continues, voice clear this time. "That's first protocol— destroy any hiding places they may have close to the city."

My unheart leaps and stumbles. But that means—

"Nightsinger," I start. "She lives in those woods. Crav and Peligli and..." I jump up off the couch. "I have to warn them."

"Because sending a message to a witch from Vetris will certainly still be possible with the city in full wartime alert," Varia drawls.

"Yes, well, I'd rather not sit here and drink tea while they *die*," I bite back.

Varia sighs. "Focus on teaching the valkerax. I'll send word for you."

"You know where she lives?"

"Approximately." The princess shrugs. "I could feel where she was when I pulled your ownership from her. I'll have my people send her a dried rat's tail—a witch warning. If she's still there, it will reach her, and she will know to flee."

"Do you promise?"

Varia sighs. "Yes. I promise. She's a citizen of Cavanos, and I'd be remiss not to save her life."

Her words are echoes of Lucien's—or is it the other way around? "Are you sure it'll get to her? Don't you think they'll tighten security around the city?"

"Worry about the valkerax." Her voice is hard. "I'll take care of everything else."

"Until you can't anymore," I say. "Until the burden becomes too big for your shoulders."

"'Too big a burden'? A d'Malvane doesn't know the meaning of those words." She laughs, but the sound is somehow thin. "I heard your inquiry was interrupted. I'm nearly certain that with the war in full swing, Father will have no time for it anymore. You got lucky."

"Is that what being your flesh puppet is called these days? *Lucky?*"

Varia laughs again and heads toward her bathroom, the steam of an already prepared bath billowing through the open door. I watch her pull out the bag with TRAITOR on it and the bag with LEECH. Gavik's heart and mine. My blood races at how close my heart is. She puts them down onto a small table, throwing me a smirk.

"You're aware, of course, that your witch must put your heart back into your body for you to become human again."

I scoff. "I spent three years in the woods with Nightsinger. Of course I know that."

She's quiet before she turns, walking into the bathroom. When I hear her slip into the water, I walk over to the table, stroking the TRAITOR bag. It's so warm. I can feel the soft lump of flesh. I can feel my own heartbeat, and I fight back the tears it brings to my eyes. My other hand grips Father's rusted sword.

"Soon," I whisper.

My hand glances over something else in the bag—something hard and sharp. I nearly jolt back—it almost speared me. Whatever it is in there is sharp enough to cut. Curiosity buzzes through me, and, gingerly and listening for Varia's movements the whole time, I pull open the strings of the bag. There, glimmering next to the pinkish lump of my heart, is a clear splinter. I reach in and touch it warily—it's smooth in an unmistakable way. *Glass.* What is glass doing in a witch's heart bag?

"Please don't," Varia calls from the bathroom, and my hand retracts instantly.

"Why is there glass in there?" I snap.

Varia's laughter is low. "There's always glass, Zera. That's how Heartless containers are made."

"But," I start. "Nightsinger had glass jars, and no splinter on the inside—"

"The splinter was in the jar itself," Varia answers lightly, like I'm an infant asking about the alphabet. "Melted down alongside regular glass. Why do you think so many witches choose to use jars instead of more economical bags? Because it's a far more elegant solution to combine the two."

I gnaw my lip, careful to close the bag in such a way that the splinter doesn't pierce my heart.

"I prefer bags for their...*personalization.*" She laughs, and my eyes fall on the threaded words on my bag and Gavik's.

"What's the purpose of that glass splinter?" I demand. "It could pierce my heart in there—"

"It never will. The splinter is what enchants Heartless containers so. It's what gives them their magic. It preserves your heart and connects you to your witch. It essentially gives you your immortality."

I think back to the glass jars in which Nightsinger kept Crav's and Peligli's and my hearts. That glass—each of those jars had a splinter melted down into it? Where did the splinters come from in the first place?

I shake my head. It doesn't matter how I'm kept a prisoner. All that matters is getting out.

"Lucien's asking about what I'm doing at South Gate," I call. "Aren't you worried I'll tell him?"

"Worried?" Varia muses. "Why should I be? No one who works for me will tell him; I've seen to that in numerous ways. And you, certainly, won't tell him, because he would try to stop us. And that would only imperil your chances of getting your heart back."

I glare at the fancy carpet. She's put in words what I've always known. I'd keep quiet about the valkerax forever if it meant getting my heart back. But Lucien's stubbornness alone isn't the biggest problem.

"They'll find out what you're doing," I insist. "They've learned a lot about sussing out secrets while you were away. He has the know-how and Fione has the sheer cleverness to sniff out any plot you might have."

"If that's true," Varia says with a sigh, "why haven't they done so already?"

Because they're enamored with you, I want to say. *They love you like a sister, like a lover. They look up to you.*

Except Varia knows that already, doesn't she? She's using their love to her advantage. She's using everyone's love, utilizing the past like a smokescreen. I must be the only one in Vetris who doesn't think the utmost of her. It's the only thing Gavik and I will ever have in common.

I turn on my heel and leave the room. Before I reach the door, Varia's voice rings out from the bathroom. "Lucien will recover in several days time. If you cared to know."

Warm relief floods me again, for the second time. "I didn't," I call back.

From the fading apartments behind me, I hear something that sounds faintly like a weary snort, and then, *"Juvenile."*

The next morning, I wait for my carriage on the balls of my feet. It doesn't take a polymath to realize that the number of guards stationed in the palace has soundly tripled now that a war has been officially declared. The watertells around both the palace and the noble quarter are constantly going off, spewing great sparkling fonts into the tense air as messages are passed back and forth. The nobles themselves are strangely absent from walking the palace's gardens, and that disturbs me more than anything. They're creatures of habit, no matter how bad things get. If they're restricting their decadent, unaffected selves, the war must truly be here.

When the carriage comes, I watch the preparing city out the window. The ornate tailoring and jewel shops of First Street are closed, the lights off. The bakeries still deal in bread, but in a hushed way, as if they are irrationally afraid that making too much noise will summon the witches from over the wall and straight to them. The smithies and the temple are the only ones who dare to make sound above a whisper—the blacksmiths pounding mightily on their anvils and the priests crowing about the justice and retribution of the New God.

It's there on the temple steps that I finally find the nobles, clinging fervently to the priests' robes, begging their reassurances that they'll be safe in the coming war. The commoners, meanwhile, are bidding their enlisted children and spouses and siblings tearful, hard goodbyes. I try not to think about their faces bloodied by my kind, scarred like Y'shennria has been scarred.

But they will be. It's only a matter of time.

teaching this valkerax to Weep is only a matter of time, the hunger speaks.

South Gate is effectively abandoned, cold and ashy. The perimeter of the witchfire has been cordoned off by the lawguards, nervous lines of them tracing the fire's scars. It's at least a three block radius, encompassing what must be forty buildings at the minimum. The few caravans that are normally here in the mornings are gone, and yet the two lawguards guarding the door in the wall are still present. The devastation curdles my stomach, but I force a smile as I approach.

"Still hanging in there, gentlemen?" I ask. Neither of them responds, but one of them obliges to nod at me. They're clearly on high alert with the war, and concerned only about business, so I give them the password and go in.

Yorl greets me with a sword when I walk into the brassy innards of the great wall. And not just any sword. The blade is pure white, and unmistakable. It's Varia's white mercury sword.

"We will retain the sword here, in the lab," Yorl says. "You may ask for it whenever you see the need."

I raise a single brow. "No payments with interest or anything?"

He snorts and starts walking. I follow him, dumbstruck, as I look the white mercury blade over. It's one of only four blades in the world that were ever smithed with pure white mercury—a tricky process no one's ever been able to replicate, though Gavik tried. The polymath who forged them disappeared before the Sunless War thirty years ago. White mercury inhibits magic, and pure white mercury even more so. If I cut myself with it, the link between Varia and I would weaken enough for me to Weep again, to regain just a little bit of control over myself.

I hover the blade over my forearm, but the command rings. **"You will not allow yourself to be cut with a white mercury blade."**

I nearly throw the sword into the darkness before I remember just how precious it is. I need to cut the valkerax with it for it to learn how to Weep properly. If I can do that, I'll have my heart back, and my own Weeping will become a moot point.

The war just above my head—curling like a viper ready to strike—will become a moot point.

A thousand valkerax, fangs dripping, crawling over the white wall of Vetris.

Straightening my shoulders and shaking off the terrifying image, I cling to Yorl's paw as he leads me down the pitch-black steps. Our breathing echoes, joined by the valkerax's deeper, louder, much slower breathing, like the respiration of the world itself. The clank of armor resounds as Yorl orders the gate opened.

"Don't come in with me this time," I lilt to him, downing the serum in one gulp. I feel his tail thrash in the air.

"Don't tell me what to do," he says.

"Please." A celeon guard to my right wheezes. "J-Just go in. Before I drop the gate."

They can lift five times their own weight, there are two of them, and yet they're struggling—the gate must be incredibly heavy. I duck under it and hear Yorl's claws scratching the dirt as he ducks into the arena after me.

"If you die, can I use your pelt as a cape?" I ask lightly.

"If you die, can I use your skin as a shirt?" he fires back.

"Afterlife *yes*," I hiss. "That sounds so fashionable. Three caveats: wear a ruffle collar with it, dye it bright pink, and flay it off when I'm not-alive."

"No promises," Yorl grumbles. The great, deep breathing all around us suddenly gets closer to me, and the sound of hard scales slithering across dirt stops in front of my feet. It's breathing properly—none of the weak gasps I've gotten used to.

"Starving Wolf." The valkerax's booming voice rasps over my ears. *"You have made safely the journey back."*

I'd shift my gaze to Yorl if I could see anything at all in the darkness. Is it addressing me? If so, it's a vast improvement from the four days of nothing but aimless thrashing and speaking in nonsense.

"Yorl," I swallow and call out. "Did you—"

"Focus, Heartless," he barks. I inhale hugely.

"I'm going to keep returning every day, my good valkerax," I chime, smiling into the utter blackness. "Until you learn how to Weep!" I hold up the white mercury blade. "See this? This is the physical part I was talking about. You've gotta be cut by this for the Weeping to work."

"This small thing, like a spear made of snow——" A gust of hot, rancid air blows over me, concentrated near my hand holding the sword. *"With a scent of dying stars. This is the blade we will hold to the throat of the song?"*

"Yeah. The song will be louder, almost too loud to resist, but it'll also be prone to your control. Which means I have to teach you how to go into the silence first."

I pause and shake my head. I'm the one who sounds mad now. There's a quiet, the chitter of Yorl's quill scratching madly on his parchment pad faintly interrupting.

"*The chime,*" the valkerax says finally. "*We heard a chime above us yesterday, when the sun was moving to meet the sea.*"

Chime. The valkerax has blabbed that word enough for me to know what it means for sure: a witch.

"A chime above you?" I freeze, staring into the dark. Could it mean the witch that started the witchfire?

"*How? How does one silently cut the throat of a song?*"

I snap out of my own thoughts. Whatever unnerving coincidence is going on, it's not as important as teaching this thing, as getting the warm memories in my heart back.

"All right." I sit on the dirt. "First, you should relax."

"*A mountain-task made for the smallest rodent. A rodent without a loudly screaming voice within.*"

"We'll take it slow. That's the whole point." I think back to that jump across the pipes, to the moment in the clearing before I transformed into the monster and defended Lucien. "That's how you get silent. You can't think about many things at once. It has to be just one thing."

"*One,*" the valkerax repeats. "*One root, not the whole plant.*"

A little thrill runs through me as I realize it's getting what I'm saying. This is huge, compared to the last few days. "Exactly! Think of just one thing, and let that one thing become your whole world. Your whole reason for being alive."

"*A purpose of being.*" I hear the valkerax curl around itself. "*To defy the song that sings of barren immortality. This, we understand.*"

"Great. Well, that officially makes you the smarter one, which means I'm the pretty one. Um. Not that your giant fangs and claws aren't pretty. Because they are."

I swear from the other side of the arena, I hear Yorl smack his paw to his forehead.

Reginall made it seem so easy when he first taught me. I tell the valkerax to listen to its own breathing, to focus on the places in its body where it feels an aching emptiness. There's even a moment where it lets me approach, and with tense awe and fear, I run my hand along the smooth white scales of its chest, below the tuft of lionlike mane, to find the breastbone. It's so incredibly big—one scale is as large as my entire palm. And it has *thousands*. The smell of it is no less rank up close, but feeling it for the first time after only hearing it flail and gnash its teeth for so long is incredible.

After a few misses in which I almost lose an arm for touching the wrong spots, we narrow down exactly where the valkerax feels empty—its left back leg. That's got to be where the Old Vetrisians took a bone from it to add to the Bone Tree. It's grown back since, but it feels thinner somehow.

I pan my hand back up its body, and my fingers catch on something wet on its ribs. The valkerax's muscles twitch below my skin as I gingerly run over the spot one more time—it's a hole.

"Yorl," I start. "What's a hole doing here? It's like it's missing one of its—"

"Scales?" Yorl offers, voice cool. "We removed a few and dropped them down Dark Below approximate shafts in order to stabilize the valkerax's mind. The more of its body obeys the command, the saner it becomes."

"Y-You—" I sputter.

"The war is here, Heartless, earlier than any of us expected. The world moves, and we must move with it," Yorl insists.

"*You* sound like the valkerax now," I mutter uneasily.

"*What does the Ironspeaker say, Starving Wolf?*" the valkerax asks.

Half disgusted at the valkerax's wounds, my words come out short. "Why do you keep calling me that?"

"*Those are the true names of you.*" The valkerax pulls away from me, its body heat fading into the cold darkness. "*You are the Starving Wolf. The warmblood watching us with many eyes is the Ironspeaker. True names hold your power.*"

True names—didn't Malachite say something about those? They were important to the beneathers, right? Varia's true name was scratched into the pipe walls where she killed Gavik's valkerax—the Laughing Daughter. That's her witch name, too. Beneather runes always know true names and fill them in automatically, like magic. Old Vetrisian magic, to be more precise.

True names hold your power.

I simply thought Varia adopted that name as her witchname because she was pleased with how it sounded. But if it's her true name, something she can't choose...does that mean every witch uses their true name? Is Nightsinger's true name Nightsinger?

"So you give these names—" I start.

"*We do not give,*" the valkerax insists, voice tearing with a growl on the end. "*We merely read, but where the chimes can read only their own name when the time comes for them to find their power, we can read all.*"

Is it saying witches can figure out their true name? *Do you know how a witch becomes?* I'd asked Fione that once, unknowing myself.

In the midst of my reeling, the valkerax continues in its jagged voice. "*The script is large and endless and there* is *power in it, and always will we read, for it is our duty.*"

"Duty?" I whisper. "To who?"

I wait on hooks, on needles. We breathe together in the darkness, and somewhere between breaths, I die.

Yorl is there at my bedroll's side when I come back to life, the mosslight gleaming in his dilated eyes as he hands me another vial wordlessly.

"We're getting somewhere, finally," I say. His muzzle pulls into a sliver of a grin as he scribbles on his parchment.

"I could tell."

I down the vial. "You look like a kid whose mother just gave him a whole year's worth of sweetrounds."

Yorl's smile fades as he leads me back to the gate, but when I sense it lifted by the other celeon, I don't hear Yorl immediately try to walk under it.

"What's wrong?" I ask.

Yorl swallows audibly. "It's— The valkerax is already waiting for us, just before the gate."

Suddenly a hot breath billows out and over us—so close it could probably slip its head out of the gate easily. But it doesn't. It just waits, and breathes, and then asks in its eerie voice, "*Does it hurt, when the Starving Wolf dies?*"

Yorl and I duck beneath the gate warily, and the celeon drop it closed with a frantic *thump*. The valkerax slithers back a little as I walk away from the gate, following behind me.

"Yes. But I'm used to it by now." I shrug.

"*We die only once,*" it says. "*But you die forever. That is your duty.*"

"It's a treat," I agree, then realize sarcasm might not be the way to go with a valkerax, seeing as I can barely communicate with it at all. "Wait—why is dying *my* duty?"

The sound of something heavy whipping through the air, and then, *"Life is a garden,"* the valkerax insists. *"In which death is required to flourish."*

mad fool, the hunger sneers. **speaking of things it has no power over.**

Bile rises in my throat, and the strangest part is I'm not sure why. Anger, confusion, sadness; all of it whirls in my head.

"Are you telling me I *deserve* being Heartless? That suffering is my *duty*?" I clench my fists. "That my mother and father deserved to die so that I could become one? Or are you just spouting nonsense again?"

There's a long silence wherein it doesn't offer anything else. I breathe in. No matter how incensed I am, this isn't helping teach it Weeping. *Priorities, Zera.*

"Do you have a name? Something I can call you by instead of 'Hey, valkerax'?" I ask.

There's a moment of silence, and then, *"Evlorasin,"* it says, drawing the syllables out with its ancient, raspy voice.

"Evlorasin." I try it on my tongue as I settle down in the arena cross-legged. I hear Evlorasin curl around me, long sinewy body circling over the dirt in all directions.

I breathe in, feeling the emptiness in my chest with every inch of my being. Lingering in this moment, and only this moment, clears out my head from the valkerax's angering words. It's nice, somehow, to practice remaining in the silence, even if it is gods-know-how-many feet below the ground and enclosed with a bloodthirsty valkerax barely kept at bay. To breathe and let everything else drift into the background—Lucien, Varia, the war—and just focus on the familiar void of my own unheart is the closest I've come to experiencing true peace in a long time.

I try to detail how to breathe, and the valkerax does the best it can while pained, and for a scarce moment its huge breaths even out completely, dulling to quiet inhales and exhales.

I'm so inwardly elated—*we're really, honestly getting somewhere!*—that I barely hear the change. From between the silence, Evlorasin's breathing collapses, and there comes a low growl. It reverberates into the ground, up through my bones, and into my chest. I faintly feel a shift in the still air of the arena—the valkerax isn't curled around me anymore. It's low, tensed, and I can hear its claws scraping the ground, rhythmic and impatient.

"Yorl?" I try calling out. "*Yorl?* What's going on?"

His voice floats to me, too calm. "The painkilling concoctions are wearing off. It needs much more with the scales removed."

"Give it some, then, and be quick about it." My voice cracks dry as I feel hot breath coming closer to my back.

"Just stand up," Yorl says carefully. "And make your way to the gate."

I'm not imagining things—I can feel the hot breath burning down my spine now, as if Evlorasin has its mouth right against my back. I won't die, but the thought of getting digested, *alive*, through the wyrm's entire body, has suddenly jumped to number one on Zera Y'shennria's Comprehensive List of Ways in Which She Prefers Not Dying. Faintly, through my terror, I catch the screeching of the gate as it opens, and as calmly as my shaking legs allow, I get up and walk with ginger steps toward it.

"That's it," Yorl encourages me. "You're almost there."

"The song," Evlorasin pants, its voice more distorted than I've ever heard it—more agonized than these last few days combined. *"The song calls for you."*

Shivers snap-freeze my nerves, my rational thought, and I start sprinting. Evlorasin lunges, its claws scrabbling over dirt, its huge maw snapping up air as it tries for me. I make a dive for what I think is the gate, hitting the ground hard, and almost instantly I feel displaced air as heavy metal slams down just behind the soles of my feet.

"Come back!" The valkerax laughs, and I can hear it pacing behind the gate, mewling kindly one moment and snarling the next. *"Come back, little wolf! We are alone in the song! But we can be together! The tree of bone and the tree of glass, together at last!"*

My incisors nip my tongue out of pure shock. Bone. Glass. That line—it's so similar to the one Gavik sang. This is more than coincidence. Something is bashing against something else in my head, trying with all its might to line up and slot into place. It could be the terror or the near-digested experience, but my body goes cold, my eyes roll back in my head. I try desperately to hold on to consciousness, to ask Evlorasin about what it means, but death always has its due.

The world goes black.

Yorl wakes me up on the small sleeping mat, and I've never been happier to see someone so colorful and illuminated and with slightly fewer teeth.

"Is Evlorasin going to be like that from now on?" I wipe the remnants of cold sweat off my forehead.

"Evlorasin?" Yorl furrows his brows.

"That's its true name."

Yorl thinks on this, then offers his paw to me, and we start to ascend the stairs. "I misjudged the amount of painkiller required. I'll adjust, and tomorrow it will remain sedated for a little longer."

"Isn't that gonna push into our teaching time?"

"Yes." He shakes his head. "We'll have less time. And time is crucial now, in the valkerax's last days, more than ever. But—" He winces.

"But what?"

"I have…" He winces again. "Faith."

"Faith?"

"I don't have it often," he snaps, as if I've thrown a punch at him instead of a word. "I hold little stock in the imaginary, baseless, unprovable belief that has all but turned this country against itself. But for some infuriating reason, I have it now. I have faith in…in, well, *you.*" He manages to finish with a great flinch.

A smile curls my lips. "Well then. Let me just jot you onto my list of people I'm trying desperately not to let down."

The dark stair climb is becoming less and less taxing on my body. Yorl barely has to drag my unseeing self up the stairs by the hand at all—I remember how the steps go.

"It said something about the tree of bone and the tree of glass," I say, and with a great swallow, I press on. "Your grandfather—his name was Muro Farspear-Ashwalker."

I can't see him, but Yorl's whole body goes rigid next to me.

"How did you—?"

"He went to King Sref once," I push forward. "The king was worried about Varia's nightmares. Your grandfather sang them a song, and it had a line like that in it. A tree of bone and a tree of glass." There's a beat. "Lucien told me."

Yorl's absolutely silent, and I swear the air between us is suddenly a thousand times colder.

"What does it mean—?" I start, but Yorl is faster.

"'The Hymn of the Forest,'" Yorl interrupts, every word cutting. "Grandfather based all his research on it. And he was called a fool for it."

"Yorl—"

"That's enough," he barks. "You don't need to know it. Forget you ever heard about it."

"But that's not—"

His warm paws suddenly grip my hands. "I'm serious, Zera." Not *Heartless* but *Zera* this time. "It's nonsense. It drove my grandfather to ruin. You have to drop it before it ruins you, too."

He waits. As if I'm going to forget about a coincidence like this. But he's not going to budge unless I assent.

Finally, I nod. "Okay. All right. I'm sorry I brought it up."

He sighs. "It's fine. Just as long as you have the good sense not to go pursuing it."

After a long, mostly silent journey, we reach the top of the stairs. For once, I'm not a panting mess.

"As much as I hate to admit it, you did good work today," Yorl says in the doorway.

"Aw, I appreciate you, too." I reach to bop his black nose, but he lifts his chin out of the way.

"Don't."

I stamp my foot. "Why does everyone in this city hate *fun*?"

"Do you think a stranger sticking their fingers up your nose is fun?"

"*Up* your nose? Gross. I was just going to tap it. Who's been trying to stick their fingers up your nose?"

"The human children," he grumbles. "Every chance they get."

I laugh. "Well, don't walk around all sour and hunched, and maybe you'll be too tall for their grimy fingers to reach."

"Goodness. Do you give advice for a living?" Yorl drawls.

"You know, it told me your true name." I ignore him. "Evlorasin did."

His huge green eyes light up like twin shooting stars, and he pushes his glasses on his nose. "It did?"

"Yeah. Ironspeaker. Then it started spiraling, saying something about its duty to *read?* And that my duty is dying." I sigh. "Was that just rambling? I mean, you put its scales into the Dark Below so it would ramble *less*, right?"

Yorl's muzzle frowns. "I don't know. My grandfather liked to say they are mystifying creatures. They live for roughly five hundred years, but most of my research indicates they predate humans and beneathers by over ten thousand. By all accounts, they were here at the beginning of the world, and they will be here at the end."

The song that sings of barren immortality, Evlorasin had said. Barren immortality - five hundred years. I can't imagine living as long as a valkerax. Except I can, actually, and that's why I'm teaching a valkerax for my heart.

"The Ironspeaker." I point to Yorl, then to me. "The Starving Wolf." There's a beat as I think it over and put on a horseshit-eating grin. "My true name is way better."

Yorl rolls his eyes. "Just because you say something once out loud doesn't make it true."

It's a moment of lightness before I have to trudge through the ash-laden South Gate and return to the teetering, frantic humans plunging into war, and I bask in it as long as I can—which isn't very long, considering Yorl is obsessed with his work and leaves me nigh-instantly to go back down to the valkerax. But I do hear him happily muttering "Ironspeaker" to himself as he goes, like the name is a coat and he's trying it on in the dressing room.

The valkerax. Everything it said swirls, diaphanous and enigmatic, in my mind. I know so little about witches and valkerax and true names, and yet they all seem intertwined. But what good does knowing do? I'm not a witch. All I need is to teach it. Everything else is pointless.

On the way back to the palace, a vendor still open amid the war crisis is selling steaming hot maple-glazed sweetrounds. There's something deeply familiar about the smell, so I buy one. I cup it in my hands knowing I can't bite it—I'd weep blood tears after ingesting such a human food, and too many lawguards are around, all of them on a knife's point and searching rabidly for signs of Heartless. A girl dabbing her eyes too much could be one of them.

"Look at me, being smart and worrying about my own well-being," I marvel. I settle for smelling the sweetround, the mere act of keeping it close by me somehow strangely comforting.

My feet take me home. Not to the palace but to Y'shennria's manor. I stand in front of the severe darkwood architecture clutching the black iron gate in one hand and the sweetround in the other. The smell of black roses cloys my way—heavy with honey and licorice. The windows are empty, lifeless. I stare at Y'shennria's bedroom window at the very top, quiet and bitterly still, and close my eyes. For a moment, the window is lit in buttery light, and against it is the regal silhouette of a woman with puffed hair, a teacup in her hand as she stares at the night, looking out for someone.

The patrolling lawguards will find the maple-glazed sweetround lying on Lady Y'shennria's porch, and wonder.

15

THE HYMN OF THE FOREST

I wake up the next morning to a terrible wine headache and thick billows of smoke in the distance.

I sip chocolate drink—blood tears be damned—to be rid of the taste of last night's mistakes and watch the clouds of smoke smolder on the horizon: not inside Vetris this time but far east and west of the city. Those must be the forests burning.

How many witches are losing the last home they have right now?

Varia wakes up later than I do but not by much, and she watches the smoke with me in her silk bathrobe, the two of us silent for a long moment.

"Try not to worry so much about Nightsinger. I sent word," she says as she turns from the window to get ready for the day. "She should be in Windonhigh now, if she wasn't already."

I swallow the relief, refusing to let her see it. She has me at a disadvantage enough already.

"You'd think they'd name the last witch enclave something,

oh, I don't know, more intimidating," I say. "Witchier. A lot more 'dark' and 'blood' words involved."

Varia says nothing to this, wordlessly letting her maids in to dress her, which inherently forbids any more heretical talk of witches. Fione comes in soon after, and we wait together, awkwardly sitting on the couches facing each other while the maids finish Varia's hair. Her cane with the valkerax head on it gleams in the morning sun, and I marvel that such a seemingly small thing can transform into a fully fledged crossbow.

"Bonbon?" I offer her a chocolate from the plate of them. She stares at the ground, determined not to meet my eyes. What do I say to her? *Don't be scared*? *It's all right*? She *should* be scared. And nothing is all right.

"Did you make that thing yourself?" I jerk my head to the cane, and Fione finally nods.

"Yes. Using my uncle's materials and blueprints."

I whistle, impressed. "You ever consider being a polymath if the whole 'archduchess' thing doesn't work out?"

"It…it sort of will always work out," she says softly. "Because I was born into it."

There's a beat of awkward but somehow ridiculous silence, and to my surprise when I burst out laughing, so does she. We lock eyes over our laughter, hers much quieter but still there, and for a moment it's like everything is back to normal. I savor it as long as it lasts.

"How could I forget?" I wheeze. "About how fairly nobility works?"

"Extremely fairly," Fione rolls her eyes through her laugh. When we've calmed, I inhale hugely.

"I'm glad, you know," I try. "That you got the chance to tell Varia how you feel."

This gets her eyes to stutter up to me, and I smile. She starts to open her mouth to say something when Varia walks in, putting a hand on Fione's shoulder and grinning at her.

"Are you ready to go?"

Fione looks between her and me and then nods up at Varia, taking her hand and rising. They leave, and I see Fione pause at the door.

"Something wrong, darling?" Varia asks her gently.

Fione shakes her head. "No."

I stare at the place where she used to sit, the remnants of our laughter still ringing in my ears. It's then I notice something sticking out of the cushions of the couch she was sitting on. Brown, leathery. I walk over and pluck it out. It's a notebook of some sort. I open it up and parse through the wild scribbles, the diagrams of strange contraptions and a sketch of a sword I recognize—Varia's white mercury sword.

This...this is Gavik's diary. Fione actually brought it for me.

My unheart leaps as my fingers leap faster, flipping through the pages frantically. I calm down enough to realize being hasty isn't going to get me anywhere, and while I finish my drink, I read the whole thing.

The writing style is, of course, insufferably full of itself. Most of it is boring day-to-day details of what it takes to keep the royal polymaths operating. Lists of materials like copper, silver, acid, and base, notes rife with equations and numbers on hundreds of experiments pursued in the name of making the Vetrisian army stronger against witches. Even more of it is inane notes scribbled about certain nobles: their weaknesses, their "uses," things Gavik can employ to manipulate them. Dated two weeks ago, he talks about insinuating to the Priseless twins that I needed to be "taken care of." It lines up perfectly with when the Priseless twins tried to tie me and scarify my face during my very first banquet. Malachite saved me that time.

Scoffing, I move on. Gavik's hatred for witches and Old God worshippers permeates it all, calling them every bad name under the sun. One page utterly shocks me; it talks about how Y'shennria refused Gavik's hand for marriage once, a long, long time ago. That's why the old rancid arsehole hated her so much. I always thought his vitriol was excessive toward her—more than just a hatred for her religion. My own hatred for him burns even hotter now.

There are some pages I just can't read at all—written in some sort of glyphic code. And there are other pages entirely covered in numbers that are too long to be equations. More code, maybe.

Finally, *finally*, I find what I'm looking for.

It's a page tucked away at the very end of the journal, faded and water stained. It looks like it was torn out of another book, a book much older than this journal. The letters are unreadable, but I recognize a few of them. They look exactly like the beneather runes I saw in the pipe with the valkerax skeleton. Old Vetrisian runes, like the ones carved over the arches of each one of the four gates of Vetris. Mercifully, between every line, Gavik has scribbled translations:

> *An empire of untold greatness, a rich land built in mirth,*
> *Made strong in the ashes, of the wyrms sealed at birth,*
> *By the bones that reach sky, magic wrought clear*
> *Glass made as a blade, to defy the deaths of those we hold dear,*
> *Two trees grown, great roots between the stone crawl,*

The happiness of the once-great empire they did maul,
A funeral for the hands held, our Vetrisian flags at half-
mast,
The tree of bone and tree of glass, will sit together as
family at last.

I gape, my mouth fishing for the words I can't find. I read the sentences over and over. This is the "Hymn of the Forest" Yorl talked about. I can gather the bare gist of it; Old Vetris seals the valkerax with the Bone Tree. But then, glass? Glass made as a blade, to defy death?

My mind flashes to the splinter of glass in my heart bag. No. No—it can't be *that* glass. But Varia said herself the splinters are what links me to her and gives me my immortality.

A tree of glass, like in my dream.

I have to find Gavik.

I don a simple brown cloak and race out of the palace. Varia's carriage is gone, taking the princess and Fione to their breakfast, so I walk off the palace grounds myself. It's probably for the better—I won't be able to find Gavik in a carriage that can't fit through tiny alleys. I comb the underbelly of Vetris, weaving through roads and side alleys, asking stall vendors and guards if they've seen a man in a gray robe. Nothing—they've seen him around, of course, but all the haunts they point me to are empty. The city is taut and wound around itself, King Sref's declaration of war plastered on every pillar and empty space of wall. No matter where you turn, soldiers choke the streets, marching to the shouted orders of their superiors, their bright jade-green uniforms with silver trim gleaming in the sun.

I slump against the wall of a shop in Butcher's Alley,

clutching the diary close to my chest. Where would he *be*? I know he's been ordered to pass out bread, but how hard can finding a hunched man with a big basket of bread be?

"You look lost." A deep voice makes me look up. There, standing in front of me, is Lucien in his Whisper outfit, the leathers sleek against every angle of his body, his eyes weary and thick with dark circles though his cowl. His posture is a little worn but refusing to look anything less than strong. My unheart sings, begging me to run forward and ask him if he's all right, inspect him to make sure he's healed. That he's real, alive, and not going anywhere. But I'm not his Spring Bride anymore. I gave that mantle to Tarroux yesterday.

I clench my fist, struggling to make my voice sound light.

"And you look terrible. Any particular reason why you're out of bed and moving around against the wishes of your polymaths?"

"I made the mistake of telling him I saw you run out of the palace in a tizzy," Malachite's voice drawls as the pale beneather steps into the alley.

"Well, good morning to you, too." I blink at Malachite.

"I'm fine," Lucien insists to both of us.

"'Fine'? You inhaled so much smoke, you were coughing up black!" Malachite argues.

"Could an injured person do this?" Lucien asks, promptly bracing his legs for what looks like a flip so quickly that he winces. He suddenly thinks better of it, and straightens. "All right. New plan—moving as little as possible."

"Let's go back to the palace," Malachite growls. "You need to rest."

"What I need is a friend, not a second mother." Lucien chuckles. His obsidian eyes focus on me. "Who exactly are you looking for?"

"How do you know I'm looking for someone?" I sniff.

"You were asking vendors questions. The only time anyone does that is when they're looking for someone."

"For all you know, I could be looking for some*thing*," I argue.

"Like what?" Lucien quirks a brow behind his cowl.

"A warm bowl of soup, maybe," I offer.

"A sense of dignity," Malachite counteroffers.

"A sense of humor," I fire back at him. "Since you seem to have lost yours."

"Lost? No," Malachite scoffs. "You stole it from me right around the same time you tried to kill my best friend, *sarvett*."

"Ooh." I smile at his beneather word. "I like the sound of that one. What does it mean?"

"Conniving cave scorpion." Malachite smiles back at me for once.

"Enough." Lucien's princely voice cuts between us. "As much as I enjoy watching you two fight over me like toddlers over a sweetround, I *am* supposed to be in bed. We have limited time before someone notices I'm gone." He looks to me. "So. How can we help?"

"*We?*" Malachite squawks incredulously.

"By leaving me alone, and sleeping." I turn on my heel. "Oh, and be sure to drink all the medicine the polymaths tell you to."

"I will," he agrees, catching up with my stride easily. "Just as soon as I've found who you're looking for."

"Because you're nosy." I sigh, trying not to notice just how close his body is to mine, his chest just behind my shoulder. I can almost feel his heat.

"Nosiness, caring." He waves a hand. "It's all the same thing."

"It's really not."

"Now." He ignores me imperiously. "Hurry up and tell me who you're after. Your prince can find them. But your prince is also a very busy person."

"If I do, will you leave me alone?"

"Verily," he agrees.

"Gavik," I say. "He's in a gray robe—"

"Handing out bread, right," Lucien finishes for me. "I know."

I watch him walk to the mouth of the alleyway.

"Luc," Malachite exhales. "We really don't have time for this—"

Lucien lowers his cowl and raises his fingers to his mouth and makes a distinct, birdlike whistle comprised of three notes. There are nearly thirty seconds of quiet, Lucien and Malachite and I standing still in the alley. Suddenly, seemingly from out of nowhere in the dense crowd, a child emerges, grimy and no older than Crav's twelve years. He grimaces like Crav does, too, but when he sees Lucien, his face brightens. This isn't the first urchin I've seen Lucien with—there was a little girl he gave trinkets to, trinkets he'd stolen from nobles. How many of them does he know? And do they all look this happy to see him?

The prince kneels at the boy's eye level and hands him a few gold coins, murmuring a question. The child points toward West Gate and then disappears into the crowd again.

Lucien turns back to me, a smile outlined in the dark fabric of his mask. "Gavik's near the old brewery around West Gate. Come. We can still catch him if we're quick."

"Again, with the 'we'!" Malachite exhales. Lucien just starts off, and of course Malachite follows. I trail behind the beneather, catching up with Lucien as best I can.

"You never told me your information network was comprised entirely of urchins," I say lightly.

"Not entirely but mostly," the prince agrees. "They don't try to lie for their coin as much as the adults do. And they tend to notice things adults overlook. Besides, the city is hard on them most of all. It's all I can do right now to ease that."

I scoff, but the sound has no teeth. My unheart feels somehow warm. Proud. I shake it off, and a sudden jostle in the thronging crowd shakes me, too. I stagger back, losing Lucien and Malachite quickly in the swarm of heads. They might be tall, but I can barely see over the sea of people.

"New God's tit," I swear. Someone else bumps into me, this time so hard that cobblestone rushes up to greet my face. I brace myself, but something catches my hand at the last minute, and I make a frantic clutch onto it for dear life. I blink up at the help, only to see black leather. Lucien's hand, holding my elbow. He pulls me up, the smile under his mask so lopsided, it makes my unheart skip a beat.

"Don't fall behind," he says.

I'm so stunned that I can't get words out, and the few words that start to come are cut off by the feeling of his gloved hand slipping into mine. He holds my hand, guiding me through the crowd as I stare at his back disbelievingly. The old affection for him starts to rear its head, my whole body punctured pleasantly by the fizzy, sugary sensation.

not again, the hunger demands. *never again. he is tricking you with the promise of love, and you will fall for it again because you are weak.*

It's just a hand. Just one moment. One moment can't hurt, can it?

you asked for moments two weeks ago, the hunger snarls. *and he ruined you for it.*

The hunger's right. I rip my hand from his, and he thankfully doesn't try to grab it again. Soon, we're at the foot of West Gate, a much busier place than South Gate, but the area near the old brewery is relatively calmer. Lucien stops in front of it, the air ripe with the viscous, pungent smell of yeast.

"There!" Lucien points at a figure in gray in the distance. "That's him."

"Finally," Malachite says. "Can we stop cavorting and go back to the palace now?"

"By all means." I wave my hands. "Go on."

"Not even a thank-you kiss?" Lucien smiles. The word "kiss," coming from him, stabs right into my lungs. That's not what he really wants, is it? Nothing can go back to the way it was between us. I know that now. I can't change the past. All I can do is move forward—with him, with everyone. I pause, and then hold out the diary page to him.

"Here. This is my thanks."

Lucien takes it, his dark eyes bewildered, but as he reads the lines, his gaze grows sharper until he looks back up at me. "This is the song—the one Muro sang that day in the throne room. Where did you find this?"

"Fione gave me Gavik's diary. That was inside it. I thought you should know."

He looks back down at it, and then hands it to me. "What does it mean?"

"I'm about to find out," I say, raising my chin toward Gavik. There's a quiet as Lucien looks between Gavik and me, and then he exhales. It quickly turns into a cough, the sound racking his body as he doubles over. Malachite shoots a worried look at me, and I reach into my cloak and pull out Lucien's handkerchief. I unfold Y'shennria's picture from it and hand it to him.

"I'm returning this to you in your hour of need."

The prince's dark eyes flash as he looks up. "That was meant as a parting gift for you."

The feel of his hand in mine just moments ago, the pride in my chest welling up for him. The warmth that spreads through my body simply because I see him. No matter how badly I want to be ruthless, I can't bring myself to do it. I can't bring myself to rip us apart all the way. I'm hopeless.

weak. disgustingly weak and pathetic—

"Yes. Well." I clear my throat. "I'm returning it."

Lucien's gaze softens. No. *No, Zera.* Stand strong. You will not love him again. You can't. Your heart is more important than anything in the world—than even love.

"I'm returning it," I correct myself, sniffing haughtily, "until you can find me a better parting gift. Something made of gold and with a few more gems on it, preferably."

Malachite bristles. "You insolent little—"

Lucien suddenly laughs. The sound is amused, but not in that hollow way he reserves for nobles. It's sincere, and light, and yanks at the very marrow of my resolve. Malachite looks as shocked as I am.

Lucien smiles at me, taking the kerchief from my hand with the slightest of bows. "Very well. I'll keep an eye out."

I fight the flush moving up my cheeks and round on my heel, striding toward Gavik with the page clutched in my hand.

16

FLESH WILL FEED ITS FURNACE

Gavik hears my footsteps on the cobblestones and looks up. His bread basket is nearly full this time, a few drifters gathered around it as he hands them the loaves. In that moment I remember his true name—it was on the pipe wall where the valkerax skeleton was, too. The Man Without Mercy. If only they could see him now. When Varia is done with him, he'll have plenty of mercy—one way or another.

"What are you doing here?" Gavik asks, his voice suspiciously lacking irritation. Perhaps sensing the impending conflict between us, the drifters take their bread and scatter as I approach.

"I have a gift," I say lightly, throwing the diary at him. He catches it in his basket, picking the breadcrumbs off as he opens it. His aged face contorts as he scans a few pages.

"This—this is my diary."

"And here I thought you were the clever minister of the bunch," I say. I point at the ancient page where he'd copied down the translation of the hymn, and he squints at it. "You're going to tell me what this means. It's called the 'Hymn of the Forest.' Half your diary is in code, so I couldn't figure it out myself. Which is why I'm here."

Gavik knits his brows. He reads through the hymn and then shakes his head.

"That is indeed the song about the Bone Tree I know. Part of it, at least. The other parts—it must be in these coded passages, along with why it's so dangerous." He frowns. "I can— Yes, this looks like something I can solve. But it will take time."

"You made up the code in the first place." I snort. "Don't you know it already?"

"I don't remember anything of my old life. All of it is hazy, except that one sentence of the hymn. This code looks complicated. However," he says with a sneer, "you're correct. If I wrote it, I can unwrite it. But I need time."

"I don't have time." I fold my arms over my chest.

"We have all the time in the world," he mutters. "After all, we are immortal."

"I'm going to teach the valkerax how to Weep as fast as I can. It's starting to learn. Varia will have the Bone Tree sooner than you think."

"You can stall," he says. "You can stall for just a few hours. The command doesn't let me do anything but hand out bread until sunset."

"The valkerax is wasting away," I insist. "It's dying much faster than anyone thought, and if I can't teach it, I don't get my heart—"

"You hate me," he asserts. My frown is deep, and I watch his hand dart into the basket and offer a loaf to a ragged passerby almost automatically. The passerby takes it, but Gavik's watery eyes never leave my face. "I hate you. But we are both bound to one person. That person has our leashes. We have a common enemy, Zera, no matter how much you wish to deny it."

"She's going to give me my heart," I argue. "She has a sense of morality, unlike you—"

"That doesn't mean she is innocent," he says resolutely.

I burst out in cruel, frigid laughter. "You'll have to forgive me if I don't take you seriously, considering this is coming from the man who *drowned* innocents."

"Something is not right," Gavik snaps. "I know that. I know that the same way I know that one and only line of the hymn. I can prove it to you. A few hours, that's all I ask. I know you don't trust me; I don't expect you to. But at the very least, you should know what kind of person your witch is before you go handing her the key to a valkerax army, don't you think?"

"She's just going to use them to force a standstill in the war." I fight with everything I have against his logic—I don't want to agree with a genocidal coot.

"I can assure you, as someone who spent his life chasing power," Gavik says, "when absolute power presents itself, there are no 'justs' anymore. It is all or nothing."

He's not wrong. He's not wrong and *I hate it*. My heart is all that matters, right? So why am I even entertaining the idea of stalling out the valkerax teaching for him?

Varia's thrashing in her bed. Her voice murmuring about the Tree. My own nightmare. Lucien's worry on his face and Fione's denial on hers. The coincidences, piling on top of one another.

If something's wrong with my witch, then where does that leave the people who love her? My friends?

former friends, the hunger corrects oily.

This. This can be my parting gift to them.

"Fine," I bark. "You have your day. Make sure you don't waste it."

Evlorasin doesn't want to talk today. It wants to be in the silence. And so do I, frankly, but we all have jobs to do.

I distract it as best I can without really damaging its teachings up until now—I ask it all sorts of harmless questions. What it'll do when it's free, where it will go. Evlorasin wants to fly, mostly. It loves flying. I'm a little surprised—I didn't know they could fly, and I spend an exorbitant amount of time grilling Yorl about it when I die for the first time. It works like a charm—at least for a while. He gets so caught up in telling me about every Old Vetrisian text that talks about them flying that he nearly forgets to give me my next vial. He remembers eventually and snarls at me for distracting him. I apologize profusely, and we walk into the arena again together.

"What did you mean?" I ask Evlorasin. "When you said the tree of bone will always call out to the chime strong enough to be its roots?"

The valkerax thrashes its tail, clearly irritated that, for the third time in a row, I've interrupted its silence.

"We are like the river over stones; we say many things that are true and do not recall them."

"You were in a lot of pain," I agree. Evlorasin snorts out a violent breath of air through its nose.

"Pain is nothing and everything. The Starving Wolf knows this, too."

I feel the valkerax move the air as it circles around me, a puff of hot breath wafting against my shoulder. There's a long, heavily breathing pause, and then Evlorasin speaks.

"The song that calls to us comes from the tree of bone."

"Right," I say softly. The song means the hunger. The hunger that forces Heartless and valkerax to obey commands, that feeds on our own doubts and fears.

"A tree cannot grow without the sun or the rain," Evlorasin hisses. *"The tree of bone is no different. Sun is not its food. Water is not its nourishment."*

"Then," I murmur, "what is?"

"Power." The wyrm's whiskers beat the air. *"Power all around, floating like clouds and falling like earth. Power that cannot be held by a tree without hands. A chime must hold it, offer the cup of it to the lips of the tree."*

I knit my brows in the darkness. *A chime must hold it.* By power, Evlorasin means magic, doesn't it? Which means the Bone Tree needs magic. Magic from a chime—a witch.

"We can hear its hungry cries," Evlorasin growls, low in its throat. *"It has not been fed sun or rain for many moons. It hungers for a great, grand chime, ringing clear and loud and sweet into the world. It will call to this chime, as it calls us and pulls us below the earth."*

My whole body feels suddenly stiff. The first thing my mind flashes to is Varia's magic. My wounds. It takes her magic seconds to heal me—it's stronger and more potent than Nightsinger's magic by miles and miles. When I was burned alive by witchfire, my bones nothing more than ash, it took Varia's magic not hours to heal me. Killing a Heartless by fire is known to slow down their healing significantly. The witchfire started roughly at sunset. But Varia's magic had me alive again during that same sunset.

She is *wildly* powerful.

Varia's nightmares about the Tree—it's calling to her. If what Evlorasin says is true, then everything lines up.

The Bone Tree wants Varia's magic. And it's *calling* to her.

I walk out with Yorl after the session, feeling his tail whipping the air beside me as we ascend the stairs.

"We can't afford to waste time like you did today." The celeon's voice has a snarl in it. "The valkerax might sound improved, but that doesn't mean it's any better physically. Death is not—"

"The Bone Tree feeds on magic from a witch, right?" I lilt. Yorl goes quiet, letting go of my hand. I may be able to find my way on my own now, but it's the gesture that hurts the most. What little trust I've built with him feels suddenly strained, but I press on. "The Bone Tree is more like an Old Vetrisian relic, you said. They pumped so much magic and polymath engineering into it that it's developed a mind of its own. What if it's manipulating Varia? Is that possible? She's a strong witch, and if it's hungry—"

He stops me on the stairs, something slightly sharp poking into the empty void of my chest. A claw from Yorl's paw. He's pointing at me. I can't see his gaze, but I can feel those huge emerald orbs on my face.

"Do you want your heart in your chest again or not?"

My own hackles raise. "Obviously."

"Then why?" he asks carefully and softly. "*Why* are you asking these questions?"

I exhale, frustrated. "Because it's important! Varia said she wants the Bone Tree to control the valkerax and stop the war, but what if the Tree is manipulating her instead?"

"And if it is?" Yorl argues. "No exchange in Old Vetris

was unequal. Varia will get her valkerax army. And the Bone Tree will feed off her magic. She knows that."

My flesh will feed its furnace.

"My grandfather knew that. He told the king and queen that, but they didn't believe him. They didn't *want* to believe him—that their daughter would hurt herself in her sleep every night until she was dead, or until some Old Vetrisian relic consumed her magic."

A coldness seeps into my veins. Yorl pulls his claw back from my chest.

"The truth is just the truth, Zera. It affects nothing. What matters most is what Varia wants. If she gets it, then we get what we want, too. Focus on that. Center your mind on that."

My unheart sinks. "If she gets the Tree, is she going to die?"

Yorl starts walking up the steps, his footpads soft, and I walk with him, feeling for the cold stone walls.

"I don't know," Yorl admits. "There isn't much documentation on how the Tree feeds, only that it requires a strong source of magic every so often. But I'd hazard a guess that it doesn't take all the magic at once from a witch—Old Vetrisian inventions are complex and often don't work instantaneously. It most likely would siphon her magic from her slowly."

"And kill her?" I ask.

Yorl is quiet, and then, "Yes. Eventually. By my grandfather's calculations, a witch cannot survive having all their magic taken from them."

I can't bring myself to walk forward anymore. Varia will die. Lucien and Fione will lose their loved one all over again. Their pain will come back tenfold. And I'm helping that happen.

Lucien's suspicions were right. And something else gnaws at me.

"If she dies, what happens to the valkerax? Are they just free to roam?" I ask.

"No," Yorl says. "The Bone Tree will always default to forcing the valkerax into the Dark Below. If...when—" His voice catches. "When she dies, in theory all the valkerax will return beneath."

I'm silent. So Varia's doing all this just for temporary power. The conversation between Yorl and me dies and doesn't resurrect until we reach the surface-level door.

"None of this concerns us, Zera," he says, his pupils slits in the light. "Keep your mind on your own goal. Not hers. Not mine. Your own."

I breathe in. Every fiber of my being knows his logic is sound. But I can't help but think about Lucien's face, how broken it will look when Varia dies again. And I will have helped her to her grave with my own two hands.

Nothing distracts me from my own thoughts better than a book. And I need distraction now more than ever. I need to read someone else's words to clear my head of all the ones buzzing around in my skull.

My time at the Vetrisian court didn't allow me to visit the library as much as I'd have liked. I had Y'shennria's library, which served me well during the scarce few moments of rest time between trying to steal the prince's heart, but I'd never set foot in the palace's library. Most of my time here was piddled away on boring things like pretending to be interesting and making other people like me.

A waste, in the end.

A waste, always.

But now, a few weeks older and wiser, I step into the most beautiful library I've ever seen. The windows are kept small and modest to keep sunlight from damaging the books. A brass globe in massive proportions hangs from the ceiling, suspended by cables and rotating slowly. Huge rosewood shelves tower over us, laden with every book I can imagine—from the sweeping epics to the children's bedtime stories to the written history of every civilization on Arathess—it's all here. The basics of polymathematics, the famous odes of a poet-general during the Helkyrisian War, the sweetest, most breathtaking romances ever written by a noblewoman with too much time on her hands and too little action in her bed—my hands can't flicker through the pages fast enough.

But of course, there are no books left in the palace library about witches.

Cavanos hates them, after all. No doubt their libraries have been purged of all literature pertaining to magic and witches. The only indication witches even exist are the children's books, in which (witch, I am *terribly* clever) a Heartless or three hunt and eat the parents of the hero-child, their long limbs and gnashing teeth puncturing through the page and directly into my unheart.

I tilt one such children's book as I look at a picture. "They got the knees all wrong. And is that— No!" I hiss softly. "We do *not* have furry underbellies!"

In utter disgust, I put the book back on the shelf, the old wood thing wobbling angrily as I do.

"There, there." I pat it to still it. "I know. These humans

never get history quite right, do they?"

"Except when someone wrongs us." I look up at the voice at the end of the aisle and see Fione standing there. I pretend not to notice the way her hand grips her valkerax-headed cane as if her life depended on it, or the way her head is held a little too high. The hunger can smell her fear even through her riding coat, and I tamp it down with extra fervor. Her noble mask is otherwise perfect, impassive as she walks a mere one step closer. I try to make myself small, unthreatening.

"Lovely weather we're having." I start with something harmless and trace my finger over the spine of a book. A fine cloud of gray particles spins up into the air. "A little dusty, though."

"I gave you my uncle's diary. So—your end of the bargain. What is Varia having you do?" Fione isn't distracted in the slightest, her voice strong.

I wipe my finger on my simple flax dress and smile. "You really care deeply about her."

I watch Fione draw herself up to her full archduchess height, her mouse-curls gleaming in the library's sun. It hurts my unheart to see her so protective of Varia, so determined to figure out what's going on.

"Answer me," she demands.

I hear no warmth in her words at all. Why should I? I'm helping her lover kill herself.

"You're right." I sigh. "I suppose I don't deserve pleas-antries."

I must hallucinate it, but something like pain runs through Fione's composure. And then, between the swirling dust, she says softly, "I need to know. That's all."

"I've been trying this thing lately called 'getting wiser,'

and I've decided there's a difference between enlightening people and hurting them with knowledge."

"Zera!" Fione's voice is firm. "I beg of you; in the name of the friendship we once had, in the name of the friendship we can still have, *please*—tell me what Varia is having you do."

I startle, deep down in my soul. *The friendship we can still have?*

lies, the hunger sneers. **all of it. lying to manipulate you like she was born to do, lying because she fears you...**

I knit my lips. I burn to tell her the truth—that Varia is planning to force a ceasefire by controlling every valkerax in the Dark Below. But what girl wants to hear her lover is on the verge of effectively becoming the most powerful—and most feared—person in the entire world? Fione's illusion of happiness would be shattered. I *could* tell her the truth. But isn't it better to let her live out her happy dream with Varia for as long as she can, the one she wanted all these five hard years?

Isn't it kinder, in the end, to be cruel?

So I laugh. "I'm sorry. But you're just not convincing enough."

Her mask slips. She blinks a dozen times, wounded. "Our friendship isn't convincing enough?"

"Not particularly." I stroke the spine of another book. "All I did was lie to you for two weeks, and all you did was use me for two weeks to get the information you needed from your uncle."

"We were more than that," Fione insists. "I felt like I could be myself with you."

I nearly smile and agree with her. So did I.

But I'm helping to kill the person she loves the most. And I won't stop. I'll keep doing it—all for my heart.

I really am the monster.

"Oh dear." I smile at Fione. "You fell for my lie just like Lucien did."

She makes a sudden staggering motion, flinging out her hand to catch herself on the nearest bookshelf. The wobbly one. It groans and creaks, and in one horrifying moment I realize exactly what's going to happen.

if you touch her, there will be pain—

The hunger's voice is too late—the bookshelf tips backward and then comes hurtling forward, a frozen Fione poised with deer-wide eyes between it and the ground. My hand catches her shoulder first, and I shove her as hard as I can in the other direction.

The shelf looms, inches away, and I brace myself against the impact, against the command's rising demand that wrenches control from my body, leaving me numb.

You will find a secluded place and stab yourself three times in the stomach with something sharp—

The heavy pain of the shelf never comes. Something else hits me, something much less dense, something warm and that moves on its own. A person. They throw me to the floor, my head hitting the wood and my ears ringing, drowning out the sound of the bookshelf crashing to the ground.

Dark, disheveled hair, dark eyes peering down at me fiercely. *Lucien.*

Dust swirls between us in the aftermath, his face close to mine. A shaft of sun enamels him in white-gold light, one dark eye molten gold, red strands illuminating his otherwise midnight hair. Vaguely, through the command's numbness, I feel his arm around my shoulders, as if he'd tried to cushion my fall.

lovestruck fool.

If I could stay in this moment, looking up at his stern expression, his arms around me, I would. The girl in the other timeline has, many times already, savored his presence in ways I'll never be able to.

I smile to myself and up at him. *She's so very lucky*, I think.

"That's the second time you've pushed me out of the way of imminent danger," I chirp, and I'm sure my eyes are sparkling deviously. "But at least this time I don't have to pretend to be impressed by it."

Faintly, behind him, I see the outline of someone else—someone with milk-blond hair and a hand over her delicate mouth. Lady Tarroux. Were they walking in the library? Gods, I ruined their time together, didn't I? She's frozen, and before Lucien can speak, the real world pierces the moment. The command demands, and I push him off and rise to my feet. I can hear Fione scrabbling to stand up, Lucien, too, and Lady Tarroux calling out after me, but my command-rigid gait is already halfway out of the library. By the time they've gotten their bearings, I'm down the hall, passing the guards who run toward the commotion of the shelf falling.

The command takes me into the sweltering kitchens, snatching a fruit knife from the table smoothly as I go. The chef and her many assistants embroiled in broiling don't even notice it's gone as I slide out of the kitchen and into the darker, cooler wine cellar.

The command is terrifyingly smart, *efficient*. It places me behind a row of barrels, over one of the drains they use to flush out old, bad wine. The blood will not be noticed.

Nothing ruptures this time. The jabs are clean and quick. I gnaw the inside of my mouth, cold sweat beading my forehead and my legs grinding against the floor in some attempt at relieving the agony. Shouting or groaning isn't an option anymore, not when I can't afford to be seen, to be caught. I can't show anyone how I really feel.

Perhaps I never could, in this city.

I wait for the wounds to heal with Varia's magic, the blood seeping into my bodice, over my stomach, and slinking down the already darkly stained drain.

it wasn't worth it, the hunger snarls.

As the cuts mend, I laugh softly. "What would you know...?" I wince as I sit up. "About what people are worth?"

The sound of creaking wood makes me stagger to my groggy feet. A human? Gods forbid a human sees this—Varia will have a time of covering it up. But it's not just any ignorant human. There, from between the barrels, steps Lucien, his handsome face strict and pale, as if he's watching the world end. How much has he seen? The stabbing? The talking to myself?

I clutch my stomach in some vain attempt to hide the massive bloodstain there, my voice nervous as I motion around with my other hand. "And here I thought the place where they hide all the merrymaking liquids would look a little cheerier."

His gaze doesn't waver, his posture stock-still. "Fione said Varia has ordered you to stab yourself if you touch her. Is that true?"

I shrug one shoulder as lightly as I can. "It's for Fione's peace of mind—"

"Is. That. *True?*" he repeats, harder. One last grain of truth, then. One last shard of truth, if he wants it so badly. He's so serious, so drastically different from the irreverent thief who offered me the black rose in the ruined house.

"Yes," I murmur.

He's there one moment and gone the next, and I follow the sound of his boots over the stone, into the kitchen. Where is he going? I pull a discarded apron off the dirty laundry pile, donning it to hide the bloodstains and dashing after him to catch up. He's so far ahead of me I can only hear his footsteps, not see him, but they lead right to the Serpent's Wing, and to the only apartments I'm allowed near—Varia's. He's dismissed the usual royal guards outside the room, the door left slightly ajar.

"—so why would you do it?" Lucien's voice singes the air—not quite a shout but nowhere near low.

"I wanted to make sure Fione felt safe." Varia sighs.

"And what about Zera?" he barks. "What about her safety?"

I hear Varia pause, and then she bursts out laughing incredulously. "Her safety? She's a *Heartless*, Luc. She's safe no matter what."

"She's not safe from pain," he retorts. "She feels it just as much as we do! Why would you inflict that on her?"

"I told you." Varia sighs deeper. "Because I care about Fione."

"And you care nothing for Zera. Because she hurt me. That's it, isn't it? She lied to me, and so you're exacting some kind of sick revenge on her for it."

"She's breaking your heart!" Varia's voice suddenly pitches up, half hysterical. "And I'm watching her do it every day! I'm watching you *let it happen*!"

Lucien is quiet, and that quiet rings throughout the room. The longer it reverberates, the more I feel sick to my stomach.

"She's a *Heartless*, Luc," Varia repeats finally, softer. "She will always value her heart above yours."

truth, the hunger laughs. *truth from the Laughing Daughter, always—*

"You're wrong," Lucien growls. My unheart sinks into the depths of the Twisted Ocean.

no, dear prince, she's so very right—

"Am I?" Varia asks coolly.

"She saved me," he says. "She could have let Gavik kill me in the clearing and taken my heart then and gotten her own for it. But she *defended* me. She killed those men to protect me."

No. No, no, no. The wrongness crawls over me, pinching my skin as it goes. That memory is for me and me alone. That memory is for me to keep, forever, by myself, so that no one else can use it as some false proof that I'm worth saving. Just like he's doing now.

one good deed does not forgive a lifetime of mistakes.

The royal siblings are silent, and then, "When she's human—" Lucien starts, voice ragged.

"When she's finally human, she will *leave,*" Varia interrupts him smoothly. "Because that's what any self-respecting person who's been magically enthralled for years would do. You are trying to hold on to grains of sand, brother."

Her rightness about me hurts worse than the three stabs—far worse, as if they've blown through my flesh and left gaping holes ten times their size. I will leave. I have to leave; there's nothing for me here anymore, just people I've hurt and betrayed and left bleeding trust all over the floor.

But the crown prince of Cavanos has never known when to give up.

"What are you making her do?" he demands.

"Luc, I love you," Varia says, and I can hear the swish of

her stiff skirts as she stands. "But that's between her and me."

There's a beat, and then Lucien says, "Undo her command about Fione."

Varia laughs. "When did you get hard of hearing? Was it while I was away? You know as well as I that Fione is terrified of Heartless, and I'm going to do everything in my power to—"

"Undo her command about Fione," Lucien says again, ironclad. "Or I will tell Father what you are."

I feel my face go cold. He wouldn't…for me? Varia might be his sister, but she's still a witch, the most powerful witch I've ever met. He's making an enemy out of her—his beloved sister—just for my sake! And I won't have it.

I stumble through the doors. "New God's bulging tit!" I brace myself from falling on the back of a couch and blink my eyes at Varia and Lucien. "Oh my! Is that an interrupted argument I smell, or did I step in something on the way back?"

As the d'Malvane siblings glare at each other—Varia sharp and Lucien fiery—I spot another decanter of wine and snatch it up gleefully.

"Princess Varia." I sink onto the couch and tip a little wine into my mouth sloppily. Nothing like a slovenly drunk to defuse a situation. "I'm starting to run out of those dresses you gave me. Any chance I could get some new ones? Stop me if you've heard this one before: covered in diamonds, made of the purest Avellish silk, and all black so I can bleed without panicking the entire palace."

Still the d'Malvane siblings stare at each other, like two street cats posturing defiantly against each other. Finally Lucien breaks off, walking out of the room with clipped strides. He passes just shy of touching me on the couch, and I linger weakly in the clearwater smell of him. I'm almost weak enough not to notice the scent of white mercury following it. Almost. Has he been hanging around polymaths often or something?

When the click of his boots on the marble fades, I look to Varia. "Is everything okay?"

Varia turns back to her makeup boudoir calmly. "You were outside the door. You tell me."

I scoff. "Do you always know where I am?"

"I know where you are the way I know where my own foot is." Varia picks up a wax-pencil, drawing careful lines on her cheeks.

"What, so I can't even play hide-and-seek with you? Boo." I blow hair out of my eyes. "I've suddenly decided magic is cheating."

"You and Gavik have been speaking with each other, haven't you?"

My spine goes stiff. If she can tell where her Heartless are at all times, then there's no use denying it.

"We ran into each other and decided to get tea together," I say.

Varia doesn't respond, applying her makeup with precision and focus, but even through the strokes, I can see the way her hand trembles. She's going to die. She's going to sacrifice herself to stop this war. That's all I can think. There's a grand ball gown on her dressing mannequin, a deep crimson with silver stars embroidered into the bust and skirt. There must be some banquet tonight, but the idea of banquets rings hollowly in what I know she plans to do.

She speaks eventually. "I want you gone as soon as possible, Zera."

the longer you linger, the hunger lilts, *the more he risks.*

The coldness with which she says it is like the deepest winter ice. I shiver, once, and breathe in to steady myself. I laugh and take a swig of wine.

"This is why I've stuck with you, my dearest princess. Partly because I have no conceivable choice in the matter, but mostly because you and I are written on the same page of the same bad book about terrible people."

17

MOONSKEMP

I was wrong.

I know, shocking. Me, of all people on the two gods' green Arathess, *wrong*? But I am—it isn't a banquet Varia is getting ready for tonight. It's Moonskemp.

I'd almost forgotten about Moonskemp with all the valkerax and Lucien feelings and war preparations going on. Moonskemp comes the week after Verdance Day. Verdance Day marks the changing of seasons, but Moonskemp marks the mythological day in which long ago the Old God sundered the too-bright single moon—which allowed no one on Arathess to sleep—into three moons. Vetris, of course, has modified the story, in that they celebrate the New God sundering the moons.

I'd been so busy worrying in the carriage this morning that I hadn't given any thought to the garlands of pale yellow moonflowers being hung about in the city or to the dishes of red-and-blue-dyed sea salt left out on the doorsteps. Usually there's a midnight feast of thin buckwheat pancakes in which fresh summer fruits and vegetables are wrapped, and a roast red-tailed duck to signify a change for the better, but with the war enacted and rationing already in effect, the only people who can conceivably indulge in the traditional duck are, of course, the nobles.

The maids who help Varia dress won't stop chattering about the "dance" tonight, a Moonskemp dance in the grand ballroom. Apparently the nobles are intent on making this last holiday before the breakout of the war a decadent one.

Varia dons her dress—quiet the entire time—and leaves around sunset, dripping clear quartz jewels and leaving me to the empty apartments. I flit my fingers over her boudoir, where a strange bracelet and earrings lie—made entirely of ivory of some kind, carved with flowers and vines. Varia obviously chose the quartz gems over this pair.

Feelings aren't jewelry. But neither are they scars. They aren't fleeting, but neither are they permanent. I think of Y'shennria, of the scars on her neck, and then of her gentle smile at me.

Even scars can fade.

I still feel terrible about being so cruel to Fione, and Lucien's anger toward his sister because of me pushes the guilt down my throat even more. They're going to be at the dance—they have to be, as Firstblood nobles. As an Y'shennria, I suppose I should be there, too. I pull out the last dress left to me from Varia's old things—a soft cream one of flax and lace. I catch my reflection in the boudoir mirror: thin dark circles, thinner lips. What does Lucien see in me? Is there anything in me worth more than standing against his beloved sister? Is there a light in the world strong enough to shine through the dark things I've done?

I don't know. I wish I knew, but these questions just hang, invisible, with no answer.

you will never have an answer. The hunger laughs. ***all you have is me.***

I touch the ivory jewelry, slowly pulling the bracelet on and clipping the earrings in.

Nobles meander the halls on their way to the ballroom, and a familiar gentle voice breaks through the sparse crowd. "Lady Zera!"

I turn to see Lady Tarroux running toward me, out of breath but dazzling in a cool pink dress with a layered skirt, the shape emulating a rosebud just opening. Nobles murmur as she passes—running won't do for a lady. But now more than ever, she doesn't seem to care.

"Lady Tarroux." I make a bow. "You look as if a groundskeeper just picked you fresh from a bush!"

She blushes pink enough to match her dress and offers me her arm. "Thank you. Will you walk with me?"

It's a gesture so reminiscent of Fione, of the way she and I walked in the garden, that it makes my unheart sing with longing. If only she were Fione. If only she knew what I really was, she would be so afraid of me, just like Fione. Softly, I take her arm, and together we make our way to the dance.

"Out of curiosity and admiration," I start, "I've heard running is good for you, but I've also heard the other nobles hate it."

"Oh." She waves her hand dismissively. "I am not overly concerned about what they think."

This time I do laugh, and she blinks.

"Is something funny?"

"Sorry. I just spent two very exhausting weeks training to

be extremely concerned with what the other nobles thought of me, so to hear you put it like that…it's a bit like hearing a celeon say they can't grow hair."

It's Lady Tarroux's turn to laugh. "Forgive me, but that's because you're a Firstblood. How you conduct yourself is your social currency. But mine is, well, *currency*."

It hits me then. "The war! Your father is funding a good amount of it, which means—" I smirk at her. "You're the only one of us in the palace who can do whatever she wants."

She becomes hesitant, lowering her lashes. "I would never do irresponsible things in the eyes of Kavar, but yes. Before the declaration of war, my father was funding Archduke Gavik's white mercury research. So I've never had to concern myself overly much with public opinion."

"Well." I sigh. "That'll make being queen a wee bit harder for you, won't it?"

She stumbles in her pale pink shoes. "Q-Queen? What are you saying, Lady Zera?"

I chuckle and pull her by the arm playfully. "Come on. There's dancing to be done."

The Moonskemp ball is by no means a banquet—there's much less decorum to it. No one is announced as they walk in. The grand ballroom is less extravagant than the banquet hall, smaller and yet just as packed with nobles. Moonskemp forbids the use of any light except for candles, colored with blue and red flames thanks to polymath powders, so the usual brightness of the oil and white mercury lamps is absent. Thousands of ruby- and sapphire-flamed candles drip and flicker on top of columns, tables, and statues, like thousands of miniature moons—the Blue Giant and Red Twins. A balcony stretches out beyond a wall of opened glass doors, the banister lined with melting candles. The ball is in full swing by the time I arrive, the scents of perfumes and wine heavy on the air.

I lean in to whisper in Lady Tarroux's ear. "Y'shennria always taught me nobles do their best to remain reasonably sober during parties, but this is clearly an exception."

She nods, her cinnamon eyes wide. Whether it's the stress of the war or something else, a number of nobles are staggering around, sloshing their drinks and laughing far louder than is acceptable. I watch a noblewoman lean too far over some candles, and she shrieks as blue fire catches to her silk collar. She beats it out with her kerchief, laughing.

King Sref and Queen Kolissa are with Varia and Lucien, of course, glowing with pride and gathered with the ministers and a few other Goldblood nobles near the punch table. There's a very good-looking Goldblood nobleman, and the queen seems intent on getting him and Varia to talk. I can't see Fione, but I'm certain she can't be happy about it. And Varia knows better than to let her displeasure show on her face. She smiles affably, but behind her smiling gaze I see daggers.

I watch my witch converse with her parents, her smile strained. She won't tell them she's a witch, and apparently she won't tell them she's in a relationship with Fione, either. They haven't exactly been quiet about their relationship—the guards ordered to follow Varia around by King Sref no doubt have talked at some point—so I'm sure there are rumors I haven't heard yet. But knowing how much noise was made around the Spring Brides and me for Lucien, I have no doubt the crown princess's match will be enforced and celebrated in equal measure by her parents.

Unless, of course, she surfaces with an army of valkerax. With that much power, no one would dare tell her who to marry ever again.

But she would be dead soon after, wouldn't she? A year? Maybe two? If Varia gets the Bone Tree, any marriage to Fione wouldn't last forever, and that shreds my lungs like broken glass.

Lucien stands beside his parents, dressed in something bloodred, but my eyes skitter over him guiltily. He talks to the king and queen, but he won't engage in small talk with Varia. He won't even look her way. Because of me.

My guilt is short-lived as Lady Tarroux's father—a tall man with a bright blond mustache—waves at her from the refreshment table, and she waves back.

"I'm jealous," I admit. "I'm an orphan, so I can't remember my father."

"Oh." Tarroux's face falls. "I'm sorry."

"It's okay. It happened a long time ago." I smile. "Are you on good terms with him?"

She sighs. "Usually, yes. But lately..." She shoots me a look. "I'm sorry. You probably don't want to hear me complain."

"Are you kidding? I complain all the time to anyone who'll listen. The least I can do is give back. I promise—your secrets are safe with me."

"It's...it's not really a secret," she corrects. "It's just... Father is afraid of the war. He wants to move the two of us back to Helkyris before it fully breaks out."

My unheart sinks. If she moves, my plan to push her closer to Lucien will fail. The tenuous threads that are reaching out to bind them will be cut clean.

"Do you want to move?" I ask.

She shakes her head. "Absolutely not. The temple is here and there are"—her eyes skirt over to Lucien's frame and soften—"people whom I care for."

I laugh a little under my breath. She practically has stars in her eyes over him.

"I hope you stay," I say, nudging her knowingly. "I think you two would make a very cute couple."

The words burn coming out, but some part of me knows they're sincere. I want Lucien to have a peaceful, normal life, with a peaceful, normal girl. Tarroux just stares wistfully at Lucien. Finally, her father motions at her from the refreshment table, and she bids me a shy farewell and trots over.

I let out a hard, small breath. There's a full musical stand in the corner, firehorns and windlutes chiming prettily into the dim room. The song changes to something more upbeat, easing a fraction of the tension in my chest, and suddenly the drunken nobles are clamoring to pair off and crowd the dance floor. I watch them twirl like colorful flowers over the marble, their loveliness eclipsed by the fact the open balcony shows the lights of Vetris below, and the thousands of crowded fires beyond the wall where the army sleeps.

Still, the smoke of the wartime forest razings lingers in the night sky.

"Lady Zera?"

I look up to see none other than Fione. She looks pensive but beautiful in a gray organza gown that makes her blue eyes seem more silver. She isn't standing close to me, though it's closer than usual. But that means little.

I smirk at her and nod over to where Varia's standing. "Ah, parents. They're truly clueless, aren't they? Not that I would know. Or remember. But I imagine they can be."

I don't expect her to speak to me. After all, I can see her fists tightening in her skirts.

"Your jewelry is very pretty," Fione offers finally, her words stiff. "It's valkerax bone, isn't it?"

I blink. "Is it?"

She nods, holding out her valkerax-headed cane so I can see it clearly beyond her sleeves. "You can tell by the way things look dimmer around it. Valkerax bones suck in light. See?"

I look at my bracelet and her ivory cane—I hadn't noticed before with so much light around, but with only the candlelight, it's easy to see the haze of dimness that surrounds the bones, as if the slightest of shadows is hanging over them and only them.

"It's why the darkness in the pipe the valkerax skeleton was in seemed so oppressive," Fione says.

"Oh!" I marvel. "I can always count on you to help things make more sense, Your Grace."

A waiter passes with a tray of fruit, and Fione takes a delicate snowfig and rolls it around in her fingers with all her nervous energy. "Thank you." She clears her throat after a moment. "For saving me, earlier."

"Oh, psh." I wave her off. "Don't worry about it."

"I do. I have been. You knew you would stab yourself for touching me," Fione insists. "But you pushed me out of the way anyway."

for selfish reasons, the hunger snarls. *to assuage your own guilt.*

Fione speaks more quietly. "You said our friendship meant nothing. But then you saved me. So what am I supposed to believe now?"

It's hard to bite my tongue rather than answer her. She

can believe whatever she wants. But her beliefs are better off without me in them.

"Oh! Lord Grat." I bow to the huge noble boy as he passes, his shoulders so broad they barely fit in his coat. He's the perfect distraction. He was part of the duel nearly two weeks earlier, where he'd promised to win it for me, and he looks no less eager to see me now.

"Lady Zera!" He smiles. "I had no idea you were attending."

"Neither did I, until a half ago." I laugh, lacing his arm in mine. "Would you care to dance with me?"

Using Lord Grat as an excuse, I bid farewell to Fione stiffly and head to the dance floor. Lord Grat's body is so big and distinct, it's easy to get us space on the dance floor, so the only pair of feet I have to worry about stepping on are his. The music is so loud that it almost drowns out the hunger. It's like hearing someone shout at me from another room—I know there's hostility, but I can't distinguish the exact words.

I haven't danced since those clumsy lessons in Y'shennria's manor, with Reginall leading me. But my body remembers slightly better than I do, and soon Lord Grat and I are moving smoothly over the floor.

"I know it's rude of me." Lord Grat shoots me a shy smile. "But everyone's been dying to know..." He trails off, waiting for me to approve, and I nod.

"Ask me anything. As long as it's not my measurements. I require compensation in the form of massive amounts of gold for those."

He laughs, twirling me around, and then when I come to face him again, he blurts, "Are you still Prince Lucien's Spring Bride?"

"Straightforwardness, here in the court? Why, Lord Grat, you must be *terribly* curious."

Lord Grat's cheeks tinge red, and he turns me again. There's a break in the dance where we have to switch partners with the people diagonal to us, and it comes up just then, so Lord Grat lets me go. I spiral into the arms of another noble, thankful for the time to think of my answer and ready with a disarming smile for the stranger. Until I look up into his face.

Lucien.

He poses a striking figure in a red-breasted coat, his hair slicked back and his high cheekbones on full intimidating display, like two blades jutting out against the darkness. His posture is perfect, his eyes icy in their stillness. He's beautiful. And I can't bear to tear my gaze away. No matter how much I know I should, no matter how much I know I need to push him away, I can't bring myself to.

Neither of us speaks.

His hand rests on the small of my back, feeling as if it's burning a hole through my dress. Part of me shivers at the feel of our palms pressed together, so close to something like that night at the Hunt in his tent, when he kissed me.

The kiss. Suddenly, it's all I can think about, my memory throbbing. I know those severe, dour lips that frown at me right now. I know the feel of them, how gentle and intoxicating they are.

"I have a confession," Lucien says softly, his voice rumbling into my chest.

I compose my face, make it as unaffected as possible as I look up at him. "There's someone I'd like you to meet, Your Highness. You've seen Lady Ania Tarroux around lately, I'm sure—"

"Do you remember," he interrupts me, "the night we stopped Gavik's raid, and you protected those people?"

Of course I remember. I remember every inch of the terrified screams, of Gavik's cruelty. I snort. "A hollow sacrifice, considering I wouldn't have died if I'd been shot."

He pulls me closer then, our chests flush now in a way totally inappropriate for the court. His mouth is dangerously close and above my ear.

"I am beginning to tire of the way you belittle the selfless things you do."

A sharp pain runs through my unheart.

selfless? The hunger finally breaks through to me, growling. *we are incapable of selflessness.*

"Whether you had died or not, you were willing to take the pain for them," Lucien continues. "For once, Lady Zera, I ask of you: be as merciful with yourself as you are with everyone else."

The dance demands a turn, but it's abruptly and incredibly difficult to breathe deep. Lucien whirls me, and I woodenly move with the motion, returning to his arms.

"Lady Tarroux"—I make my voice strong—"is a lovely girl. I don't usually say anything positive about nobles at all, for the obvious reasons, but she's very different from them. And I know how much you appreciate difference. She's honest, and sweet, and not at all hard to look at—"

"I won't let Varia hurt you anymore," he says, ignoring me bluntly.

"Miss Tarroux has never murdered anyone," I say, soft and yet still loud enough for him to hear it. "She's too upfront to ever lie to you. And best of all, I'm fairly certain she'd never try to kill you and take your heart for her own selfish needs—"

We stop. In the middle of the whirling ballroom, every

color imaginable flitting by us, he tilts his head, his sharp jawline illuminated by the candlelight. I know what's coming, as a hunting hound knows a foxhole, as the rooster knows the sun is coming, as a fish knows the tides. Some deep, old part of me—older than nineteen years by far—knows he is going to kiss me.

Lightning draws our bodies together—invisible fingers of lightning entwining around each other and locking us in place, hips to hips, chest to chest. The warmth of his lips, the soft insistence of his hands as they hold my waist—I can feel a strange fever building in me as his lips press to mine. He moves to my ear, the hollow beneath it, and kisses it gently, and I know then this is not the kiss from the Hunt. That kiss was a moon, longing and sweet. This kiss is the sun, blazing hot and brighter than the apex of sunrise, prickling my skin with sweat, nothing sweet or subtle about it. The heat wave nearly buckles my knees, and I hold fast to his coat to keep standing.

Half of me is screaming to pull away—this sunfire kiss will keep him running after me, not moving on. Half of me wants nothing more than to stay here, in this moment, embraced and wanted, the doubt and loneliness in my soul burning away.

He parts from me first, his dark eyes piercing down at me. "I will not kiss you a third time, Lady Zera, without you kissing me back. My pride will not allow it."

A bittersweet taste lingers in my mouth, and the heated curtain lifts from my body. I can see—out of the corners of my eyes—people watching. Fione, Varia, Lady Tarroux, the furious king and shocked queen.

He isn't giving up. Godsdamn him, he isn't giving *up*! Have I not been obvious enough? What will it take for him to realize he's better off without me? He is a prince; I am a Heartless. He has the world waiting for him, and I have only my regrets waiting for me. I will only pull him down.

It dawns on me slowly—I know exactly what I have to do.

unless you show him the darkness, he will never understand, he will never fear, he will never run.

The sound of the slap reverberating is the only thing that makes me realize I've actually done it. The numbness in my hand stings, and I clutch it. Lucien's head rotates slowly back to me, the red handprint bright against his cheek, but his dark eyes gleam brighter than ever in the candlelight. His expression is set, unmoving.

It's then I realize the windlutes and firehorns have stopped playing. The dance floor has stopped moving, the nobles staring in half-drunk horror at Lucien's face. The whole of the ballroom is looking our way, but I don't stop to see any expressions. My feet, wiser and less flustered than I, take me out of the grand ballroom as fast as they can.

Varia's room is, in some sick way, becoming the only safe place for me in the palace. My hands are shaking wildly as I walk in, shed the valkerax-bone jewelry, and throw it aside.

Anger simmers beneath my surface. What kind of person kisses someone who's lied to them and murdered people in front of their very eyes? What about me is so worth ignoring these things?

For once, Lady Zera, I ask of you: be as merciful with yourself as you are with everyone else.

"Shut up!" I snarl at the echo. "Shut up, *shut up!*"

who does he think he is, telling us who we are? telling us what to think of ourselves? arrogant!

I can feel my teeth starting to grow long and sharp and hear my breath as panting, blood rushing through my ears. The urge to reach for the wine decanter hits me, but I pull myself away. That won't help. It's never really helped. I can feel some horrific pain welling up in my chest, building like a bubble of gas below a marsh, pressure crushing my lungs. The hunger pounces on it as an opportunity.

he is ruining his life with his sister because of you. he is ruining his future because of you.

I collapse on the couch, my head in my hands. The hunger's words are crystal clarity—pure, logical, and undeniable. There's a sudden knock at the doors that has me standing. One of the guards comes in, holding a piece of parchment in his hand.

"Ah, pardon me, milady, I thought Her Highness had returned as well," he says. "She's received a letter marked extremely urgent."

An urgent message? Something so normal and routine breaks through my spiraling mind.

"I can bring it to her," I say.

"Thank you, milady." The guard bows and hands me the parchment. I take it, and he sees himself out. When I'm sure he's gone, I flip the parchment over—it's a letter with no wax seal. Not from another noble, then. Curiosity is a welcome distraction, and so I open the letter carefully.

The handwriting is instantly recognizable—I see it every day. Or the shadows of it, at least. Yorl's. It's thin and small, every letter perfect.

Varia, it reads. *There's been a breach near the dog's*

kennel. *Your presence is required.*

The dog—he means Evlorasin, obviously. But what kind of breach? I thought Yorl had the valkerax contained? There's another letter within that letter—the watertell must've sent both of them, one after the other in quick succession.

The next one reads simply: *The dog has escaped. Bring help.*

My eyes bug out. Escaped? Evlorasin has *escaped*?

My insides drop with a sickening velocity. Is it digging below the city even now? It could collapse the city in on itself. People could die. And every chance of getting my heart back resides with Evlorasin. If it escapes back to the Dark Below...my deal with Varia won't be called off, but who knows how long it'll be before she finds another valkerax for me to teach?

At the same time, part of me thinks, quietly, that it would be better if Evlorasin did escape. If Varia never finds the Bone Tree and never dies for it.

But I know she'll never stop. Letting Evlorasin escape now would only slow her down.

I bolt up from the couch. *Bring help,* the letter said. Apparently Yorl thinks one witch won't be enough. Which means one Heartless won't be enough, either. Varia is entrenched with her father and mother—pulling her away from the queen and king discreetly won't be easy, especially considering I slapped the prince. And by the time I bring her the letter and she manages to get away from them, Evlorasin could already be gone for good.

I need someone who can help, and fast.

There's only one other person in the city who knows valkerax better than Varia does, better than Yorl even, and certainly better than I do.

I lunge out of the door and look at the guards. "Where's Malachite?"

"The prince's guard said he would be patrolling outside the Moonskemp party, milady."

I dash back to the last place I want to be, hiking my skirts up to run. Sure enough, I find Malachite walking outside the ballroom with his usual lazily striding alertness.

When he sees me running toward him, he narrows his bloodred eyes. "Not you. Not tonight."

"Me," I assert. "Definitely tonight. I need your help. And quickly."

His white brows knit. "Why would I help you? You just slapped Luc; I could hear it all the way out here, for spirit's sake."

"You're the only one I can think of who can stop a valkerax."

Malachite's expression detonates, his anger blown to smithereens by shock. "A valkerax? Lying once spectacularly wasn't enough for you?"

There's no time to argue with him. "There's a valkerax below this city. Are you going to help me stop it or not?"

There's a long beat of silence. Malachite frowns. "You're serious?"

"Not often. But right now? Yes."

The beneather darts his eyes over to the dim candlelit party. He looks back to me and nods. "Fine. But if this is some trick, I'm arresting you."

"Yes, yes, you're very important." I grab his cool, marble-white hand and pull him down the hall, out of the palace, and into a carriage. I pound on the carriage roof the whole way, demanding the driver go faster, and thankfully he obliges, the wheels screeching over the cobblestones and the cobblestones themselves bouncing Malachite and me violently around.

"A valkerax was kept beneath South Gate," I shakily admit to Malachite, the bumpiness of the ride making my teeth bite my tongue. It heals too quickly to be of consequence. "But it's escaped. We have to get it back."

"Dark Below," he swears, voice chopped by the vibrations. "Now's probably not the best time to admit I never completed my culling practice, then?"

"It's fine—you did it, at least, right?"

"Enough to tell the mane from the tail," he asserts.

"You're the direst threat in the city I can think of besides myself," I say. "It'll be fine. It has to be fine." He scoffs, and I ask, "What? What is it?"

"You've got so much faith in me, and none in Luc."

Lucien. Godsdamnit—he's going to know there's a valkerax below the city once Malachite helps me. His best friend will surely tell him. They'll inevitably start to suspect what I'm doing for Varia involves the valkerax, and with Fione's talent for acquiring information—and all of Gavik's research at her fingertips—they'll certainly find out she wants the Bone Tree, and what that means.

But no, it doesn't matter right now. The first priority is to stop Evlorasin running before it hurts anyone, no matter who learns of its existence.

South Gate comes into view sooner than I ever thought possible, and I leap out of the carriage before it even begins to slow down alongside the curb. Malachite tumbles out after me, regaining his footing far faster. I point to the door in the high white wall, and together we dash for it. The guards are still here, but they look rattled, their gazes needling out from beneath their helmets, and even when I give the password, they don't relax a single inch. Yorl is waiting for us inside by the door down to the arena, his claws clicking over the grating as he paces anxiously, his tail thrashing. He glances up when he hears us coming, his green eyes going from frantic and searching to flat and annoyed.

"Where is Varia?" he snaps.

"Held up." I waste no time offering my hand to Malachite. "This is Malachite. Where did Evlorasin run off to?"

Yorl looks Malachite up and down, and, obviously realizing he's a beneather, the displeased thrash of his tail dies down slightly. But only slightly. Malachite just gives Yorl a cheeky wink as the celeon stares at him, and I press past the two boys and head for the door.

"Are you going to make a lady capture an escaped valkerax all by herself?" I call. Yorl and Malachite follow quickly and easily, their dark-vision impeccable. Yorl offers me his hand, and I take it. I can practically feel Malachite staring at it.

"Gave up on your friends up above and made some down here in the dark, huh?" the beneather scoffs. I flinch, my hand squeezing Yorl's harder.

Surprisingly, the celeon snarls. "You talk exceedingly much for one whose job is only to guard."

"And you use too many big words for somebody who smells like cat piss," Malachite fires back.

"You can be nasty to each other when the valkerax is secure. Yorl," I insist, "what happened? How did it get out? I thought you had this place under control?"

"I did," Yorl argues. "But a few minutes ago, there was a localized quake—it cracked all the beneather runes on the walls of the arena."

Malachite whistles. "And cracked runes can't hold a

valkerax in, or out, anymore."

Yorl presses on. "The valkerax sensed a fissure made by the quake behind the arena wall and burst through."

"Sounds like your security stinks," Malachite drawls. "I offer my consultations for free, you know."

"I checked with the Crimson Lady." Yorl ignores him with a snarl in his voice. "And the readings confirm it—there was suspicious magical activity the very moment before the tremor struck."

"A witch?" I ask.

I feel Yorl nod next to me. "I assumed as much the moment I went to the surface. The quake was enough to fracture only the arena walls, and it touched none of the city. If I was to guess, whoever cast the spell was attempting to flush us out knowing roughly where we are, but knowing nothing about what's actually down here."

"So it wasn't Varia?"

Yorl answers my question with silence, and then, "No."

"Something wrong, celeon?" Malachite chirps. "You sound suspicious."

"It's just…" Yorl exhales. "The data on the spell we collected from the Crimson Lady—it wasn't intentional."

"What are you talking about?" I frown.

"Magic has a pattern," Yorl says. "And that pattern can be detected by the Crimson Lady. I've seen many such patterns. But this one wasn't tight. It wasn't well-constructed. It's almost as if it was…unintentionally done. Instinctually. Fueled by emotion, not by concentration."

"So your rogue witch can fly off the handle," Malachite scoffs. "So what? We still have to clean up their mess."

Reminded of the immediate valkerax emergency once more, we take the steps as fast as possible, but about halfway down, we hear the clash of armor and the horrible cacophony of dozens of celeon roaring in pain and anger.

The deep, loud breathing—I notice chillingly—is gone.

Yorl starts walking faster, dragging me along by the hand with his urgency. We reach the bottom of the stairs, and I'm shocked to see actual oil lanterns lit along the walls. The lights illuminate something far more sinister—blood smearing in vivid crimson banners for far longer than blood has any right to. The smell of burned fur singes the air, blackened scorch marks enveloping what looks like the smoldering skeletons of celeon. My stomach revolts, and I grip the hilt of my father's sword hard enough to bite skin.

Malachite's irritated expression instantly dissolves as he turns to Yorl. "How many have we lost already?"

"Six." Yorl's flinch is so well disguised by his picking up of a nearby lantern that I almost don't see it. A true professional—or a young man barely managing to hold on to his failure. He hands it to me. "The breach is obvious. I want you two to follow it and stop that thing."

He pulls a heavy brass weapon off his back, handing it to me. It's a spring-loaded crossbow of some sort, loaded not with bolts but with glass phials that glimmer with a clear substance, their tips ending in sharp needles.

"Get these shots in as close to the throat as you can. Not the chest or the spine—the bone is too thick there. The *throat*. Inside, if you can somehow manage it, is the most effective. Five should be enough to knock it out cold."

I nod and turn to see Malachite already jogging toward the massive arena door, raised and waiting. I start to follow after him when I feel claws nip at my hand. Yorl holds me back, the pupils of his green eyes slit by the bright lamplight. There's something soft in his features, a new and strange thing coming from the cold polymath.

"Please," he pleads. "Don't let anyone else die."

I see myself in him, standing there, pale and reflected in his orb-like eyes. I see the girl who can't bear to think of fourteen men, or any more dead because of her. The guilt has him. But it's not his fault—how could wanting to make his beloved grandfather's name known be his fault? How could he be expected to keep perfect control over one of the most ruthless, powerful beasts in the world?

I squeeze his paw and smile reassuringly at him. "I'll be only a sec, honey. Get my tea ready."

I sprint to catch up to Malachite, seeing the arena with clear vision for the first time: deep scratch marks littering the floor, old bloodstains and decaying animal carcasses scattered around and piled high. Dull, chipped teeth long shed and great clumps of stringy ivory fur. The localized quake Yorl talked about is clear on the walls—little fissures pulling the iron apart, insinuating themselves between the carved words of familiar beneather runes and rendering them inert. There are impact craters in the walls of the arena from the valkerax's thrashing, so deep I can see where the very earth of the ceiling strained to stay together.

How could I be expected to keep perfect control over a relentless, bloodthirsty hunger that preyed on my every weakness? That knew me better than I knew myself?

you are only human, after all, the hunger taunts, an odd edge of pity to its voice.

"Only human, after all," I whisper.

The breach yawns open before me—bent metal rimming a crevice sundering deeply and darkly into the earth. I hold my lantern high and press into it. It's absurd, to only realize certain things much later than they need to be realized. I thought I had half a brain. I thought I knew things, the *important* things. But there are bits and pieces of thought that fall from life, and we scoop them up and desperately try to make a whole picture of them, sometimes long before we're ready to see what that picture is.

Pushing into the dark tunnel, I slide the last piece into its slot. Yorl is not the valkerax. And now, for the very first time in my Heartless life, I start to think, solidly and wholly and clearly:

I am not the hunger.

18

THE WYRM
AND THE
BENETHAR

When I finally catch up with Malachite, he's so far down the tunnel, I can smell the stale age of the dust in the air. I'm panting with the effort of so much running and so little oxygen, but the beneather is making no noise at all, crouched low even though the scar the valkerax made is wide and tall enough to accommodate him.

"So," I start breezily. "Got any tips? You know, from your entire culture of professional valkerax killing?"

For a moment, I don't think he's heard me, and then he speaks, low and hoarse. "If you feel the air grow hot, you're about to die."

"Good." I draw Father's sword, my hand only mildly shaking. "I was hoping you'd say something sweet and sultry like that."

He doesn't laugh. He doesn't so much as look back at me. But I can see his eyes glowing, the red irises spilling a bloody haze of light in the otherwise utter pitch-black in front of him.

"I-I thought you said your eyes glowed only on full moons?"

"Or if we catch the scent of valkerax," he manages, every word sounding labored, as if he's trying to keep his mind together in one place. He suddenly holds up a pale hand, and I freeze. "The light," he demands. "Put it out."

I scrabble with the oil lamp, extinguishing the tiny flame. Instantly we're plunged into perfect darkness. Malachite's breathing is suddenly close to my ear.

"There should be eleven others of my kind standing here with me," he says. "But all I've got is you."

"I'll do whatever you want."

He's silent.

"I'll put on a funny hat and dance a godsdamned Helkyris waltz in its mouth if you need me to," I insist. "Anything. Anything at all. But we have to get Evlorasin back."

"You've said that word before." Malachite's voice frowns. "Is that its true name?"

I curse myself. "Look—just tell me what to do. I'll do it. I'm immortal. Whatever you need, I can *do it*."

"You've been talking to it," he muses. "That's the only way you'd know its name. Why? They're madder than a drunk old man on New God's Night. They speak only non—"

"We just need to find it." I make my voice hard. "Now."

To my relief, Malachite backs off with the questioning and darts ahead of me. The ground of the hastily dug tunnel isn't level, but even when I skid and fall on the rock and dirt, I jump to my feet again. Warm blood on my gravel-skinned knees and stone-cut shins lasts only a second as Varia's magic heals me. The pain is nothing.

we've been through far worse, the hunger slithers loudly. *we* are *far worse.*

"You," I quietly correct it, gripping Father's rusted sword tighter to my side. "*You* are far worse."

"We've got visitors ahead," Malachite warns me. Sure enough, in a few spans, panting and groaning that isn't mine or Malachite's resounds from up the tunnel. I can't see them, but they sound like celeon. I hear Malachite speaking with them lowly, and situate myself against the tunnel wall until his voice makes an appearance in my ear again.

"Ten of them and two of us are much better odds."

"Normally I'd agree with you, but we should send them back." I frown and turn the lamp back on. "They've been through enough already—"

"With every beneather bone in my body, I can tell you right now that you and I alone will not be enough to retake this valkerax. It'll ignore us completely. We need sufficient body heat to draw it in, tempt its predatory instinct."

I bristle. "These guards aren't toys, Malachite—"

"And they're not children to be coddled, either," he fires back. "Everyone here has made their own choices. Do you want it to run? Or do you want to capture it?" He throws his hand up. "You make the decision—I'm just the muscle. I'm telling you how it is; two people won't be enough to make it stop running. And at the rate it's digging..."

He trails off. Father's sword suddenly feels ice-cold in my hands, my eyes skittering over the furred faces of the apprehensive celeon in the tunnel. They're royal guards. They serve the royal family unerringly, until they die. Varia ordered them here, to guard the valkerax. I can feel the strings attaching my hopes to my heart growing thin, fragile, unsteadier the farther away Evlorasin digs. Mother's face is a blur, but it had been so clear. So *perfectly* clear, better than a painting.

I clench my fist and look back at Malachite. "The moment I tell you to run, you take them and *run*."

He rolls his eyes. "And of course leave you behind, right?"

"I'll make it out somehow." I change the subject quickly. "What did you talk about with them back there?"

Malachite pauses for a moment, and I just faintly see his long, bladelike ears twitching in the light emanating from his bloodred eyes. "They were saying the valkerax dug in a bunch of different directions trying to find a way out, so all the tunnels look the same. They lost the trail. The scent of Vetris's wastewater system is strong right here. It cuts everything off. But I've got better hearing than a celeon. It's far to the west. It's digging, and injured."

I think back to the six celeon bodies—with their strength, their sacrifice, there's a good chance they *did* injure Evlorasin. Malachite orders the celeon to file out in front of us, quietly, and we move as one stealthy group, my human gait the loudest against the stone by far.

"My fellow guards." Malachite's voice is thin and yet audible in all the quiet. "You'll harass the thing. Strike any lanterns you might have, any torches—its eyes don't do well with bright light. Stab between the webbing of its feet if you can—it's a weak spot. I'll try to get on its back in the confusion and go for its neck."

A murmur of assent goes around the celeon group, and they ready their lanterns and halberds.

"We need it alive!" I hiss up ahead to the beneather. Malachite's chuckle is like his old self, before he knew of my betrayal—golden and cheeky.

"And I clearly need a raise. But here we are."

"Mal—"

"If you think a few neck stabs will kill it, then I'm the

spiritsdamn Emperor of Pendron." He sighs. "I'm aware killing Varia's pet would be the best way to book myself a caravan ticket back to Pala Amna and away from Lucien. So relax."

I can't relax. Not when Evlorasin is getting farther and farther away from me. Not when my heart is tied flush with the valkerax's very fate.

"So what do *I* do?" I ask. "Stand there and look tasty?"

"Yorl said to get those shots as close to the throat as possible, right?" Malachite tilts his head. "Inside it? If I can create an opening, you should go for it."

A cold sweat beads my neck, and it starts to run in rivulets when I pick up the sound of deep, sonorous, fragmented breathing. I'd know that sound anywhere—Evlorasin. From the complete darkness ahead that we march into, a pinprick of orange light starts to grow, and a crackling wave of heat evaporates my sweat in a flash.

The air is growing hot. But that means—

Malachite turns, eyes a blazing red, and shouts at the top of his lungs, "Get down!"

The celeon all scrabble backward in a frenzy, pushing past me and down the tunnel's slope as the smell of burning air gets stronger. The celeon hit the ground, curling around themselves in a protective stance. The telltale paper-rip noise of the fire as it tears through the tunnel quickly turns deafening. I throw myself to the ground before the cluster of celeon, some panic-numbed part of my brain knowing I could take the brunt and soften it for everyone behind me, but I feel someone slam themselves down beside me and pull me into them, cradling my body within theirs.

The fire screams over us as a jagged plume, bright yellow and blazing so hot in the middle, it appears white. The heat scrapes against our skin—singeing what feels like the very flesh off my face—and yet it's gone in an instant. I hear the celeon scrabbling to their feet, and then a voice echoes in my ear.

"As if I'd let you take all the glory."

I roll over to see Malachite sitting up, brushing the gravel off his chainmail. He...*protected* me?

He straightens and calls to the celeon, "Stand and take up your arms; the valkerax is here!"

I leap to my feet, and the celeon press in around me, drawing their swords and holding their halberds aloft. All of us stare at the tunnel where the fire came from, the tension making the musty air suffocatingly thick. I'd seen Evlorasin's jaws, and the image of them haunts me now—that mouth could come barreling down the tunnel at any moment, open wide, the spiraling teeth ready to consume us all. There'd be barely any room to run or maneuver.

The tight knot of mortals and their scared breaths are dwarfed by Evlorasin's broken, thunderous breathing, and a sound I recognize starts making itself known—the sound of valkerax claws scrabbling frantically over stone and dirt.

Out of the blackness, Evlorasin comes.

It's just a white blur at first, but with every blink of mine, it gets rapidly bigger. The celeon growl, their hackles rising as it approaches at a breakneck speed. The lantern light catches the feathered mane flaring around its head, taking up the entire tunnel's width. Evlorasin's six white eyes catch the light, one of them badly bleeding, but its wounds don't deter its speed as it scratches madly for us. Its mouth is open, its long spiral of shin-long teeth gleaming.

Malachite pulls his broadsword from his back and raises it high, waiting unflinchingly. The thought of the mortal celeon behind me has me walking forward, too, the heavy brass crossbow raised in my arms.

I can't understand Evlorasin's words because I haven't drunk the serum, but I can hear its voice, screeching and hissing in equal measure as it barrels closer. I pray for it to stop, to the Old and New God to listen for once. Nervously, I check Yorl's crossbow. Even though it's not a weapon I'm familiar with, I think I can handle—

My finger catches on the trigger on the bottom, and a single vial shoots out, shattering on the stone floor.

"Vachiayis!" I spit the swear. I have only five of those! Yorl said it would take all five—

"Tragya!" Malachite shouts next to me, starting forward and pointing his hefty blade at Evlorasin with one spidery hand.

"What?" I can't tear my eyes away from the approaching valkerax, but I can see him grin out of the corner of my eye.

"It's a swear beneathers use when they drop something expensive. It means *'damn the ground.'* Much more fitting than 'ox balls' in this case, don't you think?"

He's so calm, even here. *Especially* here. Our back-and-forth eases just a fraction of my nerves; the valkerax is so close now we can smell its rotting breath, the strength of it vibrating the dirt free from the ceiling in great clumps. We stare down death, flickering in and out of oil lamplight. It's huge. I knew it was huge this whole time, but seeing it now, in the light...it's so incredibly enormous, it feels like ten times a giant. It's the color of old ivory laced with blood. And it's not going to stop.

In this moment, Evlorasin is the thing that brought the world to its knees a thousand years ago.

But in this moment, Malachite is the thing that has

hunted Evlorasin for a thousand years.

Malachite pushes me out of the way and makes a great leap at the approaching valkerax, sinking his blade into Evlorasin's open mouth. Evlorasin rears its upper half, suddenly in pain, white feathers from its mane flying, the momentum throwing the rest of its long body forward. I barely manage to avoid the thick coils of white muscle as they fling past me. A flood of white scales crash into the celeon guards, who thankfully all have the incredible reflexes to dodge in quick measure. Faster than any human, they spread out in the seemingly impossibly small tunnel and descend on the valkerax, jousting with its flailing body parts before I'm even on my feet again.

I spot Malachite perched atop Evlorasin's back, huge double-handed swings of his broadsword biting into the valkerax's thickly armored spine. I aim down the sights of the crossbow, right at Evlorasin's rearing throat as it tries to get Malachite off, but suddenly I feel the air grow hot again, and I manage to get behind Evlorasin's mouth just as the valkerax belches forth another gout of white-hot flame, scorching the walls I was standing in front of not moments ago to ash and cinder. The heat has nowhere to run, baking into the dirt, and I watch the dry walls collapse in on themselves, completely burying one, two—too many celeon.

"Move!" I shout at a celeon close to me, but she's too busy stabbing at Evlorasin's feet to see the earth behind her shift, surge forward, and bury her whole.

It hits me then; Evlorasin is not trapped in here with us—we're trapped in here with it.

This tunnel is far weaker than it looks. The earth displaced in the valkerax's thrashing will kill us before its fangs do. Malachite sees that, too—our eyes meet in an impossibly quick moment. That one lapse in concentration is all it takes, and Evlorasin slams its back into the dirt, Malachite peeled off like a fly. He hits the ground hard and doesn't move, and it feels like all my blood drains out through my feet at once.

I bolt for him, but as if it's slowed time on a sandclock, Evlorasin raises its massive paw, claws hanging sharp, and hovers just above Malachite before slamming down on him.

I grip Father's sword, knowing it's not meant to be thrown, knowing it's all I have left of him, and give a mighty heave, the blade spiraling over itself. My aim is only half true, the blade sticking into Evlorasin's knuckle, but it's enough. It's *enough*, and the valkerax makes an ear-splitting shriek, recoiling away from Malachite. The beneather is still one moment and then stumbling to his feet the next. He blearily squints at me, the red glow thinned, and then he regains himself.

"The mouth!" His shout pierces, simple and straightforward and leaving me to make guesses. He turns on his heel, broadsword in hand, and I understand only when he draws Evlorasin's attention by stabbing it in the chest. The metal of his blade barely sinks beyond the scales, but it sticks there, irritating, and the valkerax does a complete turn on him instantly and roars, its mane bursting forward around its face in its full intimidating, pearly-white spectacle of a million feathers. The beneather rams himself, shoulder first, into the mouth of the valkerax, the countless razor teeth stopped by his sheer strength. I've held that same mouth open, once, as best I could, with all my desperate hunger-strength, and I could barely hold it aloft a few inches.

Malachite holds it above his head, fully open.

"Now!" he bellows at me, every muscle in his wiry body

beating out against his paper skin.

I'm not Fione. I can't make a shot with any accuracy, especially not at a target that's writhing in incredible pain, and Malachite knows that. He holds open the valkerax's mouth, the soft pink throat lining ripe just beyond him, below him. But if I miss—

He's counting on me not to miss.

He's *trusting* me.

Evlorasin's five white eyes flicker to me, the lower left one bloodied and burst, and in that moment it's never been clearer to me that we are chained by the same thing.

Hunger.

I aim the crossbow and fire, four times, as fast as my finger will pull the trigger. One of them grazes Malachite's ear, lodging in the valkerax's gums, but the second, third, and fourth all land squarely down its throat, disappearing into the salivating darkness.

Malachite's ears prick at the fourth shot, and he collapses backward, his bite-pierced hand and both his feet bleeding through his steel boots and gauntlets. Evlorasin gives a gasp, its thrashing suddenly taking on a random, twitching quality, spasms running through its body as Yorl's powerful concoctions make themselves known. I run to Malachite's side, but he just ruffles my hair with his unbloody hand, laughing breathlessly.

"You did it. You actually did it, you little whelp!"

I grin back. It feels good coming from him, but it doesn't last long—he catches himself, remembering who I am and where we are, and his laughter fades. The two of us watch warily as Evlorasin's panting slows. I lost one of the vials, but thankfully, just four seems to be affecting it. Those five huge white eyes droop, rolling back into its skull and showing the black of its sclera. Finally, *finally,* its gargantuan body collapses to the ground, bleeding softly from its wounds, its velvet nose at Malachite's feet.

The beneather, looking too exhausted to move, suddenly sits up with a perfect posture, knees beneath him, and makes a gesture with both his hands—reverent, careful, precise.

"Af-balfera, ansenme kei-inora," he says.

We dig out the royal guards buried—a few legs broken but none of them dead, and I thank the gods with promises of excessive spiritual kisses—and bandage their injuries. Malachite won't let me bandage his, instead doing the dressing himself. Eventually we help the injured make it down the tunnel, two celeon leaning on Malachite and one on me.

"What was that thing you said?" I ask between breaks. "In beneather?"

He shrugs lightly, his eyes no longer glowing red. "It's something the culling leaders customarily say to the valkerax that get away—the valkerax they can't kill."

"What does it mean?"

He breathes in. *"'The next time we meet will be a happier reunion.'"*

19

THE MEMORY OF A BLADE

Before we leave the unconscious Evlorasin in the tunnel for Yorl and his celeon to retrieve, I go to the valkerax's foot and pull out Father's sword.

It's broken.

The blade is warped back on itself, bent nearly flat and in half with the force of Evlorasin's stamping, and when I pull, the rusted metal finally gives out. I hold the cracked hilt in my hand, the oil lamplight dancing on the sharp edges of the dagger end that is now the blade. It hurts to see it so broken after everything I did to keep it well—the sharpening, the constant whetting. It was there for me when I felt terrible in court; it was an anchor among all the sadness in Nightsinger's woods. I fought Crav so many wonderful times with it, our laughter ringing in the forest. I scared off so many huntsmen with it, and I dueled Lucien with it.

Even if I have no memories of Father attached to it, I've made so many memories of my own, wrapping them around the hilt like ribbon. My old memories are in this sword, but new ones are wound about it, too. In a way, holding it now feels like seeing my heart again. My heart is full of old memories. But in my unheart, in the void in my chest, I've collected so many new ones—of Lucien, of Malachite and Fione, of Vetris and the whole new world I've been thrust into.

"That…" Malachite hobbles up to me. "That was your pa's sword, wasn't it?"

"Don't worry about it." I shuffle the hilt away and wipe my tears off my cheeks. He doesn't say anything, and I'm thankful for it.

Yorl is so incredibly relieved to see us and the other celeon alive as we come out of the breach. He doesn't show it, his green eyes placid behind his glasses, but after nearly a week with him, I can tell.

"Honey!" I smirk at him, flinging my arms out and approaching him with an insistent hug and a kiss on the cheek. "You didn't have to wait up for me."

This snaps Yorl out of his relief, and he pushes me off while glaring mightily, his whiskers twitching. "Who ever said I was worried? I knew you'd all get the job done. That's why Varia pays you."

"Wait a minute, you guys get *paid* for this?" Malachite feigns shock and looks back at the celeon, and a rumble of laughter runs through even the injured ones.

"I'll have the polymaths repair the tear and a new team bring the valkerax back here," Yorl says, his expression falling. "And we will bury our fallen well."

I know that expression. I put my hand on his shoulder. "Hey, it wasn't your fault—"

He pushes me off abruptly. "I'll say this only once, Zera, so listen carefully." He clears his throat, starting and stopping a few times. "Thank you. For your help."

"That's what friends do." I pause. "You've had friends before, right?"

"Of course I have," he snaps, but it's too quick, and I laugh, though I peter off quickly.

"So a witch did all the disrupting tonight? An emotional one?"

Yorl nods. "Undoubtedly. A strong one, too, if the ability to insulate the city from the quake subconsciously is any indication. I'd check with Varia's contacts in the Crimson Lady and pore over the data with them, but they despise me."

"Too smart for them, are you?" Malachite chirps.

"Too *celeon*." Yorl says it like it's been used as an insult against him more than once.

"Ah," Malachite nods. "I know that feeling."

"They might hold disdain for me, but they are not altogether hopeless at their jobs. With any luck, they'll be able to pinpoint where the magic came from in a few days' time. In the meantime, you—" He looks to me, then to Malachite. "You can take a day off while I settle everything back in its proper place."

I get the message to not spill any details of what we're doing down here in front of the prince's bodyguard, but I can feel Malachite's red eyes boring into the both of us. Malachite and I bid Yorl goodbye, leaving him to bandage his fellows more properly, and start up the steps. We walk slowly in the ashes of South Gate, Malachite's wounds still affecting his gait, though his hands are positioned casually behind his head.

"I don't know why he keeps trying," Malachite admits up at the stars. "If I were him, I would've dumped you the second you tried to kill me."

He. Lucien. I laugh, half despairing. The memory of the kiss tonight sends little flames licking at the underside of my belly, but I quash them angrily. "Yeah. I would've, too."

"The king's not too happy about it," Malachite continues. "Back when Varia told him you were Heartless, he wanted to make some kinda formal announcement right away that you weren't Lucien's Spring Bride anymore, but Luc refused. He threw a fit, ruined the whole 'happy family reunion' and everything."

I kick a pile of wood ash, black flaking away on the wind. "The last thing I want is for him to lose family over me. For him to lose anything over me."

"You know," Malachite says after a beat, "I'm actually inclined to believe you—you, the greatest con man Vetris has ever seen—this *one* time."

"That's a very impressive-sounding title for only having put on a few dresses and talking about potatoes," I grumble. This ekes a laugh from him.

We trudge through the char and back to the more untouched streets, where people and carriages roam. The Red Twins are high in the sky, both of them crescent slits of rust. It's almost curfew, which went into effect the same day the war was declared, and so people are hurrying to get home. A group of lawguards shouts at us to hurry home, too, but Malachite holds up one bloodied hand. There can't be too many beneathers in Vetris who aren't the prince's bodyguards, and sure enough, they leave us alone after that.

"How do I get him to move on?" I ask after we cross the bridge to the noble quarter. "He won't give up."

"That's the problem with Luc. He's as stubborn as a hunk of granite. He never gave up on Varia, either—reading her old papers all the time, chasing after that Tree she kept mentioning. Not until you came along. You helped."

"Did I?" I whisper. "It feels like all I did was hurt."

"Listen." Malachite sighs. "I'm not the best at love. I had it once, when I was a half-sentient grub in the Dark Below, with some kid who ran around the mosspig pens with me. We rolled in the clay a lot. It wasn't very romantic." I catch his eye, and he clears his throat. "Just...do you like him?"

"*Yes,*" the hunger and I answer instantly as one, and it fades, leaving me to defend myself. "I like him. But someone returning that affection, when I'm like this"—I motion down to my dirty clothes, to my empty chest, to the murderer, to all of me—"It's not fair to him. Or to me."

Malachite laughs again, the most I've heard from him since the reveal of my betrayal. "Love isn't fair at all, *ever.*"

"You've hurt people to protect him," I press. "Killed people to protect him."

Malachite nods.

"Then you know what it's like," I say. "What if someone who'd never killed wanted to love you? Someone who doesn't know what it's like to wake up in the middle of the night in cold sweats? Someone who doesn't know what it means to make a mistake they can never take back?" I breathe in, looking up at the stars. "Lucien deserves someone who doesn't know these things. Someone like him. Innocent."

The beneather is quiet, his eyes shining under the gentle caress of the moonlight.

"What if you were made for war," I continue, hot tears annoying the corners of my eyes, "and that war is now?"

I can see the blurry arm Malachite is extending to me, but just barely. "Zera—"

"I have to do something." I dodge away, and my hands shake as I reach out for a passing flower on a bush, burying my face in its soft petals so Malachite doesn't see me crying. "I have to do something he'll hate so I can get my heart back. And when I do, I'll have to piece together who I really am. I don't even know—" I stop. "I don't even know what I'll want after that. The hunger will be gone. I'll have nothing moving me forward anymore. I'll have no immortality. I'll have to be scared of death again. I thought that's what I wanted, but... That's why I'm special, isn't it? That's why Varia keeps me around. It's the whole reason the witches sent me here, the whole reason I met Fione and Lucien and you. It's why I could kill Gavik and protect Lucien. It's what makes me strong. Otherwise, I'm just a girl with a sword."

together, stronger than alone.

My laughter sounds cold and mad even to my ears.

"But when I get my heart back, I'll be alone in my head. All alone. *Weak*."

Moonskemp lights up only one part of the palace, the candlelight glowing softly through the high windows, the nest of luminescence perched above us on the hill.

I stare up at it longingly. "I've just been careening toward my heart all this time, I haven't given any real thought to what comes after. And I'm terrified of it. I have all these vague, nebulous ideas of peace but—if Varia gets her way, the peace will be only temporary."

Malachite freezes. "What do you mean?"

It's too hard to tell him the truth—that Varia will die if she gets the Tree. It would drive Lucien to stop us, I know it would. And if he did, there's a chance he could succeed.

I'm being forced to choose again. Between my heart and him. But this time...*this time* I'll make the right choice.

I pat my eyes dry, picking up my pace. "I despise crying, don't you?"

Malachite grabs my arm then, pulling me back. His face is more serious than ever, white brows furrowed. "Zera, c'mon. You have to tell me. Luc's worried sick about what's going on with Varia and you down there—he's barely been sleeping with all his gallivanting around on the streets trying to figure out what it is. If he keeps going like this—"

That's where all Lucien's dark circles are coming from. I frown. "You're his bodyguard, not his body...body-not-guard. Do something! Drug his water if you have to."

"You think I haven't tried?" Malachite insists. "We've been together for five years. He knows all my tricks. He's not going to stop until he finds out what you and Varia are doing down there. If it's something dangerous—"

"You can tell him exactly how dangerous it is," I insist. "Tell him the truth—it's a valkerax."

"That won't be enough for him, and you know it. It doesn't make any sense," Malachite argues. "What is Yorl doing to it? Why are you talking to it? I get it—you're Heartless, so they're using you. You drink its blood, and then you can understand it. But what are you talking to it about?"

I blink. Its *blood*?

Malachite sees my confusion and frowns. "Haven't they told you? If you get enough valkerax blood in your digestive system, you can understand them. But it kills you almost immediately after you've ingested it."

So *that's* what the serum is based on. I had no idea valkerax blood could do that to someone.

"Thank you." I offer him the flower. "For your wisdom."

He bats the flower aside, the blossom hitting the cobblestones. "You can thank me by telling me what in the afterlife you're talking to a valkerax about."

I start to walk away, Malachite's grip breaking as I finally wrench my wrist out of his grip.

"Zera, please!" He grabs my shoulder, and I see something I've never seen in his eyes before. Fear. "Lucien is...going through it right now. Please just make his life easier this once."

Why is he scared? What is he scared of? Lucien himself? They're like brothers. Why would he fear Lucien?

"Sorry, Mal." I force a grin. "I can't."

"He and Fione are never going to give up!"

"Then that makes three of us," I say. He's quiet, letting me go slowly, a hardness materializing on his face.

What is a Heartless, with their heart returned? A human? No—not entirely. They've tasted the hunger. They can still remember what it feels like to die, to be cut up, to be burned.

A Heartless with their heart is a human who's been injured and has injured in return. And though the wounds have been healed magically, the memories still remain, stabbing and slicing better than the instruments of pain.

Heartless are an instrument of pain.

Who will I be, when my heart is returned? I consider it as I eat a lamb's lung and sip a mug of chocolate drink to cover the repugnant taste in the dawn, on Varia's enclosed balcony.

a murderer, a liar.

I'll be a girl who can't do anything but wave a sword around and quip emptily. A girl who has no idea what it means to be mortal anymore. A girl who has no idea what it's like to be alone in her own head. The next time she throws herself in front of valkerax fire for ten celeon guards, she will not live to tell the tale.

The hunger has made me miserable. But it's made me bold, too. It's made me irreverent and brave. It let me protect others and myself. Even in my lowest moments, it's given me a twisted sort of confidence, in that I always knew I'd live no matter what happened. No matter what happened, I could always rely on the hunger being there. Steady. Constant.

everything you are is my doing.

I am not the hunger. But it has made me in its own image. If I leave it behind, what is there left to lean on?

20

THE SPLINTER

When Varia returns from the Moonskemp, I tell her what happened with the valkerax before her maids come in. The crown princess is utterly silent for a good half. She peels off all her jewelry, placing it carefully on her armoire, before she finally speaks.

"Lucien has asked for your presence at his breakfast."

"I'm not going," I retort automatically.

"You misheard me, Lady Y'shennria." She refers to me with my family name intentionally. "His Royal Highness Lucien d'Malvane has requested your presence at his breakfast."

It's a not-so-subtle flaunting of the royal family's power over the other noble families. The prince is calling. And so, if I am still intent on being an Y'shennria, I must go. She calls for the maids, and they swarm in through the door. She stands from the armoire, going over to her closet and pulling out a simple peach muslin dress. She presses it to my dirt-smeared chest.

"He knows," I say. "Malachite must have told him by now. Lucien knows I'm talking to—" I dart my eyes over to the maids. "To Evlorasin."

"But he doesn't know why," Varia says coolly. She nods to the maids, and they take the cue instantly, undressing me with quick, sure fingers. I squirm out of the dirty dress, only half offended when they gently urge me into a silver tub of steaming herb-laced water in the bathroom and scrub me clean.

Varia picks up the letter from Yorl I'd left on the table, reading it as she speaks. "You still have feelings for him, don't you?"

I open my mouth, but she interrupts too quickly.

"I saw it last night. The entire noble court saw it." She pauses, dropping the letter and instead picking up a brush. She patiently combs through her own dark hair, the strands shining like polished onyx. "I'll give you a word of warning— he's not who you think he is."

The warm bathwater on my skin burns like acid. What does she mean? He's Lucien. He's Lucien d'Malvane, Prince of Cavanos and the Higher Reach. I dunk my head under the water, scrubbing my hair free of soap. I come up wiping water from my eyes.

"Be wary, Zera. My brother loves me," Varia says. "And he desires you. But there is something he values more than either of us. And that is his people."

The crown princess lets that linger, like a cut in the fabric of reality. Of course he values his people more than anything else. I've seen that countless times. He worked himself to exhaustion during the witchfire. I stand, gesturing for a maid to give me a towel. She obliges, and slowly I dry off and pull on the soft muslin dress, much softer than the world waiting outside.

"How much does he know?" I ask.

"Not enough," Varia says. "And yet more than enough."

"He's going to get in the way, isn't he?" I ask, the thought of Lucien standing between my heart and me tearing me apart at the edges.

"Not if we move quickly. Yorl has informed me there will be no visits today," Varia answers. "But tomorrow, I expect your best effort. Especially considering Lucien is aware of such efforts now."

The meaning isn't lost on me. She's gone from confident he wouldn't be able to do anything about her getting the Bone Tree to wary. Something has changed, and not in our favor. Did it have to do with the valkerax's escape maybe? Or is she finally realizing just how determined her brother has become in her years away from the court?

"You," I start, then lose my courage. But it comes back around. "You're going to die, aren't you?"

Varia's eyes flash in my direction, and I press on.

"The Bone Tree. It's going to feed on your magic and kill you."

Varia's still, and then she throws her hair over her shoulder. "Yes. But I told you that at the very beginning."

She did. The passage she recited from one of her favorite books, *The Midnight Gifter*. *My flesh will feed its furnace.* I didn't know just how true to life those words were. But now I do, with the full, cold impact.

I watch Varia leave for her bedroom. Reality creeps in again—I have a full day of nothing ahead of me. No obligations, no visiting Evlorasin. All I want is to finish teaching the valkerax as soon as possible. To end all this anxiety and sadness as soon as possible.

I've waited three years. One day is nothing in comparison.

I've stalled for Gavik long enough—he should have decoded his own journal by now, and the details of the "Hymn of the Forest." But if I go to find him in the city, Varia will know. I sigh. What does it matter? If she truly didn't want us to talk, she'd command me to stay away from him. And she hasn't.

But first, breakfast.

First, Lucien wants to talk to me. About the valkerax, no doubt.

The walk to Lucien's apartments isn't far from Varia's, but he's far closer to the king's chambers, which means the security is tenfold here. Lucien must've informed them of my coming, because all of them nod as I pass, opening the doors the moment I approach.

The gilded struts of the room give it away first as a royal chamber. A generous, fluffed goose-down bed with four posters and dark blankets sits in the middle. But it's the books that catch my eye. They dominate the room—piles of them stacked neatly on the plush carpet, careful towers of them built on the redwood tables, and little blocks formed on stately black chairs and couches. No inch of the room goes without at least a scroll or parchment or a book open on a surface. Lucien must love reading; the Midnight Gifter books were something that brought us closer two weeks ago. Varia loves those books, too. The series is so important to both of their childhoods. I spot gold-embossed versions of every book in the series on his shelf.

In front of me, situated just so that anyone walking in would see it, is a small table and a beautiful ceramic vase. Inside the vase rests a bouquet of black roses, so fresh and vibrant they look like they were picked from the bushes of

Y'shennria's manor just this morning.

"It's my attempt at a heartfelt apology." The voice comes from the corner, and I see Lucien stand from a desk. He's dressed simply—a white dress shirt and black breeches, the morning sun kissing his golden skin awake. "Malachite called it corny."

The beauty of the roses tugs at me. I reach one finger out to them, then pull back. No—I can't accept such a gift. Not after what I've done to him. I look around for Malachite, but he's nowhere to be seen. It's just us.

"You called for me, Your Highness?" I lower my gaze as any noble might. His cheek doesn't have any residual sign of my slap, and for that I'm glad. He pauses for a moment, and I don't dare look up, but I know he's surprised at my demeanor. I was furious enough to slap him last night, and yet here I am, docile as a lamb. Uncharacteristic of me, to be sure.

"I heard you saved Malachite," he says. "At the cost of your father's sword. I know how much it meant to you."

The broken hilt of the sword hangs at my hip even now, heavier than even the void in my chest. He and I talked of the importance of holding on to dead family members' swords in that tavern so many nights ago, our faces close and flushed. A sweet memory, long gone.

"It's nothing, Your Highness," I say. "Metal is replaceable. People are not."

There's a pause, as if he's debating pushing it, but he lets it go and changes the subject swiftly.

"Did you ever find out from Gavik what the song we discussed means?" he asks.

I incline my head. "No, Your Highness. I hope to today."

We're quiet, and it goes unsaid; he wants to know what it

means, too. Perhaps desperately. Is that what all the books around are for? Has he been trying to find information on his own?

"I've been studying," he says, the sound of his boots walking closer. His body cuts the air like a hot knife again, my own hyperaware of every single movement he makes, even without being able to see him. I watch his boots stop at a nearby table piled with parchments. "And considering you know more about Heartless than I do, I wished to ask you some questions. If you would let me."

Varia warned me very clearly about him. Is this a trap? The fact I have to doubt him, scrutinize him at all—it makes my bones ache.

"Of course, Your Highness." I bow lower. "My knowledge is at your disposal."

"The white mercury of the four swords that polymath made in the Sunless War," Lucien says instantly. "And the white mercury daggers of Gavik. These weapons will sever the connection between a witch and a Heartless, correct?"

He'll know if I lie. The books all around him—has he been reading up on this sort of thing? Is this sort of thing even recorded in Vetrisian books, or did the humans get rid of all of them? He could already know the answer and is just asking me for show. To test me—and my honesty toward him.

An honesty I've never given him.

Until now.

"No, Your Highness," I say. "White mercury simply weakens all magic in the body of the afflicted. The only magic in a Heartless is the connection between them and their witch. The white mercury weakens it. It doesn't sever it. Severing isn't possible, unless—"

"Unless the witch shatters the Heartless's heart

themselves, yes," Lucien finishes for me. "I know that part."

I feel one of my brows raise. Does he? Where would he have learned that? Certainly not from any of the books in the palace library, or, dare I say, any book in Cavanos. It's not exactly common knowledge, but neither is it a secret. Someone could've told him, I suppose. Someone with knowledge of how witches work.

He picks up a parchment, inspecting the blueprints there. "And a weakened connection between a witch and a Heartless lets the hunger inside you roam free. You can use that to disobey a witch's command. Is that correct?"

My head snaps up, my eyes roaming over his languid posture as he reads the parchment in his hands. He knows much more than I ever thought possible. Has he *read* all this? No—there's no way the things Reginall talked to me about, the things only he and I and the dead Weeping know, were ever written down. And even if they were, they were surely burned—if not by the witches who hate Weeping then by the humans who hate witches.

Lucien sees the naked shock on my face and laughs softly. "Ironically, the more we tried to develop white mercury weapons and use them in the war, the more we freed the Heartless. An unintended side effect but not an unwelcome one. Fewer Heartless following their witches' commands means less trouble for the human soldiers on the field."

He puts the parchment down and approaches me, so close I can see the streaks of brown in his dark eyes. He leans casually on the back of a velvet-trimmed couch.

"But you—" He swallows, strong throat bobbing. "That night in the clearing. The monster in you took over and killed those men. But it wasn't just the monster, was it? Your eyes... they were still yours."

My blood is slush, icy cold and red hot all at once and thrumming beneath my skin. He reaches one arm out and I stay still, waiting. Watching. Not daring to breathe. His fingertips graze my cheek, and my body clamors for more, honing in on the feel of his skin with a magnetic frenzy. I watch the prince's eyes change when he touches me—his patient gaze turning shadowed, turning bitter. It's just for a moment, and then he reverts to normal.

"Weeping," he says, breaking the silence. The word jerks me away from his touch instantly. How did he—? "What you did in the clearing was called Weeping."

How does he know that? It's impossible—the witches know of it, surely, but humans are far less aware. How does he know the exact name for it? Has he spoken to a witch in Vetris? The one who started the witchfire, maybe—the one who caused the earthquake last night? Varia would never tell him about Weeping—it's the key to her plan with Evlorasin, and she's assured me she's made certain none of her associates would talk about it. He couldn't have spoken to a *Heartless* who knows of Weeping—I'm the only one left.

I'm the only one who knows. And I haven't said a word to him about it. He read it. He must've read it somewhere, in one of these books. Someone must've written it down during the Sunless War, the tome scuttled away.

He knows too much, and his touch is intoxicating to my traitorous body, still. I have to get away from him.

"Is there anything else"—I struggle to make my voice even—"Your Highness wishes to ask of me?"

Lucien is quiet, his eyes catching the morning sun and fracturing with warm brown. "Just one. Will you forgive me?"

"For what, Your Highness?"

"The kiss last night," he says. "I acted out of turn."

I raise my head slightly, just enough to look into his eyes. "There's nothing to forgive. I've already forgotten it."

My lie sounds smooth, and it tests the very limits of my ability to spin a web. I'm terrified the truth is gleaming out of my blank expression—that I enjoyed it. That I remember every second of it. That I wish for another, and another, and another—

His eyes flicker with some emotion I can't read—disbelief? He regains himself, turning to a table and picking up a small leather-bound book from it. He hands it to me.

"Then at least allow me to give you a gift."

I look down at the book and take it, careful not to touch our fingers together. I make a proper bow.

"I'll be taking my leave, then."

Every bone in my body wants Lucien to stop me as I walk away. I want him to pull me back, to kiss me senseless. I want to feel not so alone in this moment, to be with him like that other timeline version of myself certainly is right now.

Stiffly, I walk to the door and leave. Once I'm out of sight and down another sun-drenched hall, I open the book. It's a picture book. I inhale sharply—there, on the page, a grisly scene is sketched. A village sits on a tranquil hill, but the hill is fractured, the shelf sliding down into a massive chasm ripped straight into the earth. And from that chasm are rising familiar shapes—serpentine, bright ivory-white scales. Valkerax.

They surge out of the ground like snow-colored yarn spilling out of a basket, twisting around one another, curling around the buildings of the village. White-hot fire blasts out of their mouths, burning the people fleeing from their homes that are rapidly sliding into the abyss.

I flip the page, and the next picture is equally horrific: the flat grasslands of Vetris, completely charred to ash. The earth is naked, not a tree or blade of grass in sight. There should be verdant vegetation, and yet the only things growing from the ground are white bones—*thousands* of them. Hundreds of thousands of human skeletons poke through the black char as far as the eye can see, frozen in their death poses, until the very foot of the Tollmount-Kilstead Mountains. Clutching their heads, rolling on the ground to get rid of the fire, curling around themselves helplessly.

"Kavar's eye," I hiss. The book is full of these terrible sketches and, according to the few pages with words on them, these are the drawings of an Old Vetrisian artist who traveled the Mist Continent to cover the devastation of the valkerax rampage a thousand years ago. Her drawings were reportedly used as a piece of evidence to encourage the Old Vetrisian alliance to form in the first place. An effective piece of evidence even now—I can't tear my eyes away, a sour chill running up and down my spine.

Lucien gave this to me because he knows about my speaking to Evlorasin—Malachite most definitely told him about the valkerax escape last night. But there's no way Lucien could know about the Bone Tree and how Varia is planning to take control of it, so is he just trying to warn me in general? I know valkerax are dangerous—everyone does. That's why they're locked in the Dark Below. But I'm not going to stop talking to Evlorasin, gruesome historical pictures or not. My heart is waiting—no matter how terrifying the idea of living without the hunger is, the idea of going on living as a monster is even worse.

Gavik is waiting. I head out of the palace, a cloak wrapped tightly around me. This time, I find him on my own—a glimpse of a gray robe at West Gate pulls me into an alley.

"Kreld!" I call his fake name, and he turns. The bread basket on his arm is nearly empty this time around, his beard growing shaggy and white over his chin. His watery eyes are, for once, not entirely furious to see me. It's not anger in his face, but something more disturbing: excitement. He pulls away from a man and walks over to me.

"I've done it." Gavik pulls the diary out of his coat pocket. "I unraveled the various codes I used. Some of them were incredibly complex, but with a little effort—"

"Stop blowing your own horn and tell me what it said," I snap. Gavik's mouth twists into itself. He steps in to me, and I brace myself to tolerate his oily presence.

"The 'Hymn of the Forest'—it's not a religious hymn."

"Then what is it?" I press.

"It was originally an Old Vetrisian bardic song," he says. "In Old Vetrisian culture, bards were responsible for shepherding information among towns as they wandered the kingdom, singing for coin. They were given this song about four hundred years ago, around the collapse of Old Vetris." Gavik inhales sharply. "It's a warning song. It details how and why the kingdom fell apart."

I frown. "We know why it fell apart—the emerging New God religion tore it apart."

Old Vetris fell because of belief. The Old God and New God believers began to war, and that was the end of them. Everyone knows that.

"Yes." Gavik smiles, but it's not a pleasant smile. "But where did the split between the New and Old God begin? And why?"

"I have no clue." I snort. "How does this have anything

to do with the hymn?"

"Ten years ago, I met a historian of Old Vetrisian culture. A celeon, by the name of Muro—"

"Muro Farspear-Ashwalker," I finish for him, swallowing hard. It feels like I've said that name so many times. Yorl's grandfather is at the center of everything somehow.

Gavik narrows his eyes, but nods. "Sref and Kolissa asked his opinion on a sickness of Varia's."

"Her dreams about the Tree, right?"

Gavik blinks this time. "You've been investigating on your own. Did my clever little niece help you?"

"How did you meet Muro?" I ignore the patronizing surprise in his voice.

Gavik collects himself like an archduke, imperiously. "Muro gave an explanation to Sref and Kolissa. But they didn't believe him. I saw him as a man of learning, and as he was leaving the palace, I convinced him to tell me his theory."

Gavik proceeds to tell me about the Bone Tree needing to feed on magic from a witch, and luring a powerful witch in through their dreams when it gets hungry. At one point I let out an impatient sigh.

"I stalled for a day for you to tell me things I already know?"

He pulls out the diary suddenly and points to the coded passages with one knobby finger. "Muro told me there isn't just one Old Vetrisian tree. There are two."

I knit my brows, my nightmare resurfacing of those two naked tree rosaries. "Two?"

"The Bone Tree was created to subdue the threat of the valkerax," Gavik insists. "But Muro says, in the following years, there was a small sub-section of Old Vetrisians who wanted to use the technology that made the Bone Tree to push the envelope of creation. The Bone Tree commanded the valkerax to the Dark Below. But they wanted to make another tree. One that could command people to remain immortal. A tree made of glass."

My hands start to shake. Immortality. He can't be talking about...*Heartlessness*?

"The tree of bone and the tree of glass." I repeat the line from the "Hymn of the Forest." The glass shard in my Heartless bag—the glass jars most Heartless hearts go into. The jars witches make, the bags witches make. Varia told me they work only because of the shards of glass included in them. Those shards give us our immortality, she said.

your heart, the hunger sneers. *tied forever to me.*

Gavik nods feverishly. "The Old Vetrisians created the Glass Tree. But other Vetrisians thought the idea of immortality was wrong. Immoral. Against God's teachings. They drove out those who made the Glass Tree. They labeled themselves the New God worshippers—forging a new path forward, one without immortality. And those who were driven out of Old Vetris were called the Old God's followers."

"The witches?" I whisper.

He frowns. "Most witches became Old God followers; by giving just a few drops of their magic to the Glass Tree, they could bind their loved ones to them forever. It was a tempting prospect." Gavik pauses, then looks at the sky. "And it ripped Old Vetris in two. Muro told me: that is how the old hatred in Cavanos began. That is how the wars between humans and witches started."

"How?" I swallow, my throat so dry it feels like sand. "How was Muro the only person who knew this?"

"The wars have been hard on Cavanos's history," Gavik

admits. "Books have been burned. Historians have written about the victors, not about the truth. Even the Black Archives don't have much on Old Vetris's fall. Muro had to go to the old, ruined Palas—beneather cities, infested with valkerax—for what he found out."

That would explain why Yorl knows so much about valkerax. Muro must've seen everything about them, observed the valkerax closely on his trips to the Dark Below, in an effort not to be killed by them. And he passed that knowledge down to Yorl.

Gavik suddenly leans in more, his voice low. "That isn't the worst of it. The Old Vetrisians—they made the Glass Tree by taking a piece of the Bone Tree and transplanting it. All the magic inside the Bone Tree, all the sentience it developed, it replicated itself onto the Glass Tree."

Sentience. Like the voice in my head? Like the hunger? Like the song Evlorasin talks about? Is that the "mind of its own" Yorl talks about?

"The Glass Tree," I manage to say. "It's still around?"

"Yes. We're standing here," Gavik says, thumping his empty chest. "As unliving proof of its existence."

"And the 'Hymn of the Forest' talks about all this?" I ask.

"Yes. The temple of Kavar has the only remaining copy that we know of. I was afraid people would find it, so I had them change the lyrics and seal the original in their library."

"Why didn't you want people knowing about it?"

He lets out a breath. "I didn't want word spreading about it, and somehow finding its way to Varia. Muro told me the Bone Tree had chosen her to feed off, and he told me if it fed off her, she would control the valkerax in turn. I couldn't have that."

"So you tried to kill her, too," I muse.

"Make no mistake," he says shortly. "I hated her. I hated Lucien. I wanted Varia's sword dearly, to arm my country appropriately against the witch threat. I wanted the witchblood d'Malvanes gone, because I knew they would ruin the country. And they will. Varia will succeed at it, if you help her get the Bone Tree."

"It's an army of valkerax under her control," I argue. "And the Bone Tree will take all her magic and kill her eventually, and then the valkerax will just return underground. It's not as much of a danger as you—"

"Think with that silk-and-lace-addled brain of yours," Gavik spits. "The landscape of Cavanos isn't the only thing that will change. A valkerax army will destabilize world politics as we know it. Cavanos will simultaneously become the world's enemy and the world's arbiter. The rest of the Mist Continent—the Pendronic emperor, the Helkyrisian sage-dukes, and the Avellish queen—will unite together for their own safety against us. And in other continents, alliances will form and fall around the world because of us. Every spear will be turned against Cavanos in self-defense."

The sand in my throat turns to molten lead.

"Varia thinks she's ready for that level of power," I whisper.

"No one is ready for that level of power," Gavik insists. "It is beyond all imagining."

Suddenly, I spot something out of the corner of my eye—a shadow, lingering at the mouth of the alley behind a pile of discarded pig iron. They're too close to us, and too hidden, to be doing anything but listening. Gavik starts to talk again, but I hold up one hand in his face, and he pauses. The pause is too long, and it spooks the shadow. Before I can blink, the shadow pivots and is gone, and I rush to the throat of the road just in time to see a scrap of darkness disappear around a corner.

I dash around it, and come face-to-face with the wall of West Gate, so high and tall that nothing could jump it, flanked on either side by similar brick walls, smooth and free of hiding places. The shadow is gone. But where? There are no places to duck into, no holes to disappear down. It's like it simply...*vanished*.

Anyone could've followed me. But only one person would want to. Only one person knew I'd be going to talk to Gavik today.

"Lucien?" I whisper at the looming white wall.

But I get no answer.

When I return to Gavik, he tries to convince me, once again, to refuse to help Varia find the Bone Tree. But his pleas fall on ears long closed to him. I walk back to the palace, stopping in front of Y'shennria's manor. The black rosebushes tug at my unheart as they wave beneath the immaculately blue summer sky, the fluffy white clouds so innocent and sweet.

Even under a sky that looks this peaceful, war is happening.

Varia has been throwing me at the valkerax. I've died over and over again, and no one has mourned. The witches throw their Heartless at the human army even now, but they won't mourn them. War only means something because death does. Death only means something because life does.

Life—that tenuous, bright thing that humans take for granted. Each moment, a possibility. Each day, a new beginning.

All of that, stopped only by death.

The Old Vetrisians back then were right to be afraid of the Glass Tree. The real monster is not death. It is immortality. It is nothing changing, ever. It is that choking gray haze. It's remaining the same for three years, trapped in a forest. It's death being reduced to a joke. It is death meaning nothing, because then life, too, means nothing.

I want to be human.

I want to *mean* something again.

"Lady Zera?"

I start, and look up at the voice to see Lady Tarroux peeking her round face out of a decadent passing carriage draped on the sides with gold-plated eyes of Kavar. A long caravan precedes her, each bed bursting to the brim with trunks and bags and furniture. Guards flank the procession, their swords ready and their faces grim. There must be fifty of them—their ranks bolstered by heavily armored mercenaries.

"Good afternoon, Lady Tarroux." I smile. "Where are you off to with all your things?"

Her eyes are downcast. "Helkyris. Father couldn't wait a day longer to leave."

My lungs deflate. "I see." There's a pause, and then, "Do you want me to kidnap you? I'm very good at crime."

The worry in her gaze falters with her soft laugh. "That would be so lovely. But I'm afraid Father would miss me if I were gone."

"Isn't he worried about attacks on the road?" I ask. "The war is in full swing."

She motions all around her to the mercenaries. "Father's spared no expense. We'll be fine, I think."

"Surely," I agree with a small laugh. "By the looks of it, he's hired a small army."

She laughs, too, though it sounds sad. "I'm sorry, Lady Zera. I feel as if we've just become friends, and I'm abandoning you."

I smile brightly at her. "You'll be back. The war might be over sooner than you think, and you'll come right back here and marry Lucien."

It doesn't hurt to say it as much anymore. Maybe I'm getting used to the idea. *Finally.*

"How—" she squeaks, her cheeks going red. "How do you know that?"

"Call it a...*vision*." I smile. "Sent to me from the New God."

Her blush fades, and then her face lights up. "Oh! I just remembered."

I watch her rummage around inside her carriage for something, before she leans out the window and hands it to me. "Here. Please give this to Prince Lucien. He was asking after it, and I'd hate to leave without giving it to him."

I look down at my palm to see a carefully folded paper. "Do you mind?"

Tarroux shakes her head. "Not at all."

I unfold it and read: it's a picture-guide to a certain sewing technique. I quirk a brow up at her. "What's this?"

"Oh, well." Tarroux goes red again. "The prince asked me to teach him to sew."

I blink. "Sewing? *He* asked you to teach him?"

Her blush fades only marginally as she looks up. "Yes. He said he wanted to make a gift for someone, and so

I obliged." She suddenly bows her head, bobbed hair sweeping over her shoulder as she blurts, "I'm sorry, Lady Zera! I know you are his Spring Bride! I didn't mean to have such feelings while there is a connection between you and His Highness!"

I'm struck again by how straightforward and kind she is. *Silly girl*, I think. *Don't be sorry. You're doing exactly what I need you to do.*

I reach up and clasp her small hand in mine over the carriage windowsill and grin wider. "Can I let you in on a secret?" I ask. She nods, wide-eyed. "I'll be gone soon. The court is no place for me, I've decided."

Her eyes get even larger, and I fight back the hot haze behind my own that threatens tears. She can't see me cry, see me show any emotion other than glibness. I must look sincere, deathly so. The words come easily, even if my expression doesn't.

"He can be very prickly," I say. "And stubborn. And he's convinced—" I laugh. "He's convinced he's the only one who can save anyone. Maybe that's why we got along at all in the first place—him with his savior complex and me with my martyr complex."

"Lady Zera—" Tarroux starts gently, but I cut her off.

"Speak your mind whenever you can—he hates platitudes most of all. Don't try to get him to drink. Oh, and he likes the city much more than he likes the palace."

My hands start to shake as everything runs through my mind—every time I've seen him, touched him, laughed with him. Only two weeks. It was only two weeks, so I really have no right to be this sad. Two weeks is nothing. A flimsy infatuation—lust and lust only. Two weeks means *nothing*.

I let Tarroux's hand go so as not to betray myself, my

words spilling out faster.

"Please, Lady Tarroux. When you come back to Vetris, please watch over him. Protect your prince as I cannot anymore."

Lady Tarroux never gets to answer me. Her caravan begins to move again, pulling her toward South Gate. I wave and wave, until her carriage is nothing more than a golden dot on the horizon. Then I drag myself back to Varia's apartments at a slow crawl. I should be happy—what I wanted has coalesced. I've pushed Tarroux toward Lucien, and myself away.

She's innocent. She's free of blood. She's human.

I coax my miserable self into Varia's sitting room, surprised to find her already there. At this time of night she'd usually be out to dinner at Fione's estate. But she sits on an ironwood couch in a grand feathered bathrobe, staring into a glass not of the imported brandy from Avel that's so popular among the Vetrisian nobles but some clearer liquid. It's strange, to see someone so in control relaxing for once.

She looks up with subdued eyes as I walk in and sees me staring at her cup. She waves it at me with a flourish. "Can't stand the Avellish stuff."

"What is it, then?" I ask, eagerly welcoming any change of discussion at all. "I would say bogwater, but I know you're not that kind of witch."

She gifts me a half-scathing, half-amused glance. "*Yolshil.* Celeon liquor. It's got more burn but less bite."

"Which makes it perfect for you, because you have enough teeth already."

It's a vague allusion to the valkerax, but even slightly

buzzed she gets it, and to my surprise she throws back her head and laughs. When she calms down, she drinks the rest of the liquor.

"Father really did miss an opportunity to make you his laughing boy."

"Why are you still up?" I ask warily.

The princess shrugs. "Sleeping is difficult for me, as you've seen." In a bid to change the subject, she motions to a table next to her. "You've received gifts."

I walk over to the table laden with two things: a letter and a long package wrapped in brown paper. I quirk a brow and approach suspiciously, peeling the letter open. It isn't sealed with wax, which means it's not a letter from a noble in Vetris. The handwriting strikes me as familiar, but I can't quite place it.

Zera,

I hope this finds you well. Considering I am sending this letter to Vetris once I am finished, I would hope, too, that you are practicing and executing your manners within court sufficiently.

My unheart swells. It's so much more than a chilly sentence. I know instantly who wrote this—Y'shennria. Suddenly the paper I'm clutching and each word on it become more precious than gold.

You should know that I and the others who came with me are safe, and we have been since our departure. I wish that you could be here with us, so that I wouldn't waste whats left of my life worrying into the night about you.

She's worried about me? My chest feels like it's glowing from within. Reginall, her driver Fisher, her cook Maeve, and her stableboy Pierrot—all of them are safe. All of the people who helped me immensely, who were kind to me in different ways. It's a huge relief to know they're out of harm's way.

Our mutual friend who sent you to me originally has told me something precious to you now belongs to someone else in Vetris.

The sentence is vague intentionally, no mentions of witches or Heartless. She means Nightsinger, and my heart.

If you see a chance to depart from Vetris someday and find yourself alone, I will leave some direction for you at the place you have seen, where the birds fly.

Where the birds fly? Ravenshaunt—*of course*, her ancestral home that was all but destroyed by witchfire. She pointed it out to me when we first met, in the carriage to Vetris. A deep burden I didn't know I was carrying suddenly lifts off my shoulders, and a true smile pulls at my face. She's saying if I manage to get my heart back, I should head to the ruins of Ravenshaunt to find her.

I want that more than almost anything.

Finally, an anchor. A point on a map to walk toward.

The letter is too short.

What you have done took great strength. Know that I am proud of you.

I await, steadfast.

The smallest of her sentences rings with great impact in my head. Her words are a tiny glimmer of hope in the mire I've been wading through, and the urge to get my heart back explodes, brighter than ever. Crav and Peligli are waiting for me. And now a third person. I have somewhere to go out there beyond the walls, beyond the war. A home. A real *home*.

Varia's watching me, but at some point she turns away to refill her glass. No doubt she's already read it, but still I wait until she's not paying attention to fold Y'shennria's letter over the fragments of her wanted poster I keep in my chest pocket.

I pick up the paper-wrapped package. It's long and thin, and I open it quickly. My eagerness withers the moment I see what's nestled in the wrapping.

A blade. The blade of a sword without a hilt. And not just any blade. I almost don't recognize it because of the lack of rust until I see the blood gutter down the center leading to a distinctive sheaf of ivy carved into the bottom of it.

My father's blade. A perfect replica, new and shining.

But who would—? Only a few people know my sword broke at all. Fewer know what it looks like up close. Malachite. Did he—?

Varia makes a disgruntled noise over my shoulder as she peers at the blade. "Fool."

I look back at her. "Who?"

She downs more of her fresh yolshil, sighing tiredly. "Pendronic silvered steel. The same stuff the d'Malvane ceremonial swords are made of."

d'Malvane. Does that mean…Lucien did this? He'd seen Father's sword more than once, but I had no idea he'd paid that much attention to it. I pick up the blade, matching it hesitantly to Father's rusted hilt. To see the sword whole again, to feel its exact weight in my hands—I run my thumbs over the hilt, the blade. It's so familiar, comforting.

In this city where I am the enemy, the air suddenly doesn't feel as cold anymore.

I tuck the blade and hilt into the box and turn to Varia.

"Tomorrow morning I'm teaching the valkerax again, right?"

She nods, tightening the belt of her grand feathered robe. "Obviously."

I watch her beautiful face. I know she knows I went to see Gavik today. I might as well come clean.

"Do you know?" I ask. "About the 'Hymn of the Forest'?"

Varia smiles wanly at the glass of jade-colored yolshil. "How do you think I found Gavik's pet valkerax in the pipe below the East River Tower? I scoured every inch of this city before I faked my death, looking for ways out. Of course I know about the temple's library and their little hymn."

"He told me," I press on. "About the Bone Tree and the Glass Tree."

There's a beat, and for a moment I swear the only noise is the sound of the three moons setting over the garden hedges outside her windows.

Finally, Varia looks to me, her smile gone, her eyes tired. "Don't bother with the past, Zera. The future is where you'll find your freedom."

With that, she stands, drains her glass, and disappears into her bedroom.

21

GOLDBLOOD

The morning sun isn't forgiving, slatting through the high windows as I walk the palace halls to my carriage. Neither is the crowd gathered on the grand front steps.

With seeing Evlorasin on my mind, I have little care for the nobles and servants knotted around a marble step until I see a woman collapse, her great skirts billowing as she lets out a strangled cry into her handkerchief. Her friends gather around her, whispering comfort and helping her to her feet.

With her absence, I can see into the center of the crowd. There, standing in blackened, half-scorched clothes, stands a young boy. He trembles from head to toe, something clutched in his hand. The crowd offers him a blanket to cover his ruined clothes, water to quench his unmoving tongue and ease his sweat-stained exhaustion. The ruined black feather in his hat marks him as the stableboy of a noble family. The crowd's whispers resound.

"It's all right, young one. You're safe now."

"Did he really run all the way back from Hardetting?

That's nearly seventeen miles!"

"Someone get the guards!"

I knit my brows and look more closely at the boy—his eyes are so tired, they look deadened, filled with lead, as if he can't hear the words or see the reality around him. The only time he makes a move of his own accord is when someone tries to touch him; he flinches back instantly, eyes flashing with pure terror.

A guard suddenly calls for room and pushes through the crowd, armor glimmering in the sun. The guard kneels, his voice low as he speaks to the boy, who simply stares at him with those dead eyes. After a long moment, the boy is persuaded to open his tightly closed fist. From his fingers cascades a golden symbol.

A gold-plated eye of Kavar.

My lungs collapse. The whispers are instant.

"Isn't that one of those decorations on the Tarroux carriage?"

"Why has he brought it here? Did something happen?"

The guard takes the eye from the boy gingerly and grimly asks a quiet question of him. The boy's answer is one word, louder than the guard, his voice cracking and hoarse.

"Witch."

The crowd suddenly unravels, people touching their eyelids and invoking Kavar's name, others turning green around the edges, and more than a few staggering back.

"Witches? Did witches kill them?"

"They left just last night. This can't be happening!"

"The roads are supposed to be heavily guarded!"

"The war, oh New God, the war has truly come."

My throat bobs. No. Lady Tarroux…I just talked to her yesterday. Hours ago. The crowd is so busy fearing for themselves that they leave a space between them just large enough for me to muscle through. I approach the boy as the guard tries to reassure everyone, maintain the peace.

"Please calm yourselves! We have no information—"

"How much more do you need?" someone in the crowd shouts back. "Look at his clothes! Look at the eye!"

My own eyes rivet to Kavar's eye in the guard's hand, the gold plating dented, scratched deeply and violently. Gold is a soft metal—it doesn't take much to batter it, but the sheer jagged pattern of the scratches is familiar. I've seen these scratches before, but on flesh. Too small to be wildcat. Too big to be wolf.

Heartless claw marks.

The boy's ashen face stares up at me, and now closer, I can finally discern on his jaw the fine spray of blood. Not his own. Someone else's. Someone whom he was standing very close to when their arteries were cut open. My unheart twists for someone so young going through something so traumatic. But worry burns across my lips.

"All of them?" I ask, my voice cracking. The stableboy's green eyes fog up, but having the eye taken from him seems to have jostled some of his shock loose in him. He's quiet, but then, slowly and with great effort, he swallows and nods.

My ears ring with my thoughts as I walk woodenly away from the boy, from the hysterical crowd.

All of them. Lady Ania Tarroux. She's dead.

We just spoke in the same spot I'm standing in right now as I flag down the carriage to South Gate. I watched her drive off, her milk-blond hair glimmering away into a mote of nothingness. I saw her blush when I brought up Lucien. Her hand was warm beneath mine.

Nothing about this moment feels real. The heat of the sun,

the scent of the fresh grass—it all mutes to a dull nothingness.

I told her the war would be over. I told her she would come back soon and marry a prince. She was kind. She was pure.

But death cares for neither.

My carriage passes the Temple of Kavar, the large metal eye symbol atop the tallest spire painting my face in shadow.

This mindless war between witches and humans—fought for their gods, for their beliefs, for their differences—has killed her. The hate that began with the Glass Tree—the splinter inside my heart bag splintered more than just my own life. It has splintered Cavanos, wedged deep beneath and between it, for a thousand years.

Religion has killed her.

And still, she loved it.

I bend my head and put my fingers to my eyes as she showed me. I pray as she showed me, that day outside Lucien's room, the two of us lit by the sun shafting through the windows, smiling at each other over a platter of bread and fruit.

"May his eyes watch you, always."

I'm thankful to be back in the pitch-dark arena with Evlorasin. Thankful to turn my attention to something other than the numb despair of death. I *am* thankful to see the valkerax—hear it, really—alive and breathing normally again. I can't see the rupture in the arena wall, but if the smell of sawdust and fresh metal is any indication, Yorl's crew has patched it up admirably.

"The beneather runes on the wall have been redone, too," Yorl explains.

"So fast? *Godsdamn*," I marvel. "How do you get everything done so quickly?"

"Varia's pouring all the kingdom's resources into this lab." He frowns. "We are capable of hiring anyone and procuring almost anything."

"Except, you know, a teacher for it to Weep." I puff out my chest.

"Yes," Yorl drawls. "You are certainly the rarest imported resource here."

He hands me the white mercury sword, the distinct handle nudging my fingers, and I take it slowly. "I don't think Evlorasin's ready for this," I admit. "Especially not after its escape."

"Varia's orders," Yorl says simply. "We must cut it today."

"But—" I start. "It's really weak right now, isn't it? It's injured—Malachite was railing on its spine with his whole broadsword. It needs to be as healthy as—"

"Its health is only going to decline," Yorl insists. "I made that clear."

"Can't we wait?" I blurt. "Just give it another day or two to heal, and for us to practice the silence together... I promise that'll be better than forcing it to—"

"I know," he admits, a softer edge to his voice. "I, too, would like you and the valkerax to be fully prepared. But the orders are clear. Progress must be made. And quickly. Our time is running far shorter, far faster than anticipated."

I breathe out, anxiousness vibrating my hands. "Is this because of Lucien? Is Varia really that afraid of him? He doesn't know much—"

I freeze, my words crystallizing in their tracks as I

remember yesterday. He knows about Weeping. And I'm convinced that shadow listening to Gavik and me was him. He knows much more than I ever thought possible.

"Come," Yorl demands. "We have no time to spare thinking."

I grumble. "Never thought I'd hear that from you, Master Polymath."

"I seem to have acquired your curious habit," Yorl admits. "Of leaping first and pondering later. Not the best stratagem, but you've shown me it can be effective at times."

I scoff, my anxiousness lessened barely by a grain of pride.

Evlorasin is wide awake when Yorl and I step into the arena, tail thrashing so violently I feel a little stone shaken from the ceiling plink off my skull.

"*Starving Wolf,*" it says, voice somehow hoarser than before. Weaker. It's under a caravan-load of painkiller concoctions but still suffering from its injuries, though Yorl insisted he patched those up.

"Good morning, Ev," I wave, perhaps in the wrong direction. "Feeling any better?"

The valkerax pauses, then, "*Ev?*"

"Yeah. I've decided to give you a nickname."

"*Nicking-name?*" I hear the confused thrashing of its tail again, feel the air displaced by it decimate my hairstyle I worked so hard on this morning.

"It's a shorter name you give someone you like. Someone who's close to you. And considering I've seen down your throat in perfect detail, I'd say we're pretty close at this point."

"*We are a river of regret after the rains,*" it admits. "*Overflowing. We are sorry for the death of many. We had to run.*"

I feel massive heat close to me and reach out blindly, my hand coming to rest on Evlorasin's haunch.

"I know. Sometimes I feel like running, too." I pull Varia's white mercury sword from my hip. I run my knuckles over the delicately woven basket handle. "But it's almost over. Today, we're going to cut you with the white mercury I talked about."

"The blade of metal to the throat of the song! We have waited eternally long!" Evlorasin's voice sounds eager, and suddenly it can barely sit still, curling around me in multiple loops. I laugh—it's almost cute. But my joy is short as I remember exactly how it rampaged in the tunnel, mouth open and ready to devour what felt like the whole world.

Evlorasin is already unstable enough as it is—the wounds Yorl has made in it, the wounds Malachite and I made on it, and its waning strength with every day it's away from the Dark Below—all of Evlorasin is held together by Yorl's concoctions and the parts he's stripped from the valkerax and thrown into the Dark Below to lessen its madness. If we weaken the Bone Tree's hold on the valkerax further, there's no telling what will happen, how desperate and dire things could become. It could run away faster and more furious than before, and I'd be left with nothing. Varia's pushing us too hard, too suddenly.

It's a risk. A risk for my heart.

"Listen, Ev," I start. "You have to remember what I showed you—"

"The silence. It is vital," Evlorasin interjects. *"The song will crescendo from the very peaks of the mountains inside us, and we must echo it in perfect stillness. There is stone, and we also must be stone. This story is understood."*

I nod, shifting to hold the white mercury blade at an angle away from me. A weighty mass pushes against my body abruptly—the softness of fur and smoothness of scales alike. I feel around—it's Evlorasin's chest, rising and falling rapidly with its excited breathing.

"The song will not beg of us anymore," it says. *"We will fly above the darkness as we have not for many moons. We will spread our pride in the blue sky-home."*

I can hear its enormous claws click as it tramples dirt in place with uncontained anticipation.

"We will fly," it says. *"Below the sun and moons. We will feel the blowing whispers, and we will know the color of light again."*

I smooth my hand up its neck, feeling the blood thrumming beneath the thinner scales of its throat. Evlorasin's rank breath washes over me as its velvet nose nudges my elbow.

"Our ears tire of the singing. We cannot wait any longer. A cut is required."

"You have to be silent!" I chide. "Remember? If you get too wrapped up in your emotions, it'll all come tumbling down."

It happened to me in the clearing so many months ago—the moment I dwelled on Lucien's terrified face, on what I'd done instead of what I had to do, I fell to pieces.

"To Weep is to control," Evlorasin says. *"Excitement is not control."*

"Exactly."

Suddenly, the gate screeches open. I start—only Yorl and I are allowed in here, and the guards are all petrified of the valkerax. So who in their right mind would brave coming in?

A spot of light blooms against the darkness, a pale purple glow clutched in a robed hand. The moss above the wall I wake up near every time—that's the same cluster. The light reveals a tall person in a robe. They hold up the moss, advancing into the darkness and toward the valkerax and me without hesitation.

"Who are—"

"Varia," I hear Yorl say shakily. "You didn't inform me you were coming."

"I am not beholden to inform you of everything, Yorl, just most things." Varia's voice echoes calmly around the arena. The crown princess stops right in front of the valkerax, not an inch of fear in her regal posture. The great white wyrm winces back at the hazy glow of the moss.

It's the first time I've seen the valkerax still and lit up—the mosslight flickering over its gigantic wolflike head brightest and getting dimmer at the serpentine neck traced by its thick white mane. Evlorasin's two seemingly infinite whiskers undulate like gentle rivers, its fangs serrated and nipping over its lips. Its scales are battle-hardened, scarred and dented with a thousand years—more?—worth of living. With the mosslight, I can even see thick white eyelashes, like a deer's, around its five pale-moon eyes, it's injured sixth socket scabbed and scarred.

Varia looks to me, the darkness in her hood making her expression unreadable. "You will translate the following for me, Zera."

I start, clearing my throat. "A-All right."

The crown princess of Cavanos looks back to the valkerax and begins, my mouth moving a beat after hers.

"Evlorasin," Varia says. "I am the Laughing Daughter."

"*Yes.*" Evlorasin sways its head. "*We know this.*"

I repeat its words, my own voice feeling somehow small all of a sudden.

"I have done this thing," Varia says, gesturing around at

the arena. "I have orchestrated all of this to free you."

I see Evlorasin curl its lips over its teeth, but it says nothing.

"You will Weep," Varia continues. "And you will tell me where the Bone Tree is."

"*The Tree of Bone,*" Evlorasin hisses. "*Great branches singing in many places at once. The roots of all evil. The beginning of the end for the Old Vetrisians.*"

The beginning of the end. I know what it means by that now.

"Yes," Varia says, impatience creeping ever so slightly into her voice. "When the song is dull, you will tell me where it's coming from. I will have the Tree."

For the first time ever, I hear Evlorasin burst out in response. It's a burst, to be sure—forceful rancid air blasting out from its maw, its lips curled back and showing all of its multiple rows of razor-sharp teeth. Its tongue lolls out of its mouth, long and forked, and it makes a panting motion. *Laughter.*

"*The Laughing Daughter knows not what she wants.*"

"That is no concern of yours!" Varia snarls the moment I translate the sentence. "I know what it means. I know what it will take. And I am willing."

"*The other chimes were just as willing.*" Evlorasin laughs, drool forming a puddle on the floor from its tongue. "*They let out such sweet noises before they slept their last.*"

"It is not your place to determine what I am capable of, beast." Varia's voice goes quiet again, every inch backed by steel. "You will tell me where the Bone Tree is, or you will not be cut today. And you will never Weep. You will give me a blood promise—"

"*The Laughing Daughter invokes ways that are long lost*

to the darkness." Evlorasin closes its mouth finally, clicking its claws as it circles Varia menacingly with its titanic bulk. *"We are the ones who laugh at her."*

Evlorasin stops circling her and comes to curl itself around and behind me, putting its head on its paws just at my feet, its five eyes lazily blinking at Varia as it settles in like a hound before a winter's fire.

"You are Starving and she is Laughing," Evlorasin says to me. *"Why do you help her seek the Tree?"*

Shame burns hot at my gills, and I keep my eyes away from Varia's as I say, "She's promised me my heart."

Evlorasin is quiet, as is Varia, watching the both of us sharply with her obsidian eyes like she's tensing, waiting for something to happen.

"Ah. This is why you are the Starving Wolf." The valkerax finally exhales a puff of slow air at my feet. *"Because your hunger will consume the world."*

"Tell it." Varia points at my confused self suddenly, her wooden finger glimmering stark in the mosslight. "Tell it I will not allow—"

The valkerax suddenly explodes next to me, languid one moment and lunging forward in a blink the next, mouth open and teeth bared right at Varia. Yorl makes a shout and I fling myself toward her *(not her, if she dies I die)*, but there's a flash of black light and then the smell of singed fur. It happens so fast I barely see it, but then Evlorasin's reeling backward, pawing at its smoking mouth and whining. Varia's panting, her robe heaving as the void-like blackness that preludes spell casting for witches fades from her eyes and the skin of her hands.

"Your gods have torn you apart," Evlorasin hisses between pawing. *"The Tree tore one god into two, and you will not*

make them whole again by taking hold of its branches."

Its rambles aren't nonsense anymore. The Tree tore one god into two. Evlorasin means the Old God and the New. It knows that the invention of the Trees is what tore Old Vetris apart, just as I do.

Varia bellows at me, her hair mussed and her eyes burning furiously. "Translate! Now!"

I do, but her expression doesn't change in the slightest, her anger blazing out. Her mouth moves succinctly, her words clipped.

"You will tell me where the Bone Tree is, beast. And I will give you your unclouded mind. This is the blood promise. If you refuse it, you will die."

My stomach curdles in on itself at the thought of killing Evlorasin after everything we've been through. *Please accept,* I silently beg. *Please say yes.*

Evlorasin's face disappears from the mossglow in an instant, a curling mass of white all I can see as the valkerax winds around itself like a snake, over and over, the snowy coils tightening and loosening and tightening again. I grip the white mercury sword, waiting for it to strike out at Varia once more. The long, continuous noise of scales over dirt, and then suddenly Evlorasin's maw returns to the light, returns to hover just in front of Varia, all five eyes blinking rapidly at her at different times.

"There will be a war."

"There is always a war," the crown princess asserts, her voice echoing into the darkness.

The air grows thicker than ever, dust and the smell of smoke wafting among us. No one dares to move; I barely dare to breathe.

"Life is a garden that must flourish," Evlorasin hisses,

then, *"And we will water its soil."*

I barely get the translated words out before my ears start to ring, my fingers go cold, and the mosslight dims to blackness as my eyes—and every other part of me—dies.

Yorl won't tell me what happened after I died, but I can guess from his expression when I rouse into the world of the living again: Varia isn't pleased.

"It's strange," I muse. "She was so confident about this whole thing at the beginning. She never came down and demanded promises from the valkerax before. So why now? Was she really that scared by the quake?"

Yorl adjusts his glasses higher on his nose, scribbling on his parchment without saying a word.

"Yorl," I press. "C'mon. I've saved your tail way too many times for you to ignore me like this. There's gotta be a reason she's suddenly all anxious."

His massive green eyes narrow, ears flattening. He lowers his voice and finally leans in. "We've realized there might be a leak in our unit."

I swallow. "Like, a spy?"

"Someone leaking information," he corrects tactfully.

"Okay, yes, I'll admit it; I had to tell Malachite there was a valkerax—"

"Not that sort of information," Yorl interrupts. "More detailed than just the existence of a valkerax below South Gate."

More detailed? I knit my lips before starting, "Who are they leaking information to?"

Yorl won't meet my gaze, but he sniffs and rolls up his finished parchment. "We're not sure. But we're so close to having the valkerax Weep, it hardly matters much. If we move with haste, this nuisance will become nonexistent. Which is why Varia is pushing us so."

He's being evasive. "I helped you bring Ev back, Yorl!" I stamp my foot. "I think I deserve a little more than a hand wave! Paw wave. Whatever!"

The celeon nudges his glasses higher on his nose. "We have a job to do. Varia wants us to cut the valkerax today and be done with it."

As he passes me a second vial, he gets up and heads toward the gate. I stare at the clear vial in my palm, the mosslight from the wall reflecting into the liquid as a sickly violet. Yorl is being evasive. He thinks…*they* think I could be one of the possible leaks, don't they? I would be evasive with the person I thought was a leak, too. But I haven't told anyone anything. I've been true to my word—my every command—both with and against my own will. I stayed strong, even when Lucien and Fione and Malachite were questioning me.

Yes, Lucien somehow knew about Weeping, but he didn't find that out from me. I never said a single word about it aloud. I told Fione about the valkerax but not about what we were doing down here. I gave Lucien the diary page, but that was after he already knew about the "Hymn of the Forest," and therefore about the Bone Tree. No one knows Varia is having me teach the valkerax to Weep specifically to find it. *No one.*

I get up slowly, pulling the white mercury sword from the ground where Yorl laid it beside me.

The other chimes were just as willing. Evlorasin's words

whirl in my head. I'm kicking myself now for not asking Varia what any of that meant, but if she thinks I'm a leak, there's no possible way she'll tell me. I'm simultaneously the crux of her operation and a potential threat to it, even if I still don't understand how.

Yorl orders the gate to be opened, and we duck inside. The heavy breathing of Evlorasin is audible the second we walk in, and its rancid breath heralds its approach. My hands are shaking around the white mercury sword, and I feel dizzy.

My skin tingles hot with Evlorasin's heat behind me, and I turn to it.

"Where do you want the cut?" I ask. "It should be somewhere that penetrates down to the bloodstream easily."

"The throat of the river is the weakest part," Evlorasin says. *"Where earth and water mix."*

I feel blindly, Evlorasin guiding me with the occasional push of an undulating whisker to my back. I grope for the throat skin—much thinner and slicker than its scales.

"Evlorasin will need to eat *a lot* more often," I announce to the darkness, to Yorl. "And if it loses control completely—"

"We have failsafes in place," Yorl cuts me off. Failsafes. He means ways to kill it if everything goes wrong.

"We will control the song," Evlorasin insists, as if reassuring me. I'm quiet, my thoughts loud enough for the both of us.

Evlorasin isn't ready. I'm not ready. But we have to be.

I place one hand on the valkerax's breast, holding the blade there. Once I do this, Evlorasin might Weep, and it might give the Bone Tree to Varia. She will hold command over all the valkerax in the Dark Below. The book Lucien gave me—its pictures flash through my eyes, thousands of skeletons, charred to ash. There'll be no going back. Am I just sending Ev to a new, horrible master?

Am I just sending Varia to the death she seems to want so badly?

"*The Starving Wolf is sad,*" Evlorasin rumbles. "*Do not mourn. Flesh will always meet bone.*" When I don't say anything, it hisses, "*When we are Weeping, taste of our living blood.*"

This gets me out of my own head, and I blink up at it. "Why?"

"*You have given us a 'nicking-name.' We will give you the blood promise. We will not give it to the Laughing Daughter. She is not the rain to our drought. But you, Starving Wolf, have tasted of our drought, our darkness. In you, the blood promise will remain true.*"

Varia talked about a "blood promise," and it was the point of contention in their argument earlier, but I still don't know what it is or what it means. It sounds important.

"You should give it to Varia," I insist. "She's the one who—"

Evlorasin's fangs clack against one another. "*It is the Starving Wolf or nothing.*"

I inhale, sharp. I can't have nothing. How bad can it be? It's just a little blood—it won't kill me. Nothing can kill me. I give a slow, uneasy nod, and Evlorasin seems to relax, the clacking fading.

"Commence, Zera," I hear Yorl say. "We are ready."

22

THE SONG'S END

I brace myself against the valkerax and press, white blade first, into Evlorasin's skin. I feel the thinner, more flexible scales peel apart beneath the sword as it moves. The valkerax doesn't so much as let out a whine, standing strong as the metal slices its flesh. Something so small must be like a fly's bite to something this big. Warmth oozes down my wrist, and when I pull away, Evlorasin's voice rumbles.

"Now we are promised. We feel a tremor in the earth before it arrives." There's a pause. *"The song is becoming louder and stronger."*

"You can't let it overwhelm you." I cling to Evlorasin's mane, as if I have any control over the huge wyrm at all. "They'll give you a lot of food, and that helps, but you have to practice. Now, before it gets too loud. You are of the silence."

"We are in the silence." The valkerax finishes the words we've practiced. There's a growl deep in its throat that emerges from the depths, faint and only getting stronger.

"Focus!" I back up. "Just the blackness, nothing else. No

thoughts, no feelings—just the silence."

"*Silence.*" The valkerax chatters its fangs eerily again, breathing growing labored. Suddenly I'm shoved from behind by a massive coil of something—its tail? I collapse on the ground, my ribs crying out in agony. I can hear Evlorasin just above me, panting.

"*It hungers.*" The valkerax snarls. "*It hungers for everything in this world!*"

"You have to fight it!" I yell, each word knocking the breath from my aching lungs all over again.

"Zera!" I hear Yorl shout. "It's going for the gate! You need to stop it, or else I'll have to—"

"You want to be free, don't you?" I scream out to Evlorasin, jumping to my feet and staggering across the arena to where I can hear it moving. "You can't let the song win! You are the silence!"

"*It is...so loud,*" Evlorasin snarls, and a sudden earthquake jolts me to my knees as the valkerax throws itself against the gate, scales meeting metal in one powerful impact. Another quake, and the metal gate gives a mighty screech.

"It's going to break!" Yorl calls out frantically. "Ready the greatlance!"

No—no, they *can't* kill it.

I scrabble forward, following the scent of rotting things and throwing myself onto the valkerax's body. I catch its back leg, clinging to the ankle as it moves—taking steps back, as if preparing to ram the gate again.

My mind flashes; what stopped me? Back in the clearing, what was I thinking just before I Wept for the first time? I had to protect Lucien. That's the only thing I wanted. Everything boiled down to one thing, one moment; the one thing I wanted more than anything in the world.

"Evlorasin! You want to fly!" I scream. The hind leg stops moving, and I blurt, "Above the Dark Below, in the sky-home! But you have to be silent!"

The hind leg suddenly swings around, my brain careening in my skull as the momentum almost flings me off. I dig in with my claws and hold fast.

We are not the hunger.

i am all you have, the dark voice seethes.

"The song only wants to consume!" My shouts are hoarse now. "It wants you to feed it, focus on it, obsess over it! But it's not you! The real you wants to fly!"

"*It hurts,*" Evlorasin rasps. "*The song is the ocean at full tide and it hurts. It will hurt us infinitely if we are silent!*"

Doubt. Fear. Threats. The hunger's trying to drag even this majestic beast down into the depths with it.

"You can see trees again, and—and the color of sunset, and feel the wind on your face! That's what you want, isn't it? More than anything? You told me! You told me that's what you want!"

The hind leg tenses, the titanic muscles condensing for a leap straight forward, a lunge that will surely puncture through the gate like an arrow through parchment.

"*We are...of the silence,*" Evlorasin pants, sounding every inch as if it's struggling with an iron weight on its chest.

"You are in the silence!" I encourage. "You are in control. You are not the song! You are Evlorasin!"

"*The song....isn't us.*" A pause, and then a strangled sentence. "*Is...going...possible?*"

"Yes!" I yell into the darkness. "Going *is* possible!"

I cling to Evlorasin's hind leg, praying. Old God, New God, God or no God—*help this one. Help us.*

Suddenly there's movement, the hind leg stepping

forward as the sound of something huge cutting through the air follows. White light. I can see white light glowing faintly from behind my shoulder. Like I'm a rusted puppet, I turn my head to look.

There, looming inches from my face, are five white eyes fixed on me. Five white eyes, each bigger than my head and each glowing faintly, the veins gray and spidery. And in the dim light they give off, I can see the rivers below each eye. Five rivers of blood, falling and curling around one another as they wind their way down the valkerax's scaled face.

Evlorasin is Weeping.

"Starving Wolf." Its voice echoes calmly, none of the snarling hisses I've grown used to attached to it. The voice is smooth and even, clear in its bell-like reverberations and almost musical. *"I am free."*

Not *"we,"* like it says always, not *"us."* *"I."*

Tears grow hot in my eyes, and the rush of relief is so heady, I laugh. It's Weeping. All the pain, all the dying, all the sadness—it's over. Evlorasin is Weeping, and that means it's free. That means my heart is mine again.

"Ev," I breathe. "You did it."

All at once, the darkness in the arena evaporates, replaced with an ethereal rainbow glow that fills the room. My eyes adjust and I gape in awe at the light shimmering in ribbons as it winds through the stone arena. It hangs like a boreal mist, gently illuminating everything—Yorl's stunned face, the dented gate, a massive spearhead mechanism built into the ceiling poised to thrust down on us, the aghast celeon guards perched on the tallest reaches of the arena, bows and sedative-tipped arrows beginning to fall to their sides.

My breath stops when I realize the light is radiating from

Evlorasin itself, concentrated in its grand white feathered mane now standing on end, like a glowing white halo around its face. I can see the length of the valkerax properly now, in its full glory—so long it could circle the Temple of Kavar, so strong and mighty it could break any human in two with a single swipe. It's power incarnate—beauty incarnate.

Claws as thick as halberd blades scrape the ground as it stares at me. "*Drink of my blood. I give you this gift of myself, so that the Wolf might never howl alone again.*"

Shaken down to my core, I force myself to blink again, move again. The words are caring in a macabre, twisted way, and the valkerax nods its massive head toward the white mercury blade in my hand. I raise my finger tentatively to the sword, dabbing my fingers in the blood and then to my lips. It smells like acid and honey all at once. I try it on my tongue, and it smacks of brass and salt going down—much stronger than the serums Yorl's given me. Evlorasin's long whiskers whip the air in what I think might be happiness.

"*I am you,*" Evlorasin says. "*We sing the same and Weep the same. My blood is your blood. This is never-goodbye.*"

The sudden numbness of the serum's death creeps into my legs and arms as I smile wider and whisper, "Never-goodbye."

The numbness forces my grip to retract, and I fall off Ev's thick hind leg and land flat on my back on the arena floor, dust floating up all around me. I can hear Yorl yelling faintly, my eyes beginning to fail and blurring uncontrollably. With a heavy *whump* of air in my ear, something above me— long and white and glowing like a crystal refracting rainbow sunlight—starts to rise into the arena's ceiling.

Shouting. The sound of stone cracking thunderously and metal crashing. And then, darkness.

I wake up to a lighted underground—on the same bedroll I always do. The oil lamps are lit again, the whole underground brightly visible. Yorl's sitting next to me, tail curled around his feet and watching me like a hawk. Behind him, the celeon guards pass huge chunks of rock to one another, a chain working methodically to clear out the caved-in arena. My body's a little dusty but whole, healed.

I move to lean against the wall. Yorl starts, his paws helping me up even as his brows furrow.

"It escaped," he says, a tinge of marvel to his voice. "But you—I saw you lick its blood. It gave *you* the blood promise, didn't it?"

"I don't—" I massage my throbbing forehead. "I don't even know what that is."

"Where is the Bone Tree?" Yorl asks.

The Tree? How should I know where it is? I'm not the valkerax. I'm about to laugh in his face when the throb in my forehead suddenly morphs into a keening pain, like a gargantuan bell rung once, but then it clears, and I can see something in my mind—in my *memories*. It's not a new thought. It's a thought that feels as if it's always been here in my head. A huge, placid bend in a long river, a dense jungle of deep green palms and softwood trees heavy with golden fruit. On a sun-drenched stone by the river creak the branches of a bright white tree.

The Bone Tree.

It's made up of thousands of smooth, bleached lengths, the trunk formed by interlocking giant bones of all shapes—joints, long leg bones, jawbones fitting neatly into one another like a puzzle. It keeps going, up and up, glowing like snow under the high sun. Its bone roots drape over the rock it sits on, gently undulating with a life of their own. The willowlike branches arc high and jut out in all directions from the trunk as loose, drooping ropes made of huge vertebrae, shin bones, and at the very ends of each branch—like a demented fruit—a valkerax finger bone, tipped with a giant, wicked claw that sways in the breeze.

It's not just that I can see it. I'm *there*. I remember it—I *know* it. I feel like I've always known it.

I can feel the warmth of the sun on my face, the humid air on my skin, the shrieking animal cries as they emanate from the jungle nearby. And I know the tree. I understand its intent. It's going to stay here until the sun hits noon, and then it will be gone.

This is the Bone Tree. And I know where it is.

My mouth opens to tell Yorl, his wide emerald eyes waiting. His very whiskers vibrate with anticipation—the culmination of all his efforts resting with me.

I could lie. I could. It would spare Varia—unless she could command me to tell her. It could spare Varia's death, and Lucien and Fione's future pain. It could spare the drastic political upheaval the world is about to experience at the hands of Varia and her valkerax army.

But lying wouldn't stop the war. Keeping the Bone Tree in my head wouldn't keep Crav and Peligli and Nightsinger safe; it wouldn't put Y'shennria or the millions of Cavanos's people—human *and* witch—out of harm's way.

And it wouldn't get me my heart back.

Lying wouldn't get me Mother and Father, or my humanity, back.

"There's a dense jungle, hot and humid," I finally say.

"Ten spans east of a long river's biggest bend. It's sitting on a rock. Waiting. Waiting until noon."

Yorl leans back against the wall, his feline face lit up by the mosslight from the outside and with ease from within. I see him smile. *Smile,* really and truly, for the first time.

He puts his paw up to his eyes and massages them tiredly. "It's done," he whispers, sounding exhausted. "Grandfather...I did it. It's *done.*"

"Why—" I reach over to Yorl and grab his shoulder. "What is this? What did Ev do to me?"

Yorl doesn't say anything, his body limp and soft. I shake him.

"Yorl! *Yorl,* tell me, godsdamn you!"

He looks up at me slowly, his green eyes fluttering open. I've never seen him so relaxed, so soft. He always had some metal stick up his bum, but now...

"The valkerax know where the Bone Tree is at all times," Yorl says.

"I know that!" I snap. "Varia was supposed to—she was supposed to ask the sane valkerax—the Weeping valkerax, so how do I—"

"The valkerax, before they were chained by the Old Vetrisians, communicated not with words as we do," Yorl says smoothly, "but with blood. The concoction I gave you, that was derived from valkerax blood. You drank it; it let you understand Evlorasin. And then it killed you."

"I know that," I start. "Malachite told me—"

The celeon cuts me off, not sharply like usual but patiently. "That's what ingesting blood that has been taken unwillingly from a valkerax will do to a mortal."

I swallow what feels like needles. "Unwillingly?"

"But when a valkerax gives its blood *willingly...*" Yorl

pauses. "This is called a blood promise. We would call it a conversation. But to a valkerax, it is a pact—between the valkerax and the one it is giving its blood to—to communicate openly and trustingly. But since the time of Old Vetris, no valkerax has been able to make a blood promise, not even to one another. Their minds are too submerged in the madness of the Bone Tree to willingly, clearly choose to give their blood. Which is why Varia and I needed you."

I sink to the ground, disbelieving. The cold clarity I felt in the clearing while I was killing all those men and Gavik— the Weeping gave me that. It gave it to Evlorasin, too. And now I— Now I can— If I even think about the Bone Tree, the image blossoms bright and right into my brain. I know where it is.

I've done it. My heart is waiting.

"Send a watertell to Varia, then!" I snap. "We have to move. It's going to be there only until noon!"

Yorl's laugh—a *laugh* from him—is rife with a purr-like rumble. His whiskers twitch with a smile he's trying hard not to show on his face.

"It's understandable that you think valkerax conversations end. Mortal conversations end, after all."

I start. "What? What do you—"

"It's called a blood *promise*, Zera," he drawls. "Not a blood moment."

I jump to my feet and reach for him again, this time determined to shake information out of his intentionally cryptic arse, but he cuts me off at the pass with another laugh, his emerald eyes staring up at the ceiling.

"You know where the Bone Tree is. You will always know. Now and forever. Until the very moment your human body dies for the last time."

23

A PROMISE OF BLOOD

My knees do their godsdamnedest to turn to gelatin, but I keep them strong. I focus my eyes on the celeon royal guard line as they pass more rocks to one another, clearing out the arena that's completely caved in by rubble. The gate— that one I walked under so many times to teach Ev—has been obliterated into nothing more than a twisted piece of metal by the collapse. The cracks in the rock avalanche show faint traces of sunlight peeking through.

I close my eyes and picture Evlorasin flying through the sky, a streak of pearl-rainbow-white against the blue.

Yorl sends a watertell to Varia, and we wait for the response. In the meantime, the suddenly eternally smiling celeon takes to writing, his quill scratching busily over parchment, leaving me to simmer in my newfound shock.

"The blood promise was supposed to be for Varia," I say slowly.

Yorl doesn't even look up, but he nods. "Yes. But we will adapt, as we always have."

I pause. "That means...I have to go with her, don't I? To find the Tree."

"Undoubtedly," Yorl agrees. "The blood promise will stay with you, whether you are Heartless or human. So Varia has no reason not to return your heart as she promised."

"But she could just command me to tell her where the Bone Tree is, right?"

Yorl opens his mouth, then closes it, and finally mutters, "To the gods with it—I've given her what she wants." He looks to me. "The blood promise was given to you under the effects of Weeping, remember? Anything directly involving Weeping cannot be commanded of."

My burden lifts a little upon hearing that. If that's true, he's right. The crown princess suddenly has even more reason to keep her promise that was so tenuous before.

"Where did Ev go, you think?" I ask.

"The lawguards on the wall said it rose straight up and took off to the west," he says. "Apparently the entire city panicked—a few bumps and bruises—but no one's seriously hurt."

I laugh, lying back on the bedroll. "Those poor people. I'd think a giant glowing wyrm bursting out of the ground meant the end of the world, too. Did *you* know they could glow?"

Yorl shakes his head. "I had no clue. I studied them for ten years in Pala Amna with Grandfather. I know perhaps more about them than anyone in the world, and yet after today, I feel like I know nothing at all."

"Welcome to my unlife," I drawl.

• • •

Varia's watertell response tells us to meet her at her apartments in the palace immediately.

Yorl doesn't need to escort me to the surface this time, the lights all humming brightly against the spiral stone walls as we ascend up and up. I finally get to see the damage once we reach the exit and surface to South Gate—there, outside the wall and at the foot of it, near where the army is camped and in the center of an otherwise placid patch of green grassland, is a massive hole torn straight out of the earth. Evlorasin must've erupted from it—dirt and rock scattered around like explosive detritus, lawguards and soldiers forming a circle of barricades around it to prevent anyone falling in.

"You'll hear nothing but this for the next ten years from the bards." Yorl sighs.

"Chin up." I nudge him in the ribs. "If you think about it, it's sort of like being famous."

He just groans.

"I thought you wanted to be famous!" I quip.

"I want to be a *polymath*," he corrects. "I want to make my grandfather's name rightly famous for the work he did. My own fame is optional."

"Being so selfless is no fun." I click my tongue.

He follows me through the South Gate crowd—a half-terrified, half-worried buzz humming among the people.

"Was it the witches? Can they summon the wyrms now?"

"First the witchfire, now this—Kavar helps us!"

"It was huge and glowy and long!" a child shouts excitedly to a gaggle of his peers hanging onto his every word. *"Like a moon caterpillar!"*

"They are definitely *not* moon caterpillars," Yorl sourly mutters. I laugh and fall quiet, the two of us walking back to the palace together for once.

Varia's waiting. The sooner I get to her, the sooner I get my heart.

"What happens to you now?" I ask Yorl.

"Now I compile my findings and submit them to the Black Archives. Varia will put forward my recommendation to become a polymath before the council of the Black Archives, and they will be all but forced to let me in."

"So we won't see each other again?"

His muzzle frowns. "In all probability, no."

"You'll be safe, yeah? You'll stay in the Archives doing research and stuff and won't get killed in the war, right?"

"There won't be a war," Yorl says confidently. "Not for much longer."

He's right. The whole reason Varia is after the Bone Tree is to stop the war. And yet Evlorasin said there would be one, and Varia agreed with it. Even I'm convinced the impending peace won't last long. I'm about to bring this up when I spot someone very familiar cut out of the crowd—Lucien's hawk eyes glaring from the cowl's slit at me.

"The valkerax escaping—was that your doing?" he demands. As he gets closer, I can see his hands are clenched tight at his sides.

Yorl blinks his huge green orbs at the prince. "Just who are you?"

The cowl makes it hard to see Lucien's face properly, but if he didn't have it on, Yorl would instantly know who he is just by how similar he looks to Varia.

Lucien rounds on him. "Who am *I*? Who are *you*? Did my sister hire you?"

Yorl scoffs. "Not unless your sister is the crown princess."

Lucien is suddenly a black blur and Yorl a yellow blur

as the prince pins the celeon to a nearby wall. "My patience is thin, polymath. One of my Goldblood families was killed today, and I just saw a valkerax dig out from beneath my city and terrify my people. *Who are you?*"

Lucien's on edge in a way I've never seen before, not even when I revealed my monster form in the clearing, and I nervously start after the two of them. One of his Goldblood families, killed. Then he's found out about Tarroux. He's never had any love for the nobles, but neither is he the sort to ignore the injustice of death. And Tarroux—the last time I saw them walking the garden together, he'd managed a small, amused smile at her. My unheart sinks. No wonder he looks so strained.

Yorl struggles to twist out of the armlock, his celeon limbs with their extra bones and sinew maneuvering like flowing water from Lucien's grasp. Yorl flattens his yellow ears to his head, pulling back his gums to show all his teeth.

"My name is my own. Cross me again, and we will see who bleeds easier."

"Stop it!" I flail my arms between them. "Both of you. Lucien, this is Yorl. Yorl, this is Prince Lucien."

Yorl freezes as Lucien narrows his eyes further at him. "Your Highness? In that gaudy getup?" He pauses, looking down. "With pants *that* tight?"

"It's better than no pants at all," Lucien snarls. Yorl shifts in his robe, his barely formed hackles raising straight off his neck in a golden ridge.

"I'm not a naked ape," Yorl fires back, "who needs them to begin with!"

The competitive pride is so thick I can practically smell it. People are staring. I clap my hands as loud as I can, like I'm trying to break up a feral-dog fight.

"That's enough," I snap. "If you two are going to act like rampaging babies with full diapers, the least you could do is be considerate about it."

Lucien flinches, his eyes roaming over the staring crowd. Yorl's ears go even flatter on his head, his tail thrashing over the cobblestones. I let go of them both and they straighten, still glaring daggers at each other.

"There was a valkerax under the city!" Lucien demands. "Why? What were you doing to it?'

Yorl shoots me a look, and the words go unsaid; no matter what, Lucien can't interfere anymore. The blood promise is with me. There's no real benefit in lying or deceiving anymore, and that thought alone lifts a weight off my chest.

Yorl dusts his shoulders begrudgingly. "I was studying the valkerax for roughly eight days." The celeon shrugs. "But you don't have to worry about that anymore. It's gone for good."

The crowd slowly starts diverting their attention from us and, determined to keep heading for the palace and my heart, I pivot and continue walking, making sure my pace is near impossible to keep up with. The boys trail after me fervidly.

"You're a real polymath?" Lucien finally asks Yorl.

"I'd like to be," Yorl scoffs, his agile feline legs keeping up with me more easily than Lucien's. "But it seems you've forgotten your father's policies prevent celeons from ever becoming polymaths in the first place."

Lucien quirks his brows in a *fair enough* way as he swings around a lamppost to turn the corner with me.

"The valkerax is gone, then?" he presses. "For good? You're certain of that?"

"Mildly," Yorl says drily.

"And I'm sure you're not going to tell me what my sister got out of you studying it," the prince continues.

"Hardly," Yorl agrees.

The three of us walk near the bridge to the noble quarter, Lucien keeping up with me easily. I can feel him at my side even if I can't see him—his presence like the thick, unbreathable pressure before a summer storm.

This could be the last time I see him.

This walk could be the last steps I ever take around him. The last air I breathe near him.

Something soft and warm suddenly slips into my hand— skin sliding across skin. Steadying. Gentle. Fingers hook around mine, and I look over to see Lucien's hand entwined in my palm, his eyes soft behind his cowl. The urge to squeeze his hand hard, to make sure it's really real, fills me to the brim, but I resist it.

Why? Why is he doing this to me? Doesn't he know it's cruel? Doesn't he know I'm going to abandon him the moment I get up those palace steps and into Varia's room? The moment my heart is in my chest again will mean the moment his sister inherits her doom.

His thumb traces the back of my knuckles thoughtfully, slowly, and part of me gives in. This one moment is all I could ever ask for. It is all I will ever have, and I tattoo it into every part of my aching flesh.

When I am old and gray, forgetful and alone, I am certain this will be the only memory that remains.

I dare myself to look up into his face, only to find the gentleness in his eyes is gone. His face is *ashen*. Not just pale, not just green around the edges, but ashen, completely and totally drained of all blood and color. His hand around mine tightens slowly but inexorably. Something's wrong.

"Lucien?" I murmur. "What—" I try to pull my hand away, but his grip is too strong. And Lucien doesn't react to my attempts to get away at all—his eyes staring off into the distance as if he's watching something happen far away.

"Lucien, let me go." I yank my hand, hard, but he doesn't budge. "I said let me *go*!"

My shout breaks him out of his strange trance, and I manage to free my hand just as he releases his grip. His eyes snap back to the present, to me, and they waver over my shoulder to a paused Yorl. Then back to me. Then to Yorl again. He stutters between us, and the coldness in his obsidian orbs isn't anger. It's...*fear*. What is he so afraid of from touching me? But it's there for only the second, and then his princely demeanor shutters it off. Lucien draws himself up to his full height.

"Is something amiss?" Yorl asks languidly. I can't take my eyes off Lucien, and neither does he look away from me. The celeon clears his throat. "We have places to be, Zera."

our heart, the hunger keens. *we can feel it beating, so close...*

The hunger reaches me through Lucien's gaze where Yorl's words can't. My heart. My heart is waiting. No matter how good it feels to hold his hand, no matter what strangeness is going on with him right now, no matter if this is the last time I see him or not, I have to go. I tear my eyes from Lucien's face and trot after Yorl, over the bridge to the noble quarter, but the lawguards hold their halberds down on Lucien, dressed more like an outlaw than a prince, and he doesn't follow.

"Zera!"

Lucien's shout has me pivoting on the cobblestones. He stands there, behind the halberds, his dark eyes burning now. All the coldness of fear is gone from his face, replaced by dark flames, roaring with determination.

The prince holds out his hand to me.

"Say my sister's name," he says simply.

"Princess Varia?" I frown. "There. Happy?"

Lucien's eyes bore into me. "Her true name."

All the hair on the back of my neck stands on end. We stand on opposite sides of the bridge, the wind whistling between us as the crowd moves, ignorant of the gravity of the moment.

Her true name. Her witch name. Why? Why would he want me to say it to him aloud like this?

"Did you know"—Varia's words ring in my head—*"that a Heartless is never supposed to say their witch's name aloud to another witch?"*

My eyes start at Lucien's boots, and slowly, terrified, work their way up his legs, his hips, his chest, up his strong neck and to his face, his sister's words echoing all the while.

"If a Heartless says their witch's name aloud, you're essentially giving other witches permission to steal you away. We can use the sound to create a spell to transfer ownership."

No. I take a step back. No—that's impossible. He's from a witchblood family, but...a witch has to discover their true name. Evlorasin said that much. Has he...? No. There would've been some indication. He would've told me—

why would he? he can barely trust you.

He's asking me to abandon Varia to be with him. To choose him over my freedom.

Part of me refuses to believe. But part of me knows, deep down. He's asking me to abandon Varia to become his Heartless. His thrall.

Not again.

we will never be chained again, the hunger spits.

The kisses, the dance, those tender moments shared

between us—all of them come crashing down on me. The girl in the other timeline who loves him and whom he loves back, openly and beautifully, is closing in. I could be her. I could make the choice to be her, here and now.

I could give up my enthrallment, only to be leashed again. Would he give me my heart back? Would he free me? Can I trust him to do that?

trust a human? after what you've done to them? The hunger laughs. ***to him?***

Fear grips me, cold and wintery and absolute.

"We can help," Lucien insists. "Fione, Malachite, and I—we've been working on finding a way to free you from my sister. And we came across this. If you say her true name, I can free you."

They've been...working? For me? Putting in effort to try to free me from a bond that cannot be broken? Inane. Pointless.

I force an unaffected smile at Lucien. "You're all so smart." I laugh. "Why would you do something as illogical as waste your time on me?"

"Zera—"

The sound of my name on his tongue is poisoned honey.

"I betrayed you," I snap. "I betrayed *all of you*! How can you offer me anything, when I lied so much? So terribly? None of you should still care—" I swallow and pivot on my heel.

Enough. I've done them wrong. I've proven myself unworthy. They need to move on.

coward, the hunger sneers. ***a coward who won't trust anyone, who won't do the hard work of atoning, a cowardly girl who wants only to run away, where things are easy—***

Yorl's green eyes are narrowed squarely on Lucien. He

looks over at me, and then mutters, "We need to go."

I'm so close to my heart that I can feel it beating in my chest, vestigial and eager. Lucien suddenly flips himself forward, landing gracefully on the bridge's railing and scaling up it to get around the guards. I start—he's mad. It's so high up! He'll break his spine if he falls! Where is the carefully calculating prince of Cavanos, the one who made sure to never make waves as Whisper, to stay low and quiet and always in the shadows? The lawguards clamor, shouting and brandishing swords and gathering below the rail, just waiting for him to come down so they can arrest him. On the very top of a brass pillar of the bridge, Lucien stands, looking down on Yorl and me, his gaze fixed on my face.

"You don't have to be alone anymore, Zera," he says clearly, his words ringing down like rain. My unheart throbs with a spear of pain.

always alone, the hunger snarls. *relying on others is a fantasy. a lie. unsafe.*

Yorl adjusts his glasses and starts walking away in defiance of the commotion, toward the road to the palace. I take one step after him, and Lucien's shout is molten iron.

"If you leave with him, there is no going back. No matter how much I despise the idea of it, if you walk away with him now, you will become my enemy."

Enemy. Not just a traitor but an enemy?

we have always been your enemy, little prince. The hunger laughs riotously, as if it's the funniest thing in the world, even as my unheart is breaking. An enemy of Lucien's, once and for all. It's the last thing I ever wanted, but here, now, I realize it's what must be done. It's what I should've done, that night in the clearing.

My unheart screams to trust him. I want to more than

anything. To accept his tempting offer, to believe in the idea
that he wants to help me. That Fione and Malachite have
forgiven me. But I know better. Forgiveness isn't that quick.
It isn't that easy. I haven't even forgiven myself for killing
fourteen men, for the five men when I was turned three years
ago. But forgiveness looms so small in the face of reality.

I won't be anyone's thrall, ever again. Not his. Not
anyone's. I'm so afraid of losing the hunger, but I'm more
afraid of being a monster again. Someone else's monster.
Two sides of my unheart war with each other in the span of
a second.

He is Lucien—the kindest, noblest boy I know.

He is a witch.

He could be *my* witch. He could give me my heart
back once and for all if I became his. If I am his, he could
command me to do anything he wanted. He could command
me to stay with him when I don't want to. He could command
me to believe his every word. To smile, to kiss him. He could
starve me, force me to fight.

he is a witch, the hunger laughs. ***and magic is a terrible
temptation.***

My heart. *My heart.*

I want to trust him. But I can't.

I've learned the hardest way that I can't trust anyone but
myself with my freedom.

I look up at him, the wind whipping my hair around my
face, and smile with the last tears I will ever shed for him.
For me.

"*Af-balfera,*" I say. "*Ansenme kei-inora.*"

24

THE HEART
AND THE BONE

Walking away from the bridge in that moment is the hardest thing I've ever done. Harder than leaving Crav and Peligli. Harder than walking into the palace when I was introduced to the court for the first time. Harder than parting from Y'shennria for the last time. My legs are ballasted with granite, marble, the heaviest stones in the world slowing me down, pulling me back.

I put one boot in front of the other until the cobblestone of the bridge fades and the gravel of the palace replaces it.

A normal girl, an innocent girl, would cry inconsolably after leaving behind the only person she's ever loved. But me? My eyes are dry after just two tears.

I am used to leaving people behind by now.

you are better off alone.

I walk up the palace steps and down the hall to Varia's apartments, my chin held high. The palace is in disarray, the guards sprawling around every corner in some attempt to prepare the palace for a valkerax attack. Yorl and I approach the Serpent Wing just as someone is coming out—someone in a high-backed red velvet dress and her mousy curls in a single braid.

Fione turns from closing the doors and our eyes meet. She approaches like a true archduchess of Cavanos—her back ramrod straight and her face perfectly neutral.

"Lady Zera." She inclines her head. There's no fear in her, not of the valkerax, or of me—or at least none that I can see. She's either learning to hide it or ignoring it. I make a full bow—the last one I'll probably ever have to make, to any noble, ever again, under this beautiful white marble ceiling. All of Y'shennria's training goes into it.

"Your Grace," I say. "You're looking ravishing, as usual. Did you get new makeup, or is it all that unconditional love? I must admit, I'm a little jealous."

Fione doesn't answer me, preferring to nod at Yorl instead. The celeon in turn makes a cursory bow appropriate as a commoner. She finally focuses her cornflower blue eyes back at me.

"You're here," she says softly. "Which means you refused Lucien's offer."

My heart is just on the other side of that door, behind her, so close I swear I can feel it sink in its bag.

"We want to help you, Lady Zera," she insists, murmuring softly. "Being what you are is a hard thing; I realize that now. All three of us—Lucien and Malachite and I—want to help you."

I laugh under my breath. "And what, pray tell, can you do to help me?" I walk up to her, whispering over her shoulder so the guards can't hear. My denial bubbles up, hot and strong. "You're not witches. A witch is the only person who can help me now. One specific witch, to be exact. And you happen to be courting her."

"There's a way," Fione insists. "Lucien is—"

"Lucien," I interrupt her, "is a deluded fool. C'mon, Fione. We both know you're smarter than to follow fools."

Fione pulls away from me, her face riddled with shock. "He's done nothing but think about you this whole time, and you call him a fool? What's—" She looks me up and down. "What's *happened* to you?"

I smile at her. "Haven't you heard? I'm heartless."

The irony sends me into a fit of despairing giggles. Fione looks frozen, unmoving even down to the slightest blink, and a tendril of guilt worms through my hard ice wall. She was so afraid of me, and yet despite all that, she's offering her help.

One last time won't hurt.

I know Varia hasn't lifted the command, even at Lucien's insistence. She loves Fione too much to do that. I move toward the archduchess, slowly, and she doesn't move away. As gently as I can, I wrap my arms around her shoulders. An embrace. One last time. She smells like a hundred clover flowers soaking in the sun. But beneath that is some other scent—barely noticeable but just metallic enough. White mercury. I shake my head—it doesn't matter.

"Thank you," I whisper into her hair. "For trying."

Her body is stiff, but when she hears the words, she relaxes ever so slightly. I pull away and walk past her, Yorl leading me into Varia's apartments. The command regarding Fione is starting to take hold, but I rein it in as much as I can.

"Zera!"

I pause at the sound of Fione's voice calling my name. But she's behind me. All of it is behind me now.

"Are you sure," I say without looking back, "that you want to call your enemy by her first name?"

The silence is thunderous. When it lingers too long, I push into the doors of Varia's room and close them behind me.

Varia stands from the couch instantly when we walk in, her silver silk dress pooling around her like a waterfall. "You're late."

"Or perhaps you're just five years too early." I smile at her, the command twisting my limbs into a rigor. "Take back the command on me about Fione."

Her brow raises. "Excuse me?"

"You can't command the Bone Tree location out of me." I raise my voice. "So take back. The command on me. About Fione."

Her eyes snap to Yorl and, if I didn't know better, I'd think she looks betrayed. Yorl merely keeps his usual cool expression behind his glasses, and just as my feet begin to march away to a secluded place, I bark at her.

"Now!"

The crown princess doesn't startle, but she instantly snaps her wooden fingers, the tips of them growing black and dark. Like a dog straining to be let off a chain, the command runs away, dissipating into nothing more than air as the hunger fades out from behind it, my limbs growing soft again as my body becomes my own. It's a hollow victory, but when I've eaten defeat for so long, it tastes the same as the real thing.

"There," she says. "Now, enough wasting time. It's done, Yorl? Truly?"

He nods. "Without a doubt. I saw Evlorasin give her the

blood promise myself."

Varia strides over to me, her heels clacking ferociously on the marble. She comes to a stop inches from my face, her own expression direly serious. Everything about her expression rings so true of Lucien that I'm almost winded.

I've chosen her. Over him. I've chosen my heart over everything.

Does that make me a monster?

"Where is the Bone Tree?" she asks, soft and yet decisive. I've got no reason to hold back on her, not if I want my heart. Her words bring a deluge of thoughts running through my mind unbidden; I can see the Tree again, instant and whole, its surroundings glowing brightly green all around it.

"A jungle," I say. "Hot and humid and dense. There's a long river, the longest I've ever seen. In the biggest bend of that river, ten spans east. It's sitting on a rock, waiting for noon."

For some reason, Yorl laughs a little hearing me say it again—incredulous, maybe. Varia just stares at me, like she's delving into my eyes for the truth, and when she finds what she's looking for, she swears.

"Gods almighty."

I watch the crown princess of Cavanos teeter for the first time, uncertain and unsteady. She stumbles, clutching the back of the couch to brace herself. The shock of accomplishing what she's been after all these years—what she faked her death for, what she has nightmares of, what she killed her bodyguards for, what she tortured a valkerax for, what she became a witch for—must be crushing.

"Most probably the jungles of Gutroth," Yorl offers from the corner of the window he's staring out. "And the Golden River."

"We can't go there today." Varia regains herself admirably quickly and whirls sharply around to him.

"No," he agrees. "It's too far a journey to make by noon, even for a teleport spell."

"Then I wait," she asserts. "I wait for the Tree to go somewhere near Cavanos, and I leave the instant it arrives there."

"Agreed." Yorl nods. "The paperwork you promised me—"

"Patience, Yorl," she insists. "You've been waiting for five years. Surely you can wait for another few hours."

"I've enjoyed our time together as much as you have," Yorl snarks. "But my grandfather's legacy has waited fifty years—it cannot wait another moment more."

"*When* I get the Bone Tree," Varia recites. "That was our agreement. No sooner and no later."

Yorl lets out a feral snarl. "I gave you what you wanted! I gave you everything I promised, down to the letter. I did the impossible—I did what no polymath in a thousand years has been able to do, and I deserve what is mine!"

"Settle. Down." Varia's voice is cold. "Or I'll have Zera here settle you down for me."

She could do it—and I know that better than anyone. I'd have no choice but to lash out at him. I flash an apologetic smile at Yorl, who's suddenly looking at me warily. He spits what sounds like a swear and folds his arms across his chest.

The waiting is always the worst part.

I learned this in Nightsinger's woods, waiting for something to happen for three years. The nothingness drives you mad eventually, the way it did to me—talking to animals and trees and constantly throwing jokes to entertain myself in the dead air of the forest. Varia spends the time packing some clothes and other essentials into bags: parchment, quills, candles, dried food. Where has she been keeping these supplies tucked away in her room? She's packing like she's never coming back.

"Is your wife not joining us when we leave?" I ask lightly.

Varia looks up sharply at me, then snorts. "No. She's staying here in Vetris, where it's safe."

"And your father?" I run my finger along a dusty vase. "How does he feel about you becoming the most powerful person in the world? Have you asked him? Or is it just a given that he won't mind, as long as you're alive? Does he know how long you'll be alive for? Does anyone?"

This gets to her. I can see the stitch in her mouth, no matter how desperately she tries to hide it. She's close to her goal—the one she's had nightmares about since she was small—and that's making her sloppy. It would make anyone sloppy.

She pulls my heart, still in its bag, out of her breast coat, and grins like a hungry fox at me. My body goes on point in a split second, every hair standing up on my arms, my skin vibrating with heat and anticipation. My muscles twitch toward the bag, pulled like one of her eerie dolls on a string. I've never been more elated to see the word "traitor" in my life. My eyes roam over the stitching on the bag, over the way it thumps gently as my heart beats beneath the cloth.

Mother. Father. Human life. It's all resting in that tiny bag.

"I still have this," the crown princess reminds me. "So play nice, would you?"

I glower but say nothing. She might not be able to command me to tell her about the Bone Tree, but neither can I refuse her. We're at a dangerous impasse, the two of us standing on the same knife's edge.

It's an hour that lasts longer than three days. Varia packs, she and Yorl going over details and minutiae. I sit in the only moveable chair in the room—a simple wood thing— positioning it in front of the sandclock on the mantelpiece over the fireplace. I wait one more hour after waiting for three years, watching the sand grains of the clock fall, each golden dot pushing me further from Lucien and closer to my heart.

"Will we be followed?" I hear Yorl ask faintly.

"There's a possibility," Varia agrees. "But only by a witch, and only if they're familiar with my magic."

"The rogue one in the city that started the witchfire," Yorl says. "They may know."

"No. It has to be a more intimate knowing, repeatedly exposed to it—"

I tune them out, my eyes fully focused on the clock but my ears wandering. Outside, through the open windows, I can hear the palace in a quiet uproar. The word "valkerax" drifts up, said with fearful nervousness, as if people are unsure whether merely saying the word will summon it to their doorstep.

Reality starts crashing down around me as the clock's sand fills the noon slot to brimming. Where will I go? No, I've always known where—back to Nightsinger, Crav, and Peligli. Her forest is gone, razed by the human army, which means she has to be at Windonhigh—that witch city Varia mentioned. But how do I *get* to a witch city, especially one Vetris hasn't even discovered yet? My only hope is to follow Y'shennria's letter and visit Ravenshaunt. If I can find her, safe with the witches who are her allies, then surely I can find a way to Windonhigh. It will be hard. But I've lived and died through the worst injuries, the worst deaths. I've survived—with most of my sanity intact—three years without my heart. I'll find the people who matter most to me. I'll find them no matter what.

"Zera."

Varia says my name shortly, hard and sharp, and I know what she wants. The Bone Tree comes up in my mind differently this time, like a windblown cloud transforming in the sky each time I look at it. The Bone Tree creaks, looming and white and lonely, on top of more white. Snow. The Bone Tree is on a mountain peak, the wind howling bitterly. From the peak, I can see all of Cavanos—the gentle green hills rolling, interrupted only by the charred black swaths where the army has burned the forests. And on the other side of the peak, the Helkyris side, I can see a city farther down, strung between smaller peaks and constructed almost entirely of towers. An intricate web of bridges connects every tower in the city, the abyss yawning below it.

"The Tollmount-Kilstead Mountains," I say. "One of the peaks. There's snow, and I can see Cavanos on one side, where the army's been burning the forests, and on the other side, far below, I can see a city made of towers. The Tree is going to stay there for…" I pause, staring at the Tree in my memory. Somehow, with the blood promise thrumming through me, I just *know*. "Two hours."

"Breych," Yorl says immediately. "The scholar city of Helkyris." He looks at Varia, green eyes wide. "Your gods favor you."

"They favor *us*," the crown princess insists, pulling on a cape and handing one to me. "Dress warmly and quickly."

She walks over to a box and unlocks it with a tiny key on a chain around her neck. From inside she pulls out a roll of parchment and hands it to a wide-eyed Yorl.

His paws take the parchment shakily, and he looks up at her.

Varia smiles. "I appreciate everything you did, Yorl. Never forget that."

His ears perk up and, stowing the parchment away quickly in his robe, he looks to me and nods. "Good luck, Starving Wolf."

"You, too." I grin. "Ironspeaker."

Our true names ring in the room as he leaves, the only remaining fragments of what we've been through together. The last I see of him is his yellow-tufted tail disappearing through the doorway.

I pull on the cape, and Varia motions for me to follow her. She stops in front of an oil lantern in her bathroom; to my utter shock, she tilts it forward, and the sound of something clunking into place resounds. A dark trapdoor opens in the slate tiles of the floor, just big enough to let one person through at a time. The tightness of the secret passage reminds me of the one I found in Y'shennria's manor. Varia wastes no time in climbing down the ladder on the side, and I follow.

"Is this Lord Y'shennria's handiwork, by any chance?" I ask.

"Indeed. Father thought it was so clever, he had Lord Y'shennria build one in each apartment of the Serpent Ward. They all lead to various parts of the city—mine is the only one that leads outside the wall, and only the royal family knows about it."

Belatedly, I realize these passages must be how Lucien escapes the palace and slips into the common quarter as Whisper. Thorns curl around my unheart at the thought of him. I'm never going to see him again, am I? My hands start to shake at the thought. The Bone Tree. I let the sight of it in my memory—so lonely on top of the mountain—grow huge and consume the idea of Lucien whole.

The two of us hit the bottom of the trapdoor's shaft, and Varia leads me along a thin tunnel barely wide enough for my shoulders. To illuminate it, she lights her wooden finger with fire, and I follow the dancing flame through the darkness. The crown princess is so close to me, I can practically hear my heart beating in the bag beneath her cape.

"Do the witches know about the Bone Tree?" I ask.

"Only the High Witches," she answers. "And they think it's better to leave it alone."

"I know it might be a little late to propose this, but they could be onto something."

Varia gives a withering scoff and continues forward. My voice is the only thing that breaks our silence.

"Lucien won't forgive you, you know."

She doesn't speak, but her footsteps start moving quicker down the tunnel.

"He told me I'm his enemy now. Does that mean you are, too?"

This, and only this, makes her pause. She whirls on me, the firelight illuminating her black glass eyes. She gazes at me steadily and then turns back around and starts walking at a blazing speed, her words ringing among stone.

"I've spent five years preparing myself to be his enemy."

The tunnel eventually lightens naturally as it slopes upward, and Varia finally pushes open a trapdoor. Dirt and pebbles and grass rain down on our heads as we exit into a bright blue sky. When I emerge, Varia pushes the door closed behind me with a hard click—the door covered in grass so flawlessly, it looks just like a curve on the side of the rolling hill.

"Finally," Varia breathes out. She turns to me. "Give me your hand. And whatever you do, don't move."

I put my hand in hers. It's cold and smooth where her wooden fingers are, at odds with her warm human palm. Just like Nightsinger, her eyes grow black from corner to corner, the wood of her fingers staining dark and void, completely colorless as she casts the spell. Her mouth moves, but no sound comes out, in that usual silent prayer to the Old God that accompanies magic.

One moment, the two of us are surrounded by grassland and an impeccable azure sky, and the next time I blink, the warm air turns blisteringly cold. White appears everywhere—fresh, untouched snow—and I shade my eyes to block out the sun reflecting blindingly off it. It's been so long since I've experienced real magic for myself that I almost laugh at how incredible it is. I look around only to see Cavanos far below us now, green and distant. We're on a peak of the Tollmount-Kilstead Mountains, thousands of miles up and away from Vetris.

Varia looks nonplussed. The snow crunches under her boots as she immediately starts walking, though much slower than she was going in the tunnel. I try to keep up.

"This is as close as I could get us," she says. "Stay near to me, and if you see any wildlife, I'm relying on you to kill it."

"Why? Have you run out of fireballs?" I ask lightly, striding ahead of her.

"I'm saving energy," she answers. "For the Tree."

Without Father's sword at my hip, I feel naked. I've kept the new blade and old hilt in a bag around my waist but unassembled, they're mostly useless. Giant condors, bonemoths: those are the only two animals I've heard of living so high up here. I could use my teeth to kill a giant condor or two, but a bonemoth is another story. I keep my head on a swivel and my hearing sharp.

The sun beats down on us relentlessly—no relief anywhere for miles, as there aren't any trees, and few rock formations tall enough to throw shadows. I can feel the sunburn begin to crawl over my shoulders, and I can see it happening on Varia's nose as a bridge of red. But other than discoloration, no real dangers present themselves. I'm totally unprepared for snow, but wet boots can't bother me anymore—not with my heart so close.

Varia stutters once, her foot catching in the deep snow on a sharp incline, and I bend my knee and motion to my back. "Hop on, Your Highness." I smirk. "Zera's carriage service, at your, well, service."

"I can get there on my own two feet," she snaps, her d'Malvane pride raising its quills in defense.

"With all your energy intact?" I lilt. Her brows furrow, and after a glare from her, I feel her pressure on my back, and I lace my arms around her knees. Despite being physically older than me, she's not anywhere near as heavy as I am. It could be the prospect of the Tree being so close, or it could be the way I can feel her heart—or is it mine in the bag?—beating against my spine, but no matter how tiring it is, I manage to haul her up the incline. My legs ache, my fingers and toes starting to lose all feeling, but instantly I sense Varia's magic healing me of the frostbite.

"Hey," I demand. "Cut it out. Save your energy."

"As if I have a choice," she scoffs down at me.

"Why did you bring just me?" I ask. "What about Gavik?

He could protect you, too. You're so far away from him—he's probably screaming in the middle of Vetris somewhere right now."

"Gavik is superfluous," she says. "I need only you to find the Tree."

"I'm flattered," I grunt. The sweat beading down my neck feels like a trail of ice, my skin prickling as the wind howls louder and rips faster across the snow the higher we go. My ears are open for anything condor- or bonemoth-sounding, so when the blistering crack of ice happens, I brace myself immediately and turn my head. Yet there's nothing at all— not in the sky, not on the ground. We are the only ones in this lonely white space. But I swear I heard—

"Why are we stopping?" Varia presses, nudging me with her knees. "Hurry up—it's just over that rise."

I can feel her five years of want burning through her blood and into mine. I peer over the stony edge of the peak and to the abyss below us—there, standing tall against the snow, is the web of bridge-connected towers. The scholar-city of Breych, Yorl had called it. But with the way I saw the Bone Tree in my memory, I was looking down on the city from a much higher angle. Steeling my thighs, I carve up and through the mountain snow as fast as I can without dislodging Varia.

The farther up I climb, the stronger the wind howls. The flying snow goes from kissing my cheeks to stinging them ferociously, each flake like a blade of ice. And then suddenly my feet find a flat expanse of rock, and I blink away the frost from my eyelashes.

Something white looms before me, swaying gently in total anathema to the raging wind.

The Bone Tree.

It looks so much more frightening up close—far more massive, so tall I can barely see the top of it. The wicked claws at the ends of the branches scythe the air idly, as if they're just waiting for someone with flesh to pass by. Varia stirs on my back, climbing off and staggering through the snow toward the Tree with an enraptured gaze.

"The Tree," she whispers, the white of the bones gleaming in her fervid onyx eyes. Each bone is so huge, the ivory eerie in its seamless perfection. There's a faint darkened aura around the Tree—noticeably dimmer than the high noon sunlight beating down on us from above. *Valkerax bones suck in light*, Fione had said. This isn't a tree made sloppily—every bone has its place; every one fits to make the tree a titanic whole. Its spindly shadow stretches as long as the peak, and the air around it—the closer I walk to the undulating bone roots of the tree as they clack together, the heavier the air gets. It's the same sort of feeling I used to get walking up to Nightsinger's room, some undeniable weight to the atmosphere around me.

But this...this weight isn't some light, ominous reminder. It is *crushing*. It feels as if it's trying to grind me down into nothing.

The crown princess clambers up the rocky peak, her hands out in front of her as she walks beneath the Tree's massive branches. I can barely hear myself panting over the howl of the wind, so I climb after her, the air pummeling my empty chest.

"Your Highness," I shout. "I brought you to the Tree. It's time you hand over my heart!"

She doesn't move an inch, her gaze fixed on the bones of the trunk, her hand hovering just above as if she's afraid to touch it.

"Varia!" I shout, pulling at her arm. There's an immediate sizzling sound in the air, and just over my shoulder bursts a flash of light and an intense heat. I fling myself backward, but the burning doesn't go away, and my eyes find my cloak. A lick of black witchfire blazes on it, smoldering over the wet wool. Did she try to burn me?

I reach out and grab her arm again.

"My *heart*," I insist, steeling my mind for another shock of flame. But nothing comes. The branches of the Bone Tree merely sway above us, the creaking sound identical to the creaking of ancient wood. My shoulder burns, the fire gnawing through my layers and down to my skin, but I hold fast to the princess.

"My heart!"

This gets her attention, and she whirls around. But her eyes don't look at me—she peers into the snowstorm behind me, her gaze waiting and on guard, more owlish than ever as she searches for something on the horizon that I can't see.

And then she grips *my* arm, her fingers digging like ice daggers.

"I still need you to protect me," she murmurs, face taut. Fear? Why would the Laughing Daughter fear here, at the precipice of all her goals realized? At the cliff's edge of becoming the world's most powerful person, what is there to be scared of? I turn and look to where she's looking.

Three shadows cut out of the ice and snow, their cloaks whipping in the wind. Humans. I expected leagues of bonemoths, thousands of giant condors.

"Just three?" I step forward and crack my neck leisurely. "This will take only a half, Princess. Keep my heart warm and ready."

Varia says nothing, her whole body stiff. For a moment I

think she's frozen over, and then, as the shadows grow closer, she calls out, "You can still turn back." Her words are almost instantly swallowed by the snow. The three figures show no sign of slowing, and she raises her voice. "Go back, now, and I will forgive you."

My brows twist. Who is she—?

I don't know who or what does it. It could be the Tree, or Varia herself, or the people approaching, or perhaps even merciful nature. Regardless, the wind suddenly *dies*. It doesn't just stop—it keels over dead in its tracks, the snow flitting down in soft tufts once more and silence echoing in the wake of so much howling.

Without the storm, in the midst of the peak at peace, it is easy to see the faces of the three.

A girl with mousy curls on the left, her nose and cheeks like rosebuds, her hand gripping a valkerax-headed cane. A tall, white-haired, slender beneather on the right, his eyes gleaming crimson, like two pinpricks of blood amid the snow.

And there, in the middle.

Black leather. Black hair. Black eyes. A hawk, shrouded in shadow.

Prince Lucien Drevenis d'Malvane.

25

THE SIX EYES OF THE WOLF AND THE WYRM

The snowstorm has moved inside me.

It tears at my innards with razor ice, stupor freezing me in place and making me an easy target.

Lucien? Here? He followed us all the way here so fast? But that means—

The three come to a stop just before me, not close enough to touch but close enough to hear. Fione stares straight ahead, to Varia, Malachite staring at the Tree. And Lucien looks right at me.

"Do not," the prince calls, his gaze never moving from my face, "put your hand on that Tree, Varia."

"I told you to go back, brother!" I hear Varia shout, her voice wavering. "This is my responsibility, not yours!"

I watch Malachite slowly shrug his broadsword off his back, assuming that low battle stance I saw with the valkerax. But this time, he's not looking at a white wyrm barreling down a tunnel. He's looking at me.

Lucien says nothing, his stare burrowing straight into

my core.

Fione is the first to move. She steps forward, voice clear. "No one has been able to control the Tree forever, Varia."

"Oh, Fione." Varia laughs, but the sound is uneasy. "The Old Vetrisians very much did!"

"A new witch, every month," Fione holds out an ancient-looking scroll. "They cycled them in because the magic of the Bone Tree was too strong! It would…" She trails off. "The Tree will eat a witch's magic—*until it kills the witch, Varia!*"

Her words tinge desperate on the ends, and guilt wraps its strings around me and pulls tight, trying to cut me in half.

I don't dare look over my shoulder to see Varia's face—not with Malachite and Lucien bearing down on me like this. The look in their eyes makes me feel like a rabbit standing in the middle of a snare trap, encircled on all sides by rope. I search Lucien's face for any sign of warmth, of mercy, but he is stone. I'm his enemy. I've helped his sister find the Tree that will kill her. I've betrayed him again. But did he—? Is he really—?

"I know," Varia finally answers Fione. "I've known what it will take for five years now. I'm not ignorant, Fi."

"Then you're mad!" Fione keens. "If you take the Tree, you'll…" She chokes on her words, tears pulling them apart. "You'll die!"

Varia's voice is barely audible. "I know."

"All of this—" Fione throws out her hands, pleading. "All of this to enforce some temporary peace—"

"No," Varia cuts her off. "Not temporary. You're right—I will have only a few months' time with the Tree. But I will make every second count. I will reshape the world. Not just Cavanos, Fi. The *world*. I will make craters in Arathess that cannot be filled with earth and covered up again, or forgotten. I will make craters Arathess will be forced to build cities in, and roads around."

Lucien's gaze moves from me for a bare second, his eyes narrowing imperceptibly at his sister on the peak.

"It's easy enough to destroy," he calls out to her. "You can build almost nothing in a few months of absolute power."

"No." I hear the smile in Varia's voice. "But I'm not concerned with building, Luc. I will destroy what's in our way, and Arathess will build in the aftermath. They will build for me, in the exact grooves I have left in the world, like a child tracing their letters for the first time."

death, she will bring. The hunger laughs. *so much delicious death.*

Malachite shakes his head, that *tch* sound ringing in disbelief.

"What would you have me do, Luc?" Varia snarls down at him. "What do you plan to do? Take the throne and mete out menial tasks until you die? Will helping the poor of Vetris really save them from dying in another war? The ministers, the nobles, that damnable deep-seated Eye of Kavar and its priests—all of them *want* war. They push us to the brink of it, again and again, and they will never stop."

a wheel that turns eTERNALLY, the hunger insists. I can feel my claws beginning to press through the skin of my fingertips as the dread presses into my brain. Is Varia loosening the hunger inside me?

"Holding the world's greatest power in the palm of your hand isn't the solution!" Lucien bellows back.

"But it *is*, Luc!" she insists. "The valkerax did just that! Because of them, Old Vetris was formed! Human and witch, come together at last, working together in ways never seen before. You know the songs—we made Vetris in three days with our combined power. We made this Tree, for the gods' sake! I will make Old Vetris again—I will force the witches and humans to work together once more!"

The bones of the branches clack together placidly. As she speaks, the hunger in me has been growing steadily louder. It reaches a fever pitch now, and I struggle against it with all I have in me. I won't fight Malachite, Lucien, Fione. Not them.

Not them.

ENEMY! the hunger screams. **TRAITORS. YOUR ORGANS WILL MELT THE ICE—**

Of the silence. *Of the silence!* I beg with myself, closing my eyes and sinking into the hollowness of my chest. I've had practice, so much more practice now, but the hunger sparks an inconsolable oil fire that rages through my mind. It's stronger than anything I've felt before—stronger than it was even in the clearing. This urge to make blood run, to consume hot flesh and tight sinew, to rip and tear and leave the chaos of death in my wake—it's not just a cloud of frenzy that surrounds me as it was the night of the Hunt. It's an arrow, aimed right at me and struck true.

My teeth grow long, my breath puffing out as ragged white air.

The Laughing Daughter is urging me to kill. And Lucien is watching it happen. He's watching me become the monster all over again. Not him. Not them. *Fourteen men but not them, too, not again, not again, NOT* **AGAIN**—

I crouch—*please, don't crouch, don't move an inch*—my muscles tightening as Malachite's hand on his sword tightens.

KILL. The hunger becomes my thoughts, my very breath. **ONE BY ONE, THEIR THROATS WILL BE OURS—**

"I wouldn't do that if I were you." Lucien's voice cuts through my bloodlust, but barely. I flick my claws, the hunger tilting my head with bloodthirsty curiosity as I watch the prince move to stand next to Fione, his eyes squarely on his sister.

"And why not?" Varia laughs. "Someone has to show you she's no good for you."

Wordlessly, Lucien looks to Fione. Something passes between them, and she nods her curled head back. She moves aside her cloak, her undercoat, to reveal the thin white muslin of her undergarments just over her heart.

HER HEART, the hunger screams, and I can't help the lick of my lips. *WHICH DO WE LOVE MORE—OURS OR THEIRS?*

The faint human side of me watches in abject horror as Lucien raises his hand and places it gently against Fione's chest. She's quivering, but her expression is unbreakable, her defiant, tear-studded gaze riveted to Varia.

"Step down from the Tree," Lucien says clearly. His fingertips grow black, darkness spreading and subsuming the whites of his eyes.

My mind stutters, but my body and the hunger controlling it only lowers itself closer to the snow, ready to strike.

"Step down," Lucien says again, harder this time, not a grain of pity or softness on his face, in his two pitch-black eyes. "Or Fione will become my Heartless."

A witch.

Lucien *is a* witch.

HE WILL DIE THE SAME. The hunger doesn't care

what he is, but the fragments of me still left do. When? How? What is his true name? He's blackmailing Varia with Fione's safety. Heartlessness is pain. Heartlessness is hunger, unending. She would suffer so much. She has no idea how much, and yet she's standing there, determinedly holding her clothes aside to make it easier for him to take her heart. She is terrified of Heartless.

And yet she is *willing*.

He's doing what I nearly did to him.

With his other hand, Lucien pulls out a bag from his coat. A silk bag. There, stitched with clumsy needlework, is the word FRIEND. Varia's fury—I can feel the instant she lays eyes on the bag, the instant she understands what's going on. It's as if some furious switch has been flipped in my mind.

HOW DARE THEY THREATEN US, the hunger thunders, an echo of her rage. *BLOOD WILL RAIN. BLOOD WILL SNOW. HIS LIVER TORN FROM HIM, HIS EYES PLUCKED NEATLY OUT OF THEIR SOCKETS—HE WILL BE THE BIRD PREYED UPON*

Varia plays it differently—laughing brightly, none of the nervousness in her voice anymore, each word ribbed by sharp fury.

"Is this what it has come to, brother?" I hear her boots crunching on snow. "Must we fight each other like storybook clichés?"

NOW. The hunger shoves me. I lash forward, my claws outstretched and aimed for Lucien's hand against Fione's chest. *RIP IT OFF, SUNDER THE THREAT IN TWO.*

Broad steel suddenly blocks my vision, my hard claws scraping and screeching against a broadsword's blade. From over the steel, Malachite's red eyes glare down at me.

I'm sorry, I want to say.

DROWN IN YOUR OWN BLOOD, the hunger screams.

"At last," the hunger and I meld into one and say together. *"We find a real challenge."*

"Don't get your hopes up, whelp," Malachite drawls back at me, looking me up and down as if unimpressed with what I've become. "I know I'm not."

"Was it you, then?" Varia presses. "Who started the witchfire? I had my suspicions. But it seemed far too strong a fire for a barely named witch like you. It was messy, and driven entirely by a terrible wave of emotion. I was almost worried you'd burn the whole city down. But Father was so relieved when your bodyguard brought you back—I suppose you finally passed out from all the smoke. Unconsciousness fixes witchfire just as well as death."

Lucien simply stares at her, silently, his fingertips still on Fione's chest.

"And the quake that hit below South Gate?" the princess presses. "Was that you, too? A masterful piece of magic, if I might say so myself. It was so strong and localized I was almost fooled into believing it was a far older, more experienced witch. However did you hide yourself from me? I had every polymath in the Crimson Lady looking for you."

"How else?" Lucien says. "Gavik knew best, in this case. White mercury, ingested directly."

Varia laughs. "You drank it? Straight? For days and days? Oh, you poor, stupid thing. You must've been in so much pain. But you came prepared to threaten me with Fione's well-being and everything. So someone must've told you what I was planning with the valkerax. With this Bone Tree. And yet I made sure my people kept their mouths shut. I made sure of that more than anything. I constantly checked on them, and I made sure to cut loose ties and looser tongues."

Fione suddenly darts her eyes away from me, and Lucien fixes his on me. There's a split second in which a crack in his stone shows, naked and soft and yawning open. Varia's gaze flickers to me, her face lighting from the inside with a twisted joy.

"No. Brother, you *didn't*."

My brows knit, and I ask him the question our hunger and I burn with.

"What have you done to us?"

Fear courses through me as he opens his mouth, those gentle lips moving. "I—"

Varia's laugh interrupts him. "Every witch is unique, Zera. But some patterns reoccur in powers. My brother is a skinreader. He can touch someone to see their most recent experiences. Isn't that right, Luc? You discovered your power by accident, but you used it on Zera intentionally."

The cold of the peak freezes my unheart solid. **"The kiss...our hands entwined... You used us?"**

I TOLD YOU; I TOLD YOU. THEY WILL ALL BETRAY YOU. HIS DESIRE FOR YOU, SELFISH

The hunger contorts me around myself, my hands clutching my head shaking so violently I nick my scalp with my own claws, blood oozing down. *Why?* To everyone else I was a thing—to be feared, to be used. To him, too. He never cared. The kiss, those gentle touches giving me hope—

I was alone, always.

"I believe this is called 'irony,' my dear Heartless." Varia laughs. "Isn't it just perfect?"

"ENOUGH!" Lucien bellows, deeper and more jolting

than any quake.

"No! It's not nearly enough!" Varia instantly fires back. "I have done this for you, Lucien. To protect you! I have done this all for *you*, Fione! I have done this because no one else will." She laughs bitterly again. "You hear me? *No one else will!* Those High Witches are cowards—they could end the war, they could enact peace, but they think it too dangerous. They are selfish! *I!*" She pauses, the sound of a thumping chest. "*I* am *selfless*."

"You are convinced, sister," Lucien says, voice raw, "with delusions of grandeur."

"I do this because it is a queen's duty to protect her people!" She continues. "I do this because it is a queen's duty to change the world for the better! I will not perpetuate the problem, Lucien. I will be the answer. And if I must do that alone—" Her voice suddenly softens. "If I must do that alone..."

ALWAYS ALONE, the hunger clings, resonates her weakness with my own. I push off from Malachite's sword, and he takes a swing at me, but I dodge below his blade and come up in front of him, my claws raking soft flesh as they meet his face—*no. No! Stop this!*

Malachite looks up, his face leaking blood in three jagged slices across his nosebridge, over his cheek, and to his left ear, the lobe there torn open. Silence. I must be the silence. I have to Weep, to stop before I hurt him, before I kill him, before she makes me turn on Lucien once and for all—

"How does it feel?" The hunger taunts with me. *"Tell me, is your pain ripping you apart, too?"*

I can't Weep. I haven't been cut by a white mercury blade. No matter how much silence I call up, the image of that kiss in the Moonskemp ballroom, the feel of Lucien's palm on my palm—the hunger just screams and screams, a constant echo chamber of unending torment.

HE USED US. THEY WILL DIE FOR DARING TO USE US, TO STAND AGAINST US, <u>US</u>, THEY HAVE TURNED ON US AS I SAID THEY WOULD, FILTHY, YOU ARE FILTHY FOR EVER TRUSTING THEM— YOU ARE WORTHY OF NOTHING BUT DEATH BUT THEY WILL PAY YOUR PRICE INSTEAD—

I lick Malachite's blood from my fingers, smirking at him with all my sharpened teeth. A massive force suddenly blindsides me, sweeping my legs out from under me and tackling me into the snow. I try to flip out of the hold, but Malachite's thin arms are mind-bendingly strong—his grip steel and infinitely heavy. I can barely move, but beneath his hands I feel the worst to come. My limbs are elongating.

The monster is coming.

For one brief moment, I flicker in the darkness. I surface above the endless lake of despair the hunger has dragged me into, looking up into Malachite's face looming above me, bleeding onto me.

"R-Run," I choke out. *"Take them and run."*

The beneather smirks down at me. "Not a chance in the afterlife."

"Step down from the Tree, Varia, or Fione is Heartless," Lucien shouts beside us, his darkened fingers digging into Fione's chest. Fione tenses, her mouth open in a mute cry as blood drips from the entry points. I try to lunge for her, to pull Lucien's hand out, but the hunger yanks me below once more, enraged at my efforts to break free.

PATIENCE. THEIR TIME IS COMING

"Fione," Varia says, her voice suddenly gentle. "Step away from him and come here."

"No!" Fione blurts. "I have made my choice already. This is yours!"

"Then even you—" Varia's voice cracks down the middle. "Even *you* would turn against me, beloved?"

From my place pinned in the snow by Malachite's knees, I can see Fione's face twist, fracturing with a different kind of pain in the delicate places—her mouth, the corners of her eyes. But she doesn't move an inch from her place at Lucien's side. She's so strong. So sad.

There's a beat, the Bone Tree creaking between us. And then Varia's will incinerates my mind.

TAKE THEM APART

The world goes red. Six times.

My eyesight fractures—six points blurring into one just beyond my nose. Heat. Heat above me, cold beneath me, my limbs suddenly longer and strong, faster, fast and strong enough to throw the beneather off me. Beneather. Mal. *Mal-what? What is his name?*

A CORPSE, the hunger answers, and I fling my body— claws first—into the two heats that stand connected, the ones my witch wants ripped apart. Luc...the prince. Lucien. I remember him, his name ringing like a bell. This one we remember, this one we don't want to kill—

Metal. Metal flashes in front of my face, slicing my hand clean off. Blood splays over the snow, beautiful crimson heat. A beautiful nuisance. With a low growl, I grab the metal with my other hand and fold it backward, the screech of its resistance deafening as it curls in on itself in a useless spiral. The beneather holding the ruined weapon widens his ruby eyes at my face, at his sword, and I slice at him with my half-healed hand, the bone claws growing back through the stump of my wrist before anything else. The smell of fire, and something hot and burning, collides with my face, the scent of flesh sizzling and the sound of my own roar of pain as I turn to face the witch who threw it—Lucien, his palm blackened to the wrist and held out at me, his eyes midnight orbs.

Run.

RUN, LITTLE SHEEP, THE STARVING WOLF HAS COME TO PLAY—

Run, please.

I reach to tear Lucien from the other heat, the girl. Shouting. Lucien shouts, once, and the girl holds up something in front of me—a dagger, glimmering with jewels, the metal blade glimmering a pure white, and stabs it into my chest. Too high to reach my unheart, too left to reach my lungs, just right. White-hot fire curdles my blood, numbness spreading from my brain to my toes and back again. The stump of my hand stops healing rapidly, the skin reconstructing now with near-invisible slowness.

The smell.

THEY ARE THE TrAiToRs

White mercury.

I look down at the blade in my chest—the metal is surely white. Not a vial of mercury but a blade of it, like the four swords lost in the war. Like the sword attached to Varia's hip even now, the only one left in the world. The hunger starts to crumble, the silence I'd been clinging to so hard roaring up to greet me, enveloping me like a long-lost mother in its cooling embrace. The rage is not mine anymore, my despair is not mine, and they chip away from me, leaving me light. Silent.

The hunger has stopped singing.

"No!" I hear Varia screech, indignant and furious. "Fione!

Dear heart, what did you do?"

"I did what my uncle couldn't," Fione says softly.

Lucien's dark eyes linger on mine, and I see myself in them—my monstrous form bared for all to see. My face is strange; six white eyes where two should be. Like a valkerax. Words and despair circuit unsaid between us as I loom over him. That kiss wasn't real. His touch—unreal, manipulative. He's a witch. But all that can wait. It will wait for three years as I have waited, if it must. I am in the silence. The hot tears streak down from my six eyes. Blood tears. I turn my head slowly over my shoulder, the sun throwing my elongated shadow over the blood-smeared snow as I step toward Varia, opening my clawed palm.

"My heart," I growl, my voice still dark and bestial. "Now."

"**Stay there!**" Varia demands, the command slithering through each syllable. But the Weeping has me in its still embrace. It's so quiet inside me. Nothing moves to stop me—not guilt, not magic, not hunger. I am free.

I stalk toward her, faster now, and her eyes widen. She moves her hand closer to the Bone Tree, and from behind me, Lucien shouts.

"You first, sister. Stay your hand, or Fione is my Heartless."

Surely she cares about Fione more than the Bone Tree. I've seen them so happy together—smiling and golden.

"Surely, Your Highness," I say, my monstrous voice shredding the air, "your own dear heart is more important than power."

The crown princess's fingers hover just above the smooth white of the trunk. I know the Tree has been calling to her for years, infecting her dreams. But the choice is now hers, and hers alone. Behind me, I know Lucien is tightening his grip on Fione's heart—I can smell the blood oozing from her.

The air feels so dense to me, even as a monster, the magic all around us trying to squeeze the life from me, from the moment, from time itself.

"Power isn't everything," I say to the princess.

Every sound disappears. Every movement stops except the motion of her hand trembling above the trunk of the Bone Tree. Varia's proud face wavers, stuck on the edge between timelines. Her, happy with Fione. Her, seizing a power that will destroy her. Two of her selves war with each other in this one moment.

She was ready for five years. I was ready for three.

A snowflake lands on my eyelash. The wind softly moves the Tree, the bone branches clattering together. The princess looks to me, no trace of expression on her face.

"No," she agrees. "But it is the only thing that matters."

Varia's hand touches the bark.

The next thing I see—blue sky. I'm flying through the air, backward and away from the Bone Tree, pushed by some unbelievable force, the claws and vertebrae of the branches spiraling in my vision as I roll countless times in the snow like a thrown doll.

"No!" Fione's scream pierces the insulation of the moment, and time resumes.

"Varia!" Lucien calls, his tone cracking with worry. "Varia! *Varia!!*"

She has chosen.

I stagger to my feet, squinting with six eyes as a searing light at the base of the Bone Tree, where Varia once was, grows ever bigger. Her outline is faintly visible—a humanoid shape engulfed by white light, her hand resting on the trunk. She tilts her head up, her mouth opening and light pouring out of it in a concentrated beam. I rush to stand before

Lucien, Fione, and Malachite as Old Vetrisian power blurs the snow, the sky, draining all color from the world, from our faces and clothes. It's sucking in, as if in preparation to expel, the Bone Tree's branches now twitching wildly, nonsensically—a mirror image of the way Evlorasin twitched in pain all those days below the city.

"Something is going to burst!" Fione shrieks. I can feel it, too—the heaviness in the air is compressing to that single point of Varia beneath the Tree. Something has to give, and soon.

"Varia!" Lucien's voice goes ragged, sloughing through the snow to reach his sister. *"Varia!"*

"Luc, no!" Malachite staggers after him.

The moment slows again. Me, standing with a bejeweled white mercury dagger in my chest, my six white eyes narrowed and crying blood. Malachite, reaching his long pale hand for Lucien, his injured face etched with worry. Fione, tears streaming down her cheeks, five points of blood stained into the skin over her heart, her heart that must be utterly *broken*. Varia, brimming with light, spilling it, almost consumed by it now. And Lucien.

Lucien, reaching for his sister, his hand outstretched, his legs frozen in a long stride and his expression—so stolid until now—teetering on the edge of crumbling.

To lose someone once—devastating.

To lose them again—the end of the world.

Lucien's closer to the light than anyone; he's not going to survive the blast. But neither are Fione and Malachite. This power—it's like nothing I've ever felt—not magic, not machine, but something greater than either could ever be alone.

Silence. In the silence. All that matters is the next

moment. Not what Lucien has used me for, not what Varia has betrayed her love for. Not what I have become, with my six eyes. Just the next moment.

In the perfect quiet of my concentration, I can see everything, all the heat on and in this mountain, all the coldness in it—how far the mountains go, how close the abyss yawns all around the peak.

"I am Zera Y'shennria—the Starving Wolf," I whisper. "And this is never-goodbye."

Every single moment—one after the other—is the only thing that matters as I sprint with all my speed, all my strength, toward the Bone Tree, toward the nexus of light that Varia has become—

Something catches my wrist. It's not strong, but it's burning hot, searing in a way that demands my attention. I look over to see Lucien, his black eyes sparking out at me.

"No! I won't let you sacrifice yourself again for me."

I'm stunned, speechless, as Lucien puts himself in front of me, his fingers growing dark as he raises them, palms up. A strange, unnatural wind plays with his short hair, curling it around his face.

"This time," his voice rings out, "I'll protect you."

My unheart squeezes painfully as his lips move with unheard words—his prayers to the Old God. Varia grows ever brighter, so bright I can barely see his dark outline against the light. But still he stands, and I have to fight every sacrificial urge in me not to run full tilt at Varia and take her off the mountain peak with me. But it wins out—I can't let Lucien die.

I start forward, and Lucien barks, "Trust me, Zera. Please."

"You have a life to live," I spit.

"That life is not worth living." His voice is hard. "If it's not with you."

All the air in my lungs implodes, and I turn my head around slowly to look at him. His gaze is deathly serious, but a smile pulls his broad lips as the darkness crawls into his eyes.

"I am the Black Rose," he says. "And I have the power to protect you now."

The witchfire springs out of nowhere—a roaring wall of it so high I can barely see where it ends in the sky. The black flames stretch in all directions, obscuring the light Varia's giving off and the massive Bone Tree itself. The light struggles to pierce through the wall of black fire, still growing brighter in a terrible crescendo of luminescence. Lucien claws his fingers, the darkness stretching up his wrists and to his forearms, his biceps, up over his shoulders and crawling to his neck, sweat beading on his forehead.

"I can't deflect it, only redirect it. You have to back up," he barks. "To where Malachite and Fione are."

"But you—" I watch his posture stiffen as he raises his hands higher, the flames growing denser and roaring louder.

"I'm trusting you with them!" he shouts.

Trust. Trusting me, after everything? Trusting me after I refused to trust him? Swallowing what feels like glass, I struggle through the snow back to the bleeding beneather and human. The Bone Tree is making a horrible noise now, a high-pitched shriek, like a crying wildcat mixed with a dying deer, and I splay my arms wide, dragging Malachite and Fione into the snow for protection.

"Luc—" Malachite starts.

"He'll be fine!" I shout.

"But that fire won't—"

"We have to trust him!"

Malachite stares into my six eyes, and then nods, once and with purpose. Next to me in the snow, I feel Fione slide her hand into mine and squeeze, despite how monstrous I must look.

Trust.

Here, in the silence, it's so much easier to trust.

I could die. The explosion centering on Varia could obliterate her, and my heart. She could die. Lucien could crumble beneath the force building against him. I close my eyes and pray—to who, I'm not sure anymore. Just someone, someone who can listen. Someone who can listen to my words right now as they leak from my unheart, from my *heart*.

Please. Please keep us all safe.

The black witchfire wall blocks out the sky, spiraling up and up and all around us, like a protective bubble of pure fire. The snow melts at the flames, water pooling in the ground and soaking into our clothes. The white light starts to win, sucking in even the black flames of the witchfire. Lucien doesn't move, his body stock-still and the entirety of his upper body now writhing with animate midnight, devoid of all color.

The Prince of Cavanos, the thief Whisper, the boy I fell in love with on the night of the Hunt, the witch named the Black Rose—all of them come together as I watch his shoulders, his heaving back. He lets out a jagged roar to shame even the witchfire's noise, and the flames leap back to life, stronger than ever, dancing with newfound vigor and radiating an unholy black light.

The white light's explosion rocks the ground. Even

through the fire, the light burns on the backs of my six eyelids. I hear the mountain crack with an earth-shattering rumble, the ground crumbling away outside our fiery bubble shield. Fione shrieks, and I cover her ears and hold her close. The black fire and the white light tangle over each other, battling in midair, until every scrap of heat and energy tires out, fizzling into nothingness.

When my vision clears, the witchfire is gone.

We are in the middle of a perfect circle of earth—all that's left of the mountain peak.

Lucien stands there, doubled over, leaning on a stitch in his side and panting uncontrollably. Malachite and I leap up immediately, sprinting to him, the muddy slush that was once deep snow splashing around our boots frantically.

"Luc!" Malachite looks him over. "Are you all right?"

My panic deflates when I see he looks whole, but his eyes are fixed—staring straight forward at something.

Fione catches up to us, her voice low. "V-Varia."

I look to where the princess is, to the Bone Tree. It sits on the very edge of the circle of earth, clinging with its wavering roots. It hasn't changed at all—no marks from the explosion visible. The bones are whole, untouched.

And there, standing beneath its branches with a calm ease, is Varia. Her curtain of dark hair shines, her smile discernible from even our distance. She looks whole, too, normal, as if nothing has happened at all—save for the fangs sticking out of her neck. Like a macabre piece of jewelry, like a choker gone wrong, a line of sharp, svelte fangs spreads down her neck in a perfect ring, fused to her flesh. Not big enough to be valkerax fangs, but identical in shape and serration.

She tilts her fingers up to the sky, and, horrifically, something rises. A low hissing swells like a wave as some hundred things rise from the mountain. No—*thousands*. Thousands of sinewy, wyrm-like white bodies rise slowly into the aether, feathered manes flared and tails lashing, whiskers undulating in the cloudless sky.

The valkerax.

A pillar of valkerax, writhing around one another.

"Well now." Varia smiles at us all. "I believe this is where your work ends. And mine begins."

END OF BOOK TWO

Acknowledgments

After seven years of writing, you'd think it would get easier. But the struggle is half the fun—what would my little monkey brain do if it couldn't feel that rush of accomplishment that accompanies solving a complex problem after three weeks of not seeing the simple solution on a nigh-constant basis? What I mean to say, of course, is that writing is a dream, but one of those dreams where you don't have any pants on and you're in high school and everyone can definitely probably extremely see your crotch right now. As a career author, I can assure you, it's okay to not have pants on all the time. Sometimes people will even read what you wrote without pants on!

This little space feels silly sometimes to write in, but it feels less silly when I thank people. A very big thank-you to my agent, Jessica Faust, for being a steadfast presence in my life. A bigger thank-you to my father, Michael, and my mother, Deb, for believing in me with such candid fervor it astonishes me constantly. A wonderful shout-out to everyone at Entangled for bringing this little dream to life, and to Stacy Abrams and Lydia Sharp for being keen-eyed editors to the last word.

And most importantly of all, thank you, the reader, for soaking in these brain-words of mine. You are beautiful and worth every drop of love in this wide universe. Let reading and writing be your guide, your mentor, your muse. Make the magic, be the magic. You are my magic.

take a bite

4.7.20

Everything he craves dies...

crave

New York Times Bestselling Author
TRACY WOLFF

MALICE

PINTIP DUNN

What I know: someone at my school will one day wipe out two-thirds of the population with a virus.

What I don't know: who it is.

In a race against the clock, I not only have to figure out their identity, but I'll have to outwit a voice from the future telling me to kill them. Because I'm starting to realize no one is telling the truth. But how can I play chess with someone who already knows the outcome of my every move? Someone so filled with malice she's lost all hope in humanity? Well, I'll just have to find a way—because now she's drawn a target on the only boy I've ever loved...

GLOW
OF THE
FIREFLIES

LINDSEY DUGA

Briony never planned to go back to the place she lost everything.

Firefly Valley, nestled deep within the Smoky Mountains, is better kept in her past. It's been six years since an unexplained fire gave Briony amnesia, her mother disappeared, and her dad moved them away.

But now her grandmother needs a caretaker, and Briony's dad insists she be the one to help. The moment she returns, she feels a magical connection to the valley, as if it's a part of her somehow.

And when she meets a hot guy named Alder who claims he was her childhood friend but now mysteriously keeps his distance, Briony starts piecing together her missing past...and discovers her mother didn't leave to start a new life somewhere. She's trapped in the hidden world within the valley.

Now, Briony will do whatever it takes to rescue her, even if it means standing up against dangerously powerful gods. But when saving her mother comes with the ultimate sacrifice–Alder's death–how can she choose?

entangled teen

an imprint of Entangled Publishing LLC